FROM BEHIND THE LOCKED DOOR, SOMEONE FIRED THREE REVOLVER SHOTS

There came from that room a sound so completely inhuman that at first H.M. did not recognize it as a feminine scream. But Joan screamed again, and then a third time.

The Colonel moved with coolness and quickness. He whipped the key into the lock, unlocked it, threw the door wide open and ran into the room, Sir Henry right on his heels. Bailey sat on the edge of the bed and put his arm around Joan to hold her upright.

"She was here," Joan whispered hoarsely.

"Who was here?" Bailey asked.

"The Widow. I saw her. She—touched me. She . . . I saw her teeth. She put out her hand. She was here!" Joan screamed weakly. "She was here!"

Abruptly her head fell back. As the eyelids closed, Colonel Bailey looked at the bolted windows and then turned to Sir Henry. "This isn't so!" he exclaimed, picking up the Webley .38 from the bedside table. "I tell you," he shouted, "this simply damn well isn't so!"

"I know," H.M. agreed woodenly. "But it is."

A SIR HENRY MERRIVALE MYSTERY BY

CARTER DICKSON

NIGHT AT THE MOCKING WIDOW

ZEBRA BOOKS
KENSINGTON PUBLISHING CORP.

ZEBRA BOOKS

are published by

Kensington Publishing Corp.
475 Park Avenue South
New York, NY 10016

First Zebra Books printing: September, 1988

Printed in the United States of America

For Garney and Cynthia
who are well acquainted with Stoke Druid

Chapter 1

When murder occurs in an English village, which it does far more frequently than is known by those who have not troubled to study the history of crime, people usually feel the shock worse because of the village's intense respectability.

Take, for instance, the case of Stoke Druid in Somerset.

Here another kind of crime—underground, like a fat and swelling creek of poison—still further outraged respectability. Many persons in the village were furious. Some were terrified. But it had been running on for six weeks before anybody mentioned it, or as much as seemed to notice it. By that time matters had gone too far.

Stoke Druid, drowsy and of great age, lies about a quarter of a mile off the main road between Wells and Glastonbury. Years ago Baedeker starred it, because of its fifteenth-century church, untouched by the "restorations" of the 1840's, and because of the tall group of stones, possibly Druidic, in the northeast meadows near the river.

But, in this prewar summer of 1938, the village lay forgotten in its fold of the deep green hills. And that suited the inhabitants very well.

True, there had been considerable excitement a few weeks ago. The old vicar of St. Jude's Church had died at the age of eighty-two, and there was some disquiet about his successor.

"H'm!" said Colonel Bailey (Indian Army, Retired), with a dubious frown.

"Please don't worry," earnestly said his niece, Joan Bailey. "I'm sure they won't send us anybody *very* High Church, who'll burn incense and things."

"What's the fellow's name?"

"I think somebody said it was the Rev. J. Cadman Hunter. He's a nephew of the Bishop of Glastontor."

"Reeks of ceremony!" growled the Colonel.

But Colonel Bailey was wrong. The Rev. J. Cadman Hunter, known to his friends as Jimmy, proved to be a friendly, good-natured, athletic young man, deeply devoted to his calling but so easgoing that he harassed nobody. Only the village butcher expressed qualms, thinking him too young; and all the ladies agreed he ought to have a wife. And there was one incident, though he never dreamed it and in fact looked back on it with uneasiness, which made some of the local gentry like him very much indeed.

Stoke Druid had (and has) only one street, the High Street. At one end of it ancient St. Jude's Church faced eastward along a well-paved street toward the grounds round the gray stone lump of the Manor some five minutes' walk away. For twelve generations of squires, there had been a Tom Wyatt at the Manor. No countryman ever thought of him save as "Ol' Squire" or "Tom."

And the present Tom Wyatt, an excellent landlord, was no exception.

Most of the well-to-do in Stoke Druid, or at least those who were called the gentry, occupied houses

8

inside the Squire's immense grounds. Behind the manor house, beyond even a kitchen garden overrun like the Garden of Eden, there were two hard tennis courts of which Tom Wyatt was very proud. Though he had been educated at Clifton, the Somerset ways and the Somerset speech were in the Squire's blood and bones.

Stoutish, with a red face and a large carefully curled gray mustache, Tom Wyatt would rock back on his heels and bawl out with his own speech except on formal occasions.

"Mind, Sam!" he would say to his overseer. "You make sure the tennis courts are A-1, look, or there's a a'mighty kick in the britches for 'ee! Mind, now!"

Thus it happened that, on the afternoon of a blazing June day when the River Lea sparkled amid drowsing green, the Rev. J. Cadman Hunter went to play mixed doubles with Colonel Bailey, the young and very good-looking Joan Bailey, and (finally) that laughing and dark-haired woman, Miss Marion Tyler, about whom nobody would ever think of using the word "spinster."

The vicar and Joan Bailey were matched against Colonel Bailey and Marion Tyler. Nobody, with the exception of Marion Tyler, was a machine player who could never be made to run. The others, including Joan, walloped at everything. White-clad figures streaked about the court under a hot sun.

"Good!" said the Rev. J. Cadman Hunter to himself. It is possible that he was much attracted by the blue-eyed, brown-haired Joan. She wore shorts and a sleeveless blouse, which . . . still, it is possible he did not even notice this. But certainly, as a first-class player, he was all over the court like a sprayed insecticide. Before too long he got the opportunity for set point.

At Mr. Hunter's overarm smash, the ball whistled

across the net deep to the opposite baseline. It was perfect timing, perfect direction. Then he saw the puff of yellow-brown dust which showed it had struck just outside.

"Hell!" said the Rev. James, not altogether under his breath.

There was the briefest of pauses. Mr. Hunter's face became salmon pink under his fair hair. He opened his mouth, and shut it again. Nobody smiled, nobody even appeared to have heard. At the end of the match Colonel Bailey strolled up casually. There was a gleam of pleasure in the Colonel's eye, though he spoke out of the side of his mouth like a convict.

"Happy to have you with us, Padre," he said.

It meant that the Rev. James was a good fellow. It was the accolade.

News of the incident leaked out, of course. Told in its most exaggerated form, the new parson had cut loose with a string of expletives which surpassed even those of Fred Cordy, the shoemaker; and it shocked many persons in the High Street. It shocked the butcher, the greengrocer, the owner of the General Store. But it delighted Squire Wyatt. As for the ladies, they agreed to a woman in shrugging the matter aside, merely saying—mysteriously—that they had known the real truth all the time.

"He do be needing a wife," explained Mrs. Goldfish, biting off a thread in her snug parlor above the chemist's shop.

Mr. Goldfish, the chemist, a man of somewhat superior education, hesitated before looking up over his gold-rimmed spectacles.

"Really," he complained mildly, "you women are always wanting to get somebody married. Now no man would indulge in such gossip, or link people's names with other people's!"

At this point little Mr. Goldfish paused to consider.

"Will Mr. Hunter marry Miss Joan Bailey, do you think?" he added.

Mrs. Goldfish uttered a scornful laugh.

"Miss Bailey!" she said. "Don't be daft! Miss Bailey's too far gone on . . . well! *I'm* not the one to mention people's names, like you. But Mr. West *is* a nice gentleman; and I don't blame 'er one bit."

But Mr. Goldfish, fussy and kindly, was still considering matrimonial possibilities for the vicar.

"What about Mrs. Lacey?"

Mrs. Goldfish put down her sewing and looked sinister.

"Mrs. Lacey," she breathed with dangerous mildness. "Now wouldn't you know a man would say that? Mrs. Lacey, indeed! A widow with a grown-up daughter nearly fifteen! Ah, and herself forty year old if she's a day!"

"That may or may not be true," retorted the chemist with dignity. "But I'll tell you this. When Mrs. Lacey comes into the shop—and a pleasanter lady you'll never find—she doesn't look a day over thirty. By George, I'll go further!" he said indignantly. "She doesn't look a day over twenty-five!"

And Mrs. Goldfish, in a cold perspiration of anger, prepared to lecture.

Now these were only the innocuous waters of gossip, which may be found at Stoke Druid or anywhere else. But it was unfortunate that so many people talked about Stella Lacey. For the first arrow of malice, the first stone of the persecution, was fired at Mrs. Lacey on the morning of July 1st.

Stella Lacey, whose real age was thirty-four, was a delicate and dainty woman with ash-blonde hair and large gray eyes. She was not much of a talker, but she spoke with humor when she spoke at all. Mrs. Lacey—

11

like Colonel Bailey, Joan Bailey, Marion Tyler, and the novelist Gordon West—occupied one of the four houses inside the Squire's park, with her young daughter Pamela.

On the morning of July 1st, then, she went into the post office to buy stamps. Entering that narrow little post office, which smelled of old wood and creosote, was often a nerve-racking business because of the postmistress.

The middle-aged postmistress, Miss Ellie Harris, was almost stone deaf. If you asked her a question, she read your lips and parrot-screamed a reply which was almost unintelligible. Ellie was a stickler for regulations, too. On occasion those tiny premises, with a counter and wire barrier down the right-hand side, would become packed with maddened people while Ellie spent ten minutes screaming to a customer that he hadn't done up the parcel properly, and must do it up again.

But Stella Lacey, with her most engaging smile, moved up to the counter and slid half a crown under the wire barrier.

"A book of stamps, please," she requested.

Ellie, behind the counter, was sorting the morning's mail for the postman. Ordinarily at this time she would no more have noticed a customer than she would have noticed a black beetle. But Ellie was in a good humor.

"Letter for you, Miz Lacey!" she screamed.

"Oh?" murmured Stella Lacey, startled. Everybody in Stoke Druid knew that, except when her daughter was away at school, she received no letters save a long envelope, each quarter day, from a London firm of solicitors.

Ellie's black eyes were snapping with pleasure. When Ellie smiled, her teeth seemed to swallow up her whole face.

12

"Letter for you!" she screamed again, and waved it in the air. "Like to take it yourself, 'stead of Joe delivering it?"

"Oh. Yes. Thank you so much."

Ellie slid the letter under the barrier. It was an ordinary notepaper envelope, with the address neatly typed in light blue ink. Mrs. Lacey looked at it in a puzzled and almost fearful way; then she gently tore it open, to inspect the single folded sheet of notepaper inside.

A second or two afterwards Ellie Harris glanced up, and from kindness of heart fired off a deafening scream.

"Miz Lacey! Anything wrong?"

Stella Lacey's face had first become as red as though at some insult or indecency. Then it became so pale that she looked far older than her years. The gray eyes, under ash-blonde hair, seemed sunken.

"Not that book," she said. "Not that book!"

"Book, Miz Lacey? Book of stamps?"

Stella did not appear to hear. Hurriedly putting the envelope into her handbag, she closed the handbag and ran out of the post office. Its heavy door, with the long dusty glass panel, banged after her, while Ellie Harris shrieked unintelligibly and waved the discarded half crown.

That was the first of the anonymous letters which, in the ensuing weeks, showered on the inhabitants of Stoke Druid. Even now, when all the facts are known, the police cannot estimate exactly how many of the poison-pen letters were sent.

For nobody said a word, while the poison swelled. Not a word.

One person might laugh—a little shortly, perhaps—and contemptuously throw the letter into the kitchen fire. Another might hesitate, tear the missive to small

13

pieces, and try to hide them. It was not that great crime or sin lurked behind the little gray stone fronts and lace curtains; not at all. The poison pen was using his or her wickedest weapon mostly against the innocent.

"This isn't true," they would say to themselves, "but what if people believed it was true?"

That is how the poison pen terrifies. In a village, most people would have died rather than admit receiving such a letter.

During these weeks the Rev. J. Cadman Hunter, who wanted to make friends with everybody, met faces as blank as shutters. Despite his youthful appearance and bouncing stride, the Rev. James was not without experience. He had served three years as a curate in a parish of the East End of London. When his uncle the bishop procured him this living—to a clergyman, the poorest of the poor, its stipend of three hundred a year seemed princely—he had hoped to rouse enthusiasm and jollity. But he told Colonel Bailey that he could not understand this.

"What *is* it?" he burst out, one afternoon late in July. Colonel Bailey had two hobbies: oil and water color painting, and a study of warfare from Hannibal down. At the moment he was trying a water color sketch in his back garden.

"It isn't only," continued the Rev. James, "that they scarcely speak to me. They seldom speak to each other, and look at each other out of the corners of their eyes. One can only feel it. It's as though something were about to . . . to . . ."

"Blow up?" suggested Colonel Bailey.

"Well, yes. One might say that. But what *is* it?"

"I don't know," replied Colonel Bailey, who himself had not yet received a poison-pen letter. His ragged eyebrows, brown-gray with an occasional hair protruding, drew together. "I might guess. But, so help me,

14

I don't know."

"Then can you give me a guess, sir?"

"Better not," the other said stolidly, and picked up his brush again.

Curiously enough, the Rev. James had not seen Joan Bailey since the day of the tennis match. Several times he met Marion Tyler, that laughing and sturdy brunette who cheerfully admitted her age as forty-two, but who seemed to have heard of nothing odd in the village. But there was one very badly jarring incident, when he went to pay a social call on Gordon West, the writer.

West wrote only purely popular stuff, roaring adventure romances which the British public loved. Also he had born in him the tricks of the radio writer. When he wrote a series of plays for the B.B.C., the Controller of Programmes rejoiced and Listener Research reported an audience of nearly half the British Isles. He lived alone in the smallest house on the Squire's estate, a gray rough-stone cottage of two rooms, surrounded by fruit trees.

The Rev. James, who had heard of him as the mildest mannered of men, smiled as he knocked on the cottage door. He was a little surprised by the harsh voice which answered.

"Yes? Come in!"

In a long study whose walls were completely stuffed with books except for foreign curios or other exotic junk, West sat at a typewriter desk near the green-shaded north window. He was a middle-sized, thin, wiry man of thirty-five or so, with dark brown hair, now-smoldering brown eyes, and faint hollows under his cheekbones. He wore an old sweater and flannels, and did not get up.

"Mr. West?" smiled the vicar. "I'm Cadman Hunter," he announced rather apologetically, and glanced round the room. "I think you—er—write?"

"Yes," agreed West, and looked up. "I think you—er—preach?"

Slight pause.

"Oh, I try to do as little of that as possible," laughed the Rev. James, "except when I'm in the pulpit." He was speaking with the best will in the world. "I'm afraid I haven't read any of your work, you know."

West slewed round the swivel chair to face his visitor, leaned back, and folded his arms behind his head.

"Tell me, Mr. Cadman Hunter," he said with interest. "How would *you* answer that remark?"

"I beg your pardon?"

"Well, I often meet it. ''Fraid I haven't read any of your work.' Would you, for instance, murmur, 'So sorry'? Or would you say," snapped West, "'If you haven't read it, then have the good manners not to mention it'?"

"My dear fellow! I hope I haven't . . ."

"Not at all. Forgive me."

The Rev. James instantly beamed again. "I see you've done a great deal of traveling, Mr. West?"

"I used to, yes. Not now."

"May one ask why?"

"One may. Because it was so bloody disappointing. The only interesting scenes," and West touched the typewriter, "come out of here."

Once more the Rev. James laughed. Since he had not been invited to sit down, he wandered over toward the mantelpiece. In the carriage of West's typewriter, he had noticed, was stuck the envelope of an opened letter, with West's address typed neatly in light blue ink. But the vicar paid no attention to it.

Instead, over the mantelpiece, he suddenly encountered a small picture in oils: a head of Joan Bailey, done by a brush far more skilled than her uncle's. The

16

light effect on the fleecy brown hair, wound round the head after the fashion of '38, heightened the flesh tint and brought out Joan's expression of what can only be called intense sympathy combined with a subdued heartiness, which shone in the blue eyes and put a half smile on the lips.

"Interesting?" observed West, and showed his teeth.

But the Rev. James, for some reason, did not seem to notice the picture at all. Hastily he examined the mantel shelf underneath, along which were strung a little smoked African head, the folded war bonnet of a Comanche Indian, two Spanish daggers from the sixteenth century, and a stuffed rattlesnake, coiled.

If you picked up the stuffed snake and shook it, some ingenious arrangement of the taxidermist made it emit a kind of vicious *whirr*. The vicar discovered this.

"By Jove!" he exclaimed, pleased. "By Jove!" And he turned round.

Whirr went the stuffed rattlesnake, in that stuffy little cottage among the fruit trees. *Whirr, whirr.* Abruptly the vicar, his eyes widening, seemed to remember something. The Rev. James, tall and lean in his gray country tweeds and clerical collar, quickly put back the snake on the mantel shelf.

"I quite agree," West told him dryly. "And now, since this happens to be one of my busier mornings, I'm sure you'll excuse me?"

The Rev. James, as he tramped away from the cottage, was not unduly disturbed. Time after time, in the past, he had paid a call on someone whose hostility was due merely to the fact that the person in question was not a churchgoer. In any case, he had little time to be disturbed. One of the poison wounds burst at last.

On the southern or "fashionable" side of the High Street lived a mouselike but not unattractive woman, Miss Cordelia Martin, who was church organist at St.

17

Jude's and made a tolerable living from dressmaking. And, on the night of August 12th, Miss Martin drowned herself in the River Lea.

They found her at sunrise, caught in the angle of a fallen tree. They put the poor swollen body into a cart, covering it with burlap sacks, and drew it by hand up over the lush northeastern meadows at the lower end of the High Street.

"It do seem a pity," someone growled, in a guarded voice.

"Ah, so it do," muttered another. That was all.

A red sun, unveiling mist, was just striking up behind the manor house at no great distance away. As the cart bumped over the meadow, about a hundred feet from the High Street, the red sun gleam caught the top of that tall thin group of stones—sometimes it seemed mostly one stone—which had stood there since no man knew when. It looked, roughly, like the figure of a woman with one shoulder bent slyly. As the figure rose up black against red mist, a visitor in the street would have needed no fancy to see the eyes and mouth in the head.

The farmhands with the cart were so familiar with it that they did not see it, though one man glanced up.

"Ol' Widow," he said.

Bump went the cart, and then slid easily over a smooth stone hump up four or five feet into the High Street. Its noise scratched and thudded loudly in the dawn hush, though afterwards someone declared that Fred Cordy, the atheist shoemaker, had been standing at his upstairs window and grinning.

The local constable, his bulk trembling, was compelled to phone Glastonbury. Promising that Inspector Garlick or at least the Sergeant would be sent at a more decent hour, Glastonbury rang off. Squire Wyatt did not hear the news until seven o'clock in the morning, after which he shouted curses like one of his darker ancestors. But the Rev. James—as though there were some conspiracy to keep knowledge of evil from this innocent-faced young person—did not hear it until teatime, when Inspector Garlick called at the vicarage.

The Rev. James was having tea in his study when Mrs. Honeywell, his elderly and ultra-respectable housekeeper, ushered in the police. Mrs. Honeywell hovered for a time at the doorway, and then ran as hard as she could.

"Lordy," she later confided, in an awed voice, "there's times when he *do* look like a parson, and no mistake!"

She meant that she did not know his face could become so cold, and his eyes as deadly hard, as the stone image of Stoke Druid.

"I see," remarked the Rev. James, when Inspector Garlick had concluded a brief, veiled recital. "I knew Miss Martin well. She was our organist. She . . ." His fist tightened round a penholder. "Can you explain, Inspector, how Miss Martin came to meet her death?"

"If you ask me, sir, it's a pretty plain case of accident."

"Accident?"

Inspector Garlick, a large man with narrow stolid eyes and a mole on his cheek, let his glance stray away.

"Well, sir, what do you suggest it is?"

And the other couldn't reply. Even a reasonably intelligent man may be too close to a thing to see it. Inspector Garlick observed that the vicar, inwardly, could only rage with fury. To suggest suicide, in connection with the small eager-faced Miss Martin, would be unthinkable.

"Yes, sir?" the Inspector prompted.

19

"That is all, thank you. You may go."

"Dismissed me," fumed Garlick to his Sergeant in the passage outside, "like as if he was a lord! Never mind, m'son! There's not much more for us here."

The Sergeant looked puzzled. "In Stoke Druid? But I thought . . ."

"I said," Garlick repeated significantly, "there's not much more for us here."

Of course Inspector Garlick had no illusions. A little interview at the home of the deceased woman, a drink or two at both the Nag's Head and the Lord Rodney, a little sauntering earlier in the day, and he had smelt anonymous letters. But the Superintendent, to say nothing of that sharp-clawed deity called the Chief Constable, hated this sort of thing. Loathed it. It happened too often among the high muck-a-mucks. If at all possible, they'd ignore it.

"So you just keep out, Dave Garlick," the Inspector told himself. "And don't go prying unless you've got orders from higher up, which you won't get."

The coroners from Gastonbury played straight into his hand. In fact, the sender of the poison-pen letters must have done a good deal of laughing at this time.

Since old Dr. Spenlow was away on holiday, the postmortem examination was done by his locum at Stoke Druid: a chunky, serious-minded, Teutonic man named Dr. Schmidt. He reported that Miss Martin, in addition to being *virgo intacta,* suffered from no chronic illness and had died from drowning only. But the coroner took pity. Believing Miss Martin had killed herself as the result of an unrequited love affair, and wanting to save the poor woman's face, he pressed the jurymen at the inquest for a verdict of accidental death, and got it with one shout of assent. Inspector Garlick returned whistling to Glastonbury.

20

And still nobody said a word.

It might have become intolerable, especially after a burial service at which Cordelia Martin's sister sobbed hysterically at the grave, if the anonymous letters had not stopped for some weeks.

It was a great peace. The Rev. James, though still raging, tried to lose himself in his calling and in the fifty niggling little duties which beset even the incumbent of a country parish. Then came the real explosion.

On the afternoon of Saturday, September 13th, the Rev. James was again taking tea at the vicarage, whose little-paned windows faced the north side of the church. He had just finished working on his sermon for the next day, when Mrs. Honeywell brought in the tea tray together with the afternoon's post.

There were only two letters, the topmost one in an ordinary Woolworth's envelope with the address typed in light blue ink. While he poured out tea, the Rev. James idly opened the first letter. He read it, and slowly read it again. Then he violently rang the bell for Mrs. Honeywell, who came running.

("Lordy!" she murmured as she opened the door.)

The Rev. James was standing up behind his desk, his ruddy face pale, breathing hard. When full enlightenment comes to a man, it seldom comes by degrees: it comes with a shock, in full and grisly detail.

"Mrs. Honeywell," he said without preamble, "what do you know about these anonymous letters signed, 'The Widow'?"

"Sir?"

"I should prefer to hear the truth, Mrs. Honeywell."

Mrs. Honeywell seized the lower hem of her apron and dragged it up to her lips.

"Sir, I dunno one single . . ."

"I propose to drag this whole matter into the light of

21

day," said the Rev. James, and struck his fist on the table. "God helping us, we shall know *all* the truth!"

Mrs. Honeywell did not reply, because again he frightened her. He was as inflexible as Ol' Parson at Stoneaston. But the Rev. James, looking down at the letter and reading only its first words, felt half sick at the duty he knew he must do.

"Yah! You and Joan Bailey . . . ," it began.

Chapter 2

On that same Saturday afternoon, about the time the Rev. James had made up his mind, a taxi which had traveled all the way from Bristol drew up before the church door at the top or western end of the High Street. Out of it climbed a large, stout, barrel-shaped gentleman in a white alpaca suit.

The High Street with its neat pavements, which sloped down gently to the Manor at the other end, lay embalmed in Saturday afternoon somnolence. It was deserted, except for a few parked cars. Behind little rough-stone houses, or above the premises of brightly painted shops, wives were clattering tea things on the table and calling husbands from an afternoon nap.

The stout gentleman, somehow maneuvering his corporation out of the taxi, stood with one fist on his hip like Victor Hugo, and surveyed the street with a lofty, lordly sneer. Shell-rimmed spectacles were pulled down on his broad nose. His big bald head was bare to the early autumn air, until the taxi driver fished out a Panama hat and stuck it squarely on the back of his head.

"So this is Stoke Druid, hey?" inquired Sir Henry Merrivale, with a face of disdain.

"Ah," agreed the taxi driver, in the accents of East Bristol. "But this suitcase of yours, he'm a daisy!" He tried hard to repress Gargantuan mirth. "He'm a beauty! He'm *something!*"

"Never you mind that, son," retorted the great man sternly. "You just hoick out that suitcase of mine, and stand it up endways—endways, mind!—just as I've been tellin' you all along."

"Ah. You'm the governor."

Across the street, in a dispirited huddle, stood six children ranging in age from nine to thirteen. They were accompanied by two dogs, a Scottish terrier and a black and white mongrel with long legs. When the youth of the nation had left home that day, they had been as clean and hard-scrubbed as their mother's kitchen floors. Now, boy or girl, they were all but indistiguishable from Voodoo idols. Dismally they knew that the shout for tea would come at any moment, followed by reprisals.

Yet, as they looked at the taxi, an electric shock seemed to spark and quiver through the group.

"Easy, now!" begged the stout gentleman, in a voice of thunder. "For the love of Esau take it easy!"

What appeared from the taxi, at first glance, was an ordinary brown leather suitcase of the long, heavy, oblong variety. But, as the taxi driver upended it and set it down in the road like an upright oblong, they could see—almost embedded in the leather, on each end of four narrow sides at the bottom—four stout little nickeled wheels.

"Thankee, son," said the stout gentleman, and handed money to the taxi driver.

Hooking two fingers in a leather handle at the top, Sir Henry Merrivale moved across the street at a majestic and pigeon-toed walk. He carried no weight. He merely guided. The suitcase rolled beside him, silent

24

and rather ghostly.

"*Coo!*" a voice burst out. "Look there!"

"Hem!" said the great man, and coughed a little. Conscious of eyes upon him—he did not note the fifteen pairs of adult eyes behind window-curtains—H.M. guided the suitcase casually, with one finger, as though leading in a Derby winner.

Children and dogs poured across the street, surrounding him at the tobacconist-barber's.

"Sir!" pleaded a shivering voice.

"Uh-huh?"

The spokesman was a lanky thirteen-year-old boy, wearing a Marlborough school cap and speaking with an ultra-refined accent.

"Please, sir," he asked, "why are you carrying that funny-looking suitcase?"

H.M. was stung.

"What's the matter with this suitcase?" he demanded, directing at the offender a look of such horrible malignity that both dogs barked and shied back. "I invented this suitcase, I did! I don't carry any weight, do I? Didn't *you* ever get lumbago from carryin' a ruddy great suitcase forty-five miles?"

The whole group, suddenly realizing, were so deeply impressed that they remained silent for nearly a second.

"'Ere!" butted in the dogged voice of a stocky small boy. "'E do 'ave little wheels on the bottom; ah. But who do 'e 'ave little wheels on the top too?"

This was true. There was a small wheel at each corner of the top, as this boy (the butcher's son) demonstrated by spinning each wheel and drawing artistic black patterns with his hands on the leather.

"Oh, son!" H.M. said dismally. "That's so the suitcase will be always right side up, whichever way you grab it. There's a leather handle on the under side, too.

25

All you've got to do is reverse her, and she's the same as she is now."

"Do you mean," said the amazed, admiring voice of an eleven-year-old girl, who was sucking at a lollipop, "you thought that up all by yourself?"

"Well . . . now!" said H.M., with a modest wave of his hand.

A sudden demoniacal cry, issuing from the back of the group and making H.M.'s scalp crawl, did not mean that anyone had gone amuck. It meant merely that young Tommy, Squire Wyatt's son and the dirtiest of the lot, had got an inspiration. He rushed forward, confidentially clutching H.M.'s coat.

"Listen, sir!" he hissed. "Suppose you took that suitcase, and put her down sideways like an ordinary suitcase?"

"All right," said H.M., who was nothing if not broad-minded. "S'pose you did?"

"Well, then, she's got two wheels front and back. She's heavy. She's a racer. She'd go a-flyin' down the pavement of the High Street, four hundred yards from here to my dad's park wall, like Sir Malcolm Campbell in the Blue Bird!"

"Well . . . now!" mused the great man. "Were you maybe thinking of a little race? Against the dogs?"

"Crumbs!" whispered young Wyatt, overcome by the stranger's brilliance. "Crumbs! That's it! The dogs!"

It was a near thing. What drew H.M. back to duty, stern duty, was the deafening chorus of yells.

"I bet you my dog could beat ol' suitcase!"

"Garn! *That* fat Scotch thing? But I bet you *my* dog could beat ol' suitcase!"

"You be careful, Tommy Wyatt!" sobbed a very small nine-year-old girl. "Your dad's surveying North Field today, and he said . . ."

26

"Grr!" snarled the black and white mongrel. Both dogs, bristling, were now regarding the suitcase with a mixture of suspicion and dislike.

"I bet you a thousand pounds!"

"I bet you a *million* pounds!"

"I bet you—"

"Shut up!" roared H.M., and dead silence ensued. Every child had seized at some part of his white coat in appeal; it may have indicated trust, but it did not improve the whiteness of the coat or H.M.'s temper. He adjusted his spectacles and delivered an ultimatum.

"Now we're goin' to run this race," he said, "I promise you. What's more, if you've got any other starters you fancy (greyhounds barred), you just trot 'em out and the Old Firm'll give good odds. But we can't do it now, d'ye see?"

"Why not?"

"Oh, my son! I've got to repack this good old suitcase in case she goes smash. Why, burn me, I've got a bottle of whisky in there now! You wouldn't want me to bust a good bottle of whisky, now would you?"

Despite murmurs from the girls, there was a general gloomy agreement. The Marlborough boy, Harry Goldfish, had another suggestion.

"Got any cigarettes, sir?"

H.M., outraged, puffed out his chest and glared at the four boys.

"Now don't you go smokin' cigarettes, you hear me?" he thundered.

"No, sir," said the Marlborough boy dejectedly.

"Don't *any* of you go smokin' cigarettes; got that?"

All the spirit had gone out of them.

"Smokin' cigarettes," sneered H.M., "is sissy. If you want to smoke—" here he produced from his inside pocket four excellent Havanas, each cellophane-wrapped—"you smoke cigars like me. Here's one for

27

each of you."

Up to a point of ecstasy went their morale. Fifteen pairs of adult eyes, now bulging, still watched from behind window curtains.

But the eleven-year-old girl with the lollipop lifted one shoulder, bored, after the way of the eternally feminine.

"All right, my dolly," H.M. soothed her. "Here's ten bob to split between you and the other gal. I expect you'll want to buy sweets or lipstick or something. I expect . . ."

Here he paused, glancing across to the southern side of the street. About fifty feet down, leaning carelessly with her back to a house, stood another girl about fourteen years old. She was beautifully dressed, spotless, and a miniature beauty. Her ash-blonde hair curled to her shoulders. Her gray eyes, expressing haughtiness and indifference, might have had tears in them. Seeing she was observed, she turned and strolled away down the street.

"That's Pam Lacey, sir," observed the Marlborough boy, a man of the world. "Mrs. Lacey's daughter. Neat little piece, though."

"'*Er?*'" exclaimed the revolted and practical-minded butcher's boy. "Ain't got no pop," he sneered.

"Now don't you go talkin' like that!" roared H.M., pointing a finger at him. "What d'ye mean, she hasn't got a pop?"

"We-el!" said the girl with the lollipop, taking it out of her mouth and twirling it. "There's some who says one thing, and others who says another. Pam is too intellecktal—"

"Intellectual," witheringly corrected the Marlborough boy.

"That's as may be, *Mr.* Harry Goldfish," said the girl. "Too intellectakal for the likes of me. But *my*

28

pop says—"

"Who is your old man, my dolly?"

"Mr. Cordy, the shoemaker," the girl said proudly. "And he's so intelleckal he don't believe in nothing. He says she's got a slate loose." All the time Miss Cordy was studying H.M.'s face. "Was you thinking of going after her and giving *her* ten bob?"

"I dunno what you're talking about!" lied H.M. "And, anyway," he made fussed gestures, "I've got to go now. Can anybody tell me where to find a man named Rafe Danvers?"

"Ol' bookseller?" cried a chorus. "What you want with him?"

"Never mind, dammit! (And don't you go swearing, either!) Where is he?"

"Straight down; halfway; same side of the street!"

And off marched H.M., despite pleas to remain. He marched, boldly, his hand guiding the suitcase, never dreaming what havoc it would wreak in the near future.

Indeed, he felt stuffed with virtue. Not only had he resisted temptation, but he had preached a sound moral lesson to the youth of the land. Halfway down his eye caught the gilt letters, RALPH DANVERS: BOOKS, on a rather long, dusty shop window, with a table of twopenny books outside. The curious might have wondered why that window was covered by a heavy wire grille, as was every other window in the house.

If the name of Danvers meant nothing in Stoke Druid, except to Gordon West and Colonel Bailey, it meant a great deal to many wealthy and not-too-wealthy rare-book collectors in London and New York. For twenty years Danvers's shop in Bond Street had been their Mecca. Even now they often and angrily demanded to know why he had buried himself in a Somerset village, since they missed the long talks in the

29

Bond Street shop.

"I like peace and quiet," Danvers had said over and over. "My business is done chiefly by postal order. You can order from the catalogue anything you want to look at. . . ."

"Time wasted!" had fumed one of his wealthier clients. "And look here: isn't it true you grub up some beauties you like yourself? And can't bear to put 'em in the catalogue? And we don't even hear of 'em unless we come down here and throttle you?"

"Tut, tut!" the dealer would say evasively, and hastily try to change the subject.

Thus, on this afternoon of early autumn sunshine in Stoke Druid, Sir Henry Merrivale carefully propped his suitcase against the book table outside, so that it should not run away. He entered the shop with no thought of any crime problem in his mind.

A bell pinged sharply over the shop door. Inside was a long, dusky room, with an addition at the back to give it depth. Out from the side walls were built alcoves of books, with tables of books down the middle. The room exhaled that fragrance of old books which, far more than your dull roses or any flowers, is the true breath of dreamland.

At the very back of the shop, amid tall wire-fronted cases containing treasures, a green-shaded electric light hung on a cord from the ceiling just over an open rolltop desk. The proprietor of the shop sat there sideways, his feet on the desk, reading *Barchester Towers.*

"Hem!" said Sir Henry Merrivale, clearing his throat loudly. He adjusted his Panama hat and lumbered to the back of the shop.

Mr. Danvers, carefully putting down *Barchester Towers,* dropped his feet on the floor and sat round to face the newcomer.

"'Lo, Rafe," the newcomer said gruffly.

"Good afternoon, Sir Henry," answered the dealer in his soft, husky, and yet vigorous voice.

Mr. Danvers was a stocky elderly man, whose sparse whitish hair seemed to rest on his head like thistledown rather than grow there. His face appeared dusty; but a pair of shrewd pale blue eyes, with a twinkle in them, peered over a rimless pince-nez well down his nose. Though his waistcoat was spattered with tobacco ash, his hands were shining clean.

"It's a pleasure," Danvers went on with real warmth, "to see you again after almost two years! Sit down, sit down!" He indicated a small and battered armchair, with a leather cushion, into which H.M.'s bulk dropped dangerously. "And how are you, my dear Henry?"

"Awful," H.M. said instantly. "I got a blood pressure they drag round hospital wards just so they can show off. And I hope it's not goin' to get worse now, Rafe."

"I—er—don't quite follow you."

"Listen!" said H.M. impressively. "Not long ago I got back to London from Cheltenham. At Cheltenham they got me mixed up in a murder case while I was dictatin' my autobiography. Oh, my eye! At the end of it I was a wreck. Son, I wouldn't touch another criminal case if they stuck me head first in a barrel of gold. Anyway, I went back home hopin' to lie down and cogitate for about a month. And what happens, hey? You send me a telegram."

The bookseller, looking at the floor over his pince-nez and fidgeting, did not reply.

"You say," pursued H.M., "you've got something so good I've got to see it in person. You say I've got to come harin' down to this forsaken village for it. Well, Rafe, it had better be fairly choice."

Danvers nodded. He lifted his pale blue eyes to look

31

at H.M., and then looked at the floor again.

"I think," he said, "you're interested in Joseph Fouché, the Minister of Police under Napoleon and a fine trickster even before that? I believe there's a large picture of Fouché in your room at the War Office?"

"Uh-huh. Well?"

Danver put his fingertips together and contemplated them.

"You are perhaps not aware," he went on, "that Fouché wrote a secret book of memoirs? He wrote them at the command of the Emperor. They contain the secret and very much underground history of Napoleon's court from 1804 to 1812."

H.M. stared at him.

"Oh, lord love a duck!" he breathed.

"Exactly." The old bookseller seemed to writhe with unhappiness even at mentioning a rarity he had found. "Only two copies were printed, bound in vellum: one for the Emperor and one for Fouché himself. Fouché's copy is known to have been destroyed. Up there—" he pointed to one of the wire-fronted bookcases—"I have the only other copy, annotated in Napoleon's own handwriting. Do you want to see it?"

"I want to buy it," H.M. said flatly, and put his hat on a book table behind him. "You've always hated haggling, Rafe; and so do I. What's the price?"

"The book," said Danvers, "is not for sale."

Sir Henry Merrivale closed his eyes.

"Y'know," he said, after a long and bursting pause, "it's true when they say the purpose of second-hand booksellers is to obstruct the sale of books." Presently he exploded. "Then what in the name of Esau is the idea in bringin' me down here?"

"You don't understand," Danvers told him gently. "I want to give you this book as a present, if you solve the mystery of who is writing the anonymous letters here."

Again there was a silence.

"Anonymous letters, hey?"

"They are signed, 'The Widow,' after a tall black group of stones. They have driven the villagers half mad. In my opinion, they have caused a respectable if rather neurotic woman to drown herself not half a mile from where we are sitting.

"The letters appear," continued Danvers, slightly accentuating the word "appear," "to have stopped. But they'll begin again, never fear; and with worse results. Let me tell you what has happened."

Evidently using shrewd deduction combined with a great deal of gossip, the bookseller proceeded to outline much—though not all—of what we already know. His soft, husky voice spoke monotonously. As he sat under the only light in that dusky room, you saw beyond pyramided fingertips that he had a surprisingly strong chin.

During this recital H.M. sat motionless, his arms folded and his whole expression altered. His big face was smoothed out, hard, and impassive. His little eyes were fixed on Danvers. The youth of Stoke Druid would not have recognized him.

"Henry," Danvers concluded unexpectedly, "for God's sake step in and prevent somebody else's death!"

Still H.M.'s expression did not change.

"Tell me, Rafe," he said. "Did you receive any of these poison-pen letters?"

"Yes. To be exact, two."

"What did they accuse you of?"

"Among other things, of selling pornographic books and seducing a certain village girl with them. Neither accusation is true, by the way. But, you see," smiled the world-weary old bookseller, "I don't mind such charges. The point is that the poison-pen writer thought I *should* mind."

33

Here he nodded toward the front of the shop.

"I have a small section devoted to crime and criminology," he added. "But there is no—er—literature on anonymous-letter writing."

"Oh, Rafe! There's quite a lot of it. And practical experience, too. But about these letters you got?"

Turning back to the stuffed pigeonholes of the rolltop desk, Danvers fished out a folded sheet of notepaper.

"I particularly want you to read this one. Wait, please! Don't stretch out your hand for it."

"Well?"

"My knowledge of this sort of thing, I admit, comes chiefly from the—um—popular press. But, after you have read this letter, may I ask two questions before you comment?"

H.M. nodded. Ralph Danvers handed over the letter. While H.M. read it, not a muscle moved in his face and his whole expression gave an almost creepy effect. He folded the letter and handed it back.

"I think we can admit," Danvers went on, "that many anonymous letters are written by semi-illiterate persons. Can we also admit that many anonymous letters are written by educated persons, who use bad grammar and vile spelling to hide their identities?"

"That's right, Rafe. True as gospel."

"Very well! Then consider this letter, another I received, and one a friend showed me. The grammar, the spelling, the punctuation of each one is correct to the point of pedantry. There are few obscenities; but these are used skillfully with a kind of vicious unexpectedness, like—the viciousness of the letters themselves. Yes?"

H.M. considered.

"It was pretty nasty readin', son," he agreed, and meditated again. "Now I got a low mind," he an-

34

nounced proudly, "like most people. But this isn't ordinary human lowness. It's . . ."

"What?"

H.M.'s look grew wooden again. "You do the talking, Rafe."

"The letters are those of a highly educated or at least very well-educated person," said Danvers. "Therefore, in my opinion, we can eliminate ninety-nine per cent of the suspects. The ordinary villager, the ordinary farmer or farmhand for miles about, could no more have written these letters than he could have written *Absalom and Achitophel*. That leaves us only . . ."

"Go on, son. Who are the suspects?"

The bookseller hesitated. It was plain he loathed and hated what he had to say, but that he must say it.

"First," he began lightly, "there is myself." Pale blue eyes twinkled up over the pince-nez. "For the sake of argument, let's say I am innocent. Next we have Miss Marion Tyler, Mrs. Stella Lacey, Miss Joan Bailey, Colonel Bailey, and Mr. Gordon West. Then there is Dr. Spenlow's locum, Dr. Schmidt: his spoken English is often erratic, but his written English never. At a pinch we can include Mr. Goldfish, the chemist, and Mr. Benson, the choirmaster.

"Stop, please!" Danvers added mildly, as H.M. seemed about to speak. "Let's try the pleasanter task of those we can eliminate."

"You think you can eliminate, hey? Let's hear it."

"If you've ever heard Squire Wyatt use the King's English," smiled the bookseller, "you'd eliminate him yourself. The same is true of poor Fred Cordy, for all he once bought a typewriter to write fiery letters to the newspapers, and then became incensed and threw it in the river. You understand that many of my so-called 'suspects' are very doubtful."

Reaching into his inside pocket, H.M. produced a

case of very vile black cigars. The excellent Havanas he had given the boys, cigars pressed on him at a banquet the night before, he would have disdained to smoke himself.

"Rafe," he demanded, "what's your second question?"

"Second question?"

"That's right. When you began, you said you had two questions to ask. But everything you've said since has been an appendage to that question of the psychology of anonymous-letter writers. What's your second one?"

The bookseller stood up, pushing *Barchester Towers* to one side and standing with his back to the rolltop desk.

"The letters I have seen are all maniacal on the subject of sex," Danvers replied. "They seem to show it, if only by implication, in every line. . . . Isn't it true that most anonymous letters are written by neurotic women?"

"Oh, no!" said H.M.

His big voice seemed to echo in the quiet room. Danvers looked at him in amazement.

"It wouldn't be *quite* true, d'ye see," H.M. went on, "to say that anonymous letters, on a variety of subjects, are divided about fifty-fifty between women and men. The women still have a very slight edge. Still, it's close enough to strike an average."

"But I always thought . . . !"

Puh-ping went the bell over the shop door, as though a hesitating hand had at length decided to turn the knob. And, silhouetted against fading sunshine, Joan Bailey stumbled into the shop.

36

Chapter 3

Joan walked softly, quickly down the aisle between the left-hand alcoves and the tables. She wore a plain white silk frock, with silk stockings and low-heeled shoes; she carried shopping bag as well as handbag.

She could not see H.M. sitting there by the desk, since his head was hidden by high-piled books on the nearest table. She saw only the head of the bookseller, with pink scalp showing under thin white hair.

"Good afternoon, Mr. Danvers," she said rather breathlessly. "I want to know, please, if you have a book on the subject of . . . of . . ."

Now Sir Henry Merrivale has afterwards described his first impressions when he met her, being sure who she was from Danvers's description. And those first impressions may well be worth recording here.

"Very nice-lookin' wench," he has said, as one of his higher compliments. "One of those country gals who go about absolutely exudin' sex appeal, and never once knows it. Likes to be known as a good fellow. Polite and undemonstrative in public; demonstrative as blue blazes in private. Fall for some young feller—probably has already—and never think of anybody else. Loyal; pretty intelligent; loves gossip."

Danvers had assumed that mild, moth-eaten air which in the past had deceived so many persons in London.

"Yes?" prompted Danvers. "A book about . . . ?"

Then Joan saw H.M., and started a little.

"Forgive me," said Danvers, mildly striking his forehead. "May I present an old friend of mine? Miss Joan Bailey; Sir Henry Merrivale."

"How do you do?" Joan asked warmly, deeply interested in any stranger to Stoke Druid. Then a vague thought seemed to strike her. "Haven't—haven't I heard your name somewhere before?"

"We-el!" said the great man modestly.

The lamplight shone on Joan's heavy, fleecy brown hair, bound round her head. She had so fair a complexion that it showed every rise and fall of color. Then she remembered.

"I know! You're the man who goes about solving locked rooms and disappearances and miracles. You must have come here to . . ."

Joan stopped abruptly. Her left hand moved to touch the handbag on her right arm; then the hand dropped quickly. H.M. did not appear to notice.

"Listen, my wench," he said, frankly looking her up and down. "Did anybody ever tell you you've got a figure that would make Aphrodite look like a laundry bag in a thunderstorm?"

Joan stared at him. Color flooded her face.

"Really!" she said stiffly. "No, of course not! That is, except . . . I mean . . ."

Danvers came to her rescue with his usual tact.

"You mustn't mind Sir Henry," he assured her smilingly. "That's his notion of a casual social compliment. Er—how is your uncle?"

Miss Bailey gave H.M. another glance. Despite her expression, however, it was clear that she was not really displeased by the old sinner with the unmentionable face.

"Uncle George," she answered, "has—moods. He says there's going to be another war. He says it'll be fought with tanks and aircraft rather than rifles and barbed wire. Time after time he's got after the War Office; but they just politely say the matter is in good hands. At the moment," Joan tried to laugh, "he's sitting in the meadow near the High Street trying to paint his umpteenth version of The Widow.

"And that reminds me, Mr. Danvers," pursued Joan, giving H.M. another haughty look but rattling on nevertheless. "Are you having a special display of pictures or something in your window this afternoon?"

The bookseller was puzzled.

"No, certainly not! Why do you ask?"

"Well," laughed Joan, equally puzzled, "across the street there are about twenty children, sitting on the pavement in front of the General Store, and watching this house as though they expected it to burn down. I counted eleven dogs, too."

("Cor!" breathed Sir Henry Merrivale, with guilt stark on his face.)

"They must have had tea," said Joan, "because they're all clean. What's more curious, you know, is that three of their fathers are strolling up and down there, and smoking big cigars. I never knew Mr. Bull," she referred to the butcher, "could *afford* cigars."

H.M. spoke sharply but softly, impassive again.

"You were comin' in here," he remarked, "to look for a book about something. Was it about anonymous letters?"

"No, it was not," retorted Joan, lifting her rounded chin. She turned to the bookseller. "Mr. Danvers," she went on with desperate sincerity, "is there any book with the *real* story about this—this stone monolith they

39

call 'The Widow' or 'Ol' Widow'? I think her full title is 'The Mocking Widow.'"

Danvers looked down his pince-nez.

"My dear girl, there is no 'real' story."

"Please!" begged Joan. "Please!"

"My dear girl, I assure you! That figure is older than the Dane, older than the Norman. The guidebooks to this district," he nodded toward the front of the shop, "contain little more information than is printed on the back of the picture postcards you'll find in half the shops here. Please excuse me one moment."

Softly moving behind one of the tall wire-fronted cases, which formed a sort of square round the desk, Danvers looked along the shelf of a mantelpiece and returned with a dusty picture postcard in color and a crayon sketch in a frame some six inches high by four inches across.

Turning the postcard over, Danvers read the tiny printed words in the upper left-hand corner.

"The Mocking Widow, Stoke Druid," he said. *"This stone figure, forty feet high, thirty-eight feet round the base and eight feet round the head, stands in an open meadow below the High Street. Its name is perhaps early Christian in origin, derived from the Biblical story of the Cities of the Plain; tradition stating that there once lived here a woman so wicked she was turned to stone."*

"But I've known all that since I was a little girl!" Joan protested. "What I was asking . . ."

Danvers held up his hand.

"The eyes," he continued, *"are each large enough to contain a human head. A visitor in the lower High Street, looking northeastwards, can easily discern that look of mockery and cruelty which has given the figure its name."*

Putting down the postcard, Danvers picked up the

framed crayon sketch.

"This," he explained, "is only a fanciful sketch, done by a strolling artist in the early nineteenth century, as a conception of what The Widow may have looked like."

"Put it away!" cried Joan. There was apology in her blue eyes, but fear at the pink mouth. "Please do put it away!"

"My dear Miss Bailey! Of course!"

Danvers put the sketch face down on the desk. But not before H.M. had seen the face of a middle-aged woman, with hollows under her eyes, the dark brown heavy hair falling snakily to her shoulders. In the sketch the expression of the woman was far from pleasant. The corners of her eyes were turned up, the corners of her mouth were dark red and twisted; and her whole look, against a smoky elvish background, contained that which is easier to understand than to describe.

"I've always been frightened of that," Joan confessed, "even now it's on so many postcards."

"Oi!" said H.M. sharply. "That's only the sort of imaginative hobgoblin Phiz could do so well. She never existed, y'know."

Again Joan tried to laugh.

"Of course I know it!" she answered, even when they could feel fear exuding from her like the fleshly appeal. "I was only thinking of those letters . . . the woman who wrote them; . . . if you ever met her . . ."

Conscious of a bad indiscretion, Joan stopped dead.

"But if there isn't any story about her," she rushed on brightly, "well—that's that, isn't it? So sorry to have troubled you, Mr. Danvers." Again her fingers touched the handbag. "And so pleased to have met you, Sir Henry." Her smile forgave. "But I'm afraid I must see to dinner, and it's getting awfully late. You *will* excuse me now, won't you?"

Joan almost ran toward the front of the shop, and the bell tinkled after her.

There was a long silence.

"Rafe," mused H.M., still turning over the unopened cigar case in his hands, "who's her boy friend? This feller Gordon West?"

"Certainly gossip says . . ." Danvers paused. "How do you know that?"

"Well, I was listenin' pretty closely to what you said. . . . She's a nice gal, Rafe."

"Yes! And so is everyone else. The most pleasant, the most kindly . . ." Again Danvers paused, indicating the folded letter on the desk. "And yet somebody is writing those. I ask you again: for God's sake come in and help us!"

"Looky here, son," H.M. said very quietly. "You don't need to bribe me with Fouché's memoirs. Lord love a duck, *I'm* willing to help. But I can't."

"You can't?"

"I can give suggestions, sure. But don't you see that this case, of all cases, wants police organization?"

"No. I don't see it."

"Rafe, they've got the procedure taped. The thousand questions they've got to ask, the errands from door to door: son, I couldn't do it if I wanted to! My part is the sittin' and thinkin'. Do you want me to give you an illustration?"

"Yes."

"Rafe," said H.M., scowling at the cigar case and then looking up, "of your whole list of suspects—yes, and nonsuspects—which one has received the greatest number of anonymous letters?"

"But I don't know! How can I?"

"Well, son, that's the first question the police will ask. Very innocently, d'ye see, slipped in with a lot of harmless questions. Because why? Because the person

42

who's got the biggest number of poison-pen letters, anything from five to fifteen or more, is almost always the person who's *writin'* the poison-pen letters."

Danvers touched his pince-nez and looked fussed.

"But the police, when they were here, were either too stupid or too—what shall I say?—to see in poor Miss Martin's death anything but accident. I can't summon them."

"Ho!" said H.M., with evil glee. "But *I* can. You just leave that to me."

Putting his cigar case back in his pocket, H.M. lumbered to his feet. He folded flat the anonymous letter so that he could read it again.

"They've got to find the typewriter, too," he grunted. "I say, Rafe. Do you remember, in the very early Twenties, when they were experimentin' with portable typewriters?"

"I do, yes. What bearing on this has . . . ?"

"Rafe, I had a little Formosa so light you could balance it on nothing at all. They had to have a three-line keyboard, and squeezed in letters and symbols in an awful rummy way. Mine whacked out an exclamation point every time I tried to hit a comma; and the result looked like swearin' in Esperanto."

"But there is no such error in this letter!"

"Oh, I was only illustrating," mumbled H.M., giving him a curious look. "And now, Rafe, it looks as if I'm goin' be stuck at Stoke Druid for longer than I thought. Is there a pub where they can put me up?"

"But *I'll* put you up! Of course."

H.M. looked uncomfortable.

"Y'know," he said, "if you don't mind, Rafe, no. I'd like to make this a headquarters, yes. But it won't work if I keep whoopin' in and out of here (which the blighters'll make me do) at all hours of the day or night. What about this pub?"

Danvers sighed.

"There are two. The Nag's Head, just one door above here across an alley. Then there is the Lord Rodney, facing it across the street."

"Any recommendations?"

"The Lord Rodney," Danvers spoke with faint disgust, "is one of those Olde Englyshe Tudor hotels, built a year or two ago when Mrs. Conklin believed there would be many tourists. The Nag's Head is authentic fifteenth century, like the church. It is perhaps smaller and less—er—clean. But you will prefer the authentic fifteenth century, of course."

H.M. merely looked at him.

"Well . . . now!" he said. "I got a strong yearning for the fifteenth century, yes. But I got a still stronger yearning for bathrooms that really work and doors that don't lead straight out into the open air two floors above ground. That's just my natural cussedness."

Hastily to conceal this remark, H.M. then pointed with a look of loathing at the copy of *Barchester Towers* on the desk.

"Trollope, hey?" he sneered. "Can you still read that dreary old snail?"

Danvers instantly and gently took fire.

"My dear Henry," he said, "how pleasant to have your iron-bound self-assurance! How easy to think, as you do, that no novelist except Dickens ever lived!"

"But it's true," said H.M. "Oh, my eye! One of these days I'd like to see a sketch called, 'If Dickens Had Written Trollope.'"

"You would find that amusing, I suppose?"

"Not amusin', maybe. But awful heart-warming. The mysterious dark ladies leerin' down from the windows of Framley Parsonage! The bishop stuck through with a dagger in the monkey-puzzle-tree. The wild-eyed curates and vicars bangin' open doors and jumpin' over the furniture to find the missing papers!"

"The fact is, Henry, that you like only the incongruous. Such things, I assure you, do not happen in real life. Indeed, one might say . . ."

Wh-whang! slammed the bell over the front door, which was flung so wide open that it knocked down a shelf of books in the front widow. Similar crashes ensued as the door closed.

Though faint mellow light still lingered in the street, the shadows were gathering. In the doorway appeared the figure of a tall man in the costume of an Anglican clergyman.

Seeing apparently no path and only a line of tables, the clergyman leaped over the first table with the ease of a trained athlete. Brilliantly he leaped over the second, though his heel sent two books flying, like clay pigeons.

Then, finding in front of him a table head-high with books, he seemed suddenly conscious of improper conduct. Hesitating, rather flushed, he marched up to the astonished bookseller.

"Mr. Danvers?" he inquired, breathing hard. "I must really apologize from the bottom of my heart. Sometimes, unfortunately, I—er—hurry along without thinking where I am going."

"Not at all," murmured Danvers, and bowed.

Some other idea appeared to strike the vicar.

"I must also apologize for another thing. Unfortunately, my duties have been so pressing that I have been unable to call here, Mr. Danvers," the charm of his smile warmed the room, "for a good long talk about books."

"Not at all," Danvers repeated, with a smile. His eye was very dubious.

But one subject so filled and burned the mind of the Rev. J. Cadman Hunter that it excluded all else.

Sincerity burned from him like a flame: a dangerous flame, perhaps, but still sincere.

"I came to ask," he pursued, "whether you have any books on the subject of anonymous-letter writing."

"Anonymous-letter writing," repeated Danvers flatly, and moved across so that his body hid the letter on the desk.

"Yes," said the Rev. James calmly. "I intend to preach on that subject tomorrow morning."

Dead silence.

If the Rev. James expected to produce an effect, even subconsciously, there is no doubt that he produced one. Danvers stood motionless. H.M., who had produced and lighted a black cigar, stopped with the cigar halfway to his mouth.

"I tell you this," said the Rev. James, "because it is no secret. If it were fitting, I should have it announced in the village tonight.

"Gentlemen," he went on, "I will tell that congregation the truth. I will flay them, scourge them, with every whip and scorpion at my poor command. I will tell them to their faces what I think they are. If they do not like it, I fear it is not my fault."

Danvers spoke in a low voice.

"But your congregation . . ." He paused. "Why?"

"We do not see you often at service, sir?"

"No. I fear not."

"*They* could have told me," said the Rev. James. "Many, at least, could have told me. Yet they feared scandal and did not speak. I could have saved the life of an innocent woman . . ." He hesitated, clenching his fists. "Even now I have a plan to expose this poison-pen writer, and hold her up to shame before all men. I—I must not disclose the plan until tomorrow. But I? *I?* I had no notion of this plague until I myself received a letter late this afternoon!"

"May I inquire," said Danvers, looking at the floor, "what the letter was about?"

"You may," replied the Rev. James, bracing himself. He put his hand into his inside coat pocket and found nothing. "I—I left it at the vicarage. But it accuses me of—of an illicit relationship with Miss Joan Bailey."

Having got that off his chest, he spoke strongly.

"I propose," he said, "to read that letter aloud in church tomorrow morning."

Chapter 4

Now it was so quiet that, if they had been listening, they could have heard several dogs barking across the street. But the whole matter of the waiting children had faded from Sir Henry Merrivale's mind.

It was Danvers who spoke first, massaging his face with a bony hand.

"I am not, as you say, a churchgoer," he said in his husky voice. "And yet . . . An investigation; yes, by all means! But this method . . ."

"Do you know," asked the vicar, "what will happen when I read that letter in church?"

"Sure," said H.M. briefly. "It'll raise hell."

"Except in the literal sense, sir, I hope it will. But you don't grasp the real meaning. That letter—"

The vicar stopped, with a slight frown. Only vaguely had he been conscious of a barrel-shaped figure, with a gleaming bald head and a malevolent expression, sitting in an armchair and smoking a black cigar. The vicar glanced at Danvers with interrogation.

"Mr. Cadman Hunter," murmured the latter, "may I present you to Sir Henry Merrivale?"

The vicar, with a polite nod, was about to utter some commonplace and turn away, when a half remembrance seemed to strike him. His face, which would have been handsome except for a very long nose, grew ruffled about the forehead. He passed a hand over his fair hair. Then, suddenly, remembrance came. The Rev. James's eyebrows went up.

"But you," he said, "you must be the Old Man."

He said this very quietly and sincerely, you understand, as he might have said, "You must be Sir Lancelot."

Not twice in his life had H.M. ever heard those words uttered by another person save in grudging acknowledgment or sheer ribaldry. It is a sober fact that his chair nearly fell over backwards, old man and all. But he righted himself. His cigar fell from nerveless fingers, to be stamped out by Danvers, while H.M.'s eyes studied the vicar for any sign of hidden jiggery-pokery. There was none.

"Son," said H.M., surging up out of his chair, "lemme shake your hand."

"For me it is a true honor, Sir Henry."

"I'm as religious as hell already, y'see," H.M. assured him earnestly, "and I expect this is goin' to make me go to church still more. They don't appreciate me, son: that's a fact. Where'd you hear about me?"

"From a friend of mine: an Irish barrister named Kit Farrell. Whenever he speaks of you in the Bronze Lamp case, he might be speaking of a saint."

"Oh, son, you mustn't believe *everything*," said H.M., modestly disclaiming sainthood. "But the exposure in that Bronze Lamp business; yes, now, that was a smasher!"

"Exposure!" said the vicar, seized with inspiration and also seizing H.M.'s shoulders. "That's it, of course. I won't call this Providential," he laughed, "but at least it's the luckiest accident that ever befell a poor country parson! You were sent here to help me with my exposure!"

H.M. looked at him in alarm.

"Now wait a minute, son! I came here because . . ."

"We will go at once to the vicarage," decided the Rev. James, "and together we shall examine this poison-pen letter. How odd! There *is* an aisle here." He was now impelling H.M. forward, with the zeal of a fanatic. "My dear sir, aren't you thrilled by your manifest duty?"

"Candidly, no," said H.M. "Now looky here, son! I got a very valuable suitcase outside, on wheels. I got to get that suitcase to a pub called the Lord Rodney, because . . ."

"Your luggage, Sir Henry? Have no fear for that, I assure you. *I* will see to your luggage."

"Yes, that's what I'm afraid of. Y'see . . ."

"Forward!" the Rev. James said jocosely, and the bell pinged as he opened the front door. "Ah, your suitcase!" he added.

The suitcase was propped longways against the book table, so that two of its wheels were in the air and it rested safely. But the Rev. James, seeing before him what his preoccupied mind told him was an ordinary suitcase, essayed a gallant little feat of strength. Whirling up the case with both arms, he banged and clattered it down on the pavement—face forward, on the finest ball-bearing wheels—like an ordinary suitcase. As he reached for a nonexistent handle to pick it up, his right knee accidently smote the back of the suitcase like a battering ram.

And that did it.

"There!" said the vicar—and stopped, appalled.

The good old suitcase, as though entering into the spirit of the thing with zest, shot down that smooth, sloping pavement like Sea Breeze leaving the starting gate. Across the street, from twenty young throats male or female, rose one simultaneous howl of protest. It mingled with the yelp-scream of eleven dogs of every sort from Manchester Terrior to sheep dog streaking across the street like a varicolored moving carpet.

To this day H.M. swears fervently, and truthfully, that the whole thing was not his fault. But he committed a grievous error, which he will not admit.

The moment the vicar's knee struck that suitcase, Sir Henry Merrivale had gone tearing across the street, waving his arms, to tell Tommy Wyatt's gang this was not supposed to be a race. Thus, exactly in the middle of the road, he had met the tidal wave of dogs.

It did not treat him lightly. It spun him round twice, while he clutched at his Panama hat, and then deposited him in a seated position with a thud that nearly cracked the asphalt. Three fathers rushed up to him, still with the stumps of good Havana cigars, and demanded to know what odds he was giving.

"Ain't fair!" screamed one maddened boy, apparently afflicted with St. Vitus's dance.

"Ain't fair!" howled another. "Ol' parson's kickin' the dogs!"

Strictly speaking this was neither true nor just. The Rev. James, seeing what had happened, decided that the only possible course was to catch the suitcase. And at St. John's, Oxford, he had been a mighty sprinter. In the dogs' minds, of course, was never a thought of a race; they wanted only to pull down the evil object and worry it. If some of them got in the vicar's way, that was merely unfortunate.

And Danvers, rushing out into the road to help H.M., saw the possibilities for a new horror.

"Sir Henry!" he pleaded.

H.M., his Panama hat crushed over his eyes, lifted both fists to heaven. From his lips issued such a torrent of profanity, such a picturesque arrangement of obscenities, that upper windows flew up along the street like a trick effect in a musical revue.

"I beg of you!" moaned Danvers.

"_____!" said the great man.

"Colonel Bailey down there in the meadow! It's all heading straight for him! If anything happens to the Colonel—"

"So?" demanded Sir Henry Merrivale, suddenly yanking the hat up from his eyes.

Ordinarily, of course, he would have sat for twenty minutes in that street and described irreparable damage to his coccyx. As it was, the barrel-shaped figure arose and raced down the middle of the High Street, bowlegged and pigeon-toed, still clutching the Panama hat to its head, at a speed that almost baffled the eyesight.

"Hoy!" yelled the great man above a mass of heads. "Stop it! Stop it, can't you?"

Any turf fancier could have taken in the scene without field glasses; the maddened dogs, the flying vicar—and the triumphant suitcase, running more than four lengths ahead as measured by any dog. Then up rose the stirring treble of young Tommy Wyatt.

"Goggles!" cried young Wyatt. "Goggles! Get it!"

The response was instantaneous.

Out from the welter, nearly three lengths ahead of the field in half a second, darted the mongrel black and white spotted dog which we have previously met.

The race was approaching that partly curving, smooth hump of rock. Below it, and a little way out, sat a tall straight-backed military-looking gentleman, his brush poised for some delicate touch on the canvas in

53

front of him. Beside him stood two ladies, one of them Joan Bailey, who faced the street but could only stand petrified with mouths open.

"Goggles!" shrieked the last war call.

With one bound Goggles' long legs, as he ran almost beside it, carried him to the top of the suitcase. There he stood bewildered. But the suitcase, rocked by that left-hand jump, swerved its direction. It raced straight up to the top of the rock hump and burst open.

A spotted dog flew in one direction. A bottle of Scotch whisky flew in another direction. The suitcase, seeming to unfold huge and evil leather wings as it leaped amid a surge of H.M.'s clothes, knocked the back of Colonel Bailey's head, smacking his face against wet canvas; whereupon suitcase, Colonel, and easel toppled onto the ground.

For at least three seconds afterwards, every breathing thing in that neighborhood—dogs, children, spectators, parents—seemed turned to stone like the figure of The Mocking Widow some distance away. But this was not caused by the regrettable plight of Colonel Bailey.

About a hundred feet from them, speaking to two men with a surveyor's instrument, stood Squire Wyatt himself. He carried a heavy blackthorn stick, and turned slowly round. Even at that distance they could see his eyes bulge, and his paunch go in with breath for a war whoop.

"Haaah!" said Squire Wyatt.

In the estimation of Joan Bailey, there has never been anything like it since the rout of the Old Guard at Waterloo. In an instant's finger snap, almost the whole crush—dogs, boys, girls, even parents—swooped round and tore back up the High Street in one mixed mass. Their full charge cannoned straight into Sir Henry Merrivale, who stood his ground gallantly but was unable to move forward.

Of the race-meet crowd, only three tiny figures remained paralyzed on top of the bank over the field.

"Oh, murder!" whispered young Tommy Wyatt.

"Uncle Tom!" whispered the sobbing nine-year-old girl.

The spotted dog stood motionless, with liquid eyes fixed distantly, and trying to look as innocent as H.M. himself.

"I'll skin 'ee!" suddenly shouted Squire, lifting his blackthorn stick. "Dash my buttons, I'll skin all three of 'ee!"

As though inspired by the crack of a starting gun, all three took off at once in the direction of the broad gates of the park.

In the darkling meadow where so much havoc had been wrought, a panting Rev. James was trying to extricate Colonel Bailey from the trappings of suitcase, easel, and paint.

Sir Henry Merrivale, head down and drooping, still sat in the middle of the road like one who has succumbed to the cussedness of things.

The lady with Joan Bailey was Mrs. Stella Lacey. She took one look at her companion, and gently reproached her.

"Joan, please! I see nothing remotely funny in this accident to your Uncle George."

"B-b-b—" began Joan, and could not go on.

Turning her back, this deplorable girl pressed her hands over her face and began to rock helplesly back and forth. Stella Lacey seemed gently horrified.

"Humor, Joan," she said severely, "is *never* vulgar knock-bout farce."

"B-b-b—"

At this point Colonel Bailey stood up suddenly amid the debris. His face was a study in color. Traces of green, gray-black traces of the stone figure, the blue sky, were discernible on that lean background. He stood craggy and straight, in tweed coat and plus fours. Round his neck, like the blazonry of a good knight of old, was wrapped a pair of H.M.'s long red flannel underwear.

"Joan!" said Stella Lacey.

"Bu-but it's only water color! It'll w-w-wash off with a face cloth. It'll w-w-w-w . . ."

Colonel Bailey paid no attention to this.

"What," he inquired with heavy restraint, and touched the suitcase with his foot, "is this blasted contraption? And who—" a heavy, freckled, withered hand went out to point—"is that gentleman coming down the road?"

"Sir Henry Merrivale," whispered the Rev. James. "Holds one of the oldest baronetcies in England," he added.

The haughty aristocrat in question was approaching majestically. At the stone slide into the meadow, he was nearly deposited in a seated position again, but wrath, as well as a sense of outrage against destiny, held him steady as he lumbered up to Colonel Bailey.

"Listen!" he began, raising his right hand fervently to take the oath. "I hereby swear, before all and sundry, that for once in my life I am absolutely INNERCENT of all hokey-pokey. You can't pin a thing on me. I had no more to do with this business than a cuckoo clock in Switzerland. And I will now prove this."

He did. H.M., at his best, is a powerful orator with a wealth of gesture like the late Sir Henry Irving. Vividly, with long horizontal sweeps of his hand, he described the evil episode. By this time the Rev. James had trouble in keeping a straight face, but H.M. pointedly ignored him.

"And that's how it happened," he declared, "so help

56

me Jinny!"

For a moment Colonel Bailey remained motionless. Then he did exactly what would have been expected by anyone who knows the best and old-fashioned type of Army man. He threw back his head and roared with laughter.

"Damn good idea, this!" he said, again tapping the suitcase on wheels with his foot. "Come and have dinner with us tonight!" he added, a little embarrassed.

H.M. bowed with one hand across his corporation.

"Son," he said, "thankee. That's an invitation I'm proud to accept."

"Good man! Joan! Got something especially good for dinner?"

"Oh!" muttered Joan, conscious of being late. Her pink mouth fell open. "Uncle George, I . . ."

"Curry, eh?" insinuated the beaming Colonel.

Joan nodded and sighed with relief. She could feed her uncle curry three hundred nights a year, as a rule, and he noticed nothing except to pronounce it an excellent dinner.

"Can't miss the house," he told H.M. "Go in at the Manor gates, turn left on a gravel path that branches left, and it's the first house you come to. Got it? Good!"

Colonel Bailey, having no sense of false dignity, had completely forgotten the weird pattern of his face. He gathered up easel, smeared canvas, brushes, and large paint box, shoving them all under one arm. His gray-brown hair was cut close to his head, his whitening mustache close-clipped. But, under his tangled eyebrows, few saw the wit or penetration of his eyes. Anyone who called him a Colonel Blimp would have been sadly mistaken.

"Come early, eh?" the Colonel said brusquely. "Like to have a bit of a powwow. Especially with a War Office chap—oh, I know who you are!—bit less

57

hidebound than some of 'em. See you later."

And tossing H.M.'s red flannels to the Rev. James who was busy repacking the suitcase, he trudged off up the bank of the meadow. A moment later the vicar closed the clasps of the case with a sharp snap and straightened up. His handsome face showed only a smoothed-out determination. But his fine voice went ringing across that short space.

"Colonel Bailey!"

"Eh?" inquired the Colonel, turning round at the top of the bank.

"Do you mind," the vicar asked smoothly, "if I drop in tonight after dinner? It's a matter of—er—church affairs. You're the only vestryman I propose to consult."

"Hang it, man," said Colonel Bailey, with ill-concealed clucks of impatience, "can't it wait?"

"I'm afraid not, sir," said the Rev. James, in the same ringing tone. "It concerns these poison-pen letters. I have just received one myself."

Colonel Bailey hesitated.

"Very well," he answered, and tramped toward the park gates.

All the feeling and atmosphere in that group had changed. All were conscious of damp rising from the meadow toward sunset, and of the tall gray-black figure of The Mocking Widow, one shoulder humped and slightly leaning, at no great distance away.

Joan stood motionless, her blue eyes more troubled, her hands clasped together. Stella Lacey, appearing to have heard nothing, held her head in the air and looked aloof. Sir Henry Merrivale, watching everybody, noticed out of the corner of his eye that a new figure approached the group after sliding down the east bank of the meadow.

It was as well for H.M.'s temper that he had not

previously noticed this man, who had witnessed the great suitcase race and had been on his knees clasping a tree stump, pressing his face to the top of the tree stump to stifle mirth. But there was no mirth about him now.

Gordon West—thirty-five, middle-sized, lean, wiry —wore an old sweater and a pair of discolored flannels. His brown eyes glowered over what at first sight appeared to be a sulky mouth and jaw. The little lines round his eyes were those of amusement; but those round his mouth of discontent.

"Y'know," remarked H.M., "I expect this is the first time this business about poison-pen letters has ever been thrown down among you. Like a snake. Rattlin'. Hey?"

Stella Lacey intervened.

"Joan, dear," she said, giving H.M. a little smile to rob the words of sting, "I don't think we had better talk too much to this gentleman. His name is Merrivale, Sir Henry Merrivale." Gordon West stopped briefly, and then came on. Stella Lacey's voice went up.

"He caught the murderer in that Five Boxes case," she cried, "and nobody else dreamed who it was. He's hand-in-glove with the police!"

"But suppose he is?" asked Joan, though her hands tightened. "This afternoon *I—*" She paused. "What's this about more poison-pen letters, and why must Mr. Hunter see my uncle?"

The Rev. James's jaws tightened.

"Because," he replied, "I am accused of having," here he almost faltered, "of having an illicit relationship with you. In honesty I ought to have your own permission, and your uncle's, to mention your name in church tomorrow."

"In church?" exclaimed Joan.

Gordon West moved up just behind Joan at her right shoulder. He spoke quietly, but his voice was thick.

"Is it your idea," asked West, still restrained, "to preach about this letter?"

"More specifically, to read it aloud."

West slowly passed a hand over his cheek and jaw, which somewhat needed a shave. It was a large hand for a man who was not very tall.

"Have you this letter with you now?" asked West. "May Joan and I read it?"

Now here was a curious matter. At Danvers' bookshop the Rev. James had reached for his inside pocket, and said he must have left it at the vicarage. Now, as though suddenly remembering something, he reached into the side pocket of his informal gray-tweed jacket, and produced a folded sheet of notepaper. Not a muscle moved in H.M.'s face.

"You may," answered the Rev. James. He looked at West's face, and hesitated. "Merely as a matter of form," he laughed, "you will give me the letter back, of course? I have your promise?"

"Hunter," West said slowly, "I didn't like you when you first came here. I like you still less now. But I'll play fair with you."

It was Joan who took the letter, as the Rev. James handed it over without a word. Then, visibly shaken, he turned toward H.M. as though the whole subject could be dismissed.

"Of course we all understand . . . ," the vicar began in too loud a tone of voice.

But H.M. was not listening.

Westward, up beyond the High Street, the square church tower stood out against a long crimson sky. In the meadow there was a pinkish glow, where the blackening shape of The Mocking Widow leaned slyly. H.M., crushed hat on the back of his head, was leaning back and looking up at the top.

"Tell me, son," he growled. "Could you climb up that figure?"

"Climb . . . ?" The vicar's puzzled brow seemed to become knotted. "Oh! That! Well, people hereabouts are—are against it. Superstition, perhaps. I shouldn't like to climb it myself. It looks rather like one stone; but it might crumble at the middle and fall down on you."

Then the Rev. James's tone changed.

"Of course we all understand," he repeated, again too loudly and with a laugh, "that insinuations in poison-pen letters are often merely ridiculous. Why, come to think of it, I have not even set eyes on Miss Bailey since the . . . since a tennis match! In July, I think it was."

H.M. swung round.

"So?" he said softly. "Then why have you been avoidin' her?"

"Avoiding? I don't under-understand."

"But you can't help it in a little place like this, son. In a matter of two months or so, you're bound to bump into somebody in the street, or at the grocer's, or anywhere you like."

The Rev. James glanced over his shoulder; first at poor Mrs. Lacey, now in despair, then at Joan and West. Emotions so seethed in that quiet meadow that the chronicler cannot try to express the occasional incoherence, the fits and starts, on the part of everybody.

Gordon West walked forward and handed the folded note to the vicar.

"Why," West asked in the same thick voice, "do you want to read this letter aloud? Hasn't there been c-cruelty enough?"

"I don't want to read it. I hate cruelty. But I must do

61

my duty."

"Why is it your duty?"

"Because I must persuade these good people that *I* am involved too. *I* am a victim, however innocent. Otherwise they will not follow me."

"What do you say, Joan?" asked West.

Curiously enough, Joan seemed the least affected save for the tinge of color in her cheeks.

"No!" she whispered. "It'd be horrible! And yet . . ."

"You notice, Mr. West, that Miss B-Bailey herself says 'and yet'?"

Arms trembled in the group. Stella Lacey turned her face away.

"Then I'd better warn you," said West. "If you read that letter tomorrow, I will quite literally break your neck."

Now we must remember that the Rev. James had spent three years in an East End parish, where he had won respect by flattening the meanest with gloves.

"My dear fellow, we must not quarrel," he suggested, with the smile of a man who knows his own record as a boxer. Besides, West was at least half a head shorter.

"No, we won't," agreed West, with the smile of one who knows himself very nearly a master at judo. "And I'll modify what I said. Read that letter tomorrow, and you won't preach for three weeks."

Then West exploded.

"Do you understand that, you swine?"

Nobody else spoke. For what seemed interminable seconds West stood looking up at the vicar, daring him to come on. The Rev. James's expression was one of unhappiness and compassion alone, his head down.

Presently West whirled round and strode toward the bank. Though in passing he glanced at H.M. and Stella Lacey, he ignored Joan. Reaching the top of the bank in two jumps, he walked furiously toward the park gates.

"Gordon!" said Joan. She spoke in a voice so gasping and heartbroken that her words were incoherent. "Wait! Please wait!" And she stumbled up the bank after him.

A blue tinge, with a touch of gold, had crept into the crimson sky. No sound seemed to issue from the High Street. Three persons stood motionless in the meadow, under the face of The Mocking Widow.

Chapter 5

Joan did not overtake West, because she was forced to stop for a minute or two at her own home. This was a square Victorian home, a hundred yards to the left inside the Manor grounds, a house with long windows and the first leaves of autumn fallen about it.

Hurrying into the kitchen, Joan almost threw the shopping bag at Poppy, the hired girl, and begged Poppy to prepare dinner because she (Poppy) knew the curry recipe thoroughly, whereas she (Joan) had another appointment.

Poppy cast up a sentimental look at the ceiling and agreed.

Then Joan ran along the curving path amid the trees, a path whose gravel here changed to earth, to West's two-room stone cottage among the fruit trees.

The door was open. Joan stopped in the doorway to get her breath. A greenish twilight still lingered in the cottage.

Inside, in the long study filled with books and dusty curios, Gordon West sat on the ancient sofa with his head in his hands. He did not look up when he spoke.

"I know," he said in a muffled voice. "It's my damned temper. I can't control it, and I don't know why. I say and do things I don't mean, and can't unsay 'em afterwards. I'm sorry I cut loose. But when you didn't seem to mind much whether Cyril-Percy-Dear-Me read that letter aloud . . ."

"Well," Joan answered tonelessly, "better accuse the wrong man than the right one."

West, shocked, stood up from the sofa.

"Joan!"

And, as usual, tears came into her eyes.

From Joan, as she stood in the doorway with her fine figure in the white frock outlined against green tracery, flowed that same fleshly allure of which she was so unconscious, but which was caused (mainly) by full-blooded youth. With such attraction she need not even have been pretty, but she was. Tears of contrition brimmed over.

"Darling!" she said, hurrying across to him and holding out her arms.

He kissed her so violently, and her response was so unrestrained, that even the village idiot (had there been one) would have noticed something more than a mere flirtation.

"You do love me?" said Joan. *"Really?"*

"You know that," West said in a thick voice, and shook her by the shoulders. "You're all things and everything."

"Then, darling . . . I've been thinking."

"What?"

"Well . . . no; wait; listen!" Joan, hating herself, clasped him more tightly and lowered her head against the neck of his sweater so that her words were almost unintelligible. *"I* don't mind, Gordon. Truly I don't! But we *are* going to be married?"

West was startled. "Of course! I've already . . ."

"Well, then . . . oh, this is the horrible part! I never even thought about it until . . ."

"Until when?"

"Never mind. Darling, listen! With these books and other things—you must make quite a lot of money?"

"I do," answered West, with a curious grim smile.

"Then why can't we *be* married? This is so—so upsetting; it's awful; I don't," she added hastily, "know why, but . . ."

"*I* know," West said grimly. "And, by God, I feel worse! Just a moment! I want to ask you something."

Gently disengaging her arms, he blundered across the room in the luminous green twilight toward the typewriter table by the north window. Since Stoke Druid was so comparatively close to the main road, an electric cable had been run here; those who could afford electricity used it, and those who couldn't burned paraffin lamps.

West, though he could well afford electricity, deliberately kept paraffin lamps because of what he called "the damnation of progress." One such lamp, with a tall glass shade, was bracketed to the wall beside the window near his typewriter desk. West lighted the lamp, turning the wick low, so that the room was filled with a warm, faint, golden dusk.

Then, bending over, he found a desk dairy and flipped over the pages with unsteady hands. Presently he straightened up.

"Got it!" he said triumphantly. "I knew it was here!"

"Gordon, what on earth *is* all this?"

West smiled under the yellow lamp, and his smile altered his whole expression. All lines of discontent or of fierce determination were gone. It was the smile of a good-natured, kindly man whose guard is down and who makes no pretense.

"Joan," he asked very seriously, "will you do me the honor of marrying me on the afternoon of Friday, the 3rd of October?"

For a moment Joan, breathing hard, could only look at him in bewilderment.

"Wh-hat?"

West repeated his question.

"Isn't that time enough?" he added, with wrinkles of anxiety going up his forehead. "To make preparations or whatever it is? I mean, I want you to go up to London and buy everything in sight." His expression froze. "Here! Stop a bit! Do you accept?"

"Of course I accept," cried Joan. "If I can't have you all the time, not just for an hour or so occasionally when we're sure nobody will call here, I think I'd rather die!"

"Then what are we arguing about?"

Joan threw out her hands helplessly. An observer could not have told whether she was crying or laughing.

"Darling, you're so *foolish.*" She did not speak as though she disliked this.

"Mrs. Wych says you won't even let her dust in here, much less let her clean. Mrs. Wych says (did you know?) she simply wouldn't endure such language from anyone but you."

"All right! Admitting my manifold imperfections . . ."

"That diary," Joan interrupted him. "I'll bet you anything you like you haven't made another note in it for the whole year. Then you solemnly put down, 'Joan; marriage,' or whatever you put down, and you never say a word about it to me!"

"I couldn't. I didn't know how soon I could get the book in good order. Let me tell you the main thing."

West's smile had vanished.

"There," he went on, pointing to a thick bundle of manuscript beside the typewriter, "is an at least tolerable novel unimaginatively called 'Drums Along the Zambesi.' When I send it off to the publisher, which will be in less than a week, I've finished my commitments for some time. And what's happened in the meantime, Joan?"

He walked slowly forward, facing her, and gripped the back of the sofa.

"By now," he went on, "my bank account is so well padded that I don't need to write as much as a single line for the next five years. Do you understand, Joan? *Not a single bloody line!"*

"But . . . but I thought you loved your work!"

"I do. I'd rather go to prison than not be able to write." He silenced her with a fierce gesture. "Some time ago our good vicar paid a call here. It was . . . a brief call. Anyway, he asked why I'd given up travel when I was a comparatively young man. I said because it was disappointing. That was a lie.

"It was because—scrimp and save, scrimp and save, to the meanest little farthing that'll get you steerage passage through the Malay Straits or a bug-filled room in San Francisco! But that's not the way to do it. If you can't afford the best orchestra stalls, then don't go to the theater. If you can't afford to travel first-class, with special tips for special favors, then don't travel at all.

"That means work. And rightly! At my job it means work, work, work; grind, grind, grind: eighteen hours a day or twenty if you can stand it. Never look away; never look up. No other activities except books; no holidays; who wants a silly trip to St. Ives when you're headed for the Mountains of the Moon? Hit 'em with book after book; force 'em to recognize you; *make* 'em know you've got quality; grind, grind, grind, for five years, ten years, even fifteen years. . . .

"Well, it doesn't take quite as long as that. About halfway through—you don't know why; nothing seems to have made a dent—all of a sudden it changes.

Streams of cash begin to come running in from all directions. Suddenly you realize you're nearly at the top. But you must make sure, Joan. You must make sure."

West paused. Joan looked at him as though she had never seen him before.

Releasing his grip on the back of the sofa, he drew a deep breath and made a face of apology.

"Well! That's all for now," he said. The likable, sympathetic smile went over his face, with any smoldering look gone. "Sorry to have been such a secretive devil. I can't help it. Anyway, the first step of our honeymoon will be a year's trip round the world. You will be severely beaten if you don't buy everything you like. . . ."

"Oh, who *cares* about money?"

"I do. At least, as far as you're concerned. D'you think you'll like it?"

"Gordon!"

Presently they were both sitting in an old easy chair, facing the black and dead fireplace, and talking such maudlin nonsense as need not detain us. Outside windows and open door, the sky had deepened to faintly rustling night. The dimness of lamplight shone on a Zulu devil mask hung at an upper angle of the bookshelves.

"It's wonderful," whispered Joan. "Everything in the world would be wonderful," she hesitated, "if it weren't for . . ."

"For what?"

"For these awful poison-pen letters."

West's shoulders tightened. It was as though the stuffed rattlesnake on the mantelpiece had emitted its vicious *whirr*.

"Oh, damn the anonymous letters!" he said.

"Gordon." Joan seemed intent on a thread in the

70

collar of his sweater. "You never said anything to me about all these letters."

"Well, if it comes to that, you never mentioned 'em to me. When the vicar began shouting about anonymous letters down there in the meadow . . ."

"You thought it meant us?" Joan shivered. "So did I. I was scared to death for a minute."

West, biting at his underlip, did not reply.

"We haven't been very—very discreet," said Joan. "I think most of the village guesses about us. You *feel* that. But they just seem to take a complacent, 'Ah, youth!' attitude, and don't mind. I don't understand."

"Look here, Joan. Have you had any of these letters?"

Pause. Joan, who was sitting in his lap, now seemed intent on ruffling down the hair over his forehead.

"Yes. I have. About seven."

"Seven? Still, I suppose that's not very many. The woman who's pouring out this poison ought to have . . . ought to have . . ."

"She ought to have fangs instead of a mouth," said Joan, pressing her own lips to his cheek. Then her voice rose: "Gordon, where's this going to end?"

At that moment, though they did not know it, a certain person looked in at the open doorway. With their backs turned in the big wing chair at the fireplace, they could not see this figure; and it made no sound on the hard earth outside. Only the Zulu devil mask, had it possessed sentience, was in a position to see. A brown moth, flapping across the room, darted in silhouette against the rattly glass of the lamp. The figure in the doorway softly moved away.

"Listen, Joan," West told her quietly. "These seven letters you got: did they all connect your name with Cyril-Percy-Dear-Me?"

"Gordon dear, you *mustn't* talk about Mr. Hunter

like that! He isn't in the least namby-pamby, and you know it!"

"Yes, I know it," West admitted gloomily. "I just don't like the fellow, that's all. What's more, you're evading the question. Did these letters concern you and Hunter?"

"Well . . . yes. They did, mostly. Except for a few little things that aren't important."

Again she felt West's shoulders tighten.

"Do you really like Hunter?" he asked. "I don't mind if you do" (liar), "but for God's sake tell me the truth. Do you like him?"

"I like him, yes."

"I see."

"No, no, you don't see! I mean: I like him as I like Mr. Benson, for instance," she meant the choirmaster, "or Mr. Danvers at the bookshop. Look at me!" Joan pleaded. "Please look at me!"

One look into the blue eyes, full of passion and tenderness, must have convinced anyone of her sincerity. Gordon West felt a warmth, almost a weakness, of sheer relief. In his heart, at that moment, he could have taken an oath that he was an idiot and a traitor even to think of Joan and Hunter. Such absurdities should be laughed at. And yet . . .

(Only in imagination we hear the *whirr*.)

"Besides," Joan broke in quickly, "you haven't told me whether you received any letters. Did you?"

"Oh, two or three. Nothing important."

"Gordon, stop it! You know it's important. What were they about? Have you got the letters here?"

"No. I threw them in the fire. As you said yourself, they concerned only a few little things that weren't important."

After giving him a quick glance, Joan settled down with her head on his chest. Her air was one of

72

casualness and indifference. So was her voice when at length she spoke.

"They were about a woman, weren't they?" she asked, as though to a child. "Oh, darling, don't lie. I can always tell. What woman?"

"Now look here . . . !"

"What woman, Gordon?"

"Oh, it was some nonsense about Stella Lacey and myself!"

And, at this moment, for the second time an unseen visitor appeared outside the open doorway of the cottage.

But the second visitor was very different from the first, and we can give her a name. Miss Marion Tyler, the good-looking brunette in her very early forties, was about to lift her hand and tap at the open door. Then, seeing various aspects of the two persons in the back-turned chair, she smiled and dropped her hand. Soundlessly her lips sketched out, "Bless you, my children," while she lifted her hands as though in blessing. Afterwards Miss Tyler slipped quietly away.

Neither of the two in the chair might have seen her, even if either had turned round.

"Joan."

"Yes, dear?"

"You know it's a lot of rubbish, don't you? About Stella and me?"

"Of course, dear. Isn't a poison-pen writer apt to say anything?"

Yet there are atmospheres. That of Joan, formerly warm and intimate, was now tepid to coldness; and, very slightly, she trembled.

"Now let's be sensible," laughed West, too loudly and with a rattlesnake whirr of doubt in his mind. "I admire Mrs. Lacey, yes. She's a nice, pleasant woman . . ."

"'Humor, Joan,'" murmured Joan to herself, with the air of one who quotes, "'is *never* vulgar knockabout farce.'"

"What the devil are you talking about?"

"Nothing, dear. And please don't shout at me."

"I was not shouting, Joan. I was merely trying to explain. As I say, I respect Mrs. Lacey very much. She's not had an easy life . . ."

"Ah, no," whispered Joan. "We all know how her husband was killed in the R.A.F., testing one of the new planes. (That was bad, I admit!) But we've heard of her terrific struggle to bring up one child. She seldom speaks in public, of course, but she tells the men all her troubles in private. Don't think I mind, Gordon! Because I don't. But it does hurt me a little to—to have you bracketed by all these horrible village gossips with a sneaky little woman like that."

"Sneaky?"

Now Joan was very English. If she saw a man with black sleeked-back hair of the sort known as oily, or with sidewhiskers even a fraction of a millimeter longer than the curt island haircut, it would have repelled her like the sight of an unpleasant insect. Similarly, her contempt was boundless for a woman who told troubles to anyone except that woman's closest circle.

"Yes, I said sneaky," repeated Joan. She rose to her feet and smoothed out her white silk skirt. "That's how I feel, and there it is. Naturally, it's of no consequence. I don't care in the least whether . . ." Her voice rose. "Oh, Gordon, *have* you been running after that dreadful woman?"

West also was on his feet.

"I keep telling you, no! Use your own test; look at me! That's it! Can you honestly and sincerely say you believe all this rubbish?"

There was a pause, while the brown moth whickered

74

and fluttered near the lamp.

Joan's eyes, tear-blurred, gave him a brief glance. Then her gaze wandered round the room.

"No," she confessed in a low voice. "I don't believe it, really and truly. But—"

"But what?"

"It's got into my mind, that's all. It won't go away. I keep thinking about you and Stella Lacey, being in here, and . . ."

"Stop it! Don't you see that's how the poison pen works? How it drove poor Cordelia Martin to kill herself, probably over nothing at all?"

Joan controlled herself. "Yes," she agreed, "I understand. I'm sorry. I'll try to be good."

"If we let the poison touch us, we're done! Even now, when I can see in reasonable light and sanity, I know this business about you and Hunter wouldn't be believed by anybody. Let alone—well, by me."

"That's just it! Take Marion Tyler for instance, who's one of the *nicest* persons alive. If the letters had accused Mr. Hunter and Marion Tyler . . ."

"What's that?" exclaimed the astounded West.

Joan, her head a little on one side, regarded him fondly but helplessly.

"Darling," she said, "you and my uncle are two of a kind. You both live in an ivory tower; you never see anything round you; you both loathe gossip."

"I hate gossip, yes! Because of all the petty, footling . . . !"

"No, Gordon. It's because you're always in the Mountains of the Moon, or paddling a canoe along the Zambesi. You never notice your neighbors."

"I see. And what is your uncle's enormity?"

"He's been after the War Office for ages. He says that in the next war, which he swears will come within a year, the Germans will rush forward with dive bombers

75

supported by tanks—oh, I know all the terms!—in a lightning drive of the kind they tried and failed with in 1914. The War Office just smile and pat him on the back; and he's old and tired."

In the imagination of Gordon West the image of commonplace Colonel Bailey, retired on half pay, acquired a curious poignancy. It was to have still more poignancy two years later.

"But, you see," Joan went on softly, "it's only natural and human to be interested in other people. *I* am. Maybe I'm a gossip; but I'm at the phone half the day. I can't help it."

"But, my dear, none of this applies to you! For the love of Mike get a telephone, with angels on it to represent you, and talk to the damn thing twenty-four hours on end! Providing, of course, you keep time for . . ."

Again she held out her arms. There was a silence.

"I really must go," said Joan. "Poppy will have dinner on, I expect, and we're entertaining that big fat man with the glasses. But there's one thing, Gordon. I resolved not to tell even you; I wasn't going to tell anybody. But—"

"Yes, poppet?"

"In this afternoon's post, I got another of those letters too. It's worse than the others. It threatens me with something, and yet it can't be possible! But, oh, God, I'm frightened!"

Her worst enemy could not have called Joan hysterical. Yet there are times when nerves snap. Terror rushed into that room, as though smashing windows and blowing out lights, in a presence which could be felt like a touch.

"Close the door and turn up the lamp," Joan begged. "Please, please turn up the lamp!"

Gordon West, struck to cold efficiency, moved softly

76

but quickly. As he turned the wheel of the wick, a broad yellow coziness spread over the book walls with duskier and heavier shadows beneath. West closed and latched the door; nobody ever locked doors at Stoke Druid. Afterwards he went back to Joan. The authority of his voice, comforting her, was as gentle as the hands on her shoulders.

"Now, then," he said, with the lines in his face again. "Nobody's going to hurt you; I'll see to that. What's this about something that 'threatens you, and yet it can't be possible'? What is it?"

Joan, gulping a deep breath, moved closer.

"Well . . ." she began.

Chapter 6

Miss Marion Tyler, as she walked briskly away from West's cottage after that brief look inside, glanced up westward at a brilliant three-quarter moon which touched the trees to deathly daylight.

Everything about Marion was brisk. This does not mean she was one of those intolerable women, brazen of voice and frigid of manner, who make everybody within earshot want to murder her. On the contrary! Let us put it like this: if several men were telling a shady story, they would instantly grow silent in the presence of Stella Lacey or Joan Bailey, but they wouldn't mind if Marion heard.

Marion, her fine teeth often flashing in a laugh, wore bobbed hair fashionably curved and without the slightest tinge of gray. She had a good and sturdy figure, and excellent clothes. She had, too, a gentle hand with children and dogs and horses. As for men, she sometimes confessed, there wasn't much room for them in her life, though she got on admirably with them.

As she moved away along the earthen path between the trees, she saw in bright moonlight that two figures were approaching from the direction of Colonel

Bailey's house further westward.

"Hul-lo!" said Marion under her breath.

One person was Stella Lacey, a light wrap thrown over her dove-colored frock. The other was her fourteen-year-old daughter, Pamela. Sir Henry Merrivale, who had seen Pam in the street that afternoon, would have given her still another look.

It would not have been at all true to say that Pam was a smaller copy of her mother, though both were slim, both had ash-blonde hair which fell and curled at the shoulders, both were beautifully dressed in adult fashion. But Pam was still rather coltish and awkward, despite her attempt at fine deportment. Pam's round face had grave, gray, intelligent eyes of the "speaking" sort: they conveyed much more than she said.

"Hul-lo," Marion repeated aloud, as they met in the moonlit path. Marion quickly glanced backwards, and it was clear she had decided to head Stella off.

"I hope you're not going to Gordon West's," she added. "I dropped in there myself, to borrow a copy of this *The Sword in the Stone* he thinks is so wonderful. But he's not at home."

"Gordon's?" Stella echoed, raising her eyebrows as though she had never heard of the place. "Marion dear, no. We were merely taking a talk. You know Pam, of course? Though she *is* so seldom at home on holidays."

Marion smiled down at her.

"Yes, I know Pam. And how are we tonight, Pam?"

The little girl's eyes looked at her gravely.

"Yes," Marion added, abruptly and unexpectedly, "I know that was a silly remark to make. But how else do they expect us to talk to you?"

A glint of real appreciation shone in Pam's eyes.

"Good evening, Miss Tyler," she said.

Stella, for some reason, was tonight a little upset and unusually loquacious.

80

"Really," she observed, "I see nothing silly in the remark. Pam *is* a trial sometimes. Aren't you, Pam? She wants to play vulgar games like hockey, if you please, and get dirty. I believe her school actually *encourages* her in this. And her reading! Can you imagine a young lady, almost grown up, who does not enjoy Dostoevski and Tolstoy?"

"Oh," murmured Marion, rather flatly.

Again Pam raised her eyes.

"Mother," she protested in a low, mild voice, "you just can't keep their names straight. Anyway, who cares what happens to people called Sonya Beerwichkov Parapourdipoff and Feodor Ireoffenskeky Varaverakinsoleovitch? They sound like a couple of stove lids; and that's what they are."

Stella uttered that soft laugh which one of her admirers (the chronicler cannot help this) had once compared to a tinkle of little silver bells.

"Pam, darling," she rebuked. "How many times have I told you? We mustn't be foolishly insular."

"I don't see why not," challenged the forthright Marion. But Stella did not hear.

"The poor child," she said, "isn't really well, you know."

"Mother!"

"She may look healthy." Stella addressed Marion, shaking her ash-blonde head darkly and seeming miles away. "I have every confidence in Dr. Schmidt. And yet, in a way . . ." She hesitated. "Do you know that Dr. Schmidt, in addition to having his medical degree from Edinburgh—?" Aruptly Stella paused, as though roused from a dream. Even by moonlight the flush on her cheeks showed as a faint sepia. "Good heavens, what on earth am I talking about? Please forgive me."

This was what Marion wanted.

"Now come along, you two," she insisted cheerfully,

as she deftly turned them in the opposite direction and hooked an arm in the arm of each. "If you're going for a walk, come with me."

"Where are you going?"

"Only as far as the church. As the vicarage, to be exact."

"We-el! I think we can manage that before Pam's bedtime."

"Mother!" Pam intervened suddenly. "Could we look in and see the Gunpowder Room?"

"Perhaps, dear. Perhaps."

Stella did not even hear the question. Since she must have observed Marion had noticed nothing, she was again her demure self. As they marched along the earthen path, sometimes kicking away a dead leaf, they were as outwardly happy as three who go to seek the Wizard of Oz.

"To the vicarage?" mused Stella. "You've helped Mr. Hunter a great deal with his church work, haven't you?"

"For months and months!" assented Marion, looking up at the moon and brimful of energy. "He has a lot of work to do, you know. Then there's this bazaar and jumble sale a week from today; he'll need a lot of help there. James—" here Stella glanced sideways at the use of the vicar's Christian name—"is so worried and conscientious about his sermons."

"Mr. Hunter," said Stella, "always seemed to me . . . so *young.*"

"My dear Stella," laughed her companion, "do you know his actual age?"

"Well, I—I never thought about it," murmured Stella, as though thinking of the vicar's age would be a kind of indecorum.

"He's thirty-eight," said Marion. "Nearly thirty-nine." She spoke happily.

"Marion!" exclaimed the other. "Are you sure?"

"Oh, it's an old story. James was the third son of a good family, you know?"

Stella, being on the ground she loved, nodded quickly.

"They didn't know what to do with him, you mean?"

"Exactly," Marion told her airily. "He wasn't sent up to Oxford until his late twenties. It meant three years at the university, and one and a half years at the Theological College. Then he was a curate for three years more. These tall fair men—" Marion lightly touched her own sleek black hair—"usually do seem very young, don't they?"

Let it be repeated that Marion was only forty-two.

"Speaking of sermons," Stella began, and obviously changed her mind. "You weren't there, were you, dear, at that dreadful business in North Meadow this afternoon?"

Marion was delighted.

"I wasn't. But Mrs. Doom at the confectioner's told me." Marion's light brown eyes, which were deeply black-fringed and her finest feature, sparkled as she threw back her head. "I'd have given five years of my li-
. . . I mean, I'd have given *anything* to have seen it!"

"It was not amusing, dear. Poor Colonel Bailey might have been killed."

"Of course, of course. Still . . ."

A faint rose-leaf smile touched Stella's lips.

"But I must admit," she went on, "that I found at least a *soupçon* of high comedy in the sequel. I'm afraid that people—only ignorant and stupid people, naturally—think Mr. Hunter was responsible for the whole affair."

"Oh?" said Marion in a slightly different voice. "Why?"

"Well! Perhaps you don't remember the time,

months ago, when Mr. Hunter was said to have stood and sworn horribly for five minutes after hitting a tennis ball out of bounds?"

"I was there." Marion spoke coldly. "James merely said, 'Hell,' as any red-blooded man might have done."

"Of course I know that," Stella assured her gently. "But many narrow-minded persons were prejudiced. Then, today, I understand they felt worse. Many say that Mr. Hunter deliberately kicked the suitcase, for a headstart, before Sir Henry Merrivale could say, 'Go!' They say Mr. Hunter ran after it, and kicked any dog that might have caught it."

Marion Tyler was shivering.

"This," she said, "is absolutely outrageous!"

"I couldn't agree more. Ironically, too, Sir Henry Merrivale, who—er—really does come from a good and very old family, is the hero of the occasion: especially with the children."

"Well, what on earth could you expect?"

"Expect?"

"He hands out cigars to the boys and lipstick to the girls." (This latter was not strictly true, but no matter.) "He says he's the Old Firm who'll give 'em odds for anything they want to bet on. My dear Stella, the kids probably think he's the only sane and comprehensible adult they ever met. And," added Marion, with a wry grimace, "I'm not sure they're far wrong. What I don't see," she concluded with dignity, "is how you should find anything funny in this about James."

"Marion! I never said anything of the kind!"

"Then what did you say?"

Stella slowly turned gray eyes of innocence past the fall of ash-blonde hair. Even her dove-colored dress seemed to shrink under the wrap across her shoulders.

"Only that there is a *soupçon* of high comedy, perhaps even tragedy, in the result. Small, ridiculous events seem suddenly to grow into things very important and deadly serious. Like . . . like . . ."

Marion looked at her.

"Like anonymous letters?" she asked clearly.

Both women stopped short, as though they had seen a snake in the path.

They had forgotten Pam Lacey, who was walking sedately and thoughtfully between them, each arm linked in one of theirs; and Pam was jerked forward like a doll. But it was not Marion's question which stopped them, with a fierce blood beat at one person's heart. It was the sound of a man's voice, clear in the night stillness.

They were now close to Colonel Bailey's home. The path, which had become gravel, ran past the front door of the house: square, built of smooth stone blocks, with long bay windows at the front and long straight windows at the sides.

Only one room, the eastern front room, showed a light. The front curtains on this room were drawn, heavy and black. But the two long side windows—less than thirty feet, diagonally, from where Marion and Stella stood—were wide open and had only light lace curtains. Through these curtains, as though through a gauze, they saw a stout gentleman with down-pulled spectacles and a bald head. He was standing, fist lifted, and orating to somebody whose head could be seen only in silhouette.

Across the silent lawn, beyond the oak trees, a heavy voice could clearly be heard:

"*. . . the truth, so help me, about these ruddy anonymous letters.*"

Marion looked round quickly, as though fearful of other listeners. But Stella was smooth and deft.

"Pam, dear!" she whispered.

"Yes, Mother?"

85

"I'm afraid we can't take our walk tonight. Just run along home, and go to bed in about half an hour. There's a good girl!"

"But, Mother! You promised . . ."

Though Pam might struggle, Stella's rose-water voice flowed over her and drowned her.

"I acknowledge, dear, but I'm entirely in the wrong. There! That's fair. And I'll make it up to you, really I will. Now run along when I tell you, or," gently threatening, "I may bring Dr. Schmidt to see you again."

Pam looked at her. It was not, you would have said, a look of hatred for her mother. It was rather a bewildered, voiceless cry, which our young poets persist in trying to utter, of "Why, why should the world be like this?"

Stella Lacey's house lay far across at the other side of the park, corresponding to the position of Colonel Bailey's here, as Marion's cottage somewhat corresponded to West's. The long, low bulk of the manor house was between. Pam, merely clenching her fists, ran hard along the gravel path.

Marion, nervous, nodded toward the long lighted windows of what both knew to be Colonel Bailey's study.

"Do you really think we ought?"

"I think it's our *duty,*" said Stella, with virtuous firmness.

So they strolled casually across to the nearest window, which stretched nearly to the ground, and they listened.

". . . which is why," Sir Henry Merrivale was booming, "I've told you what happened after you left. The parson's goin' to read this letter accusing himself of hanky-panky with your niece. He's coming here later to tell you so. I had to warn you, in case you flew up and

86

hit the ceiling."

Colonel Bailey nodded. He was sitting in a leather chair, his back to the window, with a table bearing whisky and soda between himself and H.M., who stood up glowering at him.

"The point is," persisted H.M., "how are you goin' to deal with him?"

"I'll deal with him," said the Colonel, briefly and significantly.

"But wait a minute, dammit! You can't just chuck the blighter out of the pulpit on his ear. Now can you?"

The two women outside the window heard a somewhat unnerving noise. But it was only Colonel Bailey drumming his knuckles on the table, like a skeleton's.

"H'm, no," he admitted. "Can't do that. Too undignified."

"Sure. Bein' myself a man of Chesterfieldian deportment," said H.M., sticking out his chest, "that'd occurred to me before. What about the vestrymen?"

"We can protest; that's all. Not good enough."

"Furthermore," pursued H.M., who was far more worried than the Old Maestro would admit, "this feller West swears he's going to half kill Hunter if that letter's read. Can West do it?"

"He can and will," Colonel Bailey said briefly. "But the damage will be done by that time. Stop a bit!" The skeleton knuckle-drumming began again. "You know," he added, "if West (let's say) had a bit of a talk with Hunter just before the service . . ."

"Oh, lord love a duck!"

"What's the matter with that?" snapped the Colonel.

"Looky here. You can't have West smearin' him all over the gravestones just as the congregation gets there! Even if you try strong-arm business tonight, it leaks out and you've got a worse scandal than before."

At mention of the word "scandal," even the short whitish-brown hairs seemed to prickle at the back of the Colonel's neck.

"I wish the word 'gossip' had never been invented!" he snapped, and then stated a philosophy known to them all. "I wish they'd just let me alone!"

"But we can'd do that, son. For instance: has Joan ever received any anonymous letters connecting her with the vicar?"

"Great Soctt, how should I know?"

"A lot of 'em, maybe?"

"Nonsense! That's so rubbishy," said the Colonel, "that nobody would believe it. Nobody'll actually believe that note to the Padre. But reading it in church . . . !"

"Colonel," H.M. said quietly, "there's one thing that'll be believed about any woman."

"Nonsense, I tell you! The Padre's not half bad. I liked him myself, until he went off his rocker over this business. Why, his uncle—"

Colonel Bailey stopped abruptly, and leaped to his feet.

"Uncle!" he added. "That's his bishop too. Lives not far from here. Damme, I'll phone him tonight and we'll stop this lunacy straightaway!" He drew a deep breath. "There. Got it!"

The two women outside the window did not look at each other, because both knew the truth of what H.M. had said. Neither did they step back from the nearer window as Colonel Bailey approached, because they guessed his intention.

Inside, set against the windows and stretched well past both of them, was a table holding a broad map model of greenish-brown ridges and valleys and roads, representing a more or less modern battlefield. Tanks, so small that ten would have gone into a matchbox, spread out from the roads. There were multitudinous aircraft, of all descriptions and with a black cross on many wings. The artillery ranged from light field guns to the heavy batteries behind hills.

Through lace curtains they saw Colonel Bailey's tired face as he picked up a wooden pointer on the model. Then, hesitating, he swung round again.

"Now look here, Merrivale," he remonstrated. "Dash it all! I want to help you. But what's the use fiddling while Rome burns? Look here!" And he tapped the pointer against the model. "Come here for a moment, will you?"

H.M., closing his eyes, picked up a half-finished whisky and soda and followed him.

The foot soldiers on the model were so small that they could be well studied only through the big magnifying glass which lay close at hand. Colonel Bailey reached out to touch it, but hesitated. His face, with the cropped whitish mustache, looked even more fretful.

"You'd think," he said, "that a child could see it. It's Clausewitz all over again; the Jerries worship Clausewitz. In '14 they hadn't the planes; armor wasn't invented yet; they couldn't move fast enough. But look at that map on the wall over there!"

The pointer swung round. On the wall opposite, over a Victorian mantelpiece, hung a large map of Europe stuck over with colored pins.

"In '14 (read any of their memoirs) the Jerries debated whether they'd invade Holland as well as Belgium. They didn't. But they won't fail next time. No, by God! What's more, your famous French line (and never believe in static defense, my boy) doesn't run where it should."

Here he wheeled back to the model, and the pointer flickered across it.

"You can't match infantry against dive bombers and tanks. You can't do it anywhere, let alone there . . . there . . . and there. Unless you've got fighter planes to smother the bombers and heavier armor to knock out the tanks, you're done. Don't you see that?"

"Uh-huh. It sounds awful convincing, Colonel."

"Then why can't the War Office see it?"

"I dunno," said H.M. in the same wooden tone. "By the way, about those poison-pen letters . . ."

"Damn and blast your poison-pen letters!" exploded Colonel Bailey. "Let me repeat: why fiddle while . . . ?"

"A woman was drowned, y'know," H.M. said mildly. "And I'm rather expectin' a murder."

There was a long silence. Then Colonel Bailey slowly and carefully put down the pointer on the model.

"Sorry," he said. "What do you want me to tell you?"

H.M. drew a deep breath.

"Colonel," he said, touching his whisky-and-soda glass against the model, "don't go imagining I think this isn't important. But I got an awful immediacy on my mind, as you might say. Now you," he went on, "in some ways you're as innocent as a baby, and in other ways you're as sharp as Boney and George Washington rolled together."

"Pfaa!" grunted the Colonel. But he looked pleased.

"Now take this Martin gal. If she didn't fall in the water by accident, either she killed herself or got killed. There's no evidence of murder. But nobody's bothered to ask *why* she committed suicide. Any ideas?"

"None at all. Why don't you ask her sister? Annie Martin; lives in the High Street." Colonel Bailey frowned. "You hardly ever noticed Miss Martin, somehow. Very devoted to the church. Very devoted to the Padre. What else can I say?"

H.M., by magic sleight with one hand, produced and lighted a vile black cigar. A cloud of smoke rolled out through the lace curtains.

"Uh-huh. Did you get any of these poison-pen letters?"

"I did," the Colonel said grimly. "Just one."

"Accusin' you of hanky-panky in the sex line?"

"Sex?" exclaimed the Colonel. "Good God, no! . . . Wait; stop a bit; in a way there was. The second paragraph said my wife had been unfaithful to me for years before she died."

"It wasn't true, was it?"

In Colonel Bailey's eyes was a wry, deep bitterness. The speckled skin across his temples seemed crinkly, like very thin paper.

"Eunice!" he said. "Eunice brought up Joan. Joan's my brother's daughter. Never was much of a hand with kids myself." There was a sort of struggle in his throat. "Eunice wore herself to death staying with me in India. Refused to go home. Never complained. Never dithered if we had a bit of a dust-up in the hills. Unfaithful! . . . Sorry!"

He meant, "I am sorry to have inflicted any sort of personal matter on you." H.M. glared at the floor.

"Not a bit," muttered H.M. "What about the other part of the letter?"

"Oh, that's forgotten. Western Front in '17. I commanded a brigade then. Only temporarily. I made a blunder, and it cost a lot of men."

"Now, burn me, take it easy! Any professional soldier's likely to do that."

"Well!" Colonel Bailey picked up the big magnifying glass, and looked at the swarm of microscopic foot soldiers. "Power! Anyway, that's what I like to think. But the letter laughed its head off. That business in '17 was all over the newspapers; nicely phrased, of course, though you saw through it. The point is: how did anybody ever learn about it, in a potty little village like

91

this? I didn't even tell Eunice all the details."

"I dunno," said H.M. "Some of our neighbors—some—are apt to know a lot more than we think. Did you keep the letter?"

"Yes. Kept it as a kind of double-barreled curiosity. Want to see it?"

H.M. nodded. Along the right-hand wall, in a room hideously papered with blue and pink forget-me-nots, ran a line of low bookshelves. On top of these stood a row of cardboard files, containing the Colonel's voluminous and endless correspondence with the War Office, and several files marked "personal." From one of these Colonel Bailey took a folded sheet of paper, and returned to H.M. beside the model.

"You know," the Colonel went on, handing the letter to his companion, "except for the dam' heartlessness of it, I can almost understand the (what-d'ye-call-it) the mind workings of the fellow who writes these letters."

"So?"

"I mean that! There are a lot of people in this world with black bile inside 'em. Some can get rid of it by pouring it at the War Office, like me. Others . . . well, you've got the result in your hand."

Sir Henry Merrivale, who had put down cigar and glass to scrutinize the letter through the big magnifying glass, looked up quickly.

"Colonel," he declared offhandedly, "I think that's the most important thing that's been said yet."

"Important? But it's as plain as the nose on your face!"

"H'mf, well," grunted H.M., scowling down the nose in question. "That may be. But not quite, d'ye see, in the way you think."

Now our old friend Chief Inspector Masters, had he been present, would instantly have recognized this form of mumbo jumbo, which H.M. used in all

92

seriousness. Colonel Bailey, hearing it for the first but not the last time, could only blink at him.

"There's a clue in the letter, you mean?"

"No. Only what I was hoping to find: an exclamation point where a comma ought to be. Here, you take this letter and keep it safe. It may be very helpful."

"But what about the blasted clue? Where is it?"

H.M., exchanging letter and magnifying glass for cigar and whisky, ignored the question.

"Colonel," he said, "I'm going to tell you three things that nobody knows except me. I'll tell 'em short and sweet. First, I've seen this Mrs. Stella Lacey somewhere before."

"Mrs. Lacey? Well, you may have seen her before. What difference does it make?"

"It may not be important, no. Because I've got a ghosty kind of idea it was connected with something fine and noble and exalted. Which the same," added H.M., giving a modest cough before he swallowed whisky like a shark, "I am always associated with."

"Yes, I—er—yes."

"Now for the love of Esau, don't go thinkin' I'm off my onion!" bellowed H.M., with such suddenness that the two women outside both flinched. "People are always thinkin' I'm a silly old dummy; and it's not true."

"Sorry," returned Colonel Bailey, looking at him with steady understanding. "What's the second point?"

"Your niece is in great danger. Or thinks she is."

"Joan? Nonsense!"

"I'm tellin' you, son. Where *is* Joan now, by the way?"

The Colonel didn't know, and said so. At dinner he had been conscious of a vague idea that somebody was absent, but he had been too engrossed in explaining war tactics to identify the person who was absent.

"You," said H.M., "didn't see her face, or hear her words, when she came chargin' into Rafe Danvers' bookshop to ask for some book with the true story of The Mocking Widow. Son, this is straight: for some reason she thinks about that Widow as a real person. And you didn't see her hand sort of creep out to touch her handbag almost every time we were on uneasy ground. I'll give you ten to one she received a poison-pen letter today, just as the vicar did.

"And speaking of the vicar," H.M. hurried on, to crush down his companion's protest, "that's my third point. A while ago we were talking about ways and means to prevent him from preachin' his sermon and readin' the letter. . . ."

Colonel Bailey stiffened.

"Great Scott, yes! Completely forgot it! Better phone the bishop at once."

"But, the fact is, Colonel . . . I'd rather you didn't."

"You'd rather I *didn't* phone?"

"Yes. Y'see, I've got a bit of a twisty mind. I wasn't being Honest-Injun with you a while ago. I was trying to steer you away from the subject. But I've been playin' straight ever since, so help me!"

"I see. Then what do you want me to do?"

"Let him preach his sermon. And read his letter."

There was a pause.

"Now wait!" bellowed H.M. "I'm begging you; don't freeze up and look at me as if you saw a drunk subaltern! When you've heard my reasons for asking that, I bet you'll agree with me."

Colonel Bailey did freeze up. But he still had confidence in H.M.

"And your reasons?" he asked quietly.

"It's like this. After the dog scrimmage was over, and I'd left my good old suitcase at a hotel called the Lord Rodney, I went up to the vicarage. And I found . . ."

94

Here H.M. bent his corporation over the model table and pulled back one of the lace curtains in order to throw his cigar out of the windows.

Though he might have looked straight down into their faces, this was not what caused the retreat of Marion Tyler and Stella Lacey. It is probable that they had heard enough. With dignity they strolled across the lawn, and into the gravel path; then they hurried until they were well beyond the other side of the house.

"Stella," said Marion in a breathless voice, as both stopped, "what's this about an affair between Joan Bailey and—and James?"

Her companion laughed gently.

"My dear, the report is ridiculous!"

"I know that, Stella. Joan wouldn't look at any man except Gordon. But this awfulness of talking about it in church—" She paused abruptly.

"Dear Sir Henry!" murmured Stella thoughtfully. "We must have met, as he said. Perhaps at a garden party. Buckingham Palace, you know."

Her companion gave her a dirty look. Yet Marion was too preoccupied; hard as she fought, there were tears in her eyes.

"Naturally," Marion remarked in a shaky voice, "there'll be no such sermon. The Bishop of Glastontor will see to that. Oh, and don't say your Sir Henry will persuade Colonel Bailey not to phone! When the Colonel digs his heels in, he's the most pigheaded man I ever met!"

"But why are you so upset?" wondered Stella. "Unless . . . Marion!" (Her smile went unseen.) "You're not in love with Mr. Hunter yourself?"

"H-how utterly silly!" Marion retorted, with a shivering kind of amusement. "We're good pals, that's all. Simply good pals!"

"Oh, dear," sighed Stella. "I wish I could be."

"Be what?"

"Good pals. With any man. It never seems to work somehow."

"Reading letters!" breathed Marion. "Preaching about—" Again she stopped. "Are you coming on to the vicarage with me, Stella?"

"I think not, dear. It *is* rather late."

"Well," cried Marion, with a flat shining in her eyes, "I'm afraid you'll be disappointed, Stella. There'll be nothing sensational tomorrow. James will simply preach the sermon he intended: about St. Paul on charity, I think." Her voice rose. "I promise you that, Stella! I *promise* you that!"

Chapter 7

"Our text is from the gospel according to St. Matthew, the twenty-third chapter, verses twenty-seven and twenty-eight."

Then the fine voice rolled out.

"Woe unto you, scribes and Pharisees, hypocrites! . . ."

The day was fine and sunny. The great east window glowed with entwined colors of scarlet and blue and yellow and indigo. But its radiance grew dim as it touched a brick floor and gray stone pillars which had known five hundred years of worship. Westward and inside the chancel, where the choir could be seen only as dim white garments on both sides, the altar candles were not more brightly polished than the brass paraffin-oil lamps which hung on chains from low roofbeams.

". . . for ye are like unto whited sepulchres, which indeed appear beautiful outward, but within full of dead men's bones, and of all uncleanness."

Squire Tom Wyatt, at the front in the ancient carven pew of his family, sat up straight beside his third wife and his young son. Something was wrong.

Up to this time the service had gone as easily and

drowsily as the clanging of St. Jude's churchbell. Now something stabbed the quiet; something seemed to lash even the homely, beloved walls of the church. From the moment the vicar had gone into the pulpit, up there on the left . . .

"Even so ye also—" the strong, fierce voice paused almost imperceptibly, while the Rev. James Cadman Hunter glanced down—*"outwardly appear righteous unto men, but within ye are full of hypocrisy and iniquity."*

The great Bible seemed to roll as he closed it. His hands, shaking back the sleeves of the white surplice, locked on the sides of the pulpit. He surveyed the congregation, considering.

Many faces, upturned to him from various places among the rows of pews, wore curious expressions. Marion Tyler, her mouth open, regarded him with horrified incredulity. She had already observed that Joan Bailey and Colonel Bailey were not in church. Mr. Theo Bull, the butcher, glowered angrily and wondered what was up.

In dead silence the Rev. James began to speak.

"Today," he said quietly, his fair hair gleaming and his ruddy face pale, "I wish to address you quite informally. I wish to speak to you without a wall between us, and as though no wall had ever been."

Perhaps it was the quietness of his tone which sent through the pews a faint ripple of relief. Somebody dropped a prayer book.

"I have been here among you," he went on, "since May of this year. I have tried to be a friend to you all. I have tried (bear witness!) to do my duty in so far as it lies within my poor power. Some of you—" the blue eyes moved from side to side, jaw hardening—"will not understand what I am about to say. But the many will understand only too well. And to these I say . . ."

98

Again the strong voice lashed out.

"You have been liars and hypocrites, even as it is written here; and I tell you so to your faces!"

Through the church there was a stir as though everyone had moved slightly, then stopped.

In the last pew at the back sat Gordon West, his arms folded. He alone did not move at any time, but kept his eyes steadily on the vicar. Mr. Theo Bull's face was as red as beetroot, and there were other looks of anger. The Rev. James Cadman Hunter let the full pause run out before he spoke in stillness.

"I say that you *have been* liars and hypocrites," he went on, "and you know it. Now let me add what is only fair. I do not say that you have wanted to be, or that in your hearts you are. But you have remained silent when you ought to have spoken. You have been afraid that some small, possibly unimportant secret of your own might be revealed.

"Ever since July, from what I have been able to learn since yesterday this village has been persecuted with anonymous letters. I am your only spiritual adviser here. Why did you not come to me? Why did not one of you speak out? Even if you do not like me, and I now fear such is the case . . ."

For the first time the Rev. James hesitated.

Tears were running down Marion Tyler's face. Over in the shadow of a pillar, where the light aureoled her hair under a very small modish hat, Stella Lacey's lips twitched in a sort of far-off and beatific amusement. She looked as Lilith must have looked.

"Even so," the vicar went on steadily, "I have done you no harm. You might have trusted me. By this time the letterwriter might have been captured, and dug no more fangs into our bodies or souls. I will not bring pain to the bereaved—"

His eye had caught the strange, white face of Annie

99

Martin, upraised in so startled a way that the Rev. James should have studied it more closely. He did not.

"—by stressing the fact that death has come among us, for whatever reason. But the poison pen must and shall be found. You cannot want this persecution, surely. You cannot wish to be demeaned and degraded. I tell you I can find the poison pen—on one condition. If this condition should fail, then all fails. Not only must I have help from you, but I must have help from you all."

Another person in the rearmost pew, a little dark-complexioned stubby-haired man with a grin, had never been seen in church before. He was Fred Cordy, the atheist shoemaker, who writhed with secret pleasure in his decent Sunday best.

Fred Cordy hated everybody; that is, almost everybody. There were only three persons in Stoke Druid whom he really liked: Gordon West and Colonel Bailey, who gave him money without asking awkward questions, and Squire Wyatt who, though a J.P., turned a more or less blind eye to poaching.

So the thin little man, his stubby black hair standing up like a goblin's, leaned across and whispered to West.

"Giving 'em 'ell," Fred Cordy said delightedly. "Ain't 'e?"

Perhaps the vicar's cold blue eyes reached him, for he fell silent like one stricken.

"Let me explain my meaning," continued the voice from the pulpit. "We have among us today a man who is not of the police—I see you are alarmed by the word police, but you need not be—and yet whose association with the police may be very valuable to us. This man . . ."

The Rev. James glanced briefly at a front pew where Sir Henry Merrivale should have been sitting. And Sir Henry Merrivale was not there.

It caused no break or hesitation in the Rev. James's sermon. Furthermore, it must be stated that once more the matter was not H.M.'s fault.

At the very moment the service began, H.M. was lumbering up and down his hotel bedroom at the Lord Rodney, in a fume of impatience, and occasionally consulting an enormous gunmetal watch. Since last night he had been trying to get through by phone to the Rt. Hon. Ronald Bevis-Binterton, Secretary of State for Home Affairs, at the latter's country home called Muchdelight in Sussex. And in vain.

"You might know," the great man had groaned to his landlady last night, "today would be Saturday and tomorrow Sunday. If the bounder's not there . . ."

Evidently he wasn't. As H.M. paced the hotel room, he frequently whirled to look round at the telephone between the two windows. The Lord Rodney, with its long yellow-stucco frontage, rightly boasted of up-to-dateness with tel. and h.&c. in every room. But the Exchange, a false-hearted woman who had sworn to ring, remained silent.

Then, as H.M. was resigned to despair, the phone did ring.

Mrs. Conklin, his stout and sympathetic landlady, was just hurrying upstairs to sympathize again. At the half-open door she picked up the conversation with the Home Secretary about twenty seconds after H.M. had begun.

"Sure the story's spread all over the London newspapers today. Look for yourself! I phoned all the news agencies last night."

" . . . ?"

"Because I've got a weakness for justice, Boko, and I hate to see the police slip up. Do you know what'll happen tomorrow?"

" . . . !"

101

"Don't fool yourself. People don't like this poison-pen stuff. They loathe it. There'll be questions in the House that'll burn your britches clean through. That is, unless you can show you've got the matter in hand. I know one Home Secretary whose head went poppin' like an onion over a case of this kind."

". . . . . ?"

"I'll tell you exactly what to do. Phone straight through to the Chief Constable here, whoever he is, and burn his britches to a fare-ye-well."

". . . . . ! ! !"

"I don't care if he's a goddam Field Marshal," yelled H.M., grabbing the telephone. "You make it so hot for Major Villiers Gobey-Gobey, of the Oxfordshire Gobey-Gobeys, that he can't sit down for a week. Tell him to do the same to every man down to an Inspector named Garlick."

". . . . . . . ?"

"Yes, that's it, except there's a 'k' on the end. Got it? Have Inspector Garlick here at my hotel at nine o'clock sharp Monday morning. Thanks, Boko. G'by."

Mrs. Virtue Conklin, the proprietress of the Lord Rodney, had possessed about the year 1905 a full-blown Edwardian figure and a piled mass of hair the color of a brass kettle. She still had both, as well as inexhaustible good humor. Being deeply and powerfully impressed by H.M., she waited with one hand pressed to her bosom while he bitterly fought the Exchange to put through another call.

This call was to Chief Inspector Masters, who, at the moment was entertaining his younger children with card tricks in the back garden of his new house at Peckham.

"Hello, you crawlin' snake," said H.M. almost affectionately. "How are you?"

". . . ! . . . . ?"

"Oh, I'm down in the West Country at a place called Stoke Druid. Listen, Masters. I need help, and I want you to do me a favor."

". . . . ! ! ! ! !"

"Now keep your shirt on, Masters. I know you've got an important case in town; I'm not tryin' to lure you away. I just want you to send a smart lad on an errand for me."

". . . . . ?"

"He's to go round to the Formosa Typewriter people. They're in the phonebook. Ask when they stopped makin' Formosa Jewel No. 3, where the crafty hounds switched the comma for the exclamation mark. Find out if they kept records; if so, to what dealers or private persons near here they sold any."

". . . . . !"

"Yes, I know it's practically impossible! But do it. Lastly, find out what you can about an R.A.F. Flight-Lieutenant named Darwin Lacey, and his wife. L-a-c-e-y."

". . . . . . . ?"

"Ho! You're gettin' curious now? Sorry, Masters; but I'm in an awful hurry. I've got to rush off to church."

". . . . . . ???!!!!!!!!"

"Yes, that's what I said," H.M. retorted austerely. "Hoo-hoo. G'by."

Replacing the receiver, he turned round scowling in his chair. He perceived Mrs. Conklin, her bosom heaving with interrogation, and he instantly pointed a finger at her accusingly.

"Where's my white suit?" he demanded, surveying his sober dark clothes with distaste. "Did you pinch my white suit?"

"Now, dearie," soothed Mrs. Conklin, sweeping toward him with an arch smile which indicated that her best days were not over yet, not by a jugful. "The suit was so dirty, what with dogs and children and all those times you sat down! I'm sponging and pressing it meself. . . . Now don't carry on, dearie! Let's see how your tie looks."

"Are you going' to stop fussin' over me?" roared H.M. "If there's one thing I can't stand, it's women FUSSING over me. Where's my hat? Never mind; somebody pinched it."

"Last night," said Mrs. Conklin coyly, "I told you all the gossip you wanted to know. I think you might tell me . . ."

But Sir Henry Merrivale had gone.

Despite his wish to go at a run up the High Street, he marched up to the church at a slow and majestic pace which, unfortunately, there were few to see. The immense and heavy doors were closed. If he feared that some vicious squeak (which is usual) would betray his presence like a pistol shot, he need not have worried.

For all were too tensely concentrated on the Rev. James in the pulpit.

H.M. looked uneasy. Out of that dim little church, cool and smelling of old stone, flowed such a strength of emotion that many were bending forward, hand on knee. Only Gordon West, in the rear pew, seemed unaffected.

The cold blue of the vicar's eyes never wavered. His voice rolled out slowly.

"Many of you," he was saying, "will be asking a question. You will be saying to me, 'Yes, it is all very well for you to tell us that! It is all very well for you to advise us: bring these poison-pen letters to me. But *you* have not been attacked. *You* have suffered no scathe, as of boiling water poured across the ankles. *You* do not understand.'"

His right hand, clenched against his breast, fell open.

"But I do understand," he went on, "because I have been attacked. With, considering my calling, a viler accusation than has been leveled at any of you. I cannot merely say that I am on your side. To obtain your help, to show that I am as frank with you as I wish you to be with me, to demonstrate that a lie must be cried aloud and not stifled, I must prove that I am on your side.

"Therefore I propose to read to you a letter—yes, signed 'The Widow'!—which I received yesterday. It concerns a young lady whom you all know and whom you all rightly respect. Deeply and humbly I apologize to the young lady for the lie it contains; but I cannot apologize for my duty. This is the most unpleasant task I have ever had to perform."

The Rev. James swallowed hard.

There was so deathly a stillness in the church that everyone could hear even the very tiny crinkling sound as he opened a folded sheet of notepaper. Perhaps one or two persons glanced quickly at each other in question, but no more.

"The letter is addressed to me at the vicarage, and sardonically begins, *Reverend sir*. It says . . ."

At the back, Gordon West suddenly sprang to his feet.

With unusual presence of mind the little shoemaker, Fred Cordy, reached up both hands and dragged him down. Except for a brief flick round of heads in the immediate vicnity, it went unnoticed.

Yah! You and Joan Bailey apparently believe that no eye watches you, save perhaps the figurative eye of morning. And you must leave before morning, though her bedroom—as any child in

105

the village knows—is on the ground floor, with long windows convenient of access. But forgive me! I am no moralist. Since you and Miss Bailey are both fond of . . .

Already the Rev. James's hands were trembling on the letter. He could not force himself, literally and physically could not force himself, to read the next word. He omitted it. But its absence shouted aloud. Though most people here would not have been shocked had they heard it in private, within these walls it would have been a desecration.

. . . then I shall not betray you just yet. But our comic world affords few spectacles more ludicrous than a clergyman turned Casanova, though the practice is of great age; and in your case, sir, practice makes perfect.

Your affectionate friend,
The Widow.

As he ended the reading, the Rev. James put down the letter hastily so that the shaking of his hands should not be obvious. They heard only a slight throat-clearing before his voice hammered on.

"Now I beg of you to think, as you consider that parcel of lies, of any communication you may have received yourselves. Was it worse? Could it sting more? Would any sane person believe it? For, putting myself aside, any charge against that young lady would be pure nonsense; and all of you know it.

"And so at last I return to my statement that I can find the poison-pen writer if you help me," said the Rev. James, leaning forward and interlacing his fingers. "Following the conclusion of this service, I shall go into the vestry and wait there as long as may be necessary. I ask those of you who have received a communication, or more than one, to go home and get them and bring them to me. If you have destroyed them, come and tell me what they said. Only with a large mass of material can we hope to compare, eliminate, decide.

"Do you think the task impossible? I deny it! I will not trouble you with the means, I dare think good means, by which I propose to perform it. Fortunately, the gentleman of whom I have spoken—Sir Henry Merrivale—assures me there are methods, long known to the police, by which guilt of the culprit may infallibly be determined.

"And when you come to me with the letters (if you do), I implore you not to come separately or secretly, as though ashamed. Have *I* hidden my face? Or wished to? God's light cannot hurt you. Walk in it; and be not afraid."

Unclasping his hands, he stood up straight and drew a deep breath.

"I have almost done. I must tell you frankly that this morning I was forbidden by my Lord Bishop of Glastontor to read the letter you have heard. What the consequences may be to myself I do not know. Nor, if justice be done, do I care."

Then, for the last time, the Rev. James Cadman Hunter's voice rang out both in humility and in appeal.

"But, if you will not listen to spiritual advice, then in His name listen to common sense!"

For a moment he looked down at them in silence. Then he walked slowly down the steps to the chancel.

Chapter 8

In the vestry, a large flat clock on the wall ticked slowly.

It was nearly one o'clock, a good forty-five minutes after the service had ended. But still no visitor had entered by the door leading out to the churchyard.

The Rev. James, his surplice and stole put away in a cupboard, sat in a straight chair facing the door, his head bent a little forward and his hands clasped over his face. The stone vestry had small windows, whose multicolored panes were so obscurred by ivy tendrils that not much light penetrated.

H.M., sitting in a far corner in his dark suit, remained all but invisible. A reddish-yellow glow touched the head of the vicar, who never moved.

"Tell me, son," observed H.M. in a drowsy tone. "Was there anything about that sermon that bothers you?"

"I wish I hadn't pitched into them at the beginning." The other spoke in a muffled tone, hands still over his face. "Only a few days ago I was writing on charity. I felt I had to do this. Yet I wish I hadn't."

"We-el," mused H.M., deprecating. "There's no harm in that. It stirs 'em up like a good dose of brimstone and treacle." Though still you could not see him, a movement of shadows suggested his head had turned. "But one thing did bother me. I thought you were goin' to read the letter but leave the gal's name a blank."

"What good would that have done?" demanded the Rev. James from behind his hands. "They would have suspected a trick. If I were to do any good at all, I must be absolutely frank with them."

"Anyway," said H.M., "that's how I put the proposition to the Colonel. Read the letter; but no gal's name. If it came out later, it'd be among a lot of names and it wouldn't matter. Lord love a duck, you balked and blushed at a simple little word like . . ."

"Sir Henry!"

"All right. But, d'ye see, I couldn't persuade the Colonel. He rang up the bishop." H.M. sighed. "Y'know, son, this is going to raise Old Nick."

The Rev. James sat up straight and slapped his hands on his knees.

"Do you think," he asked through tense jaws, "it would have made one farthing's worth of difference to me, if I succeeded in my appeal? But I didn't succeed. I failed. Not a single person has come to see me."

This was the point at which the door opened.

In the doorway stood perhaps the two persons whom he wished least to see: Joan Bailey and her uncle.

Joan, in a soft green frock, with tan stockings and flat-heeled shoes, gripped a green handbag in both hands. Behind her, too furious to speak, stood the Colonel in tropical clothes and a broad-brimmed hat.

Joan did not seem angry. There was little expression on her face except, in the eyes, a cool and steady dislike. The Rev. James sprang rather awkwardly to his feet, but his gaze was as steady as her own.

"Miss Bailey," he said. "I—er—did not see you in

110

church this morning."

"Under the circumstances, can you wonder?" Joan raised her eyebrows. "All the same, we got news of your great 'appeal' very quickly."

At the vicar's elbow was a long table, in the middle of which stood a flattish wicker basket.

"I suppose," Joan said, "that basket is for the unburnt offerings?"

"I really don't know. I hadn't thought exactly where . . ."

Joan moved across to the basket with her loose, swinging walk. Colonel Bailey took two steps inside the vestry.

"Young man," he began, and paused. "Don't want to make a pompous fool of m'self," he added, sounding like anything but that. "But do you know what they'd have done to you in India, thirty or forty years ago?"

"I'm afraid I don't, sir."

"They'd have left you alone with a loaded revolver, and given you ten minutes to use it."

"I am not an Army man, sir."

"No, thank God! But you'd learn not to mention women's names."

"Sir," exclaimed the bewildered vicar, "to me it was not a question of what you call 'mentioning women's names.' It was a question of duty and principle."

Colonel Bailey swung round toward the door, hesitated, and swung back.

"Stop!" he said. "Maybe I spoke a bit too strong. Maybe you're only young and green. But I'd rather you kept away from my house, in the future."

"As you wish, sir." The Rev. James was feeling the letdown after a high emotional pitch.

Joan, at the basket on the table, had opened her handbag. Her cool blue eyes turned sideways toward him.

"Here are the letters I received. Seven—I beg your pardon, six of them." Joan's fingers moved quickly in the dim red and yellow light, but fine eyesight would have seen she held back one. "Some have envelopes; some have none. The postmarks are different." She threw them into the basket. "Here is a letter to my uncle." She added it to the basket. "As for Mr. West . . ."

"Yes, Miss Bailey?"

"He destroyed his letters. But he jotted down some of the beastly things he could remember. As I was accused of having a—a sordid affair with you, Mr. Hunter, in the letters here, he was accused of the same with Mrs. Lacey."

Out of the handbag Joan took a couple of folded sheets from a notebook, as though she handled a spider, and flung them into the basket. Her voice remained casual, though her color had gone up.

"Thank you," said the Rev. James. "I was pleased to see Mr. West in church this morning for the first time. Er—he did not come with you?"

"No. I think he's pacing up and down behind the Gunpowder Room. He wants to have a chat with you when everybody else has gone."

"I shall be happy to meet him, Miss Bailey. In *any* way."

"So," said Joan, her voice rising, "since we're all supposed to be in this together, and compare notes, do you mind if I ask a question? Surely Mrs. Lacey has been to see you. How many letters did she get, and about what?"

From the doorway issued the indrawn breath noise of someone about to speak, but checking the word. Marion Tyler had appeared there. Suddenly finding herself in the midst of what seemed a large group,

112

Marion hesitated but evidently saw no polite way to leave.

"Joan!" she said, after a slight pause. "You asked about Stella Lacey, didn't you? And how many letters she got?"

"Yes!" said Joan. "Yes, yes, yes!"

"Well," Marion answered thoughtfully, "she didn't get any. Not one. She told me so herself, when we were leaving church. She laughed and said she was glad she didn't have to queue up."

"Mrs. Lacey," Joan spoke flatly, but with emphasis on the name. "She didn't get a single one?"

"No, Joan." Still Marion spoke thoughtfully.

"I see," snapped Joan, and moved quickly over to the door. Shepherding her muttering uncle before her as though he had been fifteen years old, she closed the door behind both of them with almost too much care.

Marion, it is probable, forgot them at once. Like Joan and the Colonel, she had not even seen Sir Henry Merrivale in his dark corner. Sturdy, sleek-haired, she stood there and looked at the Rev. James with her hands pressed hard together. He, after a formal bow, sat down and turned his head slightly away.

"James," said Marion in a shaken voice, "you were wonderful!" Then her whole tone altered. "But you were a bad boy! You really were a bad boy!"

The invisible bulk in the chair, as though touched with an electric wire, quivered notably.

Marion's fine contralto voice seemed to represent common sense, as Joan's light voice was eager and Stella's murmur provocative. But in Marion's tone was a note so yearning, so maternal, that it could not be mistaken.

And the Rev. James, though his ears grew red, seemed to like it. To Sir Henry Merrivale, the attitude which he called fussin' was repulsive. It was just as repulsive to Gordon West, who had often explained to a meek Joan, while he kicked at the furniture in a rage, that he would not be fussed over. But the Rev. James . . .

"I tried," he answered with dignity, "merely to do what was right."

"Oh, I know that! Of course you did!" Marion moved closer, her rebuking tone now mixed with motherly solicitude. "But last night, James, you practically promised you wouldn't do this."

"Pardon me, Marion. I promised nothing of the kind."

The vicar, conscious of the presence of a third person, had a sudden terrible notion that she might pat him on the head. He rose to his feet hastily, recovering his wits.

"But what on earth," he asked, quite sincerely, "are *you* doing here?" Then he paused in astonishment. "You don't mean to say that you, of all people . . . ?"

"Received poison-pen letters?" said Marion. She laughed shortly. "Of course I did. James, you mustn't be unworldly!"

"This is damnable!" said the Rev. James, whacking his fist on the table so that the basket of letters jumped. "Here, not ten minutes ago, Miss Bailey left six letters, all accusing her, as I was accused, of the same relationship with her."

"Indeed?" said Marion, brought up short. Her brown eyes were wide open. "Then Joan, too . . . how interesting!"

"It also seems," he told her with bitter sarcasm, "that Mr. West is involved with Mrs. Lacey. Well! Let us examine even poison. What particular crime have you committed, Marion, in the eyes of our letterwriter?"

"Can't you guess?"

114

"No. How could I?"

Over Marion's arm hung a leather shopping bag instead of a handbag. Marion's air of common sense and straightforwardness seemed to blur when she shook her black bobbed hair as though to clear her brain. Reaching into the bag, she took out a thick bundle of the familiar folded notesheets, with or without envelopes.

"I'm sorry, James," she said. "I should have told you long ago. But I couldn't bear to break off our friendship."

She threw the folded sheets into the basket.

"There they are," Marion added. "Fifteen letters. They accuse you and me of . . . well, do I have to tell you?"

The slow ticking of the clock made itself audible during that silence. Abruptly the Rev. James sat down, turning and putting both elbows on the table.

This was incredible. He had never thought of Marion Tyler, he would have told you, as anything except a good friend who helped him in his work, and whose attitude (a little mothering and jollying) he appreciated.

There returned to him, while the clock ticked, some words out of his training. Not the formal training; he remembered a wise old Canon, sitting against an ivy-clad wall with a pipe in his mouth, and the words then. *"There'll always be foolish women who mistake their interest in the vicar for their interest in the church. Sometimes you won't even notice it. But, if you're compelled to notice it, you must be a better diplomat than Talleyrand and a better man than you think you are."*

But Marion wasn't in the least like that. Marion was only a helper of whom (always in the way of friendship, of course) he was growing rather fond. While all this darted through his mind, in two ticks of a clockbeat, Marion watched him fixedly.

"Fifteen letters," he said. "All directed against you."

"And you," answered Marion, still watching. *"I* didn't mind."

"I seem to have got into a kind of jungle, and I can't get out." Again he jumped to his feet, trying to smile but not succeeding. "But we'll win through! Never fear for that!" And he pointed to the clock. "Why, look there!"

"Y-yes, James? What about it?"

"A while ago I was despondent because they didn't seem to respond to my appeal. Idiot! I should have realized they had to go home first, to get the letters. And naturally they were a little—a little hesitant. Like yourself, Marion. Why, by George, in another few minutes they'll come flocking in!" The vicar slapped his hands together. "Take Squire Wyatt, for instance. He's always been my friend. Squire Wyatt will be here, to quote only one person. . . ."

"James," Marion said nervously.

"Yes, Marion?"

"I'm afraid he won't, you know."

"Squire Wyatt?"

"No, James. Before he drove away, he was the head of the indignation meeting in the High Street."

"What indignation meeting?"

"Oh, lord love a duck!" groaned a ghostly bass voice from the dark corner.

Marion, shying back, saw faintly the outline of a bald head, and then a malevolent face, as Sir Henry Merrivale thrust forward his jaw. Across Marion's own face flickered an expression you could clearly read, "Have I said or done anything I shouldn't? No, thank the Lord!" But she was not at all cordial when the preoccupied vicar performed introductions.

116

"Squire Wyatt!" the latter was repeating. "That's impossible! What did he say?"

"Well, he . . . he sat in his car, with his wife in tears beside him, and carried on dreadfully."

"Go on, please."

"He said about four times he was the Squire, and he owned the living here, bishop's influence or no—" Marion meant that he could appoint the vicar to the parish, and in fact had done so—"and nobody was going to call him a hypocrite. Squire Wyatt said he'd buried two wives; and a lot of so-and-so people said at the time he'd poisoned them; and now these (forgive me, James!) these bloody letters were saying so too."

Marion was a superb mimic. Even in despair, or perhaps because of it, she worked her face into the lineaments of Squire Wyatt, indicating gray mustache and speech.

"'I don't mind for meself, harke'e! But, dash my buttons, when it comes to upsetting Lucy here—'" in imagination, a weeping wife was roughly banged round one shoulder—"'I say that's different. Ah, and look at 'er! The only one of the lot 'oo gave me a son!'"

All the mimicry dropped away from Marion, who looked as though she wished she hadn't tried it.

"Oh, James, don't think about it! It was so—well, Stella Lacey would say vulgar. To think of a man of old family, who ought to be a gentleman, being so stupid and uneducated!"

The vicar looked puzzled.

"But he's not . . ."

"What happened then, my wench?" asked the heavy voice of Sir Henry Merrivale, as though he pushed her with his hand like Squire Wyatt.

Marion hesitated.

"Nothing much. He drove off in his car, with the gears screaming. The indignation meeting adjourned

117

to the chemist's. Mr. Goldfish, you know." Marion glanced at the vicar, with disquiet in her eyes. "James!"

"Eh?"

"They were getting louder and louder when I came back the second time. Mr. Bull was making a speech. You don't think they'd come up here and try to make trouble?"

Emotionally exhausted the vicar might be. But for the first time a hopeful gleam, perhaps un-Christian but very natural, stirred with pleasure in the Rev. James's face.

"You think so?" he asked eagerly, and flexed his shoulder muscles. "You really think so?"

"No, of course not! They wouldn't dare! But I'm afraid you'll get little help from the village. You'll get help only from . . . from . . ."

This was the point at which the door was suddenly flung open, and just as swiftly closed again, whether for dramatic effect or not. They found themselves facing the upright, shortish, chunky figure of Dr. Johann Schiller Schmidt.

Dr. Schmidt had what he would have translated out of his own language as a "pleasure-beaming countenance." Dr. Schmidt was always exuding chuckles in a kind of perspiration, or roaring with laughter, except when he paid a professional visit, and grew so portentously solemn that he scared the patient. Looking out at the world through very large spectacles with heavy gold rims, he wore now a badly tailored cutaway coat and striped trousers which emphasized his chunkiness, and carried (as did nobody else in Stoke Druid) a silk hat.

All his pleasure-beaming countenance shone through gold searchlights at the vicar.

"I believe I have the pleasure of addressing Pastor

Hunter?" he inquired in a heavy baritone, and bowed. Chuckling all over his face, he paused. "Forgive me! I come on a serious mission, though in a sense it is a choke."

"A . . . oh, yes! How do you do, Doctor?"

Dr. Schmidt's head was covered with a light fluffy down of hair, which would soon be gone altgother. He put his head on one side.

"Pastor Hunter," he said, "often I have wished to congratulate you on your sermons. They are eggcelent. You should have been an actor."

"To tell the truth, when I was a boy, I wanted to be."

"*So?*" exclaimed Dr. Schmidt in delight. "And shall I tell you how I know?"

"No; really, I—"

"You are mal-achusted," said Dr. Schmidt.

"I beg your pardon?"

"You are mal-achusted," said Dr. Schmidt, making a small concentrated gesture as though he were tightening the top of a bicycle bell. Then he roared with laughter again.

This constant merriment was getting on everybody's nerves, already strung up. From Sir Henry Merrivale came a low growl as though he had seen something he disliked. No doubt Dr. Schmidt's shrewdness sensed this.

"However!" he went on. "We come to business. In church you ask for letters, yes?" His hand whisked to his inside pocket, and brought out four of them held fanwise. "These I have received. They accuse me, if you blease, of being a Nazi."

The Rev. James joined in his merriment, though unwillingly and unconvincingly. Dr. Schmidt looked contemptuous.

"I am a man of science," he said, making fussed

gestures. "What have I to do with politics? Pah! I serve a great new science, perhaps soon. However, I tell you."

He marched over to the table and the basket.

"The childish! The sophomoric! The dramatic!" added Dr. Schmidt, shaking his head. "However," he looked thoughtful, "perhaps it is better I say nothing. I drop them into the basket. So."

Whereupon he turned briskly, though with a hint of uneasiness.

"And now, if you will eggscuse me, I must go. But . . . Paster Hunter! As your well-wisher! I think I should warn you."

"Warn me? About what?"

"Well!" shrugged Dr. Schmidt, beautifully managing the letter "w." He nodded toward the closed door. "Out there, on the little path at the edge of the churchyard, there are many big black men gathered together. I have counted thirty; and I do not think they wish you well. They will not come in. They are waiting for you to go out."

"Are they, by George!" said the vicar, his eyes lighting up.

Marion, so bedeviled that for one brief second she lost control of her nerve, almost screamed.

"Who's doing this?" she cried. *"Who's writing these letters?"*

"Ach," muttered Dr. Schmidt giving her a keen glance past flashing gold spectacle frames. "Sometimes it may be necessary, I fear, for a medical man to speak. You agree, Pastor Hunter?"

But the Rev. James was not listening. He was striding to the door.

"Excuse me for a few minutes, will you, Marion?" he requested, giving her a beatific smile over his shoulder.

And the door opened and closed after him.

120

Chapter 9

The sun, now westering, was very warm for September. Its flat glare lay on the worn turf of the churchyard, on ancient gravestones or marbly-shining new ones, on sparse grass whose green was edged with brown.

Twenty yards away, along a small gravel path which ran southwestward from the vestry door, was a dirt path curving far westward to a point behind the Gunpowder Room. The Rev. James could understand why that group, gathered close together in a half circle on the little dirt path, had been described as big black men.

All wore their Sunday best, its lightest shade being a dark brown. They wore bowler hats, except for an occasional brown or dark gray fedora. Some had one shoulder inclined. They stood there, black against a line of poplar trees. Their eyes were fixed on him like one eye, and its current he could feel when he approached.

It was not hatred. Hatred is very deep and quiet. It was a wave of sheer uncomprehending dislike; and dislike is balanced dangerously, ready to spring with claws.

There was a faint breeze in the mild Sunday air. The Rev. James, his hands in his pockets, walked straight up to them.

"Well, gentlemen?" he asked, in the same voice he had used in church. "You won't come to me, I understand. So here I am. What's your complaint?"

Though he spoke pleasantly, his dislike sprang out to meet their own.

There were, clearly, two spokesmen just in front. One was mild-mannered little Mr. Goldfish, the chemist, now pale with anger. The other was Mr. Bull, the butcher, powerful but bulky, with far too much fat on him, glowering under a bowler hat and with his thick neck wilting his collar.

"Yes?" prompted the Rev. James.

There was a faint growl from the group, and eye-turnings for a spokesman. Mr. Goldfish was the more intelligent and educated; Mr. Bull was the bigger and heavier. So, as men have done since time existed, the eyes firmly chose Mr. Bull.

"All right!" said the butcher, squaring off as one who hears a fair proposition. "I'll tell you. First off, for me and my mates, let me say this: we wants to be fair."

A growl of approval went through the group.

"There's some things 'ee do," continued Mr. Bull in his hoarse voice, "that may be all right, maybe. But there's other things 'ee do that no decent man'll put up with; ah, or means to put up with!"

Mr. Bull's fists clenched, and he drew a step nearer.

"Such as?" inquired the Rev. James, who could have slaughtered him in one round.

In fact, as the vicar's eye studied that crowd, he felt far more disquiet at the sight of two silent heavy-boned Somerset farmers, the toughest of the tough. That was bad.

Out of the corner of his eye he noticed Fred Cordy.

122

Little thin Cordy, whose short black hair stuck up in bristles and who wore a grin from ear to ear, was perched on all fours atop a tombstone. Though Cordy did not actually bounce up and down like a monkey, he conveyed the effect of doing so.

"You were mighty fine," snarled Mr. Bull, "when you stood up there and called us hypocrites!"

"Aren't you? Have you brought me any letters?"

"No, and we're not a-going to! Most of 'em's burnt anyway, and the missuses hid the rest! Hypocrites, Mr. High-and-Mighty? When you're the damnedest hypocrite that ever set foot in this village? And I tell you so to *your* face?"

A slight uneasiness of wonder shot through the Rev. James, but it only made him madder.

"In what way am I a hypocrite? Tell me that!"

A contemptuous voice squalled at him from the back of the crowd.

"As though you didn't know!"

"But I don't know! Tell me!"

"When 'ee 'ad the nerve to put that part in the sermon about . . . ?"

"Shut up, back there!" snapped Mr. Bull. Fred Cordy bounced up and down on top of the tombstone, like a devilish mechanical figure. Mr. Bull, in a sweat of wrath, turned back to the vicar.

"By George, you'd deny it!" he said, and pointed his forefinger. "I'll tell you what it is, Mr. High-Nose! If you wasn't a parson, with them clothes and all . . ."

"Is that what bothers you?" demanded the Rev. James.

"Eh?"

"The fact that I am in Holy Orders, and wear these clothes?"

"And what else *would* bother me?"

"Then come with me, please. All of you," said the

vicar, trying to control his voice.

He turned to the right along the little path, which led due west past the graveyard and behind the church. About a hundred yards behind the back of the church, and parallel with it, was the longish shape of the Gunpowder Room.

Those words, in themselves, convey a wrong impression. It was built of very thick stone, long and rather wide, with a higher addition, at the southern end, like a stone drum or the head of an oblong key. This stone drum, its walls and ceiling nine feet thick, had stored the powder for three ancient artillery pieces which once looked out through loopholes on the far side.

For, in the dim year of 1688, the West Country was "invaded" by the thin forces of the so-called "King" Monmouth. Stoke Druid, alone except for a few other places, stood out for King James. In those days the only road to Stoke Druid lay westward, curving up through thick forest toward the back of the church. And so, with Monmouth's forces strung all along the main road, they built the Gunpowder Room to defend the village.

It was not necessary to use it. Monmouth never came. Long ago its guns had been shipped to the museum at Bristol; its loopholes for gun or matchlock had been knocked open to modern windows; it was used for church affairs which rain might spoil, such as the bazaar on the coming Saturday.

But all members of the black group, steaming in eagerness as they hoped they guessed what the vicar meant, tramped after him with the sun in their eyes. At the old, blackened stone drum of the gunpowder tower, the Rev. James turned to the left behind it into an immense flat meadow of short grass.

Instinctively he moved toward the middle, and set

his back to the wall. The black group again clustered round in a semicircle, some ten feet out from him, with Mr. Bull and the chemist a little forward.

"Good!" said the butcher. "Clever-good! What's the game?"

"You have accused me of being a hypocrite—"

"Ah, and still accuse 'ee!"

"Very well. I ask you to prove that charge here and now, or let me disprove it. Afterwards, if you don't happen to be satisfied . . ."

"Well?"

"Then stand out and fight!" snarled the Rev. James.

In the distance, cows were grazing motionless against ancient dark green oaks. In the foreground, Fred Cordy was gleefully turning cartwheels. A hiss of indrawn breath went through the group. Mr. Bull thrust out his thick neck.

"Do 'ee mean that?" he demanded.

"Just a minute, boys!" sharply interposed a new voice.

And Gordon West, rather lightheaded with rage, strode toward them from the direction of the building's northern end. His suit, though cut by the best London tailor, looked as though it had not been pressed for six months; and his tie flew out past his neck. Worry, sleeplessness, accentuated the hollows under his cheekbones and eyes.

"Won't any of you who were in church today," he asked, "admit *I* have the right to first go at him?"

There was a silence. They saw West was shorter and lighter than the parson; but they noted the size of his shoulders, and most had seen him practice judo. A smile went across Mr. Bull's face.

"Reckon you 'ave, Mr. West," he agreed, slowly and almost suavely. "Mind! Not that anybody'll believe that tomfoolery about your young lady and *'im.*" A growl of approval went up. "All the same—"

West, now nearly crazy, took off his coat, threw it on the grass, and looked at the Rev. James.

"As you said yourself," he requested, not loudly, "stand out."

The vicar looked back at him.

"Mr. West," he said, "I will meet you or anybody else in this field. But I swear I will not raise my hands until I hear why I am being called a hypocrite."

Again the vicar's denial, or rather what seemed his complete bewilderment, drove them to frenzy.

"As though you didn't know!" repeated that squalling, maddening voice from the back of the crowd.

Then up spoke the little mild-mannered Mr. Goldfish, the chemist.

"This morning, sir," the chemist stated in a shaken but steady voice, "you very unctuously raised your hand and said, 'I will not bring pain to the bereaved,' you said, 'by stressing the fact that death has come among us, for whatever reason.'"

The deep, ominous growl grew louder from thirty throats.

"And when you said this, Mr. Hunter," pursued the chemist, "you had even the cheek to look at Annie Martin. Did you notice her face, Mr. Hunter?"

"Annie Martin?" The vicar stared at him. "Oh! Miss Cordelia Martin's sister. What about her?"

"What about her?" said Mr. Bull, now so incensed and strangled that he ripped off even his wilting collar. "You didn't know Cordy Martin was killed! Oh, no!"

"*Killed?*" echoed the vicar, putting a hand up to shade his eyes. "Who killed her?"

"You did," said Mr. Bull.

Now at last the Rev. James leaned his back against the gray-black wall of the Gunpowder Room, with the long line of modern windows above his head. The sun

126

seemed to glare in his eyes. Though he still did not understand, he felt a strange numbness and weakness creeping up his legs as though toward his heart.

"You didn't know," a hammering voice went on, "Cordy Martin was clean daft about you? As lovesick as any girl of sixteen! Followed you about as if you was—I dunno who! And you never encouraged her, did you? Oh, no! Us'un's never do, eh?"

The Rev. James tried to say, "Stop," but the words choked him.

It is a literal truth that he saw the butcher's face only as a blur. That strange weakness in his legs was increasing. Back to his mind drifted certain words:

"There'll always be foolish women who mistake their interest in the vicar for their interest in the church. Sometimes you won't even notice it. . . ."

But the real voice never left off blattering in his ears.

"I dunno what you done," panted Mr. Bull. "Annie Martin wouldn't say much, would she? But she'd tell a few friends, wouldn't she? And there's no smoke without fire; and the poison pen got after her. And Cordy couldn't stand it, and she drownded herself that night. Do you think we didn't know that, when we said 'accident'?"

The Rev. James's lips moved, but no words came.

"That was cushy for you, wasn't it? Good riddance for Cordy, and you could get off with . . . no, drat me! I won't say the lady's name, except it wasn't Miss Bailey!"

"And you say," observed the chemist quietly, "that you are not a hypocrite."

The butcher breathed hard during a pause. Then he swung round.

"All right, Mr. West," he said. "Show 'im some of your foreign monkey tricks. Show the one where you use the back of yer 'and, like a chopper, on the back o'

127

the neck. The bounder won't get up again, then. Ever."

Throughout this conversation West, who had yanked off his necktie by slipping the knot, stood motionless, looking from the vicar to the crowd and back again. The rage had died out of his face, though he clamped his jaws hard. Drawing a deep breath, he walked over toward the Rev. James.

The latter, though his eyes showed mere stupor, instinctively and slowly put up his hands for defense, gritting his teeth. But West did not attack. Instead he turned his back to the vicar, facing the crowd.

"Boys," he called as clearly as his thick voice would permit, "I'm not going to touch this fellow. And neither are you."

The effect was as though a meteorite had dropped into a pond. Even Mr. Bull shied back. Fred Cordy, who had ceased to turn cartwheels, crouched like a goblin and watched.

"'Ere!" The butcher found his voice. "'R you scatty!"

"No. Listen to me! *I* never knew anything about this Cordelia Martin business. . . ."

"Ah," called a voice, "but none of you nobs would."

"Look at him!" shouted West, and stood aside. "Look at his face!"

There was a brief silence.

"If Cordelia Martin fell for him," said West, "I'll swear *he* never knew it! That's not guilt. Guilt would have come roaring out at you and let fly. Curse your stupidity, don't you see he just doesn't understand? And there's another reason why I, or you, or anybody else has got to let him alone!"

Mr. Bull, with a fist lifted for emphasis and a shout, slowly lowered the fist.

"And what might that be?"

"He's punch drunk. He can hardly see. You know that. And . . . and . . ."

128

West glared down at the grass. He would almost rather have run away in embarrassment than say the trite, foolish-sounding words he knew he must utter. But he believed in them so fiercely, as one of the few articles of his creed, that he forced them out at last.

"You can't hit a man when he's down," West said.

It took perhaps ten seconds for the words to penetrate into minds, twenty for them to sink in. Hot black coats grew hotter, Sunday hats squeezed more tightly. And, at mention of the most powerful of all unwritten laws, the men in that group turned from anger to be more ashamed of themselves than need be. There was a tendency to shuffle feet uneasily; to look at the ground or up at the sky; to express the not quite articulate.

"Do seem a shame to be fightin'," said a voice from the middle of the crowd.

"Ah, and on Sunday too," muttered another. Nobody laughed.

"My missus says . . ."

"So does mine. Still, 'e might not 'a known about Cordelia, mightn't 'e?"

"No, he mightn't 'ave!"

"And there's one thing more," West called. "I promise that the Padre here will meet any of you, with or without gloves, within twenty-four hours. I promise—"

"Ah, that's all right," growled an almost pained voice.

"Maybe; but it's a promise! For the rest of it . . . hadn't we better get off home?"

It was a suggestion passionately awaited, since nobody wanted to voice the idea first. By one, by twos and threes, they drifted away talking in loud voices about some indifferent topic. Almost the last to leave was Mr. Bull, clutching his wilted collar in his hand.

"Lad," he said, dropping a friendly hand on West's shoulder, "with the last part of what you said . . . well, I agree very 'earty. But the first part: I'm still of the same mind. Lad, you be careful!"

And, lumbering in creaky shoes, Mr. Bull moved off toward the path at the south side, shaking his head with his dark doubt.

Now in the flat, sunlit meadow there remained only West and the Rev. James. West picked up his discarded coat, slapping it on the ground with the absent-minded notion that he was dusting it, and thrust the necktie into one pocket. Then, turning round, he found the Rev. James's dull eyes fixed on him.

"Why did you do that?" whispered the vicar.

Again pouring embarrassment confused West.

"Don't ask me," he retorted. "Because I don't know myself. Anyway, you can protect yourself. But—I apologize if I ever thought you weren't honest."

The vicar's eyes seemed to catch at that word "honest."

"What have I done to the people here?" he said suddenly, as though praying. "Merciful God, what have I done?"

"Nothing!" West said instantly. "On the contrary. Somebody wants to maneuver you into a corner and cut you to pieces; and it's not Theo Bull's friends either. Look here: if I were you, I should go along to the vicarage and lie down for an hour. Then you'll be able to think straight."

"Yes. Thank you, Mr. West," the other answered after a long pause. "Nor shall I forget to keep the promise you made on my behalf."

He did not say anything more, though he seemed about to speak. With a shaken gait, exactly like that of a man who has been knocked out physically, he moved across the meadow, and disappeared round the northern corner of the building.

Mechanically West put on his coat. Pondering, he glanced round the meadow in a vague way, and then sat down with his back to the wall of the Gunpowder Room. Knees drawn up, elbows on knees and chin propped on elbows, West continued to ponder until a shadow fell across him.

His heart stirred, as it always did, when he saw Joan standing above him in her green frock.

"I'm glad you did that!" Joan said in a low, breathless voice. "Yes, dear, I saw it! According to all tradition, maybe, I should have wanted a most awful row. But I didn't. Oh, I'm glad you did that!"

"Thanks, poppet. Sit down here. Do you still love me?"

Joan sat down beside him; and that she still loved him became increasingly manifest.

"Gordon," she murmured presently. "What were you thinking about? I mean, when I walked up here a minute ago."

"Listen," said West, in fierce and fiery earnest. "Let me warn you here and now. If you keep wanting to know what I'm thinking, after we're married, I am going to strangle you. I mean that! Like this."

"You don't love me."

"The hell I don't! I was merely pointing out . . ."

"Go on," said Joan. "Go on and strangle me! See if I care."

Since this seemed rather a drastic measure, he kissed her instead as she expected.

"But, Gordon. What *were* you thinking?"

West closed his eyes, counted slowly to ten, and then gave in.

"Oh, I don't know. About Hunter, mostly. I was wondering why I'd always disliked him so much until today." West brooded, though he had his answer. "His

131

unintentional air of superiority? No; I can match that. I hate it, but I can match it. His 'boyish' attitude toward people, especially women? Yes! That's it!"

"I'm not very fond of him myself, now."

"Well," West continued, "he preached a ruddy fool sermon today, though I half admired his guts for doing it. Afterwards, his self-confidence took such a tumble you could hear it flop. You can't dislike a man after that. As for this Cordelia Martin business . . . I suppose you hadn't heard anything there?"

Joan hesitated.

"Y-yes, dear. I had."

"You *knew* about it all the time?"

"Only in a way, dear. It was common talk in the village."

"Anyway," said West, lifting his shoulders, "it's a fine situation. The poison pen, apparently, has now involved Hunter with more women than a Turkish harem."

"I don't think that's very funny, Gordon."

"Neither do I! Especially since your name . . ."

This was the point at which a very broad, very black shadow fell across both of them.

"Oi!" said a malignant voice, in such a tone that they moved apart instantly. "Oi! You two!"

It would have been interesting if a camera had caught the scene that second: West looking up, startled, his mouth open; Joan, regrettably, with her green skirt above her knees; and Sir Henry Merrivale looking at them both, carrying in one hand a wicker basket of letters like the Evil One collecting souls.

It would have struck Chief Inspector Masters as odd that H.M. made no reference (for the moment, at least) to the subject of canoodling. Canoodling is a subject on which he is apt to hold forth at length.

"Y'know," he said, "ever since yesterday evening I've

wanted a little *causerie* with you two. And now it's gettin' more and more necessary. . . . You're young West, hey?"

"That's right, sir," smiled West, as he helped Joan to her feet. "And of course you're the Old Maestro." He ceased to smile. "Can you always solve locked-room problems?"

"I hope so," H.M. replied woodenly.

Though the remark may have sounded cryptic, it was evident that both West and Joan had more than a glimmering notion of what he meant. Joan, her teeth clenched, had resolved that she would not, would *not,* show ever again the least sign of the terror she had shown last night. In her mind must always be the memory of her mother, the legend of her great-grandmother and her father's aunt: all Army wives who had looked on danger and never flinched. Joan would have told you she had banished fear by simply forgetting it.

"Durin' this peaceful Sunday afternoon," pursued Sir Henry Merrivale, swirling round the contents of the wicker basket, "I've been reading and comparing letters. With very rummy and fetchin' results, in some cases."

"Forgive the question," pleaded Joan. "But did you have any other—other contributions after I left?"

"To this? Plenty of 'em. There were," H.M. hesitated, sniffing, "quite a number of 'em sent to a gal named Marion Tyler, who's alleged to be having an affair with the parson."

"Another one?" demanded West, and then stopped to reflect. "No, hold on! Marion must be the 'lady' whose name Theo Bull said he wouldn't mention."

"I rather expected this to happen," Joan said coolly. "I told you so last night, Gordon. Of course, accusing Marion is utterly absurd."

133

"And then," continued H.M., studying them both, "there were four sets of bumptious screeds addressed to Dr. Johann Schiller Schmidt. Finally, while the shootin' proceeded out here, Rafe Danvers dropped in with his two letters."

"That nice old man?" exclaimed Joan. "What on earth is he supposed to have done?"

H.M.'s face remained completely expressionless.

"Oh, I saw one of his letters late yesterday afternoon," he said. "That was what put me onto the typewriter that wrote 'em all."

Both Joan and West looked at him.

"Rafe," H.M. cotinued to rumble on in the same expressionless way, "has got very bad eyesight. You can tell that with one look at his face. He uses a lens for professional work. But he loves to be picturesque, Rafe does. He wears a pair of pince-nez stuck halfway down his nose; and for twenty years he's trained himself never to look through 'em. So he didn't spot the exclamation mark rubbed out in place of the comma. . . . Now, my wench!"

Abruptly H.M.'s tone altered to a grim and even creepy quality.

"Yesterday," he said, "you got a letter in the same post as the parson did. Afterwards you came flyin' into Rafe's bookshop to get a book about The Mocking Widow. You've got the letter with you now, because it's the one you held back when you chucked the others into this basket. I want to see it."

Joan's body grew rigid. Never, never, *never,* any sign of fear! Yet her eyes wandered toward the sunlit oak trees in the distance, as though she wondered how long daylight would last.

"Better give it to him, poppet," West suggested gruffly.

With steady fingers Joan opened the green handbag

134

and handed H.M. the folded sheet. He read it in silence, though his large mouth tightened.

"Uh-huh," he remarked. "And what were you goin' to do about this?"

"I was going to keep it between Gordon and myself," replied Joan, lifting her rounded chin. "Gordon can take care of me! Do you think I'll let on I'm afraid?"

This was what H.M. read:

My dear Joan:
I do feel that we should become better acquainted. Therefore I propose to call on you in your bedroom at a little before midnight on Sunday. It will not matter, of course, if you are guarded.

Your would-be affectionate friend,
The Widow.

Chapter 10

Everybody said it was nonsense, of course. Everybody made light of the idea, on the grounds that The Widow must have played many hoaxes before, and here was another one. This continued until dark. But, at close to ten o'clock, they held a council of war in Colonel Bailey's study.

Amid a cloud of tobacco smoke, there was loud argument in the big square Victorian room with the pink and blue forget-me-nots. Through the mist you saw the big map over the fireplace, the big map model along the windows, and the comfortable old leather chairs.

Of all persons concerned, Joan herself was not consulted. In any case, she was in her bedroom changing her dress because West had arrived.

Sir Henry Merrivale, it may for once be stated, took little part in the argument. He sat back, his eyes closed, smoking a cheroot almost as vile as his own cigars. As the cheroot rolled rhythmically from one side of his mouth to the other, he was doubtless considering all the tricks and japes—and the name of them was legion—of which he had ever heard.

The main argument waxed violent between Gordon

137

West and Colonel Bailey, until it was agreed that the latter had the floor.

"Right, then?" the Colonel asked firmly.

West, throwing out his hands resignedly, dropped into a chair. Colonel Bailey stood beside the table, and talked curtly from behind a gurgling pipe which needed attention.

"Now, dammit, I read detective stories!" he said, with the air of one who conducts deep and scholarly research into the Chaldean roots.

"Cor!" muttered Sir Henry Merrivale.

The serious-minded Colonel—who was really fond of his niece and would have died rather than have anything happen to her, though he would have died rather than admit this either—gave H.M. a stony look.

"I know they're poppycock," he admitted. "But listen! This kind of thing often happens. And you want to say to the silly ass of a detective, 'Here, man, use some sense!' Now the Master-Mind of the gang . . ."

"You've been reading bloods, not detective stories," West interposed wearily. "But go on."

"The police get a letter. It says that . . . let's say the War Minister; that's good . . . the War Minister will die at exactly half-past nine that night, and nobody can prevent it."

"Well?"

"Well, they do it up properly. Dashed if they haven't got half Scotland Yard to surround the War Minister's study three deep. They're at the windows and up on the roof." Colonel Bailey drew a deep breath. "What never occurs to the dam' fools is simply to go *inside* the study and sit down there! Everything that happens afterwards could have been prevented. D'ye follow me?"

Without waiting for a reply, Colonel Bailey pointed his pipe at H.M.

"Merrivale will sit in one corner of the room. I'll sit in

another. I don't suppose there's any harm," he looked dubiously at West, "if you're there too. By Jove! Anybody who turns up is going to get an almighty thick ear."

Picking up a burning cigarette from the edge of an ashtray, West bent forward.

"Colonel," he said earnestly, "it won't do."

"Why not?"

"Because in that case nobody will show up!"

"But that's what we want, isn't it?"

"Look," pursued West, squeezing up his brown eyes so that the cheekbones appeared higher than they were. "How do you envisage, in your mind, the kind of figure that will show up—if anybody does show up?"

"Don't know," the other muttered uneasily. "No, stop! Fair's fair. *I* think of some kind of rum-looking thing in wig and theatrical costume, maybe."

"So do I," said West. "Do you agree, Sir Henry?"

"Uh-huh," admitted H.M.

"All right!" said West, taking a deep breath of smoke and then stubbing out the cigarette. "Now if you—either of you!—had a foolproof way of getting in and out of a locked room, without anybody the wiser except the victim inside (the victim would be bound to know), would *you* turn up if you thought another person might be there?"

"No," grunted H.M., and chewed at his cigar.

Colonel Bailey did not answer in words. But he knocked out his pipe violently against the glass ashtray.

"Then listen to my plan," West urged H.M., "as I outlined it to Colonel Bailey earlier this evening. After all, we can't sit in Joan's room every night from now until Christmas. Besides—never mind. We've got to have a shot at grabbing The Widow while grabbing's possible. Very well! Now Joan's room is on the ground

139

floor, as the poison pen well knows. That bedroom," he pointed, "is directly across the passage from this study."

"In that case," Colonel Bailey interposed stubbornly, "Merrivale and I are going to sit outside the door. And we don't move."

"All right. Though I should have preferred . . . well, that's good enough." Again West turned to H.M. "The two windows in Joan's room are both full length, with heavy sash catches that are hard to turn."

"Like the windows in here, son?"

"Yes. Both windows will be locked on the inside. I will cover the windows outside, with one other person. That'll be a guard on each window."

"So? What other person?"

"His name is Fred Cordy."

"H'm," muttered Colonel Bailey dubiously.

"Hang it, sir, you *said* he was the only other person we could trust!"

"Cordy?" repeated H.M., sitting up in the chair and taking the cheroot out of his mouth. "Here, stop the bus! I think somebody pointed him out to me. Ain't he the little dark-complexioned chap, with the hair bristles, who kept bouncing on top of a tombstone?"

West laughed, without any amusement.

"That's the man. He's a wicked little devil, to most people. But he's absolutely loyal to me, and to the Colonel and Joan too. Furthermore, he'll keep his mouth shut. Whom else can we get, if we want to keep this quiet? The vicar?"

"Over my dead body," gritted Colonel Bailey.

"A number of men in the village would help us," West pointed out, "but news of it would be all over the place tomorrow. With that guard round her, do you see any possible way somebody could get in?"

H.M., who was ruffling his hands across his big bald

head, made a grimace of protest.

"But that's just the trouble, son. Isn't your scheme more apt to scare off The Widow than Colonel Bailey's?"

"How so?"

"Like this. Are there any other ways of entrance except the door and the two windows?"

"No. Not one."

"Then you've got two men guardin' the door inside. You've got two men guardin' the windows outside. If you want to attract attention to the place, why don't you send up skyrockets or have a band playin' 'Rule, Britannia'?"

Again West was not amused. The faint lines of determination tightened in his face.

"It's not quite as foolish as you make it sound, sir. If The Widow approaches at all, she'll approach by way of the windows. The moon," he glanced at his wristwatch, "will be up; in fact, it's already up. But Fred and I will be in deep shadow. Does that answer you?"

H.M. continued to massage his head.

"Son, I don't say you're wrong! But . . . this bloke Cordy." H.M.'s sharp little eyes went up, in an oblique glance behind the spectacles. "Haven't you got somebody a bit steadier than a grinnin' goblin who likes to sit on gravestones and turn cartwheels in a meadow? What about Rafe Danvers, from the bookshop? Or that German doctor?"

"Danvers," agreed West, "would be excellent. But he's too old. As for the doctor . . ."

"Rather not have him," said Colonel Bailey in a colorless voice. Colonel Bailey's gaze moved across to the low line of bookshelves, up to the files marked "War Office," and hastily away again.

"Sorry!" he added apologetically. "Got absolutely

nothing against the chap. But there it is."

There was a long silence, while tobacco smoke seemed to thicken.

"Look here, this is a lot of rubbish!" Colonel Bailey suddenly burst out, like a man who finds himself sitting on a nursery floor and playing with toys.

"Of course it is, sir," said West. "But that's not our fault. We didn't create it. The Widow did."

Tension was growing, whether any of them admitted it or not. West got up from his chair, and paced restlessly.

"I hate this!" he said. "I wish we didn't have to do it! What I'm afraid of is its effect on Joan."

"Joan?" echoed the Colonel, surprised. A smile stirred across his speckled face. "You couldn't scare that girl with anything on earth."

"Forgive me, sir. But maybe I know her a little better than you."

"Joan's great-grandmother," said the Colonel, rapping his pipe on the edge of the glass ashtray for emphasis, "was smack in the middle of the Sepoy Mutiny in '57. Used a rifle beside her husband. Joan's own mother—"

"But things don't always run in families like that!"

"They do in ours. Why, look at this trash!" From the middle of the table, spattered with tobacco grains, Colonel Bailey fished up Joan's last letter from the poison pen.

"*I do feel that we should become better acquainted,*" he read aloud. "*Therefore I propose to call on you in your bedroom at a little before midnight on Sunday.* And the rest of it. *Your would-be affectionate friend, The Widow.* Now where's the deep threat in that?"

West tugged at his collar. Both their voices were rising.

"I'm not sure," he retorted. "But I'll bet you this: if

any woman read that and kept thinking about it, she'd be scared green."

"Joan?"

"Yes, Joan! God damn it, haven't you got the perception to understand Joan's sensitive?"

"'Sensitive.' My dear boy." The Colonel spoke very quietly. "Not windy yourself, surely?"

"For my own sake, no. But put it like this! For over three months—since July, Colonel!—we've been having poisoned darts thrown at our backs. The poison doesn't kill, except in the Martin case. But the wound swells and inflames and can give some people a bad time. It's as though you were walking along a street, and a dart stings the back of your neck. And you turn round. And there's nobody there."

The shorn words pointed the image with intolerable vividness. After a pause Colonel Bailey partly lowered his defenses, indicating this by again whacking the pipe on the ashtray.

"Too many possibilities!" he said.

"That's just it. The poison pen may be you or me, though I know it isn't. It may be the vicar himself. It may be . . ."

Shrilling out with all the clamor inspired by a new battery, the front doorbell began to ring. They heard the steps of Poppy, the maid, hurrying to answer it. In her bedroom across the passage, behind a closed door, Joan Bailey also heard it ring.

Joan, who had finished dressing except for her frock, put her head back on the pillow with a damp cloth across her forehead to ease the throb of the headache until the aspirins should work. Her white silk slip gleamed by the light of a single lamp on a bedside table, just at Joan's left at the head of the trim four-poster bed.

"It's silly!" Joan said aloud to the ceiling. "It's *silly* to

143

feel like this!"

The room was large and square and, like the study across the passage, with regrettable wallpaper which here suggested cabbages. The thick Axminster carpet was too big for it, and folded at the baseboards. There was too much furniture which wouldn't go anywhere else. But the only side of that room which need concern us was the western side, where the head of the bed rested against the wall between the two full-length windows.

The moon had risen, though Joan did not notice. But both windows were securely locked, uncurtained so that she could make sure they were locked.

The worst thing, she thought, was this horrible sense of loneliness.

Joan would have wrung out the cloth more often, in a small bowl of water beside the lamp, except that each time she looked toward her left she could see the hands of the little clock on the bedside table. The time grew nearer.

If she could have written in her diary then, she would have written something like this:

"I don't want to be the woman who stood on the burning bridge at What's-its-name. That's a man's job; let him do it. But I will, because they expect it. Anyway, Gordon will be outside the windows. If I could lean out and back and stretch out my hand through the glass, I could almost touch him."

As Joan lay there, the door to the passage was in the wall facing her, but well to her right. The shrilling of the doorbell made her start, but she sat upright only when she heard the soft voice of Stella Lacey moving nearer along the hall.

". . . in a most frightful hurry," Stella was saying to Poppy, "but I *did* promise to leave these with Sir Henry Merrivale, and at the Lord Rodney that most awful woman with the badly dyed hair said he was here."

"Yes, m'm," said Poppy. "This way, m'm."

Joan slid hastily off the bed. Slipping on her frock and shoes, hurriedly tidying her hair in the looking glass over the dressing table, she opened the door of her bedroom in time to see Stella's back silhouetted against the open door of the study, and the three men on their feet amid tobacco smoke.

". . . I knew it was Sunday night, of course," Stella's charm was reflected in male faces, her ash-blonde hair swinging at her shoulders as she turned her head, "but I had to make some purchases at the chemist's. And, if I ring the bell, and Mr. Goldfish leans out and sees who I am, he always comes down and lets me in."

"Goldfish?" boomed H.M., scowling at the stump of his cigar. "I've heard that name a lot, somehow."

"He's the little fellow with the fussy look and small spectacles," explained West, "who was with Theo Bull in the crowd. And looked as if he didn't want to be, though he was fairly steamed up too."

"Anyway," murmured Stella, "he asked me if I would bring you these. He asked me to tell you he was on your side, whatever that means. It seems *he* received two anonymous letters as well. . . ."

Whack went Colonel Bailey's pipe against the ashtray, speaking despair.

"About what?" asked West.

"Gordon!" exclaimed Stella, in mock horror. Joan could feel, if not see, her narrow-eyed reproachful smile. "Do you think I'd read another person's letters?"

("Yes!" said Joan under her breath.)

"All the same, you know, I'm afraid I did coax the story out of Mr. Goldfish." Stella started to laugh; but instantly, seeing the faces in front of her, became solemn. "Once—oh, this was years and years ago, before I came here!—the wife of a very important person died, and there was some talk that Mr. Goldfish had made out a wrong prescription with poison in it."

"Wait!" interposed Gordon West. "I've heard some of the very old gossip. I don't mind it when it's almost a legend. Was the very important person Squire Wyatt, who's buried two wives?"

"That's right, Gordon."

"This has got to stop!" said Colonel Bailey.

"Oh, but how I agree with you, Colonel!" said Stella, hurrying across to put two familiar-looking letters in H.M.'s hand. "I haven't met you formally here, Sir Henry. But I think we've probably met in London."

"I'm smackin' well sure we have, ma'am," returned H.M., with his sharp eyes fixed on her. "Burn me, it's got something to do with my wife! I say, though. Why did you get all upset, and warn people against talkin' to me, when I first saw you in the meadow here?"

Stella ignored this. She was wearing a blue "creation," with one of those black hats with the half veil popular in that year. Her gray eyes shone through the veil as she turned to Colonel Bailey.

"Now I really must fly, or Pam will be worried. By the way, you must see Pam's little book of poems. But, Colonel! You really mustn't wear those tweed coats and dig your fists a foot into the pockets. You're much too handsome to look slovenly. Now don't deny it! You are! As for . . . Joan!"

Joan, appearing as healthy and hearty-looking as ever, strolled into the study as though she had not a care in the world.

"Joan, dear!" said Stella, in a tone of anxiety.

Joan permitted her cheek to be kissed, at the same time turning her blue eyes in the other direction as though meditating a kind of innocent murder.

"You're sure you feel well?" asked Stella, still anxiously.

146

"But I'm awfully fit," laughed Joan, raising her eyebrows in wonder. "Why ever shouldn't I be?"

"Of course. Only . . . I wanted to sympathize with you for that sermon Mr. Hunter preached this morning. Joan, I was furious! I don't think I've ever been so cross in my life! I know you weren't there. Still—!"

"But, Stella!" protested Joan. "What about you? It mustn't have been pleasant to learn about all those letters . . . Gordon says there were only three, but I think a dozen . . . saying you and Gordon were going on worse."

Dead silence, though this was no longer a secret. West, determined to stamp out this suggestion, could only look far guiltier than need be.

"Or hadn't you heard about them?" asked Joan.

"Yes, dear. I'd heard," sighed Stella, a slim martyr. "Don't ask me who told me! When an absurd rumor like that goes about, you can never even remember where it came from. Why, Gordon and I have never done more than hold hands in the moonlight."

West inflated his lungs with some power.

"Woman," he suddenly burst out, and ungallantly pointed his finger at Stella, "we have never even done as much as that! I have never cast one single lecherous glance in your direction! I have never . . ."

"I hope he hasn't." Joan spoke brightly to Stella. "You see, Gordon and I are to be married on the 3rd of October. . . . Uncle George, don't sit down like that! We were going to tell you, but too much has happened in between!"

She mistook the Colonel's expression, which it must be confessed was one of relief. After all, the Colonel had only his half pay as an income, and Joan had nothing. Sitting straight-backed in the leather chair, he did his best.

"Joan. And—my dear West! Heartiest congratulations! By Jove, yes. Got it! This is an occasion which calls for a bottle of cham- . . ." Then Colonel Bailey's eye fell on the anonymous letter, lying on the table like a spider.

"No," he added flatly. "Sorry. Not yet."

"Good night, Stella," said Joan in the same tone. "Poppy will show you to the front door."

And the door of the study closed after Stella Lacey.

But this was too much for Colonel Bailey's real dignity.

"Joan!" He spoke sharply. "We're not accustomed to treat guests like that, are we? Practically ordering them out of the house?"

"I'm sorry, Uncle George."

"And Mrs. Lacey! Sweetest little woman," the Colonel rushed on despite embarrassment, "sweetest little woman that ever came to Stoke Druid! Above reproach. I know you told me some guff about her, on the way to the vestry. Tommyrot. Nobody'd believe that!"

"The trouble is," Joan began, and stopped. "At least *she* couldn't have written the poison-pen letters."

"What makes you think she couldn't, my dolly?" inquired Sir Henry Merrivale.

Throughout this conversation H.M., who had discarded both cigar stump and Mr. Goldfish's letters, was studying faces with his big chin in his big hand. Joan whirled round, her color high.

"I beg your pardon?"

"I said," grunted H.M., "what makes you think she couldn't have written 'em?"

"But Stella wouldn't have written a lot of letters accusing herself!"

"Cor, what a lot of innocents!" sighed H.M., and sat down again. "A man seldom or never does it, because

148

he's too afraid of losin' his job. That's born in him. But a woman, who doesn't give a hoot, often writes the wildest and most hysterical tomfoolery accusin' herself, because she thinks, as you thought, that nobody will suspect her. The coppers know that one, too."

"Good God," said West, "isn't there *any* end to the twists in a poison-pen case?"

H.M. did not reply. But the black shadow was back upon them: the enveloping cloud in which they could be hurt and stung to madness, and yet never strike back.

"I rather imagine," remarked Joan, and laughed, "we're going to have our experiment tonight? To trap The—The Widow?"

West studied her. "You say you don't mind this?" he asked. "Honestly, now?"

"Honestly and truly."

"Angel face," West said quietly, "you're lying."

"Darling, *I'm not!*"

"H'm," muttered Colonel Bailey, and twisted round. "Like to have a couple of my yellow sleeping pills?"

"Yes! Awfully! . . . I mean—it doesn't matter much, one way or the other. But I should be apt to sleep better, shouldn't I?"

"Yellow pills," repeated H.M. drowsily. He looked at the Colonel. "Nembutal?"

"That's it. If you'd prefer something else, the chemist would probably . . ."

"No. That's a smackin' good idea." H.M. nodded and looked at Joan. "But if you're going to take those pills, my dolly, you take 'em now. Yes, now! They work like blazes, but they're delayed action. They'll sneak up and knock you out in about an hour and a half or more; so you take 'em now."

"And this is the night," fussed Colonel Bailey, "we ought to celebrate an engagement. I'm pleased, you know. Dashed if I'm not." He said this defiantly, clearly fearful of demonstrativeness on the part of Joan or West. "But it's not right. Why, in our mess the night I announced my engagement . . ."

"There wasn't a sober man," said Joan, quoting a statement she had heard *ad infinitum,* "from the Colonel to the Junior Subaltern." Then her nerve trembled and almost snapped.

"It was my fault, sir," interposed West. "If you ask Joan, she'll tell you it was so sudden a proposal—" West stopped on a gulp, his eyes widening. "Proposal!" he said.

"Here! Confound it! What's the matter?"

"Gordon darling, please don't make me jump!"

"Where's that letter?" demanded West. He saw it on the table, snatched it up, and feverishly read it again. *"Therefore I propose to call on you,"* he read aloud. *"Therefore I propose—"* West's brain snatched at a memory which just dodged his grasp. "The poison pen is bound to slip up sometimes by using the same terms. Now whom have I heard use those exact words within the last twenty-four hours?"

Chapter 11

A clock upstairs struck the quarter hour to twelve.

Though there was no light in the downstairs passage, moonlight on the glass panels of the front door made it easy for Colonel Bailey and Sir Henry Merrivale to see each other. They sat in easy chairs, their feet almost touching, outside the closed door of Joan's bedroom.

But their vigil had not been passive, and it entailed fierce whispered arguments. After eleven o'clock—when a far-from-sleepy Joan went to bed—each of them had crept into the room alternately, at intervals of about ten minutes, to see how she was. It had been agreed that one should remain to guard the door while the other investigated, the door being locked as a double precaution against the hanky-panky of someone slipping past unseen.

Each time Joan was awake. Though the head of the bed lay in deep shadow against two brilliantly moonlit windows, Joan would lean out into the moonlight and answer in an eager whisper. Sometimes, outside the windows, they would catch a glimpse of two other restless guards.

The windows were still firmly locked. An intensive search of the room, just before they had settled down to

151

wait, revealed nobody in hiding. Presently what H.M. called this creepin' about began to annoy him wildly.

"Burn it, why don't you let the poor gal get some sleep?"

"Well, why don't you?"

"I dunno. This place is *too* well sealed. I can't see any possible . . . h'mf. No."

At twenty minutes to twelve Sir Henry Merrivale, striking a match, found her asleep. The nembutal pills had won. At ten minutes to twelve the Colonel, also striking a match, found her even more deeply locked in the grip of the drug. He also had a fierce whisper-shouted conversation, through the window, with Gordon West. Whereupon Colonel Bailey hurried to the door, unlocked it, locked it again outside, and reported.

"Fred Cordy's got a revolver," he said.

H.M., sitting in the easy chair, let his hands drop at his sides.

"That's fine," he said in a hollow voice. "That's helpful, that is. When you've got a loony shoemaker with a passion for sittin' on gravestones, then what he needs most is a loaded revolver. The gal—"

"Joan's all right. Dead-drugged asleep. I was talking to West . . ."

"Uh-huh. I could hear it. You sounded like two empty fire hoses spittin' at full pressure. Did you tell West to take the gun away from that loony?"

"I told him to, yes. Rather wish I hadn't."

"Why?"

"Well, Cordy will simply run away. Or . . . hope he doesn't take a potshot at West. Cordy's not off his rocker, you know. He really thinks he's protecting us!"

"His idea of protection," said H.M., "is a feller who shoots the guards instead of the burglar. Lord love a duck, why are you bothering about this Widow? Just

152

set Cordy up as protection and you'll have a houseful of corpses overnight."

"I happen to be serious, Merrivale."

"So am I," retorted H.M., in so soft but deadly a voice that Colonel Bailey drew a breath of satisfaction. "Y'see," H.M. explained, "I don't like this at all. I like it worse and worse. Because the motor car's now whizzin' at a hundred miles an hour; and, in this part of the case, I don't even know in which direction we're going."

"*I* can tell you," replied Colonel Bailey softly. "Got any notion what time it is?"

H.M. laboriously fetched the very large watch, which ticked like a gnome's hammer, and scrutinized its dial closely in semidarkness.

"Four minutes to midnight, I make it."

"Good!" said the Colonel, and sat down in his chair with a shudder of relief which could be sensed rather than seen.

"Now I'll tell you what," the Colonel added. "If nothing happens between now and midnight, I'm going to know this was all bluff and the blighter never intended to come at all."

"Yes, I toyed with that idea myself. It would fit in."

"Can't be anything else! We searched that room thoroughly. The windows are locked. Lord know the guards are alert. To get in there now is impos- . . ."

"Stop!" said H.M., agitated. "For the love of Esau don't use that word. You don't know the history of my life, or you might as well go straight out and whistle for The Widow. Say it's highly unlikely, if you want to. Say you'd bet Lloyds a hundred quid. But don't, don't ever use that other word!"

"Very well. Can't see—never mind; very well."

"Thanks, son. You were sayin'?"

"Look here." The Colonel was embarrassed. "I'm not an inquisitive sort of chap. You know that. But a

153

minute ago you told me you didn't understand this part of the case. Does that mean you've got a line on the rest of it?"

H.M. was sitting back in his chair, his hands folded over his corporation, twiddling his thumbs.

"Oh, that?" he said idly. "Sure I have. But it's still a bit ghosty, and I couldn't prove it to save my life."

"Since last night," the Colonel refused to met his eye, "I've heard more about you. Can't think who told me: funny thing. No impertinence intended. Anyway, I know you like to be obscure. *I* don't mind that; rather enjoy it. Like one of those clues in a crossword super-puzzle that sound dam' silly till you see the meaning's logical. If you want to be obscure, old chap . . ."

"Me?" exclaimed H.M., who had been regarding him in genuine astonishment. *"Me?* Obscure? Oh, my son!"

"Aren't you? Sorry. Heard you were. Anyway, am I out of place if I ask you what line you've got on it?"

"Well . . . now," mused H.M. "No, I'll tell you fast enough. You know most of the evidence, except one bit I've been keeping up my sleeve, and I'll tell you that. Obscure? Why, burn me, I'm the purest rill of limpidity that ever tinkled on a rock! Just listen carefully!"

In the dead stillness of the passage, while the minute hand of his watch crawled ever closer to midnight, H.M. meditated.

"Y'see," he began, somewhat unexpectedly, "I've got a landlady named Virtue Conklin."

"Er—yes," said the Colonel.

"Oh, Virtue's all right," grunted H.M. broadmindedly. "She's a fine figger of a woman, if you're like me and can't get too much of a good thing."

The Colonel nodded. Glancing instinctively round the dark passage to make sure no ladies were present, after the fashion of his profession, he spoke guardedly.

"Tell you something," he said. "I once knew a girl from Cawnpore. . . ."

"Are you goin' to begin reciting limericks," H.M. asked sternly, "or are you goin' to listen to me?"

"But I wasn't reciting any blasted . . . Oh! See what you mean. Shouldn't have said it, anyway."

"Right. Well, last night when I left this house before the vicar called . . ."

"Showed him the door," Colonel Bailey said briefly. "Then phoned the bishop."

"Anyway, I went back to the Lord Rodney. After a while," H.M.'s gesture indicated a time interval, "I sort of invited Mrs. Conklin up to my room. Shockin' business," he added hastily, with an air of unction and holiness. "But had to be done."

"Definitely."

(It was now one minute to midnight.)

"We were drinkin' Black Velvet. Guinness and champagne: cor, what a mixture! And how that woman can talk! While we were talkin', among other things, she gave me a bit of information that walloped me over the head like a hammer. That's the bit I haven't gabbled about.

"Colonel," pursued H.M., "for at least a week before I got here, there'd been a widely spread rumor that there was a big detective coming from London with a big clue. Those were the local words: 'A big detective with a big clue.'

"But, cor open an oyster, it couldn't have meant me! At that time I'd never heard of Stoke Druid. It wasn't until I got Rafe Danvers' telegram on Friday, and came harin' down here on Saturday to see a rare book—never mind that part, now—that I heard about poison-pen letters either.

"Now everybody, like that," H.M. snapped his fingers, "assumed I was the big detective with the big

155

clue. Even your niece assumed it. When I met her in Rafe's bookshop, she said: 'You're the man who goes about solving locked-room problems and disappearances and miracles. You must have come here to . . .' And stopped. There are other instances; but we can let 'em go. That's what people thought."

Out of the gloom there was a frown as the Colonel drew together his ragged eyebrows.

"But where's the dashed clue? If people make a mistake, what's the difference?"

"Ho! You still don't follow me?"

"'Fraid not."

With a faint whir of weights, the clock upstairs hit the first stroke of twelve. Colonel Bailey's fingers tightened round the ends of the armchair.

And nothing happened.

Darkness and moonlight held the house. Inside her bedroom, Joan Bailey lay sleeping peacefully, her hair spread out on the pillow, near the little night table at her left hand. The windows were still locked, as they had been since nine o'clock. Outside the guards remained even more alert.

Some distance away, in a low damp meadow where mist wreaths clung to the ground, the thin stone figure of The Mocking Widow wore its secret smile. The High Street lay sealed up in sleep amid glimmering windows. Church and vicarage seemed dead, except for the mimic life of the church clock.

Upstairs at Colonel Bailey's house, the clock rapped the last stroke of twelve. Both the Colonel and H.M., motionless, waited until another long minute crawled by. Presently the Colonel's fingers slowly relaxed their grip on the chair arm.

"Think that's finished it," he remarked casually.

"Uh-huh," said H.M., who felt more relaxed and

156

cooler of sweat than he would have admitted to anybody. "Witchin' hour and no witch."

"Have a cheroot, old boy?"

"Thanks. I don't mind if I do."

Two cheroots were lighted, the flare of the match showing a dull pallor on two faces, after which the red ends of the cigars pulsed in the semi-darkness as though disembodied.

"Mind," said the Colonel, after a comfortable pause, "we stay here till daylight. But that's only the old idea: if you play the fool, play it hard. There never was any danger!" He spoke loudly and angrily. "*I* could have told you that! Knew it all the time!"

"Sure, sure."

"By the way, weren't you doing an analysis of the case? Usually I can keep facts as straight as the lines of a book, memorize any page. But I can't seem to remember what you were saying."

"We'd got to the fine and noble point," said H.M., "where you didn't understand at all. Still, I never had any particular objection to talkin'. Lemme go on a bit, and I think you'll see it very well. We can do it with a few dates. Now, when did these letters begin?"

"July. Never heard just when."

"To be exact," observed H.M., the tip of the cigar tilting up at a dangerous angle and then rolling round again, "it was on July 1st. My Virtue—Mrs. Conklin, I mean—is the only gal who's had the persistence to have a real gossip with another woman named Ellie Harris, the postmistress here. You know Ellie Harris?"

Colonel Bailey did not shudder, which would have been too demonstrative. But his shoulders indicated it.

"Y'see," pursued H.M., "people just *can't* have a good talk with Ellie. She's stone deaf; she screams and makes 'em nervous, and most of what she says is unintelligible anyway. But the Conklin wench was born in the East India Dock Road, where in the old days everybody screamed and nobody understood. She stuck it out. Result: first letter delivered July 1st. To Stella Lacey in person."

The Colonel sat up straight.

"Mrs. Lacey! Nonsense, man! Mrs. Lacey didn't get a letter at all!"

"She was lyin'," H.M. said simply. "But that's not interesting. Now stop fussin' and lend an ear to dates. When did Cordelia Martin drown herself in the river?"

"That's well fixed enough. The night of August 12th. But about Mrs. Lacey . . . ?"

H.M. ignored Mrs. Lacey.

"So!" he said with emphasis. "August 12th. And then what, son? The letters stop dead. For a full month, as far as I can gather from the contents of my letter basket and from Mrs. Conklin's talk, there's not a single poison message.

"And how do we explain that? Because," continued H.M., "the poison pen is scared. The poison pen is ugly-minded enough for anything, granted. But this drowning, virtually if not legally, is murder. That's goin' too far. So the poison pen decides to stop, maybe for good."

"But they began again—!"

"Stop!" interrupted H.M., making mesmeric passes so that the cigar wove a pattern. "That's just what I wanted to state as the odd and rummy point. For a week, as I told you, everybody in Stoke Druid has been expecting 'a big detective with a big clue.' At the end of the week, September 13th, he's bound to turn up if the rumor's true. And on that same day, mind you, at least two anonymous letters land smack at two different places!

158

"Son, what's The Widow's game? The big detective may be somebody really dangerous. Isn't this the very time to lie doggo, and not begin sprayin' vitriol again? But we know the letters were sent. I'm asking you: *why?*"

Colonel Bailey grunted.

"That's an easy one," he said. "Braggadocio! Poison pen wants to jeer; wants to say, 'What do I care for your big detective?'"

"Ye'es," H.M. admitted. "That's the natural answer of anyone who hasn't got a twisty mind. All the same, it won't square with the notion that The Widow got scared after Cordelia Martin's death."

"But, my dear chap, that's only your own theory too! If two sides of a theory won't stick together, you're done."

"Oh, no, I ain't!" returned H.M. stubbornly, and dropped his cheroot on the floorboards and ground it out. "For instance, nobody's been asking any question about motive. The original snowstorm of letters, up to August 12th, may have been from any motive you like: maybe pure malice. But the second lot . . . burn me, I smell a different motive!"

For a moment he brooded, chin on his chest.

"So," he growled, "the old man's line of reasoning may be all skew-wiff. Which the same," he pointed out loftily, "it seldom is. But The Widow promised to turn up, and didn't. There's the gal," and he nodded toward the locked door, "sleepin' as safe as houses and surrounded by guards. So I seem to be all wrong. We've got to admit—"

H.M. stopped dead.

"God!" said Colonel Bailey.

From behind the locked door of Joan's bedroom, very little muffled by the door or by the windows

159

beyond, somebody fired three revolver shots.

The sound of those shots, from a Webley .38, was heard as far as the top of the High Street. Here they paralyzed the body as well as the mind; they opened the night with noise.

Afterwards, while you might have counted a beat of three or four, there came from that room a sound so completely inhuman that at first H.M. did not recognize it as a feminine scream. But Joan screamed again, and then for a third time. Afterwards there was nothing, except for the pounding of fists against window glass.

The Colonel, shaking off paralysis as he ground out the cheroot, moved with coolness and quickness. He whipped the key into the lock, unlocked it, and threw the door wide open.

As he and H.M. stood there, the two long moonlit windows were in the wall opposite, and something to the right, with the bedhead between. The bedroom was fairly well visible, even to two more silhouetted men— one outside each window and pounding at the glass.

The Colonel ran to the right, blundering into furniture and hurling it aside, round to the side of the bed where Joan lay with her head close to the night table. *Rattle-bang* went the fists against the windows. Gordon West, whose eyes were on Colonel Bailey not three feet away, asked some unintelligible question. H.M., still watching in the doorway, was clicking the electric switch without effect.

"She's not been shot," raved Colonel Bailey, lifting Joan's shoulders and seeing her eyelids flutter. "I don't think she's even hurt. She's just fain- . . . no, she wouldn't faint! It's the dam' drug!"

H.M., in the doorway, was bellowing for Poppy, the maid, who had promised to be awake in case of need.

160

On the bedside table Joan had left a little water bowl and cloth for her head. Her uncle, banging against the table, began gently to bathe her face and saw her eyes open just as clamor and uproar took the room.

"If you don't open this window," shouted West, "I'll break it in!"

"Merrivale!" snapped the Colonel over his shoulder. "Why the hell don't you turn on the light?"

"'Cos the switch won't work. And I'm not leaving here till there's somebody to guard the door. To blazes with footlin' house locks! Try the table lamp on your side!"

The Colonel, reaching across with one hand, found the bulb missing from the lamp and reported this sulphurously. Water slopped. Joan, who had opened her eyes dully and recognized her uncle, clung to him: Poppy, astonishingly, fell down the whole last flight of stairs without a single bruise.

"Stand in this door," bellowed H.M. to the maid. "Stick your arms and legs across it. Yell if somebody tries to get out. Understand?"

Poppy made a noise like an air-raid siren, but nodded.

"There's your blasted electric bulb!" shouted West. "On the edge of the bedside table not six inches from this window!"

Colonel Bailey groped for it and found it. Just as he was fitting it into the socket of the lamp, a high gleeful voice rose from outside the left-hand window. Fred Cordy danced there like a puppet figure in a moonlit booth.

"I shot 'er!" cried Cordy. "I shot 'er!" And Sir Henry Merrivale, who has no nerves to speak of, felt his scalp crawl.

"You didn't shoot her!" snarled the Colonel. "She's

all right! She . . ."

Bang went a fist that nearly did break the window. At that point soft but clear light flooded the room from the white-shaded table lamp.

Nobody moved except Sir Henry Merrivale. He went over and studied the locks on both windows. It may be reported that, though one was a trifle loose, both metal catches fitted snugly into their sockets and were still firmly locked.

Outside that window, however, H.M. saw the wild-eyed face of Gordon West, who was wrapping his coat round his fist preparatory to a punch against glass. H.M. unlocked and slid up the long lower sash of the window, which moved without creakings. And West, putting on his coat again, ducked over the threshold with a Webley .38 revolver in one hand.

H.M. closed and locked the window, carefully studying the room.

"She's all right, isn't she?" demanded West. "She *is* all right?"

"Yes, yes, yes!" fussed the Colonel.

West put the revolver on the bedside table.

"Forgive me, sir," he said with an indicating gesture.

Colonel Bailey, who had been sitting on the edge of the bed with his arm round Joan to hold her upright, nodded and got up. West took his place, his arm holding very tightly round her shoulder. Joan looked up at him with hazy blue eyes, and smiled.

"Those shots . . . ," began the Colonel.

"Cordy fired 'em," answered West, breathing hard and through his nostrils. "I'm afraid I didn't take the gun away from him when you told me. I thought it would be all right. But I did see . . ."

"Yes, son?" prompted H.M. "You saw?"

"Some cursed queer-looking shadow," said West, "that seemed to be creeping along the wall. That was

162

just before the church clock struck. Probably it was only my imagination, or a trick of the light; I think it was. Anyway . . ."

"Go on!" prompted H.M., his fists on his hips.

"I whispered across to Cordy. Cursed queer-looking shadow; he must have seen it too. Anyway, he cut loose with three shots. I couldn't have that. When I tried to get the gun away from him, he turned on me and I nearly had to break his arm. Where's Cordy now?"

The hammering against the other window had ceased.

"Gone," said the Colonel.

"Sulking. He thinks he's a hero. That's why he kept yelling, 'I shot her!' But never mind Cordy!" West's voice became gentle. "You're not harmed, Joan. You couldn't have been harmed. Why did you scream, my dear?"

With a violent effort, unsteadily, Joan lifted her head from his shoulder.

"Gordon," she whispered.

"Yes, Joan?"

"She was here." Joan whispered hoarsely.

In that Victorian room, stuffy because of its tightly closed windows, nobody moved or spoke. West moistened dry lips.

"Who was here, Joan?" Gordon asked.

"The Widow. I saw her. She—touched me."

Joan was taken with a violent fit of trembling, which West quietened by holding her closer. Glancing up at his companions, he saw the strange expression of their faces. West moistened his lips again. His tone was casual, as though speaking of a visitor at tea.

"Where did you see her, my dear?"

Joan's slow gesture indicated the edge of the bed, on the same side as that where West was sitting, but a little farther along.

163

"Something woke me. Bangs. Crashes. Shots. Don't know." Joan paused between each word, fighting the nembutal yet padded by it against hysteria.

"Yes, dear?"

"And there she was. Against the bed. In the moonlight. Odd." The blue eyes wre hazily puzzled. "For a second—thought it was a man dressed up. Don't know why. But it was The Widow. She . . . I saw her teeth. She put out her hand. When she touched me, . . . I don't remember any more . . . any . . ."

"You were dreaming, my dear. E-easy now! You only imagined it."

But Joan, though her mind was confused, remembered quite well what she had seen. Joan put all her strength into one last effort.

"She was here!" Joan screamed weakly. "She was here!"

Abruptly her head fell back. As the eyelids closed, West could see the white of the iris as the pupil turned up. Joan's breast rose and fell, gently and evenly under the gray silk nightgown. After a time West lowered her gently to the pillow, and stood up.

"Fainted," he said.

"Not fainted." Colonel Bailey spoke curtly. "Sleeping pills got her."

But afterwards, for a full minute at least, nobody spoke.

Serene lamplight shone on a square room, papered with vertical blue cabbages against a yellowish background. They saw Poppy, standing with arms and legs planted wide in the doorway. They saw the clutter of chairs, padded and plushbacked on castors. The only place for anyone to hide was the huge Victorian wardrobe; and this, a moment ago, H.M.'s search had proved to contain nothing but Joan's clothes. Poppy nodded firm assurance that no one had slipped out.

What seemed to glaze their eyes was sheer incredulity.

"This isn't so!" said West. Suddenly he picked up the Webley .38 from the bedside table, as though to defend himself against an enemy, and slowly looked round again. "I tell you," he shouted, "this simply damn well isn't so!"

"I know, son," H.M. agreed woodenly. "But it is."

Chapter 12

Promptly at nine o'clock on the following morning, Monday, Detective-Inspector David Garlick walked into the foyer of the Lord Rodney as he had been bidden. After a scarifying time at the hands of both the Chief Constable and the Superintendent, Inspector Garlick had decided to go very quietly and use, at the service of this very big pot from London, the considerable intelligence he had.

In fact, it might mean promotion. But Inspector Garlick did not see Sir Henry Merrivale.

In the foyer he was met by Mrs. Virtue Conklin, whose face would still have been pretty if she had removed a little of the make-up. Mrs. Conklin, patting her mass of high-piled golden hair, informed him that the great man had been out late last night and could not yet be disturbed.

So Inspector Garlick sat down to wait. That H.M. was asleep could be testified by not only Mrs. Conklin but by anybody in the vicinity of the Lord Rodney. From two upper windows issued a series of Gargantuan snores, each ending in a whistle like a peanut wagon.

But at half-past one in the afternoon, when the

Inspector had finished lunch and there had been unusual excitement in the cellar of the hotel, even Mrs. Conklin decided that the sleeping had gone on long enough.

Waving minions aside, she herself ascended to the emperor's room. It was she who woke him, saw that he was shaved, whipped him into the adjoining bath with a splash like a hippopotamus, and finally saw to it that he dressed himself in neat dark clothes.

"All gentlemen wears 'em," she declared.

But all this, of course, was not done without sounds suggesting a general fight in the saloon bar below. Once Mrs. Conklin flew backwards, struck the wall, and sat down. It is only fair to state that she did not really mind this treatment; she liked it and would have understood no other. She merely pointed out that Sir Henry Merrivale was far worse than her late husband.

Yet all grew calm. Mrs. Conklin became very dignified when a scared maidservant wheeled in a breakfast tray on a table. Indicating its place with a gesture copied from a Roman Empress in a film, she waited until H.M. had pitched into the breakfast. Then she sat on the edge of a chair and tried to wheedle him.

"Now, ducky . . . ," she began.

H.M. glared at her over his spectacles.

"Are you goin' to start talking again," he inquired, "at what's practically the crack of dawn?"

"Now don't be mean to your little Virtue. Last night somebody fired three revolver shots up at the Colonel's. Everybody heard 'em except the constable." Her large body squiggled with interest. "What was it, ducky?"

H.M. put down his knife and fork. He answered variously that (a) they were shooting at a burglar, (b) they were playing William Tell, (c) Colonel Bailey was cleaning a revolver, which went off three times.

168

Whereupon Mrs. Conklin, dropping her heavy refinement, called him everything in a wide Cockney vocabulary.

"You see that window?" asked H.M., pointing his fork at it in a sinister way.

"Gord," said Mrs. Conklin, with outward indignation but inward delight, "I bet you realy *would* chuck me out of the window!"

"Sure I would. I'm the old man."

"No, dearie," returned Mrs. Conklin very firmly. "You may be a lot of things, all of 'em mean; but you're no old man." Here she shook her head and drew a deep breath; but a wicked smile followed. "Just for your meanness," she added, "I'll tell you you missed the lovely fights in the gymnasium a while ago."

"What fights?"

"Me 'usband," said Virtue, conventionally dabbing a handkerchief at the corner of her eye, "built a lovely gym in the cellar afore 'e died. Beautiful roped ring; gloves all weights; lovely gong that they nearly broke ringing it for fun."

"But what's all this about fights?"

"His Holiness," said Virtue.

"Will you for the love of Esau tell me what you're talkin' about? Whose holi- . . . Hold on!" said H.M. "Are you by any chance talkin' about the vicar?"

Virtue's notions of ecclesiastical titles, even of churches, were much confused. She did mean the vicar, but she stuck stubbornly to her term.

"About ten to twelve," she went on, "'e came into my bar and talked to me. I said, 'Definitely,' 'cos of course it'd be good for trade in the bar. So 'Is 'Oliness walks straight up to Theo Bull's butcher's shop, when there's a lot of people there."

"Uh-huh. I can sort of guess what's coming."

"'Good morning, Mr. Bull,' says the 'Oliness, as

169

polite as butter. 'It's nearly time for noon-closing. And so,' says the 'Oly Man, 'would you like to step down to the pub and get flaming 'ell?'"

"Now listen, my wench! This pack of lies about Hunter swearing like a newspaperman . . ."

"Oh," scoffed Virtue, casting this aside as unimportant, "I don't mean 'e *said* it. It's the idea. And Theo spits on 'is 'ands and says there's nothing 'e'd like better. Only Theo sends a message to a big heavyboned farmer, Jim Somers 'is name is, to stand in Theo's corner. And Theo wants Mr. West as referee."

"West, hey?" mused H.M. "Did they have any trouble finding him?"

"No, dearie. Only they had to pull 'im out of bed like you, and some says 'e looked like death. But Mr. West said 'e'd do it.

"'Strewth, ducky," continued Virtue, in a voice of awe. "You'd think the 'ole county was a-packing into my house. Theo Bull swears 'e won't have no nance amateur three rounds. 'E wants a perfessional fifteen, and what's more 'e wants four-ounce gloves and they're the lightest anybody's allowed to use."

Sir Henry Merrivale reared up from behind the table.

"D'ye think I don't know that?" he demanded. "Listen, my wench! At Cambridge, in '91 or maybe '92 . . ."

But Virtue had now lost control of herself.

She got up from the chair arm and danced out to the middle of the room, her mass of golden hair bouncing like other parts of her, but her left fist out and her right back.

Whang goes the gong for the first round. Theo Bull charges out with round-arm swings that a babby could have dodged. The Holiness goes for Theo's wind—" she illustrated—"and then straightens 'im with an

170

uppercut. Theo was on the canvas four times in the first round and couldn't come up for the second.

"But Theo's a proper sport, I'll say that. 'E kept saying it was a good fight, and, 'Send Jim Somers against 'im!' 'e says. They was all yelling, and they did. Jim's bigger and heavier than the 'Oliness, who's no more'n cruiser weight. Jim hasn't got any science at all, see, but 'e's got a straight right with murder in it."

H.M., as deeply and profoundly absorbed as she, stood looking at her in a paralysis of fascination.

"Gord, ducky, what a fight! Jim punishes the 'Oliness a bit, and gets 'im on the floor in the fourth. But the 'Oly Man never stops throwing lefts and rights at Jim's face. By the ninth Jim can't hardly see out of either eye, and he's hitting the air.

"Then Mr. West (which was wrong, dearie, 'cos Mohammed was ahead on points; but it was good sense and it pleased everybody) Mr. West stops the fight and calls it a draw. Everybody yells and shakes 'ands. The 'Oliness shouts out and says: as soon as 'e gets a bath, can 'e stand everybody a pint of bitter in the bar?"

Virtue stopped, completely breathless, and sagged a little.

"Dearie," she added, "yesterday they hated that man like poison. Today 'e's the most popular gentleman in Stoke Druid. That's funny, don't you think?"

"Oh, I dunno. Not really funny, no."

Virtue still stood motionless, her arms at her sides. Unexpectedly, tears welled up in her eyes and smeared the mascara as they ran down. She looked at a corner of the ceiling.

"Don't *I* know?" she asked in a harsh voice. "Kid Trelawney. From Poplar, 'e was. A lightweight, and so fast they couldn't lay a glove on 'im. And me, only seventeen years old."

There was a long silence.

Sir Henry Merrivale, growling under his breath, sat down. With intense concentration he jabbed a fork at an egg fragment remaining on his plate, and continued to jab it without looking up.

But it was impossible for Mrs. Conklin to remain depressed for more than two or three minutes at a time. After repairing her face in the long mirror between the two windows, she moved quite naturally into her pose of the great lady, as she had been before the maid. Patting her back hair, allowing her eyelids to droop, she addressed H.M. in such a refined tone that his eyes slowly closed with rage.

"Really," said Virtue, "I think such an exhibition, on the part of a Holy Man, is *quite* disgusting. A common fight, upon my word!"

H.M. pointed the fork at her.

"You try any more Paula Tanqueray," he said, "and I'm goin' to cut your heart out. There's something else. D'you think any church wants its parsons to be droopy dufflebags? You bet they don't! Our Rev. James—hem!—may sort of get too enthusiastic and go a bit too far. But what happened today, burn me, is the best thing that could have happened! You tell that to every visitor."

"Visitor!" breathed Virtue, in consternation. She had completely forgotten she was supposed to be mad at H.M.

"Ducky," she breathed, lovingly and apologetically. "There have been two visitors waiting to see you!"

"So? Any phone calls from London?"

"No calls, no. But the visitors . . ."

Virtue, in danger of losing her great-lady manner, snatched it back.

"One is a mere copper," she said haughtily. "He has waited for some hours; it will not trouble him to wait

172

longer. But the other . . ."

There was a light tap at the bedroom door. Virtue swept back to a position by one window as H.M. called for an entrance.

Marion Tyler, a figure of happiness, came in and softly closed the door. She wore black slacks and a brown sweater, with a coat thrown over her shoulder. Marion's feelings emphasized the tawny color of her skin, against the sleek black bobbed hair, and the pleasure in her light brown eyes.

Yesterday she had seemed far from cordial to H.M. Today she was quiet cordiality itself. Yet there was something else—something besides briskness or common sense—in her bearing.

"I'm sorry to intrude, Sir Henry," she said, "but may I sit down for just one moment? And . . . oh! Mrs. Conklin. Please don't go. I should be very grateful if you'd stay and help me."

Virtue, amazed and flattered, yet retained her air. She swept out her own chair for Marion and a rocking chair for herself.

"Do be seated," she invited.

H.M. was regarding Marion with a very fishy expression. Possibly because of her attitude yesterday, or his own cussedness of temper, he was far from cordial himself.

"By the way," he said. "Aside from visiting me, why are you here at the Lord Rodney?"

"I came to cheer at Mr. Hunter's fight," Marion answered simply.

"Did you?" exclaimed Virtue. "I didn't see you!"

"I was up in the lounge, Mrs. Conklin. But all the bars were crowded, and they sent the news up round by round." Marion's eyes sparkled. "He—he did rather well, didn't he?"

173

"Miss Tyler," said Virtue, leaning forward fervently, "he kicked their . . . what I wish to say, he was greatly victorious."

Whereupon Marion seemed to brush this aside as though it made no difference to her.

"You see, Sir Henry," she went on with her disarming air, "I really came here to ask you a very great favor."

"So?"

"But before I do," Marion hesitated, and snapped the catch of her handbag. "That was a bad business at Colonel Bailey's last night."

"Was it?"

"But I *know*," Marion told him earnestly, and looked him straight in the eyes. "Poor Joan had such a shock that this morning the Colonel brought her over to my cottage and asked me whether I'd take her in for a day or two. He said he was willing to sit there all the time, but he'd rather have a woman in charge. Consequently, I know."

"So," said H.M.

Virtue, who was almost screaming with curiosity in the rocking chair, nevertheless remained aloof and patted her hair.

"Sir Henry," said Marion, "it *couldn't* have happened!"

"Somehow, y'know, I've heard that before."

"Yes, but this time!" protested Marion. "The windows were locked and guarded. The door was locked and guarded. Nobody was hidden in the room, and nobody slipped out afterwards. Yet this . . . this . . ."

"Say monstrosity," suggested H.M. "You won't be far out."

"This figure, either a woman or a man dressed up, actually touched Joan's shoulder and stood there as big

174

as life?"

"That's what it seems, yes."

"Can you suggest *any* explanation?"

"At the moment, no. But," said H.M. drowsily, "since both of you want to talk business, let's talk business. Mind if I ask a question?"

Marion seemed to shy away, but Virtue was agog. Though still she had made no comment, Virtue's rocking chair was swinging dangerously.

"Now you," H.M. glanced at Virtue, "can more or less speak for opinion in the village. You," he glanced at Marion, "can speak for opinion among the others. There's been too much secrecy about this business already. We've learned—" here his sharp eyes fastened almost hypnotically on Marion—"that Mrs. Stella Lacey did get at least one anonymous letter from The Widow, though she said she didn't."

"I rather thought she had," replied Marion. Her eyes were lowered, but there was a tinge of grimness in her voice.

"We don't know whether she got more than one; probably she did. But we don't know, and we don't know what was in the first one. Still! We do know Gordon West got three notes delightin' in how he was carrying on with Mrs. Lacey. West and Mrs. Lacey. Would either of you believe that?"

Virtue spoke in her most dignified voice.

"Crumbs, no!" she said. "Fancy a proper man like Mr. West looking at her, when," explained Virtue, who always looked at matters from one angle alone, "he'd got what you might call a well-built young lady like Miss Bailey!"

"And you?" H.M.'s hypnotic eye fixed on Marion.

Marion looked at the floor, looked at the long mirror with the telephone table in front of it between the two windows, looked at her handbag.

"Like Mrs. Conklin," she replied, "I say no."

"Why?"

"Really, Sir Henry, I . . ."

"Why?"

"If I give you an honest answer to that," Marion said straightforwardly, "will it help you in your investigation?"

"Yes. It will."

"Very well." Marion's lips tightened against the tawny skin. "Because Stella hasn't got enough blood in her. I doubt whether she's ever been interested in what they call 'relations,' even with her own husband."

"Miss Tyler!" exclaimed the staring Virtue. "Fancy you guessing that! Fancy—"

"You don't know much about me, do you?" asked Marion, flinging her head round.

"One final question," interrupted H.M. grimly. "I'll make it hypothetical, if you like. Suppose you fell for somebody." Marion grew tense. "What would you do about it?"

For a moment Marion considered, knowing in whose presence she was. Whereupon, deliberately, she flung aside that inner protection she had worn for years like a shirt of chain mail.

"I should go completely overboard," she answered clearly and defiantly, "and not care a damn who knew it."

Perhaps, a moment afterwards, she wished she had not spoken. Yet it may be deduced that such was Marion's mood, after the fights downstairs; and she spoke in a mood.

H.M. did not smile. He seldom did, austerely considering it beneath the dignity of the Old Maestro. But a look of serenity spread across his unmentionable features.

"By the way, ma'am," he observed. "Did you say you

176

wanted to ask me a favor, or something like that?"

Marion eagerly flung the other matter aside and became brisk. In her eyes you could see now what her original expression had been: that of a woman who sits on committees, is chairman of committees, and often really works instead of letting others do the work.

"I'm afraid it's a terrible impertinence," she said deprecatingly, as though the matter were of no importance. "But each year, you see, the church holds its annual bazaar. It's to be held this coming Saturday, in the Gunpowder Room."

The atmosphere had changed.

"Church bazaar, hey?" said H.M., with a wary look in his eye.

"Yes! We—sell things, you know. Handicraft, china, dolls, knitted wear, cakes and pastries, all made by our own church members. Each person who's really interested takes charge of a stall, a kind of table between two posts, and . . ."

"Now wait a minute, my wench!" said H.M., beginning to push his chair away.

Marion did not stop.

"This year," she rushed on, "Mrs. Doom suggested what we all thought was rather a brilliant idea. Mr. West has a lot of old fancy-dress things put away, wigs and costumes and so on, and we thought it would be most fascinating if the stall holders dressed up in imitation of the sort of things they were selling."

Sir Henry Merrivale stopped pushing his chair away. A strange gleam appeared in his eye.

"Dress up, hey?" he mused. "Sort of costume affair, is that it?"

Now, any friend of H.M. has long known his passion—in fact, his obsession—for anything even remotely to do with theatrical affairs. We need not mention his tales, true or untrue, of how he played

177

Richard the Third for Henry Irving. This passion, to the despair of Chief Inspector Masters, has often swerved him from the line of duty and created havoc.

"You see," Marion continued, "Gordon West also has a *wonderful* collection of American Indian relics. I think he has strings and strings of wampum, and a bow and arrow. I *know* he has a chief's war bonnet, with a lot of feathers, because I've seen it on the mantelpiece. And a very lifelike stuffed rattlesnake.

"As it happens," she went on, "Gordon and Joan are going to be married soon, I understand. They'll want a bigger place to live in. Gordon doesn't in the least mind giving us the relics. And, with that headdress, the costume will be easy."

"Cor!" said H.M., sitting up as though galvanized. "You want me to be an Indian Chief?"

"If it wouldn't be too much trouble, Sir Henry."

"Well . . . now," said the great man.

Pondering this for a moment, Sir Henry Merrivale rose up majestically. He went to the mirror, moving aside the telephone table to get a better view. Rearing back with a face so indescribably horrible that even Virtue was alarmed, H.M. struck an attitude as of one who stands on a lofty crag and broods on the trail beneath.

"Big Chief Roarin' Bull!" he intoned in a deep, guttural voice. "Big Chief Smack-Em-Down! Big Chief Thunder Fire! . . . *How!*" he added suddenly, lifting his right arm.

Obviously much satisfied, he returned to the chair and faced Marion earnestly.

"Ma'am," he said with his greatest dignity, "I'll be proud to help you. But look here: does West have a tomahawk? I've *got* to have a tomahawk! The war whoop, now . . . well, I can practice that by myself."

Marion, even now, had no idea of the forces she had

178

set in motion. But alarm showed in her face.

"Sir Henry!" she said rather sharply. "May I remind you that this is a church bazaar?"

But H.M. was not listening.

"I can jump up from behind the counter," he explained to Virtue, who nodded approvingly, "and pretend to conk 'em on the onion. I can . . . Beg pardon, ma'am? Were you sayin' something?"

"A church bazaar," Marion insisted firmly. "Most of the people there will be women and children. What do you think will happen if you begin war-whooping and chasing people with a tomahawk?"

H.M., who had not previously considered this, reflected now.

"You think maybe it'll be too realistic?"

"Definitely!"

"H'mf, yes. Y'know, maybe you're right. I'll tone it down so a babe in arms wouldn't be scared. Honest!"

"That's better. And thank you *so* much! But you will promise . . . ?"

"Have no fear, madam," returned H.M., lifting his hand loftily and crushing opposition. "I'll show you an Indian Chief you'll never forget."

Marion might have persisted if, at this moment, the telephone had not rung.

H.M., despite his bulk, dived for it. All his notions about Indians (derived entirely from books and films, and having small resemblance to reality) were immediately swept away as he picked up the receiver.

"Hullo? Yes. Yes, speakin'. All right." Slight pause. "Masters? Right; what did you find out?"

The telephone went on talking, while the two women pretended it did not exist.

"So!" said H.M. He took a very small notebook out of his pocket, and then juggled wildly with a pencil which seemed to dance above his head before he

179

gripped it. "Masters, that's not bad at all. That's a bit of luck. Yes, I'm gettin' it. What about the Lacey woman?"

The phone continued to talk.

"Uh-huh. That's just about what I expected. And I can see the association now. Thanks, you weasel. . . . No, no, there's too much to do in the meantime! . . . It's no good gettin' mad, son. See today's newspapers. I'll tell you later. G'by."

When he returned to his chair, his face was expressionless and smoothed out. He chewed the pencil like a cigar, and had the notebook poised in his hand. This time it was Marion who politely squirmed with curiosity. But the two women kept up a conversation, while H.M. stared rather eerily into space.

". . . and we should appreciate it so much, Mrs. Conklin, if you'd be kind enough to take a stall yourself."

Virtue was deeply touched.

"Miss Tyler, you can count on me! But . . . they never asked me before, so help me!" Her large blue eyes looked puzzled under the blonde hair. "Maybe because—anyway, they didn't. I keep wondering why they think of it now!"

Perhaps Marion's gaze strayed briefly to Sir Henry Merrivale and back again; or perhaps it didn't. But it was clear that Marion did not at all dislike Virtue Conklin. A year ago, despite her broad-mindedness, Marion might not have felt quite like this.

"It was an oversight, Mrs. Conklin. It won't happen again. Well!" And Marion smiled gaily. "What sort of stall were you thinking about?"

Virtue, in the kindness of her heart, was about to offer every bottle of booze at the Lord Rodney to make the bazaar gay-like. But instinct warned her that this

180

might not be quite the right suggestion.

"China!" she said. "I've got two sets, 'and painted, thirty-six pieces in each. Would that do?"

"Splendid! But it's really too much. We were merely . . . You seem abstracted, Mrs. Conklin?"

"Oh, I was still wondering why they didn't invite me before. I expect," Virtue said philosophically, "it was because they thought I was a . . . what I mean," she corrected herself hastily, "there were too many men in one's life, reolly. Still! They do follow one about!"

"Do they?" Marion asked lightly, as though the subject were of only academic interest. "But suppose they didn't? I mean, for the sake of argument: let us suppose one particular man didn't?"

"Dearie!" said Virtue, giving her a sorrowful look. "You don't know much about it, do you? Why, holy . . . I mean, my goodness! There's ways of making him follow you."

Marion's voice seemed a trifle higher.

"But how?" she inquired, still academic. "One can't simply—" Marion stopped abruptly.

"Listen," began Virtue, and was bending forward confidentially when Sir Henry Merrivale's fist whacked the table with a thud that made crockery jump.

"Oh, lord love a duck!" said H.M., who was still looking into space. "To think I never noticed that before!"

He glanced toward the telephone and then back at the notebook in his hand.

"What a dummy!" he groaned. "If that's not failin' to notice the obvious, I don't know what is!" He shook the notebook, dropped it on the table, and got up. "You two gals have got to get out of here. This is really important. Hop it!"

"Sir Henry!" said the outraged Marion.

"Sling your hook!" said H.M., giving Virtue a wallop on the behind which she expected and in fact hardly noticed, but which startled Marion very much.

"Never mind, Miss Tyler," soothed Virtue. "I'll tell you what. It's after three o'clock, but come and have a glass of port with me, will you?"

"Well, I . . . *Yes!* It's extremely kind of you."

"And when you go downstairs," H.M. pointed at Virtue, "send that copper up to me. Burn it all, d'ye think it's good manners to keep a police inspector waitin' all day? Send him up straightaway!"

Chapter 13

"Sit down, Inspector Garlick."

"Thank you, sir." One grunt.

Inspector Garlick, a tall heavy man with narrow eyes and a mole on his cheek, sat down gingerly and looked at his companion across a now-cleared table.

The big pot from London had both hands folded behind his bald head and was smoking a black cigar. H.M.'s eye, when he chooses it to be, can become as cold and deadly as a snake's. Inspector Garlick admitted to himself he could understand how this old beggar might be important.

All the same, he knew that lots of his officials—his Chief Constable, for instance—weren't very practical. He wondered how much this old boy knew about police work.

"I expect," said H.M., taking the cigar out of his mouth and balancing it on an ashtray, "you've had quite a lot of britches-burning about this business? Yes; I see you have. So we're goin' to forget all that and start from scratch."

A weight lifted from David Garlick's soul.

"I want to find out," said H.M., "how much you know about police work. . . . What's wrong, son?"

"Nothing, sir. Er—nothing at all."

"Most people, even very well-read people like Rafe Danvers, think that about ninety per cent of anonymous letters are written by neurotic women. Is that true or not?"

Deliberately, conscious of that cold eye, Garlick put his hat on the table.

"Sir," he answered, "I'd rather not plump out with 'Yes' or 'No.' I'd like permission to explain."

"All right. Fair enough."

"Roughly," said Garlick, determined to do his best, "there are about four different categories of poison-pen writers. Though, sometimes, one gets a bit mixed with the other."

"Uh-huh. Go on."

"First," continued Garlick, "there's the type you might call the Informer. This one writes straight to the police, or somebody in authority. Denounces the victim for anything from murder to cruelty toward children. That's the commonest: usually happens after the victim's been acquitted in a trial. Always malicious; seldom or never true."

H.M. nodded.

"The Informer," he said. "Are you forgettin' anything?"

"Yes, sir! Pretty well divided between men and women. But won't do here in the Stoke Druid business."

"Right, son. And next?"

"The second type," Garlick went on, "you could call the Avenger. This one writes blackmail letters, and demands money with threats. Usually a discharged servant, discharged employee, somebody with a heavy personal hatred for the victim. Sometimes does attack. Type—oh, very predominantly men."

Again H.M. nodded.

"The Avenger," he grunted. "That won't work here. We can throw that out; there's nothing to do with money. Fire away."

"Third," Garlick began, and stopped. "Well, sir! This type you might call the Crazy Busybody. If somebody's prominent in the public eye, even for a little time—a flyer, maybe, or the judge of a big case— this poison pen can't stand it and throws mud. Motive: envy. Sort of Hitler-love for what it can't get. Predominantly men. But that won't work here either." His pale gray eyes swung round. "Right, sir?"

H.M. remained expressionless.

"Son," he grunted, "I've given you 'yes' and 'no' too often. Though you're right about the category, and I agree that . . . Never mind! Fourth and last?"

"Fourth," the Inspector said quietly, "just what we've got here."

"So?"

Inspector Garlick's narrow eyes grew still more narrow. He tapped a finger on the table.

"So far, I admit, we've had a whole lot of men." Again Garlick tapped on the table. "But now we come to the fourth type. And it pulls down the scale to fifty-fifty; yes, and more than that, in favor of the women."

"That type being?"

"The neurotic woman with—oh, well!—some kind of sex complex. That's why I couldn't give you a straight answer a moment ago. Or didn't want to. Excuse me, sir, do you mind if I walk about a bit while I talk?"

H.M.'s almost invisible eyebrows went up.

"Burn me, not a bit! You're not in clink, son."

"Let's admit," Inspector Garlick went on doggedly, as he paced, "people have got a lot of wrong ideas about these neurotic women. People think they're middle-aged to elderly, and unattractive, and unmar-

185

ried, and un-everything. You and I know they're just as often young, pretty, married, and—whatever you like. Can you agree with that, sir?"

"Sure. That's a statement of fact."

"And have I covered all the categories?"

"You have. It's just that I'm not saying yes or no. I'm giving you a little test. . . . By the way, have you read any of these letters?"

The Inspector had too good a poker face to show that he had been stung. But his only course was the simple truth.

"No, sir. When I was here before . . ."

"I told you we were saying no more about that."

"Thank you. I talked to Miss Annie Martin, Cordelia Martin's sister, but naturally she didn't mention any letters; she was all for accidental death. Still, I took a turn round the village, with inquiries. You could see poison pen as plain as plain." Garlick snapped his fingers. "Who else would it be but a woman, maybe a pretty and attractive woman, in a little place like this?"

"Ever handled a case like this before?"

"That I have, sir!" the Inspector instantly fired back. "Though not, you might say, to handle. There was one in Cornwall when I was a constable, just before the war in '14. Another in Glastonbury when I was a sergeant. Now this."

H.M., twiddling his fingers over his corporation, glanced toward a locked cupboard with the key in it.

"In there," he said, "you'll find a wicker basket with a lot of letters in it. The vicar had to preach an uncommon rough sermon to get 'em; but I approved because there wasn't any other way. Get those letters. Study 'em; take your time. See if there's not a great big blazin' clue that jumps up in your face."

Inspector Garlick did so. He put the basket on the

table. Requesting permission to smoke, he lit a pipe, put on a pair of spectacles, and with a pencil went over every line as well as West's notations. Occasionally he made a note. He did not hurry, nor did H.M. Getting from his good old suitcase a copy of *Edwin Drood,* H.M. read quietly and finished two cigars.

The long afternoon light began to die in the street. Traffic ceased its honk and slur. A maid, who put her head in to suggest tea, was sent away by H.M. with one ferocious look. Presently Inspector Garlick put away spectacles, notebook, and pencil.

"Well, son?" prompted H.M., putting down *Edwin Drood.*

"It's a woman, all right," Garlick said flatly.

H.M. neither agreed nor disagreed. Garlick got up to pace.

"It's pretty well hidden," said Garlick. "No man would say, 'I *do* think,' or 'Good heavens, my dear,' except the kind of man we haven't got here. I'll bet you it's a woman, maybe a young and good-looking woman. At the same time . . ."

"Listen, son." Again H.M. chopped across his companion's thoughts. "You've got a lot of big words bottled up inside you. And you're afraid I'll think you're showin' off if you use 'em. Spit 'em out!"

Garlick moved his fist vaguely.

"There are—discrepancies," he managed to say. "Very often these letters from neurotic women (though not all, mind) don't make much sense. Some are—well, incoherent, except for the swearwords. And not too many obscenities here, either. But these are as clear as crystal." He scowled. "Most of all, sir, it's the way they're written. It's the . . . the . . ."

"The style?" H.M. demanded, with ghoulish eagerness. It was as though he were whistling Garlick nearer to something.

"The style! That's it! Well educated, of course. Very fancy. And yet I'll tell you, sir: I've got the idea I've heard or read that style practically every other day of my life. Or maybe it was on . . . But I can't for the life of me think what it reminds me of!"

"Think!" urged the old sinner, slapping his hands on the table.

From the basket H.M. snatched up a letter at random. It was addressed to Dr. Johann Schiller Schmidt. About to read it aloud, H.M. changed his mind and absent-mindedly thrust it into his pocket.

"You get that," he informed Garlick, "and you've got the key clue to the whole business. Come on, man! Use your wits!"

Garlick looked at him obliquely.

"Excuse me, sir, you might give me a bit of time to think."

"All right. Fair enough. Meanwhile," the voice rapped so sharply that Garlick instinctively stood to attention, "I'll give you your instructions. How many men have you got with you?"

"Sergeant and two plainsclothesmen."

"Uh. Well. A while ago I had some information from Scotland Yard." (This name seemed to act as a bracer for Garlick.) "Do you know a typewriter dealer, in Glastonbury, named Joseph Palmer?"

"Old Joe Palmer? He's been there for a donkey's years!"

"Then he may keep records. The Formosa Typewriter People, in 1925, sold him four of the Formosa Jewel No. 3, a portable which is what we want." Opening his notebook, H.M. read out numbers and peculiarities. "As I told Rafe Danvers, it's a tiny little thing you could balance on one finger."

"But if Joe's got a record—!" Inspector Garlick stopped, realizing.

"Oh, son!" H.M. said dismally. "Do you think the original's goin' to be in the hands, *now,* of whoever bought it? Still, it's a lead.

"I want you," he went on, "to make an open house-to-house search for that typewriter, looking in all the damnedest places you can think of. Be thorough. If anybody cuts up rough, you'd better have a big sheaf of search warrants with names in blank. . . ."

"Got 'em, sir," returned Garlick, tapping his breast pocket.

"Good. I'm awful sorry to give you this trouble, son. Because I don't think you'll find the typewriter. . . ."

"What?"

"And I think I've got a ruddy good idea where it really is. But we've got to go through all the moves; and the old man can't afford to be wrong. Y'see, I'm scared stiff. As I've told others, I'm afraid this'll end in murder. . . ."

"Murder?"

"You don't understand the second part of the motive," said H.M., depressed. "But you did notice, I hope, that all the letters with envelopes were post-marked here, or in Glastonbury, or in Wells?"

"Yes, sir," Inspector Garlick said dryly, "I did notice that."

"That makes the territory fairly narrow. If we can't get forrader, son, we must simply step in and nab The Widow with the oldest dodge in the game: marked stamps."

"Marked stamps!"

"That's right."

"But we can't do that, sir," protested Garlick. "To use marked stamps—that is, to have somebody at a post office deliberately give 'em to a suspected person—we've got to have a pretty dead-sure principal suspect!"

"Oh, I know the principal suspect," said H.M. carelessly, and then glowered. "Cut along now! Do what I tell you."

Inspector Garlick lowered his head. Again with great deliberation he picked up his hat from the table. And, though he kept a poker face as he bade H.M. good-by and went to the door, one puzzle stung and maddened him more than his stolid soul would have believed possible.

He was groping for the shape and form of something of which those poison-pen letters reminded him. Just within grasp, yet it eluded him. In imagination, from the shorthand copies he had made of various passages in his notebok, he saw in front of his eyes a vicious and untrue statement made to Joan Bailey.

Well, well! Following inquiries made about you, Joan, I have discovered that Mr. West was not your first lover. A certain young man, who shall be nameless and whose reign was more brief than that of the vicar (sic transit gloria amoris!) *must* surely *be mentioned before we discuss Mr. Hunter himself.*

Inspector Garlick, as he went out, almost slammed the door.

For a very long time afterwards, H.M. remained motionless with his fingertips together. A powdery twilight began to tinge the open windows; the bars could be heard opening below; and still H.M. reflected.

Presently, when it was barely light enough to see, he hoisted himself up. Virtue, he noticed, had put out for him a bowler hat to match his clothes. It was not, you understand, from the past that H.M. had anything against bowler hats. It was merely that anybody should put out anything, even with a hint that he should use it.

First he put the hat on the floor and jumped on it. Afterwards, with careful aim, he punched his fist through the remainder and finally dropped it, dusting his hands, into the wastepaper basket. Then, marching serenely, he descended the stairs.

These stairs brought into the front hall of the Lord Rodney, already much astir. On the wall opposite the stairs was a bust of that famous Admiral, with two models of Rodney's ships. Facing this wall was the reception counter, behind which Virtue Conklin was doing her nails a bright scarlet.

At this point the front door opened. Sir Henry Merrivale, about to step into Virtue's line of sight, stopped and stared with his mouth open.

"Wow!" the great man said inaudibly.

The newcomer, though not much over thirty and with excellent features, achieved his somewhat dark and sinister look merely from the fact that he wore black sidewhiskers. Though they were not Victorian sidewhiskers, spreading like fans, they were certainly thick sidewhiskers. As he moved past into the lounge, where he sat down and chastely called for lemonade, he looked exactly like John Jasper, the sinister choir-master in *Edwin Drood*.

H.M., hurrying toward Virtue, cut short her reference to hats.

"Who's the bloke that just went in there?" he asked. "If novels begin comin' life, I want to know it. Is his name Jasper?"

"Dearie!" said the puzzled Virtue. "Don't be silly! That's Mr. Benson, the choirmaster."

"What sort of feller is he?"

"We-el!" Virtue's ample shoulders indicated neither like nor dislike. "Don't smoke or drink. 'Ardly ever laughs. *Ve*-ry serious. Got a beautiful voice, though. When he sings, ducky, it's like the heavenly choir doing

'O Solo Mio' at the old Tivoli."

"H'm," said H.M., squinting back at the gentleman with the sidewhiskers. "One more thing, my wench. When did Marion Tyler leave here?"

"Only about an hour ago," Virtue giggled. "She was a bit squiffy, but that's my fault."

"Were you—hurrum!—putting any ideas into her head?"

Virtue smiled a curious smile over the bottle of nail varnish.

"Call it technique," she corrected, examining her fingernails. "There's one technique that you use when you're about thirty; dearie, you can stamp it 'never fails' and hand it to anybody. 'Course she's older, but no experience. Ducky! Got any objections?"

"Me? Lord love a duck, no! I'm all for it. . . . I'm goin' out now," added H.M., heading for the front door.

"Ducky. Your dinner's all ready for you in the dining room."

"I said I was goin' out."

Virtue's voice rose. "Ducky! Where you going?"

"To see a gal," replied H.M., instantly and untruthfully.

Leaving behind him an enraged blonde goddess, H.M. went out into the dusk and cool of the High Street. The Nag's Head, just across the street, was a-gleam and a-bustle. Otherwise there were few lights, since householders preferred to keep their front parlors dark and sit at the back.

H.M. had not gone two steps before he met Ralph Danvers from the shop across the way. The mild-mannered, stocky bookseller still wore his pince-nez down on his nose, and a black broad-brimmed soft hat covered his white hair.

"I wished," he began.

"Rafe," said H.M., and instantly swept away whatever Danvers wished to say, "I've been treatin' you shamefully. And you're just the man to help me. Come along."

"Where?"

"Colonel Bailey's house."

"As it happens," Danvers said dryly, "I have not been invited."

"Oh, son! Joan and the Colonel are over at Marion Tyler's. There's nobody in the house except the maid. And I like Poppy. If you want her in a hurry, she just falls downstairs and gives you real quick service."

"I warn you, Henry! If you are up to any of your monkey tricks . . ."

Under the light of the three-quarter moon, now rising and broadening towards its full, H.M. looked back at him strangely.

"Son," he said quietly, "I was never more serious in my life. I've got to show, to my own satisfaction, how The Widow got in and out of that locked room."

Chapter 14

By the time H.M. had finished his story of the disappearance, the west side of Colonel Bailey's house loomed up square and moon-cold, apparently unlighted. A thin mist clung to the ground. How different, in everyone's eyes, Stoke Druid looked by night!

Danvers was raving in a kind of quiet intellectual agony.

"If you have stated the circumstances correctly," he said referring to the appearance and disappearance of The Widow, "it is beyond the bounds of human reason and therefore impossible!"

"Uh-huh."

"Then somehow (unwittingly, that is) the circumstances have not been correctly stated!"

H.M., without replying, pressed the button of the electric bell at the front door.

Poppy, rather too red in her freshness of face but not ill-looking, had been sitting downstairs in the kitchen and scaring herself to death with a terror play over the wireless. She bounced up in deeper alarm when she heard the bell. But ghosts, except in the subtler variety of story, do not ring doorbells.

Hurrying upstairs, she shot along the passage in a

whirl of arms and legs, and drew a sigh of relief when she saw H.M. with Danvers behind him.

"Oh, sir!" she breathed gratefully.

H.M. explained his intention of exploring Joan's room.

"I wish you would!" Poppy told him as she turned on all the lights in the passage. "But you'd best hurry. I think Miss Joan's coming back tonight, because she says she *won't* be coddled and what is wrong with her anyway? Even Dr. Schmidt . . ."

"So?" inquired H.M. "Did they call in the doctor? Tell me, my wench, what do you think of Dr. Schmidt?"

"Oh, bosh!" said Poppy, tossing her head. "I never had an ache or pain in my life; but others has. Dr. Schmidt don't tap your chest and give you a nice bottle of medicine, like a real doctor; leastways not often. At Miss Tyler's (so Martha tells me) he gets his big glasses sort of staring at Miss Joan, and begins to use a lot of long words. Miss Joan, she don't understand. The Colonel," Poppy mimicked, "he says, 'What the devil is all this, sir?' But Mr. West, *he* understands; and he glares at the doctor and says another visit won't be necessary. Dr. Schmidt says we're all stupid; la-me, as if I cared! Howsoever, here I am talking again. Come with me."

Danvers was about to make a comment as they walked back toward Joan's bedroom, whose door was at the left near the end of the passage. But H.M. silenced comment.

"Now!" said H.M. in a significant growl. "Switch on the light, my wench. Rafe, you'll see this room just as we saw it last night. What did we miss?"

Again serene white light shone from the lamp beside the bed. All three moved a little way into the room, Poppy peering past H.M.'s arm.

The bookseller, no doubt naturally, glanced first at the pictures on the walls. They were of the Victorian be-my-Valentine school, framed in broad gilt or mahogany; and unquestionably they nauseated him.

But these could have little significance. There, between the two long windows in the western wall, was the trim bed: built rather high, with four dark wood shiny posts. Beside it stood the bedside table, with a little cupboard underneath. The bed had been made and the room swept; otherwise, there was no change. A dressing table stood against the opposite wall; and, set cater-cornered in the northwest angle of the room, was the huge wardrobe all in plain oak.

The thick carpet, too large for the room, had been folded up a little on the eastern side. In the southwestern angle, corresponding to the wardrobe, stood a fairly high chest of drawers. These, with the many chairs upholstered in purple velvet and a few tables, were all Danvers could . . .

"Well, Rafe?" inquired H.M., with a long challenging sniff. "You boast—I mean, of course, you don't boast—of being an intelligent man. You can spot one wrong letter in a first edition that keeps it from bein' a first edition. How did the witch get in and out of here?"

Danvers fidgeted with his pince-nez.

"One moment!" he said. "As you described the room to me, there is something missing."

"Where?"

"On that bedside table," Danvers pointed. "You said there was a revolver on it."

"Oh, that? I didn't finish explaining. Gordon West picked up the revolver. Afterwards he shoved it in his pocket as far as it would go." H.M. looked thoughtful. "I expect he didn't remember it himself, till he got home. . . . Solution, Rafe?"

"One question," the bookseller said in an even voice.

"Was this figure of The Widow, whoever it may have been, actually inside the room?"

For a moment H.M. considered the cussedness of all things in general.

"Yes, Rafe," he said. "It actually was."

"That is bad," muttered Danvers. "That is very bad." And he began to prowl round the bedroom.

H.M., in the meantime, was contemplating the bed from the other side, that is, the length at whose head stood the bedside table near the long window. He scowled at the tan silk coverlet, now drawn up over the pillows. With vast effort, and to everybody's astonishment, H.M. crawled on the bed and turned over on his back as though seeking repose.

"Is it possible," came the dry, husky voice of Danvers, with some sarcasm, "that you are reconstructing?"

"No, no, no! Burn it, you'll see in a minute!"

Propping himself on his left elbow, H.M. surveyed the long window at his left, running his gaze up and down. Then he propped himself on both elbows. Finally, he slid down the side of the bed; and, with a martyr's afflicted glance to heaven, he ended by going on his knees like an elastic beer barrel to study the carpet.

"Oi!" he said. "Where's that gal? Poppy!"

"Yes, sir?"

"Has this bed been changed since yesterday?"

"No, sir. I'm awful sorry, but—"

"Never mind. It's all right. Or, rather, it ain't all right." H.M. began to show signs of being bothered. "Rafe, I know you never look through your pince-nez. But have you got that lens you really do use?"

Looking mildly but patiently annoyed, Danvers drew a large magnifying glass from the pocket of his old and shabby coat. This deeply impressed Poppy, whose heart hammered in her throat with a belief that the detectives were getting down to business at last.

And it was confirmed when H.M. examined the side of the bed and the carpet. Finally he reared up on his knees to inspect the little cupboard under the bedside table. This formed a kind of painted wooden box some eighteen inches square, with a door. When he opened it, the great man found there a few old discarded medicine bottles.

This troubled him still more. Carefully exploring the floor of the little cupboard, H.M. called out again.

"Torch!" he said. "Is there an electric torch in this house?"

Poppy replied that there was. She went to get it, and returned with such speed as to suggest she had been traveling on noiseless roller skates.

Again H.M. examined the floor of the cupboard with both torch beam and magnifying glass, running his hand over it. At length, closing the door, he laboriously stood up.

"Rafe," he said with a face of despair, "I'm dished."

"Are you suggesting," inquired Danvers acidly, "that some person was hiding in that little space? Not even a midget could have done it!"

"Don't gibber, Rafe. I hate gibberin'."

"That what *do* you mean?"

H.M.'s speech grew somewhat disjointed.

"Poison pen," he said. "Easy to deduce; hard to prove if The Widow shuts up now. Locked room. Hard to deduce; easy to prove—I thought. It'd be taken away, yes, but the traces! I thought I'd solved the right problem by solvin' the wrong problem. I thought I'd opened the right door with the wrong key. Maybe I still have. But evidence!

"It all comes, of course," he added, drearily knocking the torch and the magnifying glass against his head, "of me being such a cloth-headed dummy last night!"

"Henry." Danvers spoke gently.

"Hey?"

The bookseller, who now carried his broad-brimmed hat in his hand, ran his fingers through tufts of whitish hair.

"I have often wondered, merely as a matter of psychology, why you will never give a straight answer to a straight question. Do you enjoy mystifying people?"

H.M.'s eyes came into focus.

"Sure I do!" he retorted, with unusual candor. "Who wouldn't? Wouldn't you? But I never do it, son, when there's danger to the person concerned."

"No danger? What about Miss Bailey?"

"Son," H.M. told him earnestly, "there's no more danger to that gal. Not even if you put a patent haunter, full of ghosts and steamin' like a kettle, smack in the middle of this room. It's finished. I guarantee that."

"How can you guarantee it? I am aware," Danvers interrupted himself, raising one hand, "that you are the old man. You have emphasized this point so often that I cannot overlook it. But forgive me if I do not consider it altogether an adequate reply."

"All right, then!" growled H.M.

He had dropped again into his complete absence of mind. He was blundering about the room, bumping against chairs. On the dressing table he found a pink comb, and peered into the glass as though considering sartorial adjustments to his almost nonexistent hair. He moved on and straightened a picture, entitled, "She Loves Me; She Loves Me Not," studying it as absorbedly as though it were a priceless work of art.

Finally, grunting, he handed the magnifying glass to Danvers and the torch to Poppy.

"All right!" he repeated gustily. "If you think I'm only star-gazin', I'll explain it to you. First—" and he nodded toward the window beyond the bedside table— "you've got to remember (which I didn't) that . . ."

None of the doors in the passage fitted closely to the baseboard. They heard the front door open, and the sound of voices in the hall. Footsteps raced down the passage; the door was flung open, and Gordon West appeared there with the look of one ready for anything.

"Oh!" he said, and relaxed. "We saw a light in here. We thought somebody was in the room."

"Whereas," said H.M., "there's not a single bloomin' soul, is there? . . . Is that the gal with you?"

Behind him stood Joan, carrying a light leather case and with a scarf wound round her neck. Though slightly pale, her health and vigor had left her with little or no aftermath. Putting down the leather case, she moved into the bedroom past West. But first she took a quick look round.

"Just a moment, my dolly," said H.M., taking her hands with extraordinary gentleness for such an old reprobate. "I was tellin' Rafe Danvers here . . . You all know Rafe?"

There was a pleased chorus in the affirmative.

"I was telling him," pursued H.M., "that there's absolutely no more danger to you, even if there's ever been any. The Widow'll never visit you again. You can even sleep in this room."

"Sir Henry, they've made an awful fuss about nothing at all," Joan laughed. She hesitated. "But I think I shall sleep upstairs tonight."

"Upstairs," West agreed grimly, "by all means."

"Darling, you heard what Sir Henry said! Otherwise," Joan appealed to the others, not unhappily, "I think he'd prowl round the upstairs windows, on the pretense he was serenading me with a guitar."

201

"Angel face," said West, "if I think that monstrosity's near you, I'll damn well serenade you with a trombone or a bass drum. But I'll be there."

"Gordon!" said Joan.

"Oh, lord love a duck!" groaned H.M. "Now don't you start canoodlin' again! Every time I've seen you two together," he added in despair, "you've always been canoodling!"

"But that's not true," protested Joan. "The only time you saw us—well, like that—was behind the Gunpowder Room on Sunday afternoon."

"Oh, no, it wasn't!" H.M. corrected swiftly. "It was on Saturday night. The first day I landed in Stoke Druid."

"Saturday night?" echoed West.

"That's right. I was having dinner with the Colonel, and you two were down in West's cottage. After dinner I excused myself for a couple of minutes to . . . anyway, what I did was hare down to the cottage. Because, as I told you afterwards, I wanted a talk with you as soon as possible."

Here H.M. sniffed, glancing from one to the other.

"You had two visitors, while you were canoodling in that chair with your backs to the door. Both visitors just looked in; you didn't see 'em. Well, I was the first. I didn't barge in for fear of interrupting you. I stopped because I heard you say a couple of such rummy and fetchin' things that I hared back to the Colonel's and cogitated. Your second visitor was the Tyler gal, so don't worry. She didn't see me on the path; I was playin' Indian."

Joan and Gordon exchanged a quick glance. The question in both their minds, clearly, was, "What were we talking about?" Joan, flushed and disconcerted, sought to turn the subject and hurried across to Danvers.

202

"Mr. Danvers!" she said, taking his arm with genuine friendliness. "It *is* nice to see you here! Don't you like us? We've often wondered why you haven't paid us a call before this."

The bookseller, obviously surprised and touched, pinched at the bridge of his nose and looked away.

"Thank you, my dear. I was not—er—sure of my welcome. Those are the notions of lonely men."

"Uncle George," Joan told him, "has only gone up the High Street to see whether he can get some tobacco. We've got another visitor too. He dropped in to see Marion, and walked back with us." Joan turned her head. "Where on earth . . . ?"

West grinned broadly.

"Jim!" he bellowed out along the passage. "Jim!"

In the doorway, rather hesitantly, appeared the tall figure of the Rev. James Cadman Hunter, in his usual gray tweeds and clerical collar. His face was scrubbed, his fair hair plastered flat. But his left eye, above the eyebrow, was swollen purple and almost closed. A reddish roughness stained his left cheek, and his jaw was a little swollen. In one hand he held, a little hesitantly, a raw beefsteak.

"I crept out, like Nicodemus, by night," he smiled. "Though not, of course, on the same errand as Nicodemus. Er—this beefsteak is for my eye. Miss Tyler gave it to me."

"Didn't it strike you," West asked meditatively, "that Marion was as tight as a tick when she first came in?"

"Nonsense, my dear chap!" The Rev. James instantly straightened up. "A glass or two of port: where is the harm in that? Indeed," said the Rev. James, putting the beefsteak against his bad eye and with a sort of puzzled exaltation in his good one, "it was rather odd and very pleasant. I have never been quite so conscious of Miss Tyler's—er—personality."

Gordon West gave him a sidelong look.

"Yes," West agreed, "I see what you mean."

"Good evening, Mr. Hunter," Danvers said gravely. He smiled. "We're to congratulate you, I think, on your victories today?"

The Rev. James shook his head gloomily.

"I greatly fear, sir, that I may have been precipitate and overhasty. I must learn (alas, how soon?) the virtue of self-discipline. And yet," said the vicar, "I maintain that I was right and justified in what I did! Therefore I propose—"

(Suddenly the expression on Gordon West's face altered.)

"—to defend myself before my uncle when he arrives on Saturday. Believe me, I shall be calm. But let the truth be known before all men!"

A clamor of voices—Danvers' and Joan's—rose in approval. They were perhaps a little too rapid, too babbling. H.M.'s bellow cut across it.

"Stop that!" he said. "You're all whistlin' in a graveyard, and you know it."

Dead silence.

Joan stood rigid, moistening her lips. For the first time she noticed Poppy.

"Poppy, dear!" she said. "I wonder if you could manage tea or whisky or something for all of us."

Poppy darted out of the room with such celerity that an observer, using his fancy, might not have been surprised if she had darted straight back in again with the steaming tea prepared. But she did not. Silence, as cold and dead as the white light of the lamp, held the room until Sir Henry Merrivale spoke.

"The Mocking Widow," he said, "has now got a stranglehold on this village. What do you think'll happen when this story gets about, as it's bound to? Yes, I mean what happened last night! After all, I had the police in today. . . ."

"Did you tell them?" asked Joan.

"No. But they'll hear about shots being fired last night. They'll want to know what's up. At the very smallest microscopic least, there'll be a question of firearms licenses. That's why . . ."

"Please!" interrupted Joan, in her most pleading voice. "I'm not complaining, you know. After all, there wasn't really any crime committed here last night, was there?"

"Oh, my dolly! What's going to happen when a lot of already reelin' people hear that The Widow can walk through locked doors and windows?"

"But it can't! . . . Can it?"

"No, my dolly. Rest assured! That was all mumbo jumbo and jiggery-pokery, as I told you; it won't happen to you again. But it's not what's true; it's what people will believe is true. The vicar can tell you that."

"I can," said the Rev. James.

"Then let's settle to business. *You!*" said H.M., and pointed at West.

West, who had been glancing covertly at the Rev. James with an expression in which a man says to himself, "Impossible," or, "You're crazy," woke from his dream.

"What," demanded H.M., "did you do with that Webley .38 revolver?"

"I should have explained about that." West ran a hand through his hair. "I took it away myself. But, so help me, I never noticed it until I got undressed."

"Did you give it back to Fred Cordy?"

"Under the circumstances," West replied dryly, "I thought it was better not to."

"Have you seen Cordy today?"

"Yes. He's all right. He was reading Tom Paine again. And he's always as lively as a cricket if you let

205

him recite two or three pages about the Rights of Man."

"Then what *did* you do with the revolver?"

"Well, I—" West paused. Alarm sprang into his eyes. "I put it on the table beside my typewriter, that's all."

H.M.'s big jaw dropped.

"You didn't lock it up in a cupboard, son? You didn't even lock the door of your cottage?"

"Look!" said West. "You can't lock the door of that cottage. And, so far as I remember, there isn't any kind of lock in the place!"

H.M. considered this, massaging the side of his jaw.

"Uh-huh," he said. "Now you nip back to that house, as straight as you can go, and get that revolver. Then get Fred Cordy; bring him here; don't let him get away from you until I question him. Got that?"

"Right! Anything else?"

For some time Danvers, unintentionally discourteous, had been standing with his back to the group and his face toward the high chest of drawers in a far corner of the room. His thoughts far away, he idly touched a hand mirror, a hair brush, a pair of nail scissors, nail file, and a powder bowl; then he turned round.

"Has it occurred to you, Henry," he asked clearly, "that you could spare us most of our troubles merely by saying a few words yourself?"

"What's that, Rafe?"

"You tell us the village may be terrorized by a figure which can walk through locked doors and windows. Very well. You say you know, even though you now can't prove, how the trick was done. Then tell us; and end the mystery and the fear."

"Rafe," said H.M., gripping his hand round the nearest bedpost, "I'm not going to say another word. It's not because I want to mystify anybody. It's not because I'm afraid someone's got an ingenuous dial,

206

and might betray the secret. It's because I don't dare tell the whole lot of you together."

"Are you suggesting," exclaimed the Rev. James, "that someone here . . . ?"

"I'm not suggesting anything! I'm tryin' to *tell* you that somebody is, or may be, in great danger. By the way, isn't your church clock four or five minutes slow?"

"I—yes, I believe it is. Why do you ask?"

Outside on the passge, a telephone rang.

As the double peals were still ringing, Gordon West hurried off on his errand while Joan went out to answer the phone. Joan returned almost immediately.

"For Sir Henry," she announced. "It's Stella Lacey."

H.M., muttering to himself, lumbered out. The telephone table was against the end of the passage, with the door of the bedroom on one side and the door of the study on the other.

"Sir Henry?" The voice which spoke was guarded, as though someone watched; yet it had such fierce urgency, close to the mouthpiece, that it was very clear. "Forgive me for troubling you, but I—I've been trying to get you everywhere!"

"You're not troublin' me. What's wrong?"

Now the voice was so desperately clear that the whole group, who had crowded out into the passage, could hear every syllable.

"This is Stella Lacey. You *are* a doctor, aren't you? Someone said you were a barrister, and he'd seen you in the courtroom. But you *are* a doctor?"

"Well, y'see," H.M. explained apologetically, "as a matter of fact, I'm both. But I don't work at 'em much."

"Can you please come over to my house now?" begged Stella. "Not in a few minutes, but now? I shouldn't ask, but . . . it's not a little thing. It's a matter of life and death. Please, for God's sake, come immediately!"

Chapter 15

"Sir Henry Merrivale?" whispered a woman's voice in the dimly lighted doorway.

"That's right."

The woman seemed to sag, like a dim droopy witch, as she indicated a door on the left side. "In there, please."

Stella Lacey's house, which occupied a position on the south side of the park corresponding to Colonel Bailey's on the north, was not at all Victorian. A few hundred years ago it had been the Dower House; when a young squire married, he threw his mother out of the Manor and she lived here. Outside it looked picturesque, with black beams against stone. Inside, as a witchlike housekeeper directed H.M. into the drawing room on the left, it was perhaps not quite that.

The drawing room, in which Stella Lacey and Dr. Johann Schiller Schmidt were waiting, was a long low room with walls painted a near morning-after green. Against them lurked three pictures: two of them colored blobs whose subject could have been known only to the artist, and the third vaguely reminiscent of a woman crouched mysteriously in the air with one red eye.

Along one wall, opposite the door, was a staircase. Against another stood a bookcase, descending drunkenly in a series of uneven steps. There was a grand piano, over which was thrown a silver bunched cloth held down by what appeared to be a small, heavy statue: a cylinder with an ear on one side and a wing on the other.

But, if in the Victorian bedroom there had been any breath of the supernatural, this drawing room was heavy with the weight of human fear and grief and misery. H.M.'s sharp little eyes roamed round.

"I got here as fast as I could, Mrs. Lacey," he said. His big voice was lowered. "What's the trouble?"

Dr. Schmidt, his arms folded sternly, stood with his back to an empty fireplace over which hung the vague nude with the red eye. Mrs. Lacey, her head down and the ash-blonde hair fallen forward, sat on a curiously shaped divan and stared at the floor with her slim hands clasped.

"Sir Henry," she began, swallowing hard, "I . . ."

"A moment, blease," said Dr. Schmidt.

Though clearly Dr. Schmidt did not like this, he remmbered he must always be in a perspiration of smiles and chuckles and goodwill. His chunky shape quivered with them now. As the heavy gold rims of his spectacles flashed, and the eyes were magnified, his amusement in this room of fear seemed almost horrible.

"I have not called a consultation, you observe," he said. "Still! Man must be happy with man's colleagues, yes?"

"Please, Dr. Schmidt!" Stella spoke tensely. "Let me tell this in my own way!"

The doctor waved stolid assent.

Stella looked up. Her gray eyes were smeared and red with tears, and her pretty face looked haggard.

H.M. had backed against a table, on which he noticed another weird statuette and a pack of cards.

"Sir Henry," asked Stella, clasping and unclasping her hands, "I wonder if you've ever met my little daughter, Pamela."

"I saw her in the street, Mrs. Lacey. And I've passed her a couple of times since. Very nice-lookin' little gal. I liked her."

"Thank you," said Stella. "Last night I asked you—no, it was the Colonel—never mind! I asked whether you'd seen her little book of poems. She's done it over and over, to get a fair copy, and bound it herself in heavy paper. Wait!"

Stella got up and stumbled toward the bookcase. Blinking hard to keep back the tears, she only made matters worse. From the top of some books she picked up the copy, bound and clipped together in gray paper, with the name "Pamela Lacey" neatly printed across it.

"Here, Sir Henry. Please read the third poem . . . I—I should say set of verses . . . in this pamphlet. Dr. Schmidt has marked it."

"Ach, so!" beamed the doctor, and folded his arms.

"I ought to explain," said a nearly hysterical Stella, "that there's a French song which caught Pam's fancy. If you translate the first part, it means, 'It's raining, raining, shepherdess; gather in your sheep.' It's all about Marie Antoinette and those people, when they played at being shepherdess and dairymaids at Versailles."

"I think I got it, ma'am. That's all right."

H.M. took the bound sheets, and turned to the third page. The two were written in a clear and careful, but somewhat childlike and unformed, handwriting. They were headed, "Chansenette," and ran:

It's raining, raining, shepherdess; gather in your sheep—

Pretty crook and laughing look; come, my dear, don't
  weep!
Do you smile at me, you witch, pink-white china dress,
Me so big in china wig, you a sheperdess!

It's raining, raining, sheperdess; gather in your sheep—
Don't despair if all's not fair; lay down, now, and sleep.
Ribbons pink and ribbons blue, where's the cloud
  between,
*Wake up, there, and shear your hair—that's the
  guillotine!*

There was a long silence after H.M. closed the
pamphlet and put it behind him on the table,
unobtrusively scooping up something else.

"Uh-huh," he said without expression.

Stella Lacey could control herself no longer.

"Sir Henry," she cried, "Dr. Schmidt says that Pam
wrote all these anonymous letters!"

A cold shock of silence seemed to make more
grotesque the furnishings of this room, imbuing them
with evil. Still H.M. did not move or speak.

"Don't you *see?*" pleaded Stella.

"Ach!" exclaimed Dr. Schmidt, making a little twist
of a gesture. "You understand the morbidity, the deep
rot like the worm in the apple, which shows to the true
observer in the last line of that poem?"

"The—the book," murmured Stella.

Stumbling, she rushed again to the bookcase and
returned with a blue-bound book whose pages at once
opened to the required place.[1]

"True!" murmured Dr. Schmidt, pursing his lips.
Then he waved his hand, with half-smiling modesty. "A
leedle parallel case. I was able to warn Mrs. Lacey that
this might take place, even before she has received a
poison-pen letter. Dear lady, you should have been

calm and not alarmed." The gold-rimmed lenses flashed toward H.M. "Yes?"

Still H.M. did not move or speak.

His friends could have said that in this mood he was about as innocent and harmless as a battleship's broadside slowly lifting dead to the target. But he still stood by the table.

"This parallel case," continued Dr. Schmidt, beginning to pace back and forth before the fireplace, "is that of a girl named Marie de Morell at Saumur in France. (Decadent!) That book of Herr Irving," the lenses flashed, "is the fullest account of it except in Chermany. Here iss a young girl of eggcelent family: pretty, modest, obedient, pious. A fine one, eh?

"Yet she has written poison-pen letters, obscene and abusive, which have caused the partial ruin of her family, the death of one Army officer and the ruins of another, until after many years they have discovered the author. It must not go on so long here! I much fear, alack-me, that Pam has a mind like Marie de Morell."

The book dropped from Stella's hands to the floor. Tears ran down her face.

"Sir Henry," she pleaded for the last time, *"is* this true? For God's sake can't you help us somehow?"

Dr. Schmidt, absorbed in the case, was waving his stocky arms as he paced.

"The leedle Pam," he said, "has another attack. Good, but we must cure her! These medicines? No! I must probe into the mind. She does not understand? Pah! She is fourteen; she understands well enough to write the obscene language. What she does not understand, I must find and show her. Yes, yes, yes!"

Dr. Schmidt stopped. Whirling round, he stood with his face raised and his finger pointed upwards, as in a holy cause.

"I vill again," he cried, "der psychoanalysis try!"

213

Sir Henry Merrivale lumbered slowly forward and stood in front of him.

"If you ever again der psychoanalysis try," said H.M., still mildly, "you will an awful wallop over the onion get. Understand, Jerry?"

Stella Lacey, who had thrown herself on the divan, suddenly looked up. There was a pause, during which Dr. Schmidt regarded H.M. in amazement.

"But I am a qualified analyst!"

"Uh-huh. Well?"

"For three years I have studied in Vienna and received my degree! I am permitted to practice by the British Medical Association! I do not under—" Dr. Schmidt paused. Something like horror came into his face. Incredulously he asked:

"You do not believe in der analysis?"

"That depends on who practices it, son." H.M. turned to Stella. "Where's the child, ma'am?"

"I forbid this!" stormed Dr. Schmidt. "I have not called a consultation!"

It was surprising how quickly H.M.'s bulk could turn round.

"Like the police to call one?" he inquired.

No doubt it was his own emotional heat which caused Dr. Schmidt to sweat heavily.

"I do not understand!"

"Mind your eye, son," said H.M., in a soft and dangerous growl. "Just mind your eye, that's all. . . . Where did you say Pam was, Mrs. Lacey?"

"It's the first door at the top of the stairs, there. You can't miss it! We put Pam to bed, but the light's on. Sir Henry! Do you really think . . . ?"

"It's all right, ma'am," said H.M. "You just trust the old man."

Lumbering up the carpeted stairs, he tapped on the door. They heard Pam's voice, terrified, ask who was there. H.M.'s remark was not clear, but the door

214

opened and closed.

Then they waited.

It seemed an hour, then another hour, then a third hour.

Now Dr. Johann Schiller Schmidt would have denied, and believed it, that there was any trace of the dramatic in his nature or in his whole race. But it is true that he flung up his arms, danced on the carpet, and muttered strange Wagnerian oaths.

As regards his medical practice, he was not a hypocrite. Dr. Schmidt was deeply concerned about Pam, and believed in his own methods. He said that this dumbhead Sir Henry would undo all his good work. He swore the dumbhead would frighten her still more, and that he (Dr. Schmidt) washed his hands of the consequences.

Stella Lacey, sitting on the couch and breathing shakily, did not reply. Often she glanced toward the staircase, uttering silent incoherent prayers.

Dr. Schmidt was right, of course. These analysts always knew. What he said about Pam—and there was that other matter, too—might be unpleasant and even revolting, but facts were facts. Stella could only grope back to her old faith, to that gray church on the hill, in blind hope that some help would . . .

Suddenly, upstairs, there was the creak of a door moving slightly.

". . . put it a little way open," rumbled one voice, "and get some more air in here."

But Stella scarcely heard this. She heard what she never expected to hear. It was one of the most healthy, heartening sounds in the world. There was affection in it. It was the sound of Pam Lacey whooping with laughter.

Clearly, downstairs, they could hear Pam and H.M. talking.

"But you didn't do it, really?" protested Pam, half

215

defiantly. "You didn't *really* pour Epsom Salts into the Home Secretary's soup? Just as he was sitting down at the Lord Mayor's banquet?"

"Cross my heart!" declared the other voice, with such deep sincerity that even those downstairs believed him. It was, in fact, quite true.

"But that's nothin'!" scoffed H.M. "Wait till I tell you how Pinkey Waterford bet me five quid I wouldn't go down Ludgate Hill on roller skates. That wasn't bad at all!"

"Dr. Merrivale." Pam's voice sounded faintly offended. "Aren't you going to come back here and sit down beside me?"

"'Course I am, my dolly. I say!" H.M. paused, and spoke very gravely and courteously. "I hope you don't mind me calling you 'my dolly,' do you? It's only a manner of speakin'. I'll change it if you want me to."

"Oh, *no!* I love it! It's—it's when people talk to you *sneery,* as though you didn't know anything and couldn't learn anything. I mean . . ."

"Don't I know it? Didn't I tell you about my uncle: that weasel? But there's the point: you mustn't let 'em stuff your head up with a lot of nonsense; which they're doin'. Before I explain that, watch!"

"Watch what?"

"Watch!" repeated H.M., with powerful impressiveness. "Nothing in my hands, see? Nothing up my sleeves. I raise my left hand in the air, like this. . . . Now burn me," said H.M., as though he had been struck by a bolt of lightning, "where did that jack of spades come from? Or the queen of hearts? Or the seven of clubs? Or the nine of diamonds? Or . . . here, we'd better shuffle these together."

Downstairs, during the interval, Dr. Johann Schiller Schmidt had stood rigid. Stella, on the divan, was looking up toward the door; her eyes growing brighter and brighter with hope. Dr. Schmidt prowled across and hissed at her.

"This Home Secretary, who iss he? I think I know, yes; but what does he do?"

"Well, I . . . I'm not quite sure. He's an important Cabinet member, I know. I think that technically he's the head of all the police."

"Herr Gott!" whispered Dr. Schmidt.

"What on earth is the matter?"

"This Merrivale, against an important British Reich Minister, commits a grave and serious offense. Yet Merrivale is not imprisoned or . . . or . . . ?"

"Or what?"

"It makes no matter. But—Herr Gott!"

Stella scarcely heard him. She was still trying to look at the door upstairs. Yet once more, for some reason, the door was deliberately closed. For what seemed another long, aching hour they waited in silence. Dr. Schmidt began to fume.

"I am a man of science. I haf no time," he said contemptuously, "for card tricks or chokes. Life iss a serious matter. With my patients I do not choke."

"I wish you would," said Stella, suddenly giving him a look of dislike.

"Bitte?"

"Stop! The door's opened a little way again!"

It had, for some reason. Evidently H.M. was again sitting on the edge of Pam's bed. The conversation, to Dr. Schmidt at least, was electrifying.

". . . so you see, my dolly, there's no call to be scared of that sausage-eatin' faker downstairs. He's only wind and gold-rimmed gig lamps. He sticks the gig lamps in your face and talks a lot of tommyrot. Then you get scared and upset, and it makes you sick in your stummick, and your mother thinks you're ill. But there's nothing really wrong with you; now is there?"

"Of c-course not!"

"That's right. Don't be ashamed to put your arms round my neck. And cry all you like; nobody'll know but you and me; but I bet I make you laugh in a minute."

A smothered laugh and sob.

"As I explained to you, my dolly, about half the things grown-ups tell you are just plain lies. Why they should keep on lying to you, when you're past fourteen, I'll be switched if I know. But lots of people do.

"So here's what you do, d'ye see? If they try on something you think is humbug, just think about it carefully and you'll find it *is* humbug. If it's mean contemptible humbug, either ignore it or hit it like blazes. But if it's only ridiculous humbug, like Dr. Snickenpoof downstairs, you can laugh at it and see how funny it is."

"But sometimes you can't laugh," said Pam. "You *can't!*"

"I know that, my dolly," said H.M. very gently. "You can't expect to change overnight, can you? That's why I'm here."

"How'd-you-mean?"

"Pam, that sausage-eatin' bungler is never goin' to bother you again."

There was a noise like a gulp. "Honestly?"

"Cross my heart. I'll see to that; and I promise you."

"But Mother says . . ."

"Your mother's all right, my dolly. I'll have a talk with her when I go downstairs. Don't you believe Dr. Merrivale can do what he says?"

"Oh, I do! I do!"

"Then that's settled. If Dr. Schmidt should ever come sneakin' about here again—which he won't, mind, but *if* he does—you get in touch with me at the Lord Rodney. I'll come round and chuck him out of the window. Come to think of it, why not chuck him out all the windows?"

"You—you *are* silly! You couldn't throw him out of *all* the windows!"

"Why couldn't you?" argued H.M., with every sign of reasonableness. "You could always pick him up and bring him back and sling him out again. And, speakin' of windows, here are these three Russian crutch-walkers on the table by the bed. We'd better get rid of 'em now."

There was a whirr of leaves and then three separate thuds as Dostoevski, Tolstoy, and Checkov flew out of the open window and struck the bole of an oak tree.

"The idea is," explained H.M., "I want you to read some fellers named Dumas and Mark Twain and Stevenson and Chesterton and Conan Doyle. They're dead, yes; but they can still whack the britches off anybody at tellin' a story. I'll get 'em for you at Rafe's. Your school can give you more of 'em."

"But—" Pam stopped abruptly. "Aren't you going to sit beside me?"

"Sure, my dolly. And I bet I know what you were thinking about. Your mother's always dragging you back from school, because she's afraid the diet's not right or you'll sit in a draft or some goddam—hurrum!—some quite loony thing."

"I didn't say that."

"I know you didn't, and I apologize. But we'll arrange it just the same."

Pam's voice, muffled against H.M.'s chest, sank lower and lower.

"You still don't know what they're *saying* about me! They say . . ." The voice trailed off, indistinguishable, halting many times, to a whisper.

"Now do you think I didn't know that?" asked H.M. gently. "Listen, my dolly! The only reason I'm goin' to

219

leave you now is that I've got to go downstairs and . . ." His own voice was lowered to an indistinguishable mutter which went on for some time.

"You're not!" said Pam. It was not incredulity, but a gasp of relief.

"Certainly I am. If you want to hear something interesting, keep an ear out."

"Honestly, I . . . I can't sleep anyway. I can't!"

"'Course you can't!" thundered H.M., as though the mere idea of anybody sleeping would be monstrous. "Why should you? Here, let's run an eye along this bookshelf. I can't see anything that wouldn't kill a goat with boredom, but . . . stop! This must 'a' got here by mistake. It's called *The Cloister and the Hearth.*"

"I—I saw that one. But the title sounds so awfully dull."

"That's what I thought, until I tried the first chapter or two. Don't you like sword fights, and bloodhounds, and robbers at lonely inns, and good old-fashioned blood and thunder?"

"But that's what I like best!"

"Then you take that, my dolly, and I'll say good night. There's a grand character in the book called Denys, who goes about roarin' to everybody, *'Courage! Le diable est mort!'* Naturally you know what that means?"

"Courage!" laughed Pam. "The devil is dead!"

"He is for you, my dolly," said H.M. "I'll be back tomorrow with the roller skates, and what books I can find."

Heavy footsteps creaked on a carpet above.

"Dr. Merrivale," said Pam in a small voice.

"Yes, my dolly?"

All the sophisticated air had gone from Pam's tones. "I think you're . . . you're . . ."

"Hey?"

220

"I think you're like a knight in armor," said Pam, and began to cry.

This astounding statement, which could never have been dreamed by H.M.'s wife or even by his mother when he was a child, made the footsteps stop for a second. If Pam's remark were ever repeated in any of his clubs, he would not have dared enter one of them for the next two years. Yet the old sinner was so touched, as he came out and started to close the door, that his scowl became purely fiendish. What he said to the closing door was equally surprising.

"I wish *I* thought so, my dolly," he muttered.

H.M. walked slowly downstairs. There Stella Lacey, with a different sort of tears in her eyes, stretched out her hands to him.

"Now, ma'am!" growled H.M., fussed and embarrassed. "There's nothing wrong with the little gal. She never wrote any poison-pen letters. Any country g.p. could have told you that."

"Sir Henry, I . . . I . . ."

"But I expect you won't stop worrying until I show you proof you can see and handle. That's fair enough. Let me have a little talk with Paracelsus over there."

The feelings of the outraged Dr. Schmidt, standing on the hearth rug, must not be described. On the one hand his face was purple as with dangerous blood pressure; on the other hand he shivered like a man with malaria.

H.M. sauntered toward him. The doctor found his voice.

"In all my life," he said, "nefer have I so many outrages to medical ethics heard! You haf called me—" Dr. Schmidt paused. H.M. had called him so many things that offhand he could not remember one of them. He could only shiver with wrath. "The whole medical world shall hear of this!"

221

H.M., eyes narrowed, spoke in the same low growl which had been heard before.

"Somehow," he said, "I doubt that."

"You have insulted my profession!"

"Oh, no! Only you, because you can't manage it. . . . Sit down."

"I am hinsulted . . . too much!"

"You've bungled this work, just as you've bungled," H.M. paused very slightly, "other work. By the way, didn't I tell you to sit down?"

Dr. Schmidt gave him a quick, wary look, and instantly sat down in an odd-shaped chair.

"Tell me, Doctor," pursued H.M. "Didn't you ever read any of the poison-pen letters you received yourself?"

"How many times must I speak it? I am not concerned with politics. I am not a National Socialist!"

"Here, here!" H.M. sounded surprised. "I haven't said you are. But even if you were, what's the odds? Aren't your country and my country two friendly nations enjoyin' the most friendly relations in sunshine and apple sauce?"

"Yes!" gasped Dr. Schmidt, and much of the purple color receded from his cheeks. "Yes, yes! Of course!"

"Well, then!"

"Ach, yes! I forget myself."

"Now it's a rummy thing," said H.M., fishing in his inside pocket. "Inspector Garlick and I were going over a basket of these letters this afternoon. I happened to stick one of 'em in my pocket—absent-minded, which I am—and it's a letter to you. Here, take it and read a couple of lines out loud."

Under thick lenses a suspicious glance went up at him, but H.M. remained bland.

"Your spoken English may slip a bit, son. But they tell me you never fail at written English."

"Ha ha. No, that is too much. However!" Dr.

Schmidt took the letter. "Where do you wish me to begin?"

"At the beginning. That'll do."

"Dear Dr. Schmidt," began that worthy, balancing his elbow on the chair arm because his hand was still unsteady. *"Pursuant to my last letter, I find that the exigencies of the situation compel me further to explore your career. Admittedly—* Pah! This charge is nonsense! What are you doing?"

H.M. lumbered over to the center table. He put down the pack of cards he had taken from there. He picked up the gray-bound copy of Pam Lacey's verses, folding it over to page three and the song about the shepherdess.

Then the balloon went up.

"Now, you perishin' dummy," roared Sir Henry Merrivale, thrusting the verses into Dr. Schmidt's hand on top of the letter, "read that! When you read it, remember a medical man's first duty is to use his eyes and his common sense.

"What do I mean? In those verses, including the title—from what ought to be 'Chansonette' to what ought to be 'ribbons'—there are five spelling mistakes in eight lines. The grammar's wonky: see 'lay down.' The punctuation skids all over the place. But Pam had worked on it and worked on it to get it as well as she could. Have you got the infernal, star-gazin' cheek to say those verse and the poison-pen letters could possibly have been written by the same person?"

Dr. Schmidt looked at the verses. He looked at the letter. Finally, moistening his lips, he looked up.

"And you are one," he sneered, "to speak of grammar!"

H.M.'s big hand moved out, lovingly, toward the other's neck; but it stopped, as though at a pleasure deferred.

"I'll tell you something, son," he said mildly. "As a

Jerry, you wouldn't know it. I came of a generation who said 'ain't' and 'don't' and 'gal' and the rest of it as naturally as we said huntin' or shootin' or fishin'. But you'd get an awful surprise if you knew who the people of that generation were."

Taking the letter and the pamphlet from Dr. Schmidt's hands, H.M. returned to the table and put them down.

"Now clear out!" he said. "You've done enough damage. Clear out."

"I appeal to the only berson who can make decisions! I appeal to Mrs. Lacey!"

Stella, who had been standing motionless, gave a slight shiver.

"Please go," she told the doctor. "If you ever return, Sir Henry has my permission to throw you out of every window in the house."

Dr. Schmidt, not without dignity, took up his hat and medicine case from a side table.

"You haf not heard the last of this!" he said, ending on (somewhat) a dramatic note. Then he clapped on his hat and marched out.

Stella's knees sagged, and she sat down on the divan, staring ahead.

"Ma'am," said H.M., fiddling with the papers on the table, "when I first came here, I think I misjudged you a bit. There are some things I still don't know. But I've learned a lot since."

He lumbered over and stood in front of her, again speaking gently.

"Your husband's not really dead, is he?"

Chapter 16

Stella's hands, pressed against her face, slowly fell as she lifted her head. Though there had been some damage to her slight make-up, all expression of haggardness had gone. The delicate features filled out. Yet, at the same time, that elusive mocking quirk had faded from the mouth and from the gray eyes. Just as Pam had lost all her semi-sophisticated airs, so had her mother lost her own poise and turned into a human being.

"How did you learn . . . ?" Stella began, but her voice trailed to a whisper as she glanced toward the door upstairs.

"I've been watching that door too," H.M. assured her. "It closed pretty firmly, like a riot of delight, when you slung out Dr. Schmidt. Pam can't hear anything if we keep our voices down."

"But how did you learn . . . ?"

"Through Scotland Yard." H.M.'s gesture quietened her sudden movement. "Don't worry, ma'am. Nobody knows it here. Nobody ever will know.

"Y'see," the big voice went on soothingly, almost as he had talked to Pam, "I wondered why the only mail you ever received was a letter, each quarter day, from a

London firm of solicitors. To me (but that's only a twisty mind) it suggested somebody was sending you a quarterly check without contact."

"Darwin—that's my husband—Darwin's family don't like me," said Stella, lowering her eyes. "I don't blame them! They're right! Only . . .

"You see," she went on, tightening her shoulders, "my husband's in an Air Force—well, let's call it a nursing home. He's not insane!" Stella whispered fiercely, and the truth was in her eyes. "It's a kind of (what do they call it?) psychosis they think they can clear up. The Air Force doctors seemed so . . . so . . ."

"If they're Air Force psychiatrists, they do know their job. From A to Z. Not like friend Schmidt, who's a faker in more ways than one."

"Well! Because of the others, I put so much faith in him. When he told me . . ."

The wrath of Sir Henry Merrivale, mounting into his face and quivering even in his nose, he managed to cork down as does Chief Inspector Masters.

"Did he tell you your husband's trouble could be inherited and might turn up in Pam?"

"Yes! That's why—"

"Well, it can't. That's just another lie."

Now Stella's lip was quivering again, but with a relief that made her shudder. From the floor H.M., with some labor at bending down, picked up the copy of *Last Studies in Criminology,* and returned it to the bookcase.

"Tell me," he resumed, "did old Cagliostro—?"

"Who?"

"Oh, just another quack. Did he predict, as he said he did, Pam might begin writing poison-pen letters? Even before they actually began?"

"Well, that among a lot of other horrible things. He gave me the book and said to study the case of Marie de

226

Morell. Do you know what she did, Sir Henry? It wasn't only letters. This little Morell girl said that some man, presumably this Lieutenant de la Roncière, had climbed through her bedroom window and tried to . . ."

"Sh-h!" said H.M., sitting down beside her. "Don't you know it's all lies about Pam? Don't you?"

"Yes! Thanks to the g-good old country g.p.!"

"But Schmidt," H.M. observed thoughtfully, "predicted 'em beforehand."

Stella Lacey seemed to be nerving herself desperately for the worst of confessions.

"You see," she went on, "*I* didn't know Pam's verses were misspelled, or had bad punctuation, or anything like that." A flush stained her pale cheeks. "I'm dreadfully ignorant, really. I—I never even went to school."

H.M. gave her a quick sideways glance, but did not comment on this for the moment.

"Marie de Morell," he rumbled. "And that's why, when Ellie Harris handed you the first anonymous letter, you said, 'Not that book, not that book.' You were scared out of your wits and went rushin' out of the post office."

"I suppose Scotland Yard knew that too. Yes, it's true. I was so *miserable*. But of course I couldn't tell anybody."

"No, my dol—that is, ma'am," pursued H.M. "Take a look round at the pictures and the statuary and most of the books. We'll exclude Irving; he's good stuff. What do you really think of them?"

Stella pushed back the wings of her ash-blonde hair.

"I think they're bloody awful!"

"S-h-h!" urged H.M., glancing toward the closed door upstairs. "Then why do you stick 'em all through the house?"

"But I'm ignorant! And—well! All my London friends say they're *chic* and smart and the best people have them."

H.M. closed his eyes, as though counting slowly to ten. He counted another ten, and the bottle was corked.

"'*Chic*,'" he repeated, wooden faced. "'Smart.'" Then, with an even harder effort. "'Best people.'"

"Oh, Sir Henry, please don't! This business about Pam has had me nearly out of my mind! And Pam being so delicate . . ."

"No, she's not!" H.M. said sharply. "That's more hoobusgoobus you're goin' to get out of your head. She'll play hockey and get as dirty as she likes; she'll take a fine toss on roller skates or ice skates; she'll have some childhood. I'm goin' to cut up awful rough, mind, if you don't promise that."

"But I do! I do!"

"Now we'll take this question," H.M. shivered, but steadied himself, "of what you've been callin' the 'best people.'"

"Yes! Darwin's father and mother . . ."

"Just a minute. How do you know the best people aren't sittin' on your doorstep now? Wouldn't you back the taste and judgment of Gordon West, of Rafe Danvers, or Colonel Bailey, or the vicar—no, burn me, not his judgment; but you know what I mean—against any of the droops who've been advising you?"

Stella grew very quiet. "Please don't mention Gordon West."

"Oh?" inquired H.M. "Don't you like him?"

"Yes. I like him. Perhaps too much." Stella paused. "That's why, when I know poor Pam didn't do it, I can tell you only a woman could have written those letters."

"How so?"

"Because only a woman could have guessed. I concealed it too well."

228

"Then you got more than one letter? And they were all about West?"

The most evil of shadows brushed this room, brushed the vague nude with the red eye and the cylinder statue of ear and wing.

"Yes, they were," Stella replied in a low voice. "But I lied. I wouldn't even give anyone the satisfaction of asking me questions.

"And that's not the worst of it," continued Stella, with growing self-loathing. "I've always had an awfully funny reputation here. All the men have liked me, and all the women have just tolerated or plain disliked me. Maybe they're not fond of a presumptive 'widow.' But I ask you!"

Stella's voice rose passionately, and H.M. was compelled to shush her.

"When have I ever 'told my troubles' to even one man, except just now? Nobody knows a thing. I've flirted a little, yes. But on one side they say I'm a kind of—of a Messalina. On the other side they say I haven't blood enough to be interested. Well, I'm neither! I'm an ordinary human being, with feelings and temptations like anyone else."

"Sh-h! Easy now!"

"But after the 1st of July, when those letters started . . . well, it was my fault. When you're unhappy, or at least it's so with me, you turn horrible and say the cattiest things you can think of. Half the time it slips out before you know what you've said. Shall I tell you something, Sir Henry?"

"Absolutely."

"If Marion Tyler hates me, I don't blame her. Or Joan Bailey either. Joan didn't like me from the first. But how I wish I were like Joan! A healthy, hearty girl, who really doesn't think about anything except—well, love—and hasn't got a nerve in her body."

229

H.M. shook his head.

"Oh, my wench!" he said. "She's not like that at all. Something happened last night; the gal was so scared green she could hardly talk. But she just gritted her teeth, because the menfolk expected it."

"Don't we all?" breathed Stella, summing up her philosophy. "About Joan and Gor- . . . never mind! I didn't believe in my heart, truly, that Pam wrote those anonymous letters. Where would she get the typewriter? And, so far as I know, she can't even use one!"

"Aha! Common sense rears its lurkin' head!"

"But I put so much faith in Dr. Schmidt, because of those Air Force doctors. When he said Pam wrote the letters, and there was a psychosis shown in the last line of that 'Chansonette'—about that 'meet the guillotine!'—and you haven't denied it either. . . ."

"Psychosis my left foot!" said H.M., though he used a stronger term than this. "Look at me!"

Stella looked.

"Didn't you know about a trick verse style that is, or used to be, very popular? It begins all cooey and lovey-dovey, all rose leaf and tender mist, and then it ends with 'Get to hell out of here, my love'?"

"But of course! That's—"

"Everybody liked it, because it was well done and they liked the sting at the end. Young 'uns loved it. They'll imitate it if they can. Pam did."

"Is that *true?*"

"Oh, is it true! Pam said she didn't care much for the lovey-dovey business, though a bloke named Harry Goldfish wasn't so bad, but she wasn't allowed to play with Tommy Wyatt's gang because they were called Satan's Imps and wouldn't join the choir." An evil expression stole over H.M.'s face. "So I told her about my uncle, a louse named George Byron Merrivale, and how he tried to make me join the choir, and how I fixed

230

the bounder good and proper."

"But I'm so *ignorant!*" Stella seemed to harp on this fiercely. "I—was in the chorus when Darwin and I were married."

Sir Henry Merrivale was astonished.

"Sure you were," he said. "I said I'd seen you before. I said it was concerned with something fine and grand and noble. You were the gal on the end of the front row of the 'Veradana Gaities' in 1924."

"But Darwin's father and mother . . ."

"Looky here," he said impressively, "do you know how much a gal's got to have to be in the chorus of a Chalmers revue?" He added, with modest pride: "And my wife was in the chorus of that same show in 1913."

"Your—wife?"

"Sure. Of course," H.M. explained deprecatingly, "Clemmie's years and years younger than I am. But she's little and blonde and kept her figger. And even now, when she's all dolled up, she's still a smasher. Y'see, Clemmie—"

"Clemmie?"

"My wife. Her name's Clementine, like the Darling Clementine in the song." Assuming a stuffed and detached air, H.M. strummed at an imaginary banjo. "But we don't see much of each other nowadays," he added gloomily. "Clemmie's usually in the south of France."

"I'm sorry!" Stella's gray eyes grew concerned. "An unhappy marriage?"

"Unhappy?" exclaimed H.M. "Burn me, no! That's the trouble: it's been too happy."

"But there can't be any such thing as a too-happy marriage! I—I wish there could be."

"Looky here!" H.M. said sternly. "I'll tell you. Clemmie gets bored with the south of France. She sends a cable tellin' me to expect her. Well, we go to the

231

Ivy, or maybe Claridge's or the Savoy Grill—" H.M.'s tone was still deprecating—"and we begin having maybe four or five double whiskies. See what I mean?"

"Oh, yes! My husband and I—" Stella paused.

"And about the sixth one, when we both feel we've just been met at the Pearly Gates with a brass band, Clemmie will begin to look thoughtful. And she says to me, 'Henry, I've got a *wonderful* idea. How would it be,' she says, 'if we put a stuffed policeman sittin' on top of every chimney at Scotland Yard? And we did it in broad daylight, and nobody in the building ever saw it done?'

"And me, being full of whisky and cussedness, I say, 'Clemmie, that's not bad at all. Gimme a few minutes to work out how we can do it.' We did it, too. And then there was the time we . . . But what I mean," persisted H.M., raising a finger impressively as he preached his moral lesson, "you can't go on doin' that, can you? I got my dignity to think of."

Stella looked at him strangely.

"Good heavens," she cried, "you don't mean there are *two* of you?"

"I dunno what you're talking about!" said the outraged H.M.

"Two Sir Henry Merrivales, only one small and female? I . . . I . . ."

Stella's emotions, clearly, had gone too far. The old blighter had brought her so much hope, so much handling of black mental devils as though they were comic tissuepaper, that she must inevitably take one direction or the other.

"Do you know," said Stella, "when you first came here, I was afraid of you." And she threw her arms round his neck and wept on his shoulder.

"Oh, for the love of Esau!" groaned the great man. Casting up a look of acute martyrdom, he stretched

232

out both arms straight. Though he had encouraged this in Pam, having a natural affinity with children, he considered that with Stella it was going too far. Besides, with Stellas arms round his neck, he was conscious of a position which might have looked equivocal.

Another person was conscious of it too. It has been remarked that nobody ever locks doors in Stoke Druid. Gordon West, finding the front door unlocked, had gone through the passage into the drawing room, and stopped short.

"Er—sorry," he said quickly and hastened out.

"Wait a minute, curse you!" bellowed H.M. Gently he deposited the confused Stella on the divan and hurried out after West.

The night air met him with fresh coolness. West, hands in pockets, faced him under the peaked hood over the front door.

"Tell me, you old rip," West inquired with real interest. "How many women do you want? In a few days you'll have as bad a reputation as the vicar. And wait till Virtue Conklin hears about this!"

"I am absolutely INNERCENT," said H.M., tugging at his collar. "I'm the poorest, most misunderstood ba- . . . helper of mankind that ever tried to do a good deed! I went there, I tell you, only to comfort a little girl upstairs."

"According to my line of vision," said West, "you were comforting a big girl downstairs."

"I say." H.M. lowered his voice. "You're not goin' to say anything about this to Virtue?"

"No, Maestro. I don't mind if you keep a harem. But have you forgotten about what we were going to do? And all the rush-rush instructions you gave me?"

As a matter of face, H.M. had forgotten. But he instantly attacked, dragging out his watch and squinting at it.

"I thought," he said, "I must have been in there about four hours. I expect the others did too. But it's only ten o'clock now. Never mind; what have you been doing, foolin' about all this time?"

Shadows deepened under West's cheekbones. "Fooling about?" he demanded.

"Yes. Where's that .38 revolver?"

"It's gone." West spoke flatly. "It was gone when I rushed back to my cottage. I wasn't working, and it might have been taken at any time during the day."

High sailed the white moon over Stoke Druid. Though the moon was not yet at the full, it had strengthened its light.

"And where's Fred Cordy? I told you to grab him and not let him out of your sight!"

"I couldn't find him!" snapped West. "That," he added bitterly, "is what you call 'fooling about.' He wasn't at his home, which is the last house at the northern end of the High. He wasn't at either of the pubs. He wasn't at any hangout I know."

Both of them looked round. Before them the gravel path curved from the park gates toward their left, and past Stella's house for a hundred yards before it became an earthen path. In front of them were the thick rustling trees on this side of the park. Beyond the trees, a straight wide gravel drive ran from the gates to the door of the manor house. Beyond more trees, on the side where lived the Baileys and West himself, another path curved like this one.

Thus there were three paths, the center one to the Manor like the shaft of an arrow, and the other two like the sides of the arrowhead. But nothing moved or stirred, except shadows, amid moon-painted trees.

"This is gettin' worse and worse," growled H.M. in a low voice. "After all, Cordy's got somewhere!"

234

"Unless he's deliberately hiding."

Both of them stepped out into the moonlight, but their footsteps were so loud on the gravel that both stopped.

"Hold on! Would he be—" H.M. swept an arm round to indicate the park—"would he be visiting any of our friends here?"

"No. I thought of that."

"Howd'ye mean, son?"

"After you left the Colonel's, I gather, the party broke up. The vicar went home, and so did Rafe Danvers. Well! After I'd hunted high and low in the village, I came back here on the off-chance. Joan and the Colonel were playing chess; Cordy certainly wasn't there. I went on to my own place; deserted, no Cordy. I crossed up there in front of the manor house," West pointed, "and came round this side to Marion Tyler's cottage."

"That," interposed H.M., "would be on our side now. Up to the right as we stand here?"

"Yes. Marion was just undressing to go to bed. Definitely Cordy wasn't *there*. So I came on here."

"Did you look in at the manor house?"

"The manor house?" repeated West, taking his hands out of his pockets. "What the devil would Cordy be doing there?"

"Oh, son! You haven't got a landlady like Virtue, to ladle out all the gossip."

"What is it this time?"

"Squire Wyatt," said H.M., "is one of the people Cordy likes. Squire Wyatt, in Cordy's case at least, turns a blind eye to poaching. But you're probably right," H.M. added despairingly, "and Cordy's hiding. Son, he's got good reason to hide."

"H'm, yes. You indicated he was the person in danger." West stamped his feet on the ground. "We've got to find him! But how in Satan's name can we?"

"I dunno. Maybe—The Mocking Widow."

"But how can a lot of letters have any connection with . . . ?" West stopped. "Do you mean the stone figure of The Widow in that meadow?"

"Uh-huh."

"But he couldn't possibly hide there!"

"No, son. He couldn't hide. All the same, he could . . ."

Then H.M.'s hand dropped heavily on West's arm. "Listen!" he said.

Chapter 17

After that first moment and first sound, which was like the sharp breaking or tearing of a very small tree branch, there was no reason to call for silence.

Both H.M. and Gordon West heard the noise of footsteps running on gravel—running frantically, running desperately, in mortal fear. Anyone within an even wider distance could have heard the screech that went up.

"Help! Help! For God's sake, help!" And it faded only because of the runner's gasping breath.

"That's Cordy's voice!" said West.

"Steady, curse you! Where is he, and which direction's he going?"

The footsteps came nearer and nearer, spurting gravel.

"He's on the middle path that goes to the manor house," said West, whose nerves were on wires. "But he's running like hell away from the manor house, toward the front gates!"

"Stop that!"

"What's the matter?"

"You may catch him if you start plungin' through the trees. But if you fall you're dished. Take the gravel path

237

here; it curves, but it's open. . . . For the love of Esau, come on!"

Seldom, not even during the suitcase race or once when he was chased in a reptile house, did Sir Henry Merrivale run as he ran then. Bowlegged and pigeon-toed, his legs seeming to go like a wheel, he turned a terrible face sideways. Instructions seemed to jolt or spill out of his mouth, between breaths, as he flew beside West.

"When Cordy gets to the front gates, he'll head across to The Mockin' Widow. . . ."

A heavy gasp and gurgle followed.

"Try to catch him before he gets there. Got it?"

"Yes!"

"If he does g-g-et there . . ."

"Go on!"

"And climbs up that stone, you got to stop him before he reaches the head. I mean, the eyes!"

"The *what?*"

"The eyes!" One more effort, after a heavy gasp. "I'm goin' to drop out now. Sprint for it!"

West sprinted for it, and he was no mean runner. His own crunching race for a moment drowned out the sound of Cordy's, and he could not tell where Cordy was. The shoemaker, so far as West could gather by sound, had not started as far back as the manor-house door. Cordy must have started at least sixty or eighty yards away from the door. He . . .

Then West picked up the sound of the other runner. Cordy had passed him on a straight track and screamed again. West had not reckoned on the sinew of the little man who could balance on gravestones or turn cartwheels like a professional acrobat.

West, with a kind of spring, put on a burst of speed in which he could feel the breath saw across his lungs. He was blind to everything else. He whirled into the curve, by the low park wall near the gates, not twenty feet behind Cordy as the latter raced through the open gates.

"Stop, you fool! Wait!"

That was what West wanted to shout. Whether he managed to get out words clearly, or even get them out at all, he could never afterwards remember.

Brilliant moonlight now picked out every detail of the scene before him. Cordy, as H.M. had predicted, ran in a diagonal line past the High Street and across the open space toward the bank leading down into the meadow. Several hundred feet beyond, the wicked black shape of The Widow rose up forty feet amid dull light-pallor.

Cordy was flying with his head down, spiky hair a-bristle, his patched coat and corduroy trousers clearly to be seen.

"Show you!" the thin voice screamed.

Then, behind both West and Cordy, somebody fired two revolver shots.

West knew what they were, though he did not turn his head and flew on, feeling only a hot crawling of the skin that they had missed him. Cordy, jerked forward and serving as though he had been pushed by hands, was within three feet of the bank down into the meadow. And Cordy disappeared.

"Got him," thought West, with what seemed the inhuman loudness of the shots still ringing in his ears.

But they hadn't. Either the shots missed him, or they must have caused such trifling wounds as to be of no importance. Cordy was up and pelting across the soggy meadow, in thin mist about knee-high, straight for The Mocking Widow.

West, who had slowed down a little to calculate that the bullets must have been fired either from behind the low, curving park wall or just outside it, plunged onto the bank—and made his first mistake.

He tried to save time by jumping down into the meadow, without remembering either the pitch or the depth. His heel slid into mud under tearing grass. A moment later he landed with a thud which seemed to drive his bones into his vitals and spill the wits out of his head. But, on whatever object he set his mind, he went at it with fierce concentrated directness. He was on his feet, and running hard, within a second or two.

In fact, he closed the gap between himself and Fred Cordy, who did not run well in the sodden meadow. He was only half a dozen feet behind Cordy when the latter leaped for the figure.

Then . . .

The Mocking Widow faced out diagonally toward the High Street, her sly smile set there forever. Fred Cordy was swarming up the front of the figure, carefully yet as nimbly as a monkey.

"That's done it!" was the thought in West's mind, even as he leaped over some boulders and groped along the figure's side.

Without an incident or even some minor miracle, West was finished. Cordy's particular form of acrobatics would get him to the top before West could hope to reach it. Nevertheless West groped feverishly up on what at a distance seemed a fairly smooth rock face. But there were many handholds—deep crevices, projecting rocks smooth or sharp—as high as he could reach.

He could not follow in Cordy's track. One smash from a hobnailed boot would send him down again. West jumped for the side of the figure, and began to climb.

It seemed an eternity before he had fought halfway up. If you have never done any climbing, your trouble is to find footholds that do not slip or crumble, leaving

240

you dangling, ankles stabbed and feet flailing, on the end of one wrenched arm.

To West the handholds were better, though the whole side seemed to strike back at him. It was as though The Mocking Widow, with all the malignancy of more than a thousand years, shivered and resisted. The handholds would tilt suddenly, banging your body against the side. Grope with caution, or your head would half crack against an unseen rock above.

West, in despair, decided that Cordy must have reached the top—or the eyes, an ugly image—and have started down again. He set himself with reasonable firmness, and began to edge himself round toward the front. If he could see Cordy . . .

Then West stopped dead.

Less than ten feet above him, clamped in secure holds against the rock, Cordy was leaning round the side and looking down at him.

Cordy's goblin face, between shadow and moonlight, seemed pale and with an unnaturally sharp nose. West could hear the thin whistling of his breath, which came slowly.

And West tried to speak without hard breathing.

"Fred! Don't you recognize me? I'm Gordon West!"

The teeth were visible as Cordy drew his lips back.

"Ah, Mr. West," he said almost pleasantly. "I reckernize 'ee. Did 'ee think I wouldn't?"

"Then what are you doing here?"

Cordy's smile, which seemed a trifle mad, clearly expressed the sentiment, "Wouldn't 'ee like to know!"

"If it comes to that," said West, "what are we both doing here? Come on down with me, will you? I'm your friend; don't you know that?"

Cordy considered this. The suggestion of madness faded out of his eyes, to be replaced by a shrewdness which looked even more dangerous.

241

"I've got nothing against 'ee, Mr. West. By Gearge, I like 'ee!" Cordy's blackened right hand was free, and he pointed with it. "That's why I say: go down. Go away. While 'ee've got the chance. Now."

"What if I don't, Fred?"

The goblin, peering with white face down the rock, uttered a scream of rage.

"Then I'll show 'ee 'oo's boss!"

Cordy's free right hand darted out of sight toward his left. West could guess what he would choose. It would be a heavy smooth stone, not large but weighted to the hand.

"I'll show 'ee 'oo's boss!"

West saw the man's hand and arm go back. He saw the stone fly straight and black at his face. Dodging instinctively, he lost all but one hold and swung helplessly with five bloodied fingers gripped inside a rock crevice. The stone, missing him by two inches, whacked with a dull *splash* into the meadow below.

Slowly, fiercely concentrated, West groped and groped until he found a hold. Another stone flashed past him, but Cordy was in such a rage that the stone flew wild.

"I'll get you for that, Fred."

"Think so?"

"You may get up there. You may even get to the eyes." West stressed the last two words. "But you'll have to come down. I'll get you."

Afterwards he paid no attention to the other. Clinging flat to the rock face, his forehead and the insides of his wrists scraped raw, he devoted himself to hoisting himself one foot, two, three, four, five. Cordy, climbing with inhuman agility amid a rattle of small stones, must be nearly at the top.

But West stopped a moment. For the first time he felt a sickness in the hollow of his stomach. It seemed to him that the whole figure—very slightly—had tilted sideways.

Through West's mind, in the instant that precedes a pounce of danger, flashed fragments of a conversation he had heard before. In low soft light of early evening on Saturday, he could see Sir Henry Merrivale standing at the foot of The Widow and peering upwards. Again he heard H.M. ask:

"Could you climb up that figure?"

And the puzzled jumble of the vicar's reply, from which emerged:

"I shouldn't like to climb it myself. It looks rather like one stone, but it might crumble and fall down on you."

The Mocking Widow was forty feet high. That's nothing at all, is it? Yet, when you cling to it a little more than half way up, and the imminence of the stone mass towers over you, the ground seems a long way off.

Again—but very slightly—the figure seemed to tilt sideways from West's position: actually straight forward from The Widow's face, where Cordy was climbing. If that mass came down, it would crush Cordy and probably West as well.

"Fred!" he shouted upwards.

No reply.

West glanced over his shoulder and downwards. Evidently the alarm had gone out. Across a mist-carpeted meadow, and up the bank to the foot of the High Street, several indistinguishable shapes of men had gathered. Stoke Druid had no street lamps, not being in a built-up area, but lights—electric or paraffin oil—were springing up along the High Street.

"You've climbed up once too often, Fred," West shouted, with an inspired guess. "Come down! She's tilting forward! She'll fall on you!"

From above came a strangling sound of coughing.

243

"Ol' Widder?" jeered Cordy, and coughed again. "Been 'ere before ol' Druid, Widder has! She won't . . ."

Then, without warning or even premonitory sound, The Mocking Widow collapsed.

She collapsed straight forward, breaking off at about twenty-six feet up, just at the place for which West was reaching. She collapsed amid a roll and rumble of stones which, in that night silence, sounded like an avalanche.

A tiny fragment of stone stung West's forehead like a wasp. A larger stone leaped out over him. But, just before the fog of stone grit and dust rolled out, he saw two things he will not forget.

Fred Cordy, flung outwards or more probably jumping, seemed to go past in a whirl of arms and legs, but in a kind of grotesque slow motion. The huge head of The Widow, cracked off cleanly because West could see moonlight between head and neck, turned in mid-air and looked at him with the same grisly slow motion. Out of its left eye leaped a black flattish object, which he scarcely saw.

Whereupon, after the roll and roar of the stones, the thick dust smothered down with a grittiness that made West shut his eyes as he held tightly.

The stones beneath him rocked and cracked, but held firm. By reasonable odds he should have been crushed by that stonefall, or knocked loose by the showering overflow. He escaped merely as a man may escape because a high-explosive bomb falls too close to him.

Through the healing silence below, voices rose up.

"Cordy!"

"Don't touch 'im now!"

"Ah, and look there!"

"Who's still on the side? Mr. West!"

Even through closed eyelids, West could catch the bright shimmer of light on rock as the rays of many electric torches and lanterns fastened on him. What annoyed him most was his stinging, smarting eyes when he tried to open them. Also, in the backwash of emotion, his muscles had turned watery and he wondered whether he could keep his grip on the stones. He wanted to call for help, but wouldn't do it.

After that short tremble of panic, he began to descend. It was far easier than he had expected, with the encouraging voices from below.

"You go after him, Mr. West?"

"You got him, Mr. West."

"Yes!"

"Ol' Widder's gone," a woman's voice said stolidly. "Or a lot of her. That means trouble for everybody; mind what I say."

Within easy jumping distance of the ground, West craned over his shoulder to look down. A circle of faces—indistinguishable to his painful eyes—first glanced up at him, then down at what lay amid a shifting of many lights.

Some distance away lay a very small portable typewriter, its black cover smashed off and flung still further, but its little keys gleaming white. At the foot of The Widow, under a rocklike hump spreading out, Fred Cordy lay face downwards in a thin cover of mist.

Heavy rocks and dust covered and crushed him as far up as the waist. His arms were flung wide, and his spiky hair was damp where his face pressed into the meadow. He wore his old patched shirt—and there were two bullet holes in his back.

Chapter 18

They buried Fred Cordy on Friday, September 19th, four days after his death, under a chilly sky coiling with a few smoky-looking clouds.

Few attended the funeral, since Cordy had almost no friends and his death was regarded secretly as good riddance. But Gordon West and Joan Bailey were there, together with the Colonel; so was Ralph Danvers; so was Squire Wyatt; so, rather surprisingly, was Marion Tyler.

"He dug my garden," Marion said. "He wouldn't work at his shoemaking, but he dug my garden."

Despite the late Fred's atheistical views, Mrs. Cordy pleaded for a churchyard interment; and the Rev. James could resist no woman in tears. Mrs. Cordy wore deep black. She held the hand of her eleven-year-old daughter, Frederica, who was sucking a lollipop behind the black veil. Squire Wyatt promised to take in Mrs. Cordy and Frederica for some place in his own home; and a few drops of rain fell.

Stoke Druid, taken collectively, didn't care.

Between Monday night, when Cordy was murdered, and Thursday night, following the inquest, the village went through several phases of emotion. First it was alarm, causing doors and windows to be locked. Then it was wrath. Finally it became apathy.

They expected much from the inquest. It was common knowledge that the typewriter concealed in one eye of The Widow was the typewriter which had written the letters.

Mr. Vance, the same obliging coroner who had presided at the inquest on the body of Cordelia Martin, was in charge. The coroner had a number of whispered conferences with Inspector Garlick. A few pressmen, who had come down from London over that spreading tale of the ghost appearance to Joan Bailey, ceased bedevilling Joan, to attend the inquest.

The first witness, according to custom, was Mrs. Mary Ann Cordy, who made formal identification of the body. Next to occupy the witness chair was Dr. Johann Schiller Schmidt, who really understood this sort of work and should have stuck to it.

The deceased, Dr. Schmidt explained, had died as the result of a hemorrhage caused by a bullet wound through the left lung. Two shots had been fired, and in a diagonal direction slightly from right to left. Both, missing the backbone, had lodged in the body; but only one in a vital spot.

It was unusual, but not impossible or even surprising, that a man with such a wound could have run across a meadow and climbed up the stone figure before succumbing (it could not be stated just when) to his injury.

The report of the ballistics consultant at Bristol was brief.

"Both bullets submitted were fired from a Webley .38 revolver, pattern 3. I cannot say, nor can anyone else, from what distance the bullets were fired, except that it was neither very short not very long range."

Gordon West, following the reading of this report,

248

told—he was encouraged to tell it very briefly—the story everybody knew.

Could *he* estimate the distance from which the shots might have been fired?

Well, he could only say what had occurred to him at the time; he would have guessed about thirty or forty feet. He had been running well to the left of Cordy, though in the same diagonal direction, and the bullets would not have come near him.

Whereupon the coroner, at the request of the police, blandly adjourned the inquest.

The spectators of Stoke Druid sat with bulging eyes, in stunned incredulity. For a few moments after the coroner's statement there was only hard-breathing silence. Then up spoke Mr. Rush, the ironmonger, in whose own face there was a trace of iron.

"*'Ere!*" shouted Mr. Rush. "*What about they poison-pen letters?*"

"They are not germane to our inquiry, sir. May I remind you that this inquest is adjourned?"

"*Never mind the German stuff!*" said Theo Bull from another corner. "*Who owns that typewriter? Who wrote the letters? You 'aven't said a word about the typewriter, 'cept it was hid in ol' Widow's 'ead. You've only said what we all know!*"

"For the last time, sir, I must remind you . . ."

If at that moment the coroner had been unwise, and called on the police to clear the room, there would have been very bad trouble.

"Gentlemen," he said, "I can do only what the law permits me."

There was a heavy growl and a stamping of feet. But Stoke Druid, like the rest of England, had been bred with such respect for the law that mere mention of it quietened the most malcontent, and the group disintegrated.

This, however, did not prevent indignation meetings larger and more angry than any which had followed the vicar's famous sermon. Somebody knocked off a policeman's helmet outside Danvers' bookshop; but Robert, having his orders, treated it good-naturedly and remained stolid. That night, Thursday, all bars of both the Lord Rodney and the Nag's Head were packed to capacity.

At the Nag's Head, by the counter of the saloon bar, Squire Tom Wyatt held forth to a group of admirers. His heavy gray hair, tinged with black, was parted and so carefully brushed up round the edges that it looked like a wig. His heavy gray mustache was barbered as well.

Squire Wyatt swallowed a third of his pint, his paunch moving visibly, before setting down the glass.

"I'll make a statement," he said, and wiped his mustache.

It may or may not have been a coincidence that Inspector Garlick had just entered the bar. Instead of going to the bottle and jug, Inspector Garlick leaned over the counter and asked for three quarts of George's Home-Brewed to take away with him.

Another thing, perhaps to be noticed, was that Squire Wyatt no longer used the Somerset speech. His speech, though harsh and rough-edged, was that of any country gentleman who rubbed elbows with his tenantry.

"There's a rumor in this place," he went on, "that Fred Cordy was at the Manor before he was shot on Monday night. That's a lie, and I'll tell it to any damned policeman who wants to see me."

His eye sought Garlick's in the mirror behind the bar; but, as seen against a steamed glass, the Inspector was only accepting bottles.

"You heard," Tom Wyatt continued, to an assenting

chorus, "what young West said. West said he thought Cordy tore out of bushes, or it might be small trees, at the side of the drive about sixty or eighty yards from my house. Well, that's true. I saw it myself."

Up went a babble of voices, as the Squire gulped down more bitter.

"Listen, Marty! Listen, Steve! I was just going to bed, and I opened the front door to see if the night happened to be fine. Cordy tore out of those trees— you couldn't miss him in the moonlight; I think there was somebody with him in the trees—and ran full tilt down my drive. I thought it was some more of his unfunny nonsense, screaming like that, so I closed the front door and locked it."

"Which side of the drive would that be, Squire?" asked an interested voice.

"The left, Len! The south side! *But . . .*"

Squire Wyatt's glass came down on the bar.

"They didn't call me as a witness today," he said, which clearly enraged him more than anything else. "But when I kill a man, Len, I'll meet him face to face and give him both barrels of a twelve-bore. Tell *that* to any bloody policeman you meet!"

Beer-handle pumps thumped and thumped again. Since the two barmaids seemed to spill almost as much beer as they served, even the tobacco smoke was tinged with damp. Inspector Garlick, carefully counting his change, picked up the paper bag with the bottles and went out.

The Inspector had only to walk past the entrance to the old Nag's Head coachyard, and turn in at Danvers' bookshop. Far at the rear, a green-shaded lamp burned over the bookseller's desk, where sat Danvers and Sir Henry Merrivale.

But, when the beer was poured, it became a guarded conference between Inspector Garlick and H.M.

Danvers, looking uncomfortable, sat a little distance away.

"Did you hear anything," asked H.M., nodding his head drowsily toward the pub, "in there?"

"Nothing I didn't know already."

While H.M. merely grunted in reply, Inspector Garlick squared himself with determination. Round them rose up three sides of cases with wire fronts. Garlick took out notebook and pencil to show that his words would be weighty.

"Sir Henry," he began, "did you know all the time that the poison-pen typewriter belonged to Fred Cordy?"

Danvers, who had been reaching for a book on the desk, dropped the book with a thud and sat up.

"It's all right, Rafe," H.M. reassured him. "The Inspector here won't fire off too many secrets."

"Sir Henry, I repeat my question! Did you know all the time . . . ?"

"I didn't know it, son. I thought it might very well be."

"And again! How in blazes did you know where the typewriter was hidden?"

"Oh, son! I keep sayin' I didn't *know*. I told you I didn't know. I told you I wasn't sure, and you'd got to have your intensive search just the same."

"Since this hullaballoo," said Garlick, and tapped his pencil against his notebook to indicate the murder, "I haven't had much chance for a good talk with you. Cordy bought that typewriter from old Joe Palmer, the Glastonbury dealer, in 1931. Can I hear about the rest of it?"

H.M. stuck his feet up on the desk, meditating.

In fact, he meditated so long that Garlick thought he had gone to sleep, until H.M. opened one sharp eye toward Danvers.

"The first time I ever walked into this shop," he said, "was the first time I ever walked into this village. You gave me an outline of what was generally known or deduced, and very nobly offered those Fouché Memoirs if I solved the mystery . . ."

"That was nothing!" Danvers threw the words aside.

"It's a lot, Rafe. Anyway, you showed me one of the letters. You were too nearsighted to spot the mark; but I was pretty sure it was written on a Formosa Portable. Then, while we discussed possibilities, you made a remark about Fred Cordy that was very interestin'. Lemme see if I can remember what you said about Cordy. You said, *He once bought a typewriter to write fiery letters to the newspapers, and then became incensed and threw it in the river.* Remember?"

"Yes. I remember."

"But I thought to myself, 'Oh, no he didn't! Cordy didn't throw that machine in the river. He only said he did.'"

"Why did you think that?" demanded Garlick.

"Because it's not a natural action, son. Even for a half crackpot, and Cordy wasn't a crackpot at all. Now suppose, for instance, I'm trying to drive a golfball across your river here. Suppose I try it four times. And each time," said H.M., beginning to shiver and glare with reminiscence, "the little swine goes smack in the river and sinks."

"Well?"

"Well, son, I'm goin' to be awful mad. I may chuck the golfclub in the river. I may chuck the whole ruddy golfbag in the river. So far, it's still a natural action. You may think I'm goin' a bit too far. All the same, it's natural.

"But suppose," argued H.M., in reply to himself, "you're at home—at home, mind!—with a typewriter that's up to some cussedness. You may sling it across

253

the room. You may jump on it. Most likely, you shove it away in a cupboard. But does it *ever* occur to you to carry it some distance away from home and drop it in the river? Is that a natural action? I ask you!"

There was a long silence.

"I'm bound to agree with you, sir," admitted Inspector Garlick. "I wouldn't get as mad as that, myself. . . ."

"Oh, son! Neither would I!" said H.M., and instantly looked holy. "I'm known everywhere for the sweetness of my temper. I was only givin' you an illustration, d'ye see?"

"Um—yes."

"So I thinks to myself: Rafe isn't telling lies about a report that could be confirmed anywhere. Cordy's the joker in this. But Cordy couldn't have written the letters. Then let's think for a second of The Widow. I mean the poison-pen writer, not the stone figure."

Again, for a time, H.M. appeared to sleep.

"Let's suppose (just for the sake of argument) that The Widow is writin' letters on Cordy's typewriter. The Widow's as clever as Satan. We've all discovered that. If you use a typewriter, you run all kinds of risks, from neighbors to curious servants. Follow that?"

"Yes, sir. If I may ask—"

"Furthermore, you've got to be ready," continued H.M., ignoring the interruption, "when the police come chargin' in. Sooner or later they always do. The press will dig up these cases if nobody else will. And the coppers won't politely ask, 'Have you got a typewriter?' and bow 'emselves out if you say no. Will they, Inspector?"

"Not likely," said Garlick, with a certain grimness.

"So The Widow," said H.M., "has got to have a hiding place for the typewriter. It ought to be out of the house and grounds; she's a dead duck if they find it. . . .

By the way, Rafe, have you still got the postcard, with the colored photograph of the stone figure? The one you showed us late Saturday afternoon?"

Without a word Danvers found it and handed it to H.M. H.M., adjusting his spectacles, turned it over and read from the printed description on the back.

"The eyes," he read aloud, *"are each large enough to contain a human head.* Well, they'd also contain a very small and light portable (I kept stressin' how small it was) of the kind used twenty-five years ago. But was anybody in the habit of climbin' up there? I asked the vicar, down in the meadow later. He said *he* wouldn't like to climb it; but he said there was a village superstition against it, and nobody ever did climb up.

"Cor, what a hiding place! Here's Mocking Widow, watching the village, with the source of the poison-pen letters hidden in the stone figure's head, where nobody will ever see it and nobody will ever look for it!"

"This infernal business," snapped Garlick, "begins to give me the creeps."

"Remember," H.M. reminded him with ghoulish relish, "that The Widow doesn't need to *use* the typewriter more than once in a fortnight or even more. The letters, mostly, have come in batches. The Widow won't have to do any climbing, if . . ."

"If," supplied Inspector Garlick, "she had a man like Fred Cordy, who was a natural acrobat and would have enjoyed the spitefulness of poison-pen letters."

H.M. grunted, flicking the postcard on the desk.

"Well . . . now," he protested. "I hadn't even seen Cordy, or many others, when those ideas went whoozlin' round in the old onion. But I did see Cordy, I saw some others, and the ideas began to churn again. Does daylight dawn now?"

"Cordy, of course, was The Widow's accomplice. We can't get away from it!"

H.M. looked dubious.

"In the sense of knowing most of what went on," he answered, "my vote would be no. But Cordy was an accomplice this far: he knew who was writin' the letters."

Both of them listened to the slow, measured tapping of Garlick's pencil against the notebook.

"Maybe Cordy tried a little blackmail, sir."

"Maybe he did."

"And maybe The Widow didn't like that." Garlick pointed the pencil like an imaginary revolver and crooked his forefinger twice.

"Burn it all!" said H.M., bringing his feet down from the desk. "I told you yesterday, in private, that the poison-pen writer and the murderer are one and the same person! I told you who it was. I tried to suggest lines of . . ."

"But look here, sir! Why didn't you tell me—?"

Inspector Garlick, as though catching a look from H.M., abruptly stopped. He glanced briefly at Danvers, who was looking through a newspaper. Then the Inspector put away notebook and pencil.

"There are a lot of things we've got to discuss," he said with heavy significance. "But that can wait. I don't like the attitude of these Stoke Druid people. You can't blame them if they're a bit up in the air. But they won't help!"

Both H.M. and Garlick were startled by a burst of Danvers's low, chuckling laughter. Danvers, folding up the newspaper, regarded them quizzically.

"Inspector," he said, "neither you nor our good friend Sir Henry can understand countrymen, can you? Most of them have been angry or frightened, yes; and some of them still are. But, underneath all this, they are apathetic and rather shocked."

"Shocked? By the death of Fred Cordy?"

"No, no, no, no! They are shocked because a good third of The Mocking Widow's statue has tumbled down to rubble before their eyes. They neither liked nor disliked it. But it was always *there*. It was a part of themselves and their landscapes and their lives. Men will feel much the same, I think," Danvers added, "if the bombers come to our cities."

"H'm, yes," muttered Sir Henry Merrivale. "Rafe, I didn't think of that."

Inspector Garlick, who was not interested in this, tried to sweep it aside. But the twinkle in the bookseller's eyes held him.

"Shall I tell you something else, Inspector?"

"Thanks, Mr. Danvers. If it's got sense in it."

"Tonight," said Danvers, "is Thursday. If it rains tomorrow, as the newspaper forecast says it will, you won't get one question answered—you won't even get a word—until Monday morning."

"Now draw it mild, Mr. Danvers! Why won't I?"

"Because the women will be too much occupied, and they'll lead their menfolk by the noses," Danvers replied calmly. "Haven't you forgotten the church bazaar on Saturday?"

"Church bazaar? What about it?"

"Confound it, man!" said Danvers, with a mild frown. "This bazaar means more, far more, than a visit from the Prime Minister. The ladies began decorating the room today. If it rains tomorrow, on Friday . . ."

"Oi!" interposed Sir Henry Merrivale, getting to his feet. "I'm in this church bazaar too." He inflated his chest and smote it. "I'm goin' to be an Indian Chief. But they hold it in that long stone building, don't they? Why are you botherin' so much about rain?"

"The roof, my dear Henry!"

"What about it?"

"Roughly a hundred years ago," said Danvers in a

leisurely way, "the then-vicar replaced the original stone roof, which was in bad repair, with a low-pitched shingle roof supported by boards underneath. If the vicar keeps a sharp eye on repairs, the roof seldom leaks. Unfortunately, too, there is an earth floor. Whether Mr. Hunter has kept an eye on the repairs . . ."

"All this fuss," interrupted Inspector Garlick, "about a church bazaar?"

Danvers merely lifted his shoulders. He went to the front of the shop, drew back an edge of the blind, and peered upwards past glass and steel meshwork.

"It's an overcast night," he reported.

Thus, as Danvers had looked up at the sky that night, so many heads looked up out of windows on the following morning. The sky, thought not too much overcast, showed ominous blackish patches of the I-will-I-won't variety.

Many ladies had worked hard on those decorations of the Gunpowder Room. Though they wanted very much to find out the condition of the roof, they did not want to worry poor Mr. Hunter, who for the past week had seemed so oddly distraught.

Nor had Marion Tyler inquired about it. It was past ten o'clock on Friday before Marion woke up, in her trim and well-furnished little cottage near the manor house. She must have awakened to the shock of the many duties she had on her mind, as chairman of the bazaar committee. Marion herself was distraught, and conscious of being less than her usual brisk self.

It was to be hoped that she could trust her two chief assistants, Mrs. Doom and Mrs. Goldfish. Marion dressed hastily and sat down to breakfast. She had scarcely finished breakfast when Mrs. Doom, the confectioner, arrived with news of the first crisis.

Mrs. Doom, with a name like that, should have been

tall and sinister and beetle-browed. Actually, she was a small, smiling, stoutish woman, rosy of face, with six children and a husband who couldn't keep a job. She never gave trouble unless she had what she called her nerves, which put everybody else in a dither. And Mrs. Doom approached bravely.

"Miss Tyler," she said, "I wanted to tell you, Miss Tyler, that the special costumes have arrived from London."

"What special costumes?" asked Marion, with a sudden feeling of disaster. "The costumes were supposed to be homemade! You and Mrs. Goldfish are in charge of that."

"Miss Tyler, surely you remember, last meeting, when Miss Robinson suggested we *might* have a few special costumes?"

"Er—yes. I do remember something of the sort. But I never thought . . ."

"The cost, Miss Tyler, is more than we thought. It's dreadful."

"How much?"

"Ten-pound-fifteen. We've put our hands in the till before there was anything in it."

"Oh, God!" said Marion, not aloud. Aloud she said: "Never mind, Mrs. Doom. I'm sure we shall more than make up for it. Besides," the image of the Rev. James might have been standing in the room, "it will please the bishop."

"And it's a mercy," Mrs. Doom said eagerly, "there's one costume we can send back. Theo Bull simply WON'T be Simple Simon."

This rather cryptic remark needs small explanation. Mr. Bull, always dependable, was to have a stall at which he sold strings of the sausages he made himself, and of which he was very proud, together with a great number of cold meat pies, large and small.

259

Mrs. Doom, who prided herself on her genteel manners, did not repeat the butcher's actual words.

"Simple Simon *met* the pieman," Mr. Bull had argued violently. "'E wasn't the pieman his own bloody self; now was 'e?"

"And, you see," rosy-faced Mrs. Doom beamed on Marion, "he's got a beautiful white coat. Miss Robinson's got him a big high chef's cap."

"There are a number of things we must see to immediately," said Marion, taking up a notebook whose pages were covered with her fine, neat handwriting. "Are you ready, Mrs. Doom?"

The day passed in a whirl of activity. All in the village seemed headed toward the Gunpowder Room, the men merely to have a look but at the same time curious and instantly seized upon for work unless quick enough on their feet.

It was Marion herself, finding the word ROOF in her notebook, who investigated. There were few persons outside the grim old building, with its stone drum of a powder magazine, looming up at the far end of the churchyard.

She found an unexpected source of assistance. Mr. Basset, the seventy-five-year-old sexton, had left behind a ladder for some purpose which doubtless he himself had forgotten. Propping up the ladder as best she could, Marion made an attempt to examine the shallow-peaked roof.

Afterwards, feeling much disheveled, she must rush back to her own cottage to gulp down something as a late lunch, and dress in time for the funeral of Fred Cordy at three o'clock. As she went down the High Street, the ruin of The Mocking Widow struck her with a shock. It roused thoughts which she locked away in her mind, so securely that they cannot be revealed here.

Then she passed Inspector Garlick, standing on the steps of the Lord Rodney. The Inspector was today in full uniform instead of plain clothes, wearing a shiny black waterproof though no rain had fallen. He looked defeated and wrathful.

"Excuse me, miss," he said to Marion. "If you can spare a moment . . ."

"So sorry!" answered Marion, and fled.

Afterwards they buried Fred Cordy, that afternoon of Friday, September 19th, under a chilly sky coiling with a few smoky-looking clouds. Very few words were spoken by the little group about the grave. Marion, watching the Rev. James's vestments blow in the autumn wind, was mainly glad that Squire Wyatt had promised a home for Mrs. Cordy and her daughter. At the end of it, as has been recorded, a few drops of rain fell.

Marion, glancing up at the sky, hastened to separate herself from the others when the burial service was completed. Hurrying toward the front of the church-yard, where the trees shook down a few yellowing leaves, she made for the High Street.

Much as she wanted to see the Rev. James, she did not want to speak to him in the presence of others. After a few minutes, she knew, he would walk across to the vicarage. Marion hastened into the tobacconist-barber's, and ordered many more cigarettes than she needed while she made conversation with Mr. Chandler. Next she crossed the street, lower down, and at the chemist's she talked to Mrs. Goldfish—a severe-looking woman, censor of morals for all Stoke Druid—who was on duty because Mr. Goldfish had been called away.

It was fully half an hour before Marion strolled up to the vicarage. The front door was opened by Mrs. Honeywell, the Rev. James's housekeeper, with a welcoming smile.

"I'll announce myself, Mrs. Honeywell," said Marion. "Is he in the study?"

"He is indeed, Miss Tyler!"

Marion tapped at the door.

"James!" she said earnestly. "James!"

Chapter 19

In the meantime, for the past twenty minutes, the Rev. James Cadman Hunter had been pacing slowly round his study, with the weight of many problems visible in his forehead.

By this time his left eye had returned to normal, with only a faint bluish line under the lower lid. The swelling and redness had long gone from his face. Dull September daylight, through leaded windows, showed that his study contained furniture inherited mainly from past incumbents of the parish.

Clerical faces looked down from the pictures, clerical words stuffed the books, as in a hall of judgment. But the Rev. James, tall and determined, stalked about the study with one finger unconsciously raised.

"Now look here, Uncle William!" he said aloud.

His Uncle William, otherwise the Bishop of Glastontor, would arrive late tomorrow afternoon, and had graciously consented to visit the bazaar early in the evening. Though at heart he might have misgivings, the Rev. James believed he could defend himself fluently and well. The only serious charge was his disobedience of the bishop's order. But he, Rev. James, had been in the right. Indeed, he thought hotly, he was prepared to stand on a humble soapbox in Hyde Park and defend himself against anybody.

As for other worries . . .

His eye encountered the large looseleaf notebook, with calender heads, which lay on his desk and on which his own handwriting was gibberish. He had left undone, he darkly feared, many of the things which he ought to have done.

The truth was that the Rev. James, always in a hurry and seldom paying close attention, would listen to a message, swear he had got it correctly, and then write down in abbreviations what he thought he had heard. As a result, he was never able to decipher the abbreviations concerning what he was supposed to do. True, he told himself, Marion Tyler had offered to reduce this chaos to order . . .

Marion Tyler. There lay the blackest of his worries.

For he had fallen in love with Marion, fallen past hope; and this, thought the Rev. James, was very bad.

In the depths of his mind he looked briefly at one thought which for months he had not admitted even to himself. When he first arrived at Stoke Druid, he had been rather attracted to Joan Bailey. When he learned she was tacitly engaged to another man, he had deliberately avoided her for many months. That crafty old villain, Merrivale, had seen this and commented on it. It had made the reading of that letter in church more of a nightmare than anyone knew; yet it was his duty and he had done it.

Nevertheless, long before then he had recognized that he was not suited to Joan, nor she to him. He was amazed, thinking back, at his strange fancy. But—Marion!

That was different, and he knew it. He had always liked her very much, though her reserve and coldness (the Rev. James really believed this) had put him off. Yet, since Sunday afternoon of last week, something about her—yes, personality—had made his head swim and had caused the condition they called "distraught."

Marion wished to be treated merely as a friend. It was black and hopeless.

Like many orators, the Rev. James believed he was merely pacing the floor and thinking, his lips moving soundlessly. Actually, he was talking aloud.

"I am so moved and distracted by your personality," he declared, to a stuffed owl on a cabinet, "that sometimes I cannot achieve coherent speech. I fall over things. My dear Marion, would it not be more simple, more sensible, indeed sounder policy, if we were merely to be married?"

Pacing on, he shook his head gloomily. That would never do. It sounded like a speech in Parliament. And you cannot ask a young lady to marry you merely because it would be sound policy. He flung this aside. Circling the room again, he quite unconsciously addressed a bust of some church dignitary on a marble pedestal.

"Now look here, Uncle William!" he said. "Let's get down to cases, shall we? What did I do? Tell me straight, without the wrappings! If you think . . ."

Vaguely he heard a tap at the door, and the sound of his name.

"Yes?" he called back. "Come in!" And then: "Marion! Come in! Sit down!"

The Rev. James had a sight flush on his face. Any curious spectator might have noticed that both of them were so self-conscious in each other's presence that neither noticed slight slips of speech or irregularities of behavior on the part of the other.

"I can't stay, really," said Marion. "No, really!" She allowed her coat to be removed tenderly, and then thrown in the general direction of a bookcase. "And I hate to trouble you, James. . . ."

"Trouble me? Nonsense!"

"But we really must have someone repair the roof of the Gunpowder Room!"

An expression of enlightenment crossed the vicar's good-natured face.

"By Jove, that's it!" he exclaimed, dashing at his desk and the open memorandum book. "I really could not think why I had written the expression *o-o-f*, with two exclamation points, merely after paying a call on a worthy invalid lady. The roof, of course!"

He swung round briskly, rubbing his hands, ready for anything.

"It isn't much, as far as I could see," Marion rattled on. "It's only along the sides of the ridgepole, both sides, but only a little way down. If you could get someone . . ."

"My dear Marion! I will attend to this myself!"

"Whatever you think is best, James."

"Ah, now I have it! Will it trouble you, Marion, if for a moment I walk about the room and consider this problem in silence?"

"No, of course not!"

Nodding profoundly, the Rev. James began stalking round the room and was promptly lost in speculation. Marion's light brown eyes, with their black lashes, watched him make three slow circuits of the study.

"I love you so much!" he said unexpectedly. "Could we do it with tin, do you think?"

Marion stood paralyzed.

"Wh-what?"

"I beg your pardon?" said the Rev. James, waking up at the sound of her voice. Then he saw the expression on her face. "My dear Marion! Is anything wrong?"

"Do—do you know what you just said?"

266

"But I said nothing," replied the puzzled vicar. "I was merely thinking about the roof. Forgive me!"

And off he started again, chin in hand, deeply and seriously considering. This time he made four circuits of the room before he spoke.

"Long and broad sheets of tin," he declared, while the faces of stern clergymen regarded him from the pictures, "could be bent halfway—so!—and would fit in a line over the shallow peak of the roof until proper repairs were made. Of course, there is always the question of the nails.

"Would they," he admonished the carpet, "hold sufficiently through shingle and board as well as tin? But it is not alone a question of holding tightly. It is a question of your coldness and reserve, which at first daunted me. True, there has been something different during the past week. So much do I love you . . ."

This was the point at which he bumped straight into the still-paralyzed Marion, who could not move. At the moment of collision, it was as though a blind flew up in the Rev. James's mind. He heard ringing in his ears, with the terrible clarity of a fine loudspeaker, the last sentence he had spoken.

Aghast, the Rev. James stood motionless. Marion swallowed hard, stammered, tried to look away, and then raised her eyes with a look Virtue Conklin had taught her.

"Well, if you do," she said defiantly, "why don't you tell *me,* instead of just telling yourself?"

"Is it possible—?" began the vicar. "That is to say: friendship is a fine and noble thing, no doubt. But is it possible that you . . . ?"

"Yes! Yes! Yes!"

Sheerly exalted, the Rev. James reached for Marion with all the enthusiasm in his nature, which was considerable; nor can it be said that Marion's response was in any way slow or less enthusiastic.

This was the tableau which met the eyes of Mrs. Honeywell, the housekeeper, as she wheeled in the tea wagon some thirty seconds later. But Mrs. Honeywell, who knew human nature and knew both these two, merely beamed. Nor was the vicar embarrassed in her presence.

"Mrs. Honeywell! Let me be the first to congratulate you!"

"Thank you, sir."

"That is to say," hastily corrected the Rev. James. "Let me be . . . No matter. Behold my future wife!"

"Well, now! Fancy that! Though I can't say it's what you might call unexpected, sir. You'll want a bit of a celebration, sir?"

"Celebration!" said the vicar, and whacked his right fist into his left palm. "By Jove, yes! That's it, exactly!" He pondered for a moment. "I have never, nor has my uncle, seen any objection to champagne."

"James!" said Marion, who was now in tears but suddenly alarmed. "That would be wonderful, yes! But you can't have people saying you held a champagne party at the vicarage the night before the bishop arrived!"

"Now I consider it," admitted the Rev. James, "perhaps it had better be postponed until another evening. Still! We will light a fire; we will lounge in comfort; above all, Marion, we will forget that infernal roof. Can I trouble myself about a tin roof now? Besides, it's not raining. Look out of the window! So be it; no roofs."

"We-el," said Marion.

Consequently, when Marion went back to her cottage that night, both she and the vicar were so bemused that they had forgotten the roof and the bazaar as well.

Now here is the point at which we might pause to quote improving proverbs, and preach a moral lesson as Sir Henry Merrivale does. Never put off until tomorrow, a stitch in time, and so on. For, at three o'clock in the morning, the skies opened to the deluge.

It was raining so hard that people who heard it could not see through its wall. This continued until daybreak, when heavy rain gave place to light rain. The Rev. James—who had slept soundly through it—was roused by blurted news when Mrs. Honeywell brought him his morning tea.

From the window of his bedroom, at the back of the vicarage, the Rev. James could see many persons gathered round the Gunpowder Room. All were women, and many wrung their hands. Dressing hastily and plunging into a mackintosh, the vicar met Marion, also wearing a mackintosh, in the back garden.

"It's all right," she assured him. "That is, it's come through in a deluge on either side of the roof peak. That earth floor is one awful sea of black mud in a wide aisle straight down the length of the room. But the stalls at the sides haven't even been splashed; or, at least, not much. If you get the tin now . . ."

"Like Mercury," cried the vicar, "I dash to the iron-monger's. And find that blighter Benson, with the sidewhiskers. He never does any work."

By noon the sound of the vicar's hammering could be heard near and far. By noon, while the tireless police still searched for a Webley .38 revolver which had been missing since Sunday night, when Gordon West said he last saw it beside his typewriter, a procession of cars and carts struggled up the High Street with a richness of merchandise. Rain had ceased.

At the same time, in the bedroom of her suite at the top of the Lord Rodney, Virtue Conklin was trying on her costume and contemplating her image in the mirror. Since one of the china sets she offered was brightly painted with scenes from Holland, Virtue had chosen to go as a Dutch doll.

True, the curling white cap set off her blue eyes and copper-kettle hair, as the black laced bodice and white puffed sleeves suited her figure.

Virtue had a real maid, who was also a maid at the hotel, and whom she had taught to say "Miss Virtue" like a maid in a book.

"Miss Virtue," Flossie said admiringly, "you do look a picture!"

"No so bad, eh?" Virtue inquired complacently, tilting her head in the mirror to apply lip salve with one finger. "Gord, Floss, there's life in the old girl yet!"

"But, Miss Virtue . . ."

"Lot of old cats!" said Virtue, referring to the ladies of the bazaar. "Except Miss Tyler and Miss Bailey, of course. Was you at the last Suggestion Meeting, where gentlemen was permitted? No, of course you wasn't. Some gentleman—he'd never say who 'e was, afterwards—pops up the suggestion that Miss Bailey, with 'er long hair, ought to go as Lady Godiva."

"Miss Virtue!" said the scandalized maid.

"Well," said Virtue philosophically, "it didn't seem to bother Miss Bailey none, or Miss Tyler either. They both seemed sort of thoughtful, as though they was wondering how they'd look themselves. But this Mrs. Goldfish—" Virtue's smile broadened with a look which boded ill for somebody—"she got up and went on awful. And Bill Huxtable, who's the biggest landowner except the Squire, he settled it.

"'You can't sell horses at a church bazaar,' he says, in a state; 'leastways, you can't sell mine.' Which was quite right, Floss; you can't. Give us a choc, ducks."

"Yes, miss," said Flossie, handing out a brandy-liqueur chocolate from the nearest box. "But—Miss

Virtue! This bodice or corsage or whatever it is . . ."

"Ah, that reminds me!" said Virtue. "It's like the gowns you're too young to remember. It's got stays and laces. So pull me tighter, Floss. Stick your foot against the coal box, and pull. Never mind if I bulge over a bit in front." She became reminiscent. "I was at the National Gallery, onest. A gentleman took me, and I seen the Old Masters. And, Gord, ducks! Their women hadn't got a thing on me."

"But, Miss Virtue! This is a *church bazaar.*"

"Oh, the ole cats won't like it," said Virtue, with a wicked smile. "But the men will."

"And Miss Bailey isn't really going to be . . . be . . . I mean . . ."

"No, Floss. Can't say I know just what costume they decided on."

At the moment Virtue spoke, the nature of Joan's costume was not even known to Gordon West himself. Some distance away, at Colonel Bailey's house, Joan stood before the big mirror of her dressing table, with a large, fresh, unopened costume box in front of her. Gordon West, lounging on the bed opposite, was laying down the law over a matter which had been under discussion for some time.

"No!" he said. "Can't you get it through your head, earthly angel, that I will not touch a church bazaar with a barge pole? I will come and hang about, yes. I will buy anything from birdseed to old clocks. But entrust myself to those harpies I will not!"

"You don't love me," said Joan.

"Woman, that is entirely irrelevant and you know it!"

"Come here," requested Joan, in a low voice.

"No, by God!" West said breathlessly, after about three minutes. "You can't persuade me with that argument either. This is a matter of principle. Is your uncle going among those damned women and dress up as Father Time or something?"

"No. I don't dare even *mention* it. He simply looks all stuffy and Army, and shudders."

"Well, that's what I'm trying to tell you too. What's more, do you realize I've hardly done a stroke of work at a final correction of the manuscript? Until that manuscript goes off to the publisher, we can't get married."

"Oh, yes! I'm awfully sorry! You *must* go and work on it." Joan paused, her mouth open. "Gordon! Weren't you supposed to meet Sir Henry Merrivale and talk about his costume?"

"Come to think of it, I was. About fifteen minutes ago, at my cottage."

"Then you run along, darling, while I change. I wonder if Sir Henry's there now."

He was. The presence of the great man, in West's study about five minutes later, could be demonstrated by a sound of violent argument audible as far as the manor house. West—a man now nearly out of his wits—was trying to explain.

"Now listen, Rain-in-the-Face," he said. "For the last time, let me tell you what you can do and what you can't do. Will you be quiet?"

"Ugh!" said H.M., already thinking himself into his part.

In the long dusty study, whose walls were built of books, H.M. sat on the sofa with his arms folded and a mulish look on his face. In a far corner sat Pam Lacey. Pam's ash-blonde hair was disheveled and her frock begrimed, in a way which would have horrified her mother a week ago. Over one arm hung a pair of muddy roller skates, and clutched under her other arm was a book labeled *The Adventures of Sherlock Holmes*. Pam's eyes flashed indignation at every

272

disparaging remark leveled at H.M.

"In the first place," continued West, "you can wear that Indian war bonnet. You can sell it if somebody wants to buy it."

"No sellum," said the Indian Chief decisively. "Keepum."

"All right; buy it yourself. It's not authentic, I warn you."

West, a stickler for accuracy, almost tore at his hair. He glanced up at a topmost shelf of books.

"I wish," he said, "I'd had time to make this authentic. It's an insult to the Indian. But never mind; try it in a book; you give the poor boobs of readers an authentic historical background, and nobody believes it. We've got to make a hash for the people who see films.

"Next," he went on, "you can sell the stuffed rattlesnake. You can sell the bow and arrow. But don't, under any circumstances, try to fire it. The bow *is* authentic; and it'll break. Next, do you mind stripping to the waist?"

"Burn me, no!" said the Indian Chief, immediately beginning to tear off his collar.

"Not now, curse you! Not now! The bazaar will start in the afternoon, but they won't shoot in their star turns, including you, until after teatime—say six o'clock—when there's standing room only and the bishop will be there. Here's the point:

"I can give you enough greasepaint to make you brown from the top of your head to your waist. Also the stuff for warpaint, if you want it. Yes, I see you do; don't look so greedy! But I haven't got any trousers."

"Gottum pants," said the Indian Chief. "Fine pants," he added.

"Good. You'll put on your make-up at the hotel. Sneak in behind the line of booths (yours is number 7, odd numbers on the left) so that people won't see you until you appear from behind the counter. That's all, except the things you can't do."

H.M., folding his arms more tightly, glared in silence at the door.

"You can't have a tomahawk, because I haven't got one. No war whoops, unless you give a mild one like woo-woo-woo to indicate your appearance. Not under any circumstances will you get out from behind your table and do a war dance. Finally, you can't be named Sitting Bull or Smack-em-Down or Lightning-bolt."

There was a far-off gleam in H.M.'s eye, which West should have noticed. All but the last point passed without argument. But here H.M. set down his foot.

"Why can't I be Sittin' Bull?" he asked passionately, and in real perplexity. "What's the difference what my name is?"

"Because you're selling wampum. Indian money!"

"D'ye think I don't know that?"

"Marion," West continued, "thought I had a great deal of wampum. I haven't any. As a result," his face writhed with loathing as he picked up some object from the back of the sofa, "you are going to sell as many pieces as possible of this."

Many village ladies had been busily knitting. Their notion of a string of wampum was a narrowish piece of knitted wear, some three inches long by an inch broad, to which cockle shells were sewn in a vertical line.

"Maestro," West said earnestly, "if you're going to sell thirty pieces of this, at one-and-six each, you can't scare 'em away. You've got to have Indian sex appeal. You're the kindly, crafty old chief who's got all the money. Your name," West searched his mind, "will be Big Chief Much-Wampum. How's that?"

"Awful," said H.M. "And choke me if I do it!"

"But why not?"

274

"Looky here, son. If you're having a fine time roarin' about with feathers in your hat, who wants to be on the goddamn Stock Exchange?"

"But the Indians didn't have a Stock Exchange!"

"That's what I'm tryin' to tell you. . . . Big Chief Much-Wampum!" intoned H.M., testing it in his deep, guttural voice. "Big Chief Pound-Note! Big Chief . . ."

"Maestro, you've got to do it! Not that I care a hang about this bazaar. But Joan—"

He paused. Joan had just appeared in the open doorway, wearing her costume.

Against a background of green leaves, and despite the galoshes she was compelled to wear, Joan was a trifle breathtaking. Her light brown hair, heavy and soft as fleece, was parted in the middle and rippled down her shoulders. Round her forehead she wore what might have been described as a gold fillet. Her dress, of smooth but heavy green material, fitted closely down as far as the waist, then spread in flowing lines to the ground. Round her waist was a golden rope, with tassels, loosely tied.

"Like it?" she asked eagerly.

"Like it?" breathed the half-hypnotized West. "You make me think of every dead romantic dream I ever had! Sherwood Forest! Sherwood in the twilight! In another second you'll see me turn into a ruddy pre-Raphaelite! 'The blessed damozel looked out . . .'"

At this romantic stage the very mundane figure of Colonel Bailey, a cap on his head and a pipe in his mouth, stamped in with flapping galoshes and said it was a devil of a day.

"But who are you, Joan?" asked West. "Who are you supposed to be?"

Joan was deeply thrilled. She wished Gordon would talk more to her like that. Nevertheless, though keeping a demure face, she permitted a touch of ironic

275

mirth in her eyes.

"I'm a Saxon Maiden," she replied. "At least, that's what it says on the costume box."

"Well, you look . . . wait a minute!" West said abruptly. "Aren't you in charge of the confectionery and pies and cakes?"

"Yes, dear. Mrs. Doom was afraid it would look like advertising if she did it. Anyway, she might have a nerve crisis and faint."

"But why the hell is a Saxon Maiden selling cakes and sugar mice?"

"I'm the Saxon Maiden," explained Joan, "who caught King Alfred burning the cakes."

"You know, West," said the Colonel, taking the pipe out of his mouth, "dashed if that's not wrong somewhere. Flaw in it. But these dam' women—Mrs. Doom and Mrs. Goldfish—talk twenty to the dozen. They're cracked on anything they call 'mideeval.' They'd have had me as the Pied Piper if I hadn't locked the door."

West, stamping on the floor in a kind of dance, was really tearing his hair.

"We were speaking," he said, keeping down a shout, "of history, not of legend or folklore. Even in folklore, wasn't the woman who caught King Alfred burning the cakes a cowherd's wife?"

"No glamour," said the Colonel, shaking his head gloomily.

"Glamour, sir? What do you know about glamour?"

"I don't know anything about it," retorted the Colonel heatedly. "But that's what these wild women kept saying, along with the fact that a costume's fine if it begins at the neck and ends on the floor— Something to do with films," he added.

"Yes, I thought so," West replied grimly. "The point

is, Joan, can't you persuade Sir Henry that his Indian name has got to be Big Chief Much-Wampum?"

"Wouldn't you do it to please me?" coaxed Joan, who was very good at this.

"Well . . . now," mused H.M. Considering the look in his eye, a baby could have seen he was plotting devilment. "Since a lot of concessions have been made . . ."

Over in a dark corner, where Pam Lacey clutched a pair of roller skates and *The Adventures of Sherlock Holmes,* Pam's eyes blazed with jealousy.

("Oh?" Pam thought. "You'd do that for her, would you? See if I care!")

Casually H.M. turned his big head, though no word had been spoken.

"But the final decision's with you, my dolly," he called. "I may think they're all of 'em right. But what do you think?"

At those words "all of 'em," Pam's jealousy melted. But her chin remained high.

"If you think it's right," she answered, *"I* don't mind."

"And you remember all the signals?" H.M. asked cryptically. "Just in case?"

Now Pam's great lady disappeared.

"Oh, golly, do I!"

"Then that's settled," declared H.M., turning on the others a calm and holy expression. Only West looked at him suspiciously. "No, stop the bus!" added H.M. "You told me, young feller, that the star turns, including me, were goin' on about six o'clock?"

"Yes, that's right."

"Well," said H.M., drawing himself up and inflating his chest, "who's the star turn *besides* me?"

"Didn't you know?" asked Joan. "It's Dr. Schmidt."

277

Pam Lacey uttered an exclamation, but some cryptic gesture from H.M. kept her silent.

"Is that so, now?" he mused. "It's very interestin', that is. What's he going to do?"

"He'll play the piano and sing," explained Joan. "If he plays a song you can't identify—it's got to be English or American; he could murder us with German—you pay a forfeit. Otherwise, you win. In the meantime, he both plays and sings."

"That's better and better!" said H.M., with his eye on a corner of the ceiling. "Dr. Schmidt's a fine feller. I bet he gets everything he deserves."

"H.M.," said West, suddenly standing in front of the dreamer, "are you sure you haven't got anything up your sleeve? No colossal fireworks of devilment that'll blow the roof off the Gunpowder Room?"

"Oh, son! I promised what I'd do; and I'll do it. So help me!"

"Nothing *must* go wrong," said Joan. "The vicar! And with the bishop being here!"

"By the way," interposed a slightly exasperated H.M., "just who *is* the bishop, anyway? Everybody's been yowlin' about him so much he must amount to something. What's his name?"

The others looked at him in surprise. It was Joan who said:

"He is Dr. William Waterford, Bishop of Glastontor."

"Oh, lord love a duck!" breathed H.M. after a long silence. "It can't be! No, honest! You don't mean old Pinkey?"

"I—I certainly never heard him called that." Joan moved back.

"Little feller," H.M. urged earnestly. "But big round as a balloon; pink complexion. Can't stop eatin'. Waterford!" He turned his head toward Pam. "You remember, my dolly. That was the chap who bet me five quid I wouldn't go down Ludgate Hill on roller skates!"

"You . . . er . . . know him well?" asked West.

"Old Pinkey? I was at school with the little blighter. Saw him once or twice at Cambridge. I knew he'd jumped into the golden chariot, yes; but I never thought they'd make the silly ass a bishop!"

"You're a *friend* of his?" insisted West.

"Oh, absolutely!" said H.M., who was speaking the truth as far as he remembered. "Word of honor! And I'll give you another tip. Old Pinkey used to get mad and carry on—oh, shockin'! But he never meant it. He'd back up his own nephew if the vicar had been preachin' demonology or tree worship. So don't worry too much about the vicar, because I doubt if he worries himself."

West's sigh of relief almost turned him dizzy.

"That's perfectly splendid!" cried Joan, her eyes aglow. "Then there's nothing to fear. To quote Mrs. Doom about the matter," she smiled, "it should be the happiest, jolliest church bazaar that ever was!"

Chapter 20

Anyone who entered the Gunpowder Room, then (by the northern door on the narrow side, that being its only entrance), at ten minutes to six on that same evening, would have had reason for pleasure. He might have agreed with Mrs. Doom in finding here the jolliest, happiest church bazaar that ever was.

But not so Gordon West, who at the same moment was in his own cottage, still feverishly at work correcting a manuscript.

Ever since all his visitors had left early that afternoon, West had been conscious of something wrong. It had nothing to do with Sir Henry Merrivale's possible indiscretions. It was wrong in the rain-tinged air, wrong in somebody's emotions, wrong in he could not say what.

After eating the lunch prepared by Mrs. Wych, he lighted the wall lamp over his typewriter desk, and lighted two more lamps against the gloom of a day which threatened more rain. He returned to his desk, pushed the typewriter aside, and sat down with a pen over the great part of the manuscript, "Drums Along the Zambesi."

He worked slowly and carefully, sometimes getting

up to verify a reference in a book. West well knew parts of the Zambesi as it is now, but he had set his story in 1886, before "the damnation of progress."

The scenes got into his head. He could see red light on the water, against the line of black dripping paddles as they lifted and dipped, and hear the rocking and thundering drums from the other bank. Yet persistently other thoughts swam between his eyes and the type.

Never, for instance, had he known such a change as in Pam Lacey. He saw her flying down the High Street on roller skates, ahead of Harry Goldfish and Tommy Wyatt and the others of the gang she seemed to have joined. He could see the change in Stella Lacey, regarding this with a smile and without horror.

Stella's change—why, she was a human being. Her coquetries, which sometimes in the past had annoyed him and sometimes (let it secretly be confessed) fascinated him, had been replaced by a straightforwardness like Joan's.

But the puzzle in his mind was associated with the color white, always white, while his wristwatch ticked on. Rain began to fall, brushing and rustling in the trees outside. At length he put down his pen and began to wander about the room.

And there he found it.

The envelope, bent and half crushed as from someone's hip pocket, lay on the sofa where Sir Henry Merrivale had been sitting. He remembered how many times H.M. had twisted round to consult Pam Lacey. It could easily have worked out of the pocket, and there it lay.

West picked it up.

The address read, "Sir Henry Merrivale, Lord Rodney Hotel, Stoke Druid," in small, lean fine-point-pen block lettering. It was postmarked at Glastonbury, at eleven forty-five A.M. on Friday, the previous day.

It might be some personal letter, which was none of his business and which he must put aside. But the envelope looked too familiar.

West knew, as did many others (again, never ask where these rumors originate; let Virgil talk about gossip), that the tracing of anonymous letters by their postmarks was useless. Everybody in Stoke Druid went to Glastonbury or Wells at least once a week, by car or by bus along the main road, sometimes as far afield as Bristol. And yet . . .

After a struggle, he threw principle overboard and drew out the folded sheet of notepaper. It was written in the same fine small block capitals.

My dear Sir Henry:
You begin to interest me. Though I do not regard you as a menace, since wits cannot beat me at the game I play, I will tell you what I have done. That woman has received the fright she deserved; others have been scarified according to their deserts. My work is finished, my course run. Let me salute you sincerely as
Your affectionate friend,
The Widow

For a little while, his heart bumping at the nearness yet the intangibility of this figure, West stood motionless. Then, with an idea occurring to him, he hurried to his desk. From a lower drawer he fished out a large magnifying lens. It required close scrutiny to detect, in the upper left-hand corner of the blue twopenny-halfpenny stamp, the faint little blue cross drawn there.

Marked stamps. Somebody was for it.

Whereupon, with that intensity of purpose which

could turn him almost into a machine, West pushed the folded sheet back into the envelope. He placed both on one side of his desk and went on correcting.

Montonously the rain dripped and splashed outside the open door. West had finished twenty more pages, with an occasional correction or substitution of a word, when he heard heavy foosteps in the earth path outside.

Inspector Garlick, with a gleaming-wet black waterproof over his uniform, appeared in the doorway. The uniform made him seem more businesslike, more sinister. West's watch indicated a quarter to six.

"Sorry, sir." The Inspector saluted, the peak of his cap glistening by lamplight. "I was wondering if Sir Henry was here?"

"No. He left."

West picked up the note in its envelope and handed it over as Garlick strode in.

"Would this be of interest to you? Sir Henry must have dropped it."

"Thank you." The hard face, with the mole on the cheek, became still harder. "May I ask whether you read this?"

"I did."

"You shouldn't have done that, sir. It's none of your business."

"Pardon me," answered West, looking him in the eyes, "it *is* my business. And everybody else's."

"Do you know where Sir Henry is now, Mr. West?"

"At the Lord Rodney, I imagine. Or at the bazaar."

"Can't go in to the bazaar. In this uniform. Except as a last resort."

Garlick turned to the door. He had reached it before West spoke.

"Inspector, who *is* The Widow?"

"Sorry, sir." Again Garlick saluted. "Information

284

received." And he strode away in the mud, followed by two uniformed constables.

For a time West looked unseeingly at the page in front of him. Then the wristwatch told him it was ten minutes to six.

At this same time, then, anyone who entered the Gunpowder Room—a good distance away—would have agreed with Mrs. Doom in pronouncing this the happiest, jolliest church bazaar that ever was. Success was already assured by the babble of voices, dominated, some way down the line of stalls, by the heavy banging of a piano and a hoarse voice singing *Die Wacht am Rhein* in German.

Entering the door on the narrow side, you would have been greeted by the Rev. James, handsome and beaming in brushed clerical black, and by Marion Tyler, who wore a plain gray dinner dress in place of masquerade.

They stood inside a large square rustic arbor, in whose interstices the ladies had twined lifelike artificial flowers, with a rustic roof. The floor was dry, since little rain had penetrated at either end of the room. Under the arbor were set out many tables for tea and soft drinks. Often Marion would hurry away to assist Miss Robinson, who was dressed as a medieval page except for her skirt, in serving the crowded tables. Then she would hasten back to the Rev. James, nodding proudly past the arbor straight down the central aisle of the long room.

"You must at least acknowledge," he said, "that I did a very tolerable job at repairing the roof."

A candid friend would have been compelled to say no. The Rev. James, his thoughts with Marion, had hammered much tin in the wrong places. Once he had gone through the roof bodily, being saved by the seventy-five-year-old sexton on the ridgepole.

285

Still, it was a notable display.

From horizontal beams across the tops of the walls, with the roof peak above, hung long lines of brightly polished oil lamps on chains. Their light illuminated the stalls, six on the left side and six on the right, set back against the side walls. Posts had been driven into the ground, together with a screen of vines twined with flowers, to separate each stall from the next. On the ground in front of each stall had been stretched a line of wooden planks, two twelve-inch widths set together, so that visitors should not touch the middle. For in the middle . . .

In the middle, fully fifteen feet wide, stretched a sea of the blackest, slimiest, most plastic mud ever seen outside a tropic jungle. Nor had it a chance of drying. Light and heavy drizzles, together with a sudden occasional gush like a water spout, kept it always fresh.

To the crowd, pressing along the planks on either side, it was the biggest hit of the bazaar.

"Ol' parson do have some good notions, don't 'e? One wrong step, and—*sploosh!*"

"Ah, ol' parson's all right!"

"Like me to chuck 'ee in, Gert?"

"Now don't be fresh, Frank Billings!"

From the arbor entrance, the vicar and Marion surveyed this shining mudpath.

"By Jove," murmured the former. "What is being sold at stall number six, the third down on the right? I have never seen such a crowd—curiously enough, all men—in one place."

Marion gulped.

"That's Virtue Conklin, James. I'm afraid her costume is . . . well, just a *wee bit* daring in front. But the bishop . . ."

"Ah, Uncle William! He will be here in just three minutes!"

"He doesn't have to go up the right-hand side. He can take the left-hand side."

"My dear Marion, I fear that is impossible. Our ceremony is already arranged."

"You've arranged—a ceremony?"

"Of course!" replied the Rev. James, raising his eyebrows like one who never forgets anything. "Except to say that it includes the choirmaster and a dozen of the younger choirboys, I leave it to your happy imagination. My uncle will walk first down the right side."

He nodded straight down the aisle. At the end Marion could see the roundness of the grim old drum tower, its oaken door nearly two feet thick, and a key in the door. Another key hung on a nail near the entrance. Near the powder magazine there was displayed an older fifteenth-century battering ram, smallish, but said to have belonged to Sir John de Courtenaye in 1416.

"There is plenty of dry space at the back," the vicar pointed out. "The people will give way as Uncle William approaches."

"But one thing rather worries me," said Marion, craning her neck. "Where is Sir Henry Merrivale?"

"Isn't he in stall number seven?"

"I can't see him, anyway. Where is he?"

This question could have been answered by a worried Virtue Conklin, in number six. Reaching the far end of her stall on the right—where, beyond the post and the flower screen, Dr. Schmidt was hitting each chord like a sledgehammer and trying, with immense pathos, to sing *Die Lorelei* in English—Virtue pushed aside a group of admirers to get a look out.

Across the sea of mud, facing her, sat Mrs. Goldfish as a Quaker Lady amid a fine display of needlework.

287

Diagonally to the right, stall number seven appeared empty. The counter, which was actually a long table set up on bricks to make it seem high, was covered by two Navajo blankets. Along it lay thirty strings of wampum, together with a bow and arrow and a stuffed rattlesnake, and the blankets stretched to the ground.

"Dearie!" shouted Virtue under cover of Dr. Schmidt's music.

She knew that Big Chief Much-Wampum, on these occasions as temperamental as any prima donna, would not put on his costume or make-up at the hotel. Sir Henry Merrivale must appear, like Venus rising from the seen, unseen until the appointed time.

As a result, the table was behaving as though it were at a lively spiritualistic séance—though it cursed vilely, as no table ever does at these meetings.

"Dearie! Fer gossake put a sock in it! Your langwidge!"

At that moment a messenger from Chief Much-Wampum slipped out under the blankets. Running low, straight across the mud, Pam Lacey seized conspiratorially on Virtue.

"Mrs. Conklin!" she whispered, slipping the other a folded note which was quite clean despite the mud-stained and paint-stained frock and face. "Will you give this note to the horrible mean old piano player next door? The note's from the bishop."

"Now, ducks!" remonstrated Virtue, half closing one eye.

"He says it's from the bishop," whispered Pam, glancing back toward the agitated table and then lifting wide innocent eyes. "That's good enough for me."

"Well, pretty," sighed Virtue, "I expect it's good enough for me, too."

Wherepon Virtue stuck her head round the side of the post and whistled loudly.

288

"Oi, weinerschritzel!" she called. "Heap big note from bishop. You takum?"

Dr. Schmidt's hands had fallen from the keys. Panting, streaming with perspiration, he leaned forward and took the note. He was about to announce indignantly that he spokum English as well as a native. But the whole hall had grown very still, except for whispers of "The bishop!" "'Is lordship the bishop!" "There he is!"

And Dr. William Waterford, Bishop of Glastontor —with a happy smile all over his round pink face— stepped out on the right-hand planks.

Now we must admit that H.M.'s description of him was exaggerated. He was a small man, but not as small as H.M. had suggested. His shape did not suggest a balloon, though certain balloon indications were present. The Bishop of Glastontor rightly believed in giving the crowd a good show; he wore gaiters and a very large shovel hat.

Above all, he had a commanding eye and a rich voice. They had all heard that voice, as though from the depths of a wine barrel, when he spoke to his nephew in the arbor.

"Mud?" he had laughed. "My dear James, pray don't apologize. I like mud!"

And then, as he paused at stall number two:

"Come," he said, "this is really admirable!"

He praised Mr. Vance, the ironmonger, for a display of homemade toys which would more than have done credit to a professional toymaker. Passing on, he warmly congratulated a blushing Miss Partridge on the exhibition of bottled jellies, strawberry and raspberry, the savory pickled onions and herrings. Then, at stall number six . . .

Virtue, powerfully impressed, made as low a curtsy as was possible.

The bishop took one look, and a somewhat unepiscopal thought darted through his mind. But you would not have known this. Casually he raised his eyes to the china above her head, platters and plates against the back wall in a circular pattern.

"Madam, I congratulate you!" he said warmly. "Seldom have I seen so fine and rounded a display!"

"Me lord!" exclaimed Virtue, deeply shocked.

"China has always been one of my weaknesses," said the bishop. "And have we not just beyond," he continued, pointing with a gold-headed cane to distract attention, "the maker of music at the piano? Ah, a sweet sound upon the ear! I have often wished . . ."

Well, he heard a sound.

From beneath the counter draped with the Navajo blankets, unmuffled, there rose upward a noise so blood-curdling, so freezing to the spirit and grinding against the bones, that every person in the room stood petrified.

It did contain, as faithfully promised, the sound "woo." But this particular war whoop, beginning on a deep note, seemed to rise endlessly in a kind of spiral screech to burst against the roof with every savage promise of torture and the stake.

"Her Gott!" screamed Dr. Schmidt.

Up from behind the counter, slowly and in awful majesty, rose a figure quite as horrible as the war whoop. Even Virtue, who expected it, reeled back. From the head of the figure, high-sprouting and spreading like a fan, rose the war bonnet of dusty varicolored feathers. The apparition was brown in color—from head to powerful arms, barrel chest, and corporation—down to its Scotch-plaid trousers. Shell-rimmed spectacles were pulled down on its broad nose. Horizontal streaks of warpaint, white and ocher and red, crossed its face.

Fortunately or unfortunately, there was nobody standing in front of the stall of Big Chief Much-Wampum. Only Mrs. Doom, who feared a fit of nerves again, was pushing near it with her six children ranged behind her in order of size.

The apparition, feathered and terrible, cast one evil look around. Then its deep, guttural voice rang out.

"Big Chief Wall Street!" it thundered, and slapped its hip pocket. "Makum much dibs! Paleface lose shirt. *How!* You buy?"

And he thrust a string of wampum straight into the face of Mrs. Doom.

With a fluttering loud sigh, not unlike those occasional fluttering V-1's we heard in later years, Mrs. Doom closed her eyes and swooned away against her children. The miracle was that the whole line did not sway outwards into the mud. But, as Mrs. Doom was passed from hand to hand like a fire bucket, the line held.

The good biship was furious.

"You, sir!" he shouted, pointing his finger at the Big Chief. "Who dares disturb our innocent merriment with these ill-timed jests? You, sir! You're drunk, sir!"

Mr. Benson, who had moved out on the planks beside the bishop—and who, with his sinister black sidewhiskers and pale handsome face, looked more than ever like John Jasper in *Edwin Drood*—echoed the bishop's anger.

"You're drunk, sir!" he shouted.

Something like the edge of vile glee crossed the unspeakable countenance of Big Chief Wall Street, with its lines of warpaint. He pointed his finger at the nose of the bishop. Slowly rocking back and forth, he began what must have been an old Indian chant.

"Little Chief Big Stomach, Little Chief Pinkey," he intoned. "Eatum much beefsteak; drinkum much rum;

291

eatum much pork chop, yum, yum, yum."

At that word "Pinkey," the bishop's head dropped. He peered forward, intently.

"Henry Merrivale!" exclaimed the bishop.

"Drinkum much port wine," intoned the other, one hand raised to the Great Spirit, "drinkum much sherry; face red, face red, red as a berry. Little Chief Pinkey . . ."

Whereupon the good bishop completely lost his head. Nor is it possible for any sober-minded critic to blame him. We do not, as H.M. had already indicated, see our old school friends as the undoubtedly good and great men into which they have grown. We see them as they were in the old times, long past, before honors had been thrust upon them. Decades and all that had happened in those decades were obliterated from the bishop's mind and, as a result, what happened would furnish any psychiatrist with a topic for a learned paper.

Deliberately, Dr. William Waterford, Bishop of Glastontor, dived over and scooped up a handful of rich mud. There was no time, his quick brain told him, to harden it to a mudball; a rough pie must do. Partly by luck, partly by the accuracy of his good right arm, the mudpie landed squarely in the face of Sir Henry Merrivale.

"Why, yer old perisher!" gasped Virtue Conklin.

Long ago, brooding over what she quite mistakenly considered a lewd remark, Virtue had decided that this man could not be a real Holiness. He could certainly not be a Big Holiness, like a Lord Bishop.

"Madam," exclaimed the bishop, turning round momentarily, "I have no time to . . ."

He hadn't, either. He underestimated the speed with which H.M. could clear his own glasses and eyes. Snatching up the bow and arrow which West had said couldn't be fired, H.M. drew the arrow to its head.

The bow twanged sweetly, as on some roaring plain of old. The arrow skewered the top of the bishop's shovel hat neatly to the post between stalls six and eight.

"Villain!" roared the bishop, ducking under the poised hat to make certain he was not hit. "On this night, mark me, I will make you rue . . ."

Down he went to fashion a mudball. His shot went wild, skimming a meatpie off the shelves of the furious Theo Bull in number nine.

"My lord!" pleaded the choirmaster. "This must stop!" Then Mr. Benson glanced toward his left and had an inspiration.

Down near the entrance to the inside of the arbor, drawn up on the planks in two lines of six facing each other, stood twelve choirboys holding up their music sheets. They wore no vestments or other formality. The bishop's favorite hymn, "Ten Thousand Times Ten Thousand," was to be sung when the choirmaster gave a signal to the piano player.

But H.M. had discovered mud under the planks of his booth. *Whap* went a mudball against the bishop's cheek. *Whap* went the bishop's return fire, spattering a broad black star across Theo Bull's new white coat.

"Now!" wailed Mr. Benson, raising his pitchpipe.

The choirboys straightened up with "Ten Thousand Times Ten Thousand." Nobody, of course, could hear a pitchpipe under that babble. But the peering pianist, the corners of the boys' eyes, saw Mr. Benson's cheeks as he blew. The choir drew a deep breath. And Dr. Schmidt, with all the thunder at his command, burst into "Onward, Christian Soldiers."

No blame, emphatically, can be attached to the choir. When you have one song before your eyes and in your vocal chords, you can't change immediately to another even if you happen to know the words. Some had a desperate shot at the original; some tried to be Christian Soldiers and couldn't remember the words; some merely gurgled.

"Stop!" said the Bishop of Glastontor.

So quietly commanding was his manner, so rich his voice and churchly inflection, that silence slowly descended on everybody—even Dr. Schmidt, who was puzzling over the bishop's letter.

"Mr. Benson," said the bishop briskly, "what's the matter with your choir?"

"Nothing, my lord," retorted Mr. Benson with spirit. "I imagine someone has given our pianist the wrong hymns."

"Ah!" said his bishop, his eye turning toward H.M.

Whereupon the bishop, squaring his shoulders, walked straight out into the aisle, with mud well above his ankles.

It was obvious that he was taking the offensive.

Sir Henry Merrivale, hurling aside the table and pressing the war bonnet skew-wiff on his head, lumbered out to Pulverize Pinkey. Virtue, swinging legs and skirts over the table to a flying and crashing of china, stood up firm in the mud. Out leapt Theo Bull, with a juicy meatpie in his hand. Mr. Benson stalked out with his arms folded, as though he were walking on air.

The bishop, whirling round, took one step forward in the direction of the arbor. His gaze fell upon the choirboys, and moved from right to left.

"If you can't sing," he taunted, "can you make mudballs?"

The choirboys, long repressed, let out one concerted hysterical yell. A dozen pairs of boots landed together in the middle of the aisle, sending up a huge sputter of mud.

"Stout lads!" beamed the bishop. "There stands the enemy! Let virtue triumph!"

Instantly H.M. whirled round toward the back of the room. All pose as an Indian Chief had gone. There were at least twenty members of Tommy Wyatt's gang scattered along the back. The Old Maestro stuck two fingers in his mouth and let out a piercing whistle.

"Satan's Imps!" he roared. "Get the blighters!"

And so began the Great Mud Fight, which will linger and gather legend in Stoke Druid for the next hundred years.

Joan Bailey at the cakes in number eleven, and Ralph Danvers facing her above books in number twelve, could only call to each other when the surge of the fight spilled all spectators out into the mud and the spectators joined in battle too.

"I'd *love* to get in on the side of darkness," groaned Joan. "It's this lovely dress. Do you think I could take it off and fight in my slip?" The girl was really in despair.

"I implore you, Miss Bailey, no! Observe the state of Mrs. Conklin!"

At the other end of the room, under a rustic arbor twined with artificial flowers, stood two who had not joined in the battle either. But the condition of one of them was pitiable.

Blue veins stood out in the forehead of the Rev. James Cadman Hunter. His eyes were fierce with yearning. His fists clenched and unclenched.

Marion, regarding him with watchful eyes, was ready to hurl her arms round him and cling to him if he dashed out into the mud. "James, did you notice the policemen? Three of them slipped in here, two behind the stalls at one side, and one at the other."

"Policemen!"

"Yes, James. And we mustn't let your uncle be arrested for brawling." Marion made her decision.

"Dear, I'm afraid you must go in and get him. But promise me, promise me! You *won't* push anyone's face in the mud?"

The vicar, swallowing hard, nodded and rushed in. Marion had scarcely turned when she saw at her elbow the towering uniformed figure of Inspector Garlick. Since the rain had ceased about half-past six, his waterproof was only damp. But even his narrow eyes widened as he surveyed the bazaar.

"Good evening, Inspector," said Marion out of a shaky throat. "Have you come to view our innocent merriment on behalf of St. Jude's?"

"Innocent merriment, hey?" said Inspector Garlick. Both of them dodged the heavy metal toy which whizzed past over them and disappeared. "Why, there's a woman out there—can't tell who she is; too much mud—who's half naked and smashing plates over people's heads! And another one (Miss Bailey, a sweet girl, if one ever lived) with her hair down and wearing only one of those silk things, climbing over a counter with a pie in both hands. Have you all gone clean daft?"

The Rev. James escorted out a short, tubby dignitary who appeared, at first glance, to be a mudman as conceived by H. G. Wells.

"Inspector Garlick," said the vicar, "may I present you to my uncle: the Bishop of Glastontor?"

Inspector Garlick shut his eyes.

"And now, I daresay," the mudman commented to his nephew, "you will present me with a bill of my iniquities, as a reason why I should pardon yours?"

"Indeed I will not!" snapped the Rev. James. "If you and your diocese don't like what I have done, you can go to the devil. Furthermore—" he turned to the petrified Marion—"I mean to marry this young lady, and how do you propose to stop me?"

In the expanse of mud there gleamed something like

a smile.

"James," said the bishop, "that is the answer I had hoped for and prayed for. And of course you will marry this young lady! Did you think I didn't know that, as soon as I saw you? Inspector Garlick! With regard to our mild little festivities . . ."

"My lord," answered Garlick, dodging a muddy whisky bottle which crashed outside, "I don't want, and don't intend, to shove anybody in the clink. I merely want to get the room cleared."

"Excellent!" beamed the mudman. And, as he marched out with Marion on one arm and the vicar on the other, no man could fail to admire the little cock sparrow.

Another policeman whisked in at the same moment.

"Get 'em out gently!" the Inspector snapped. "If there's a way to lower all the lights without putting 'em out completely, do that; darkness means a stampede. Tell everybody this is no arrest; just to get out."

Then Garlick raised his voice.

"Attention, everybody!"

Swiftly and without fuss the whole room was cleared, with two exceptions. The lights had gone out. Through the western windows flooded the light of the rising full moon. At the front doors, nearly shut, stood two figures both of whom had bagged mackintoshes.

"It was awful," murmured Virtue. "But, oh, Gord, *'ow* lovely!"

"It wasn't bad, was it?" modestly admitted Sir Henry Merrivale, who had pinched a towel from the tea arbor and discovered the qualities of honest mud in removing make-up as well as mud.

"But, dearie! The profits . . ."

"Oh, I dunno," H.M. said apologetically. "I shouldn't be surprised, y'know, if tomorrow the vicar gets a check covering all profits or damages, and a lot more besides. Burn it, he told me about this whole ceremony on Friday morning!"

"But . . ."

Virtue stopped. From somewhere in that dim old room, where moonlight touched ghostly stalls, had come a noise which Virtue recognized as not part of this byplay. It was the sound of a heavy thud, suggesting a weighted object swung against heavier wood.

Thud it went in the moonlight. Then some ten seconds' pause. *Thud*. Another pause, and *thud*.

"Virtue," said H.M., putting his hands on her shoulders, "you know when I'm playin' the fool and when I'm not. Get along home now. I'll see you later."

"'Smore trouble, eh? Danger?"

"Oh, spot of bother. Nothin' serious."

"Y'ol' bastard," said Virtue, with a catch in her throat. "You'd say that, wouldn't you, if you was walking right up to a ruddy machine gun?"

"Hop it, innercence. It's all right."

"Ol' barstud!" sobbed Virtue, and ran.

H.M. moved inside the doors and softly closed them behind him. His hand groped up for something on the wall; and what he found he dropped into the pocket of the mackintosh. *Thud* went the slow, ponderous noise. *Thud.*

Throwing the towel over his shoulder, H.M. advanced down the aisle of the room, his big shoes making little noise in the flattened mud. Now he could catch the gleam of a lantern, held back; but it caught the barrels of several unused electric torches.

Ahead loomed the oaken door, two feet thick, of the powder magazine in the drum tower. Though at ten minutes to six there had been a key in the door, there was none visible now. *Thud* went the slow noise. *Thud.* The old, small battering ram of Sir John de Courtenaye, a small square beam with a bronze ram's head blackened to iron color, swung on new ropes from a very low scaffold with wheels. Inspector Garlick and four constables operated it.

"I had an idea *I* was givin' orders here," said H.M. Inspector Garlick straightened up.

"If we could find you, sir. Which we couldn't. So I decided to close in. The walls are eight feet thick, and there's no other way in. The Widow fired one shot, but it couldn't slap through the door. I tell you: The Widow's gone to earth, with no other way in. . . ."

"Oh, ain't there? Clear out! All of you!"

"Sir, I protest this . . ."

H.M.'s big voice was not at all loud, but it had a concentrated viciousness which seemed to strike Garlick's face like vitriol.

"You'll obey my orders, son. Or—so help me God!— I'll break you off the Force so quick you won't even know you're out of a uniform!"

Garlick opened his mouth, hesitated, and his eyes dropped.

"What do you want us to do, sir?"

"Clear out, as I told you, and don't come back for exactly an hour. You in the plainclothes: gimme that lantern. Now! Gimme a gun."

"You ought to know, sir," Garlick observed dryly, "we're not allowed to carry guns."

"No. But the same feller in the plainclothes has one. I can see it stickin' out of his hip pocket."

"That's Mr. Meadows, a private citizen and a friend of mine. He has a license to carry . . ."

"All right; he's got a license. Gimme the gun . . . ha, thanks; it's a .38 . . . and everybody clear out."

H.M. waited, holding up the lantern, until they had gone. The wheels of the battering ram were on dry ground. H.M. gave it a powerful shove which sent it

299

backwards. Afterwards, he bent down to the keyhole of the door.

"I'm comin'," he called. "And, as I promised, I'm comin' in alone."

From one pocket—he had hidden the revolver in the deep pocket of the other side—he drew out the second key to the drum tower, which had hung on a nail beside the front entrance. He opened the door, went inside, and closed it. He held up the lantern with his other hand.

The rough-stone walls, as Inspector Garlick had said, were eight feet thick and had no aperture for light. But a broad stone ledge curved partway round the opposite wall.

On the ledge, legs crossed, Webley .38 held carelessly flat on an open palm, eyes regarding the newcomer inscrutable from under the peak of a tweed cap, sat Colonel Bailey.

Chapter 21

Slowly H.M. lumbered across and put down the lantern not far from Colonel Bailey on the ledge.

"Evening, Colonel," he said casually.

"Evening, Merrivale." Colonel Bailey might have been muttering greetings at a club.

"I wish an awful lot this hadn't to happen," growled H.M., not facing him. "There's a great deal of good in you. And a man ill-treated by his own country . . ." He paused.

"If you think," the Colonel spoke stiffly, "I mind being hanged for the murder of Cordy—"

"Oh, the murder of Cordy!" said H.M., disconsolately sweeping out his hand as though this were the mere peccadillo he thought it. "Killin' a greedy blackmailer? If that's all you'd done, Colonel, I might have dished the evidence against you and maybe I still can.

"But there are other things, d'ye see, I can't forget. You're The Widow. You've been The Widow all the time. I can't forget the death of Cordelia Martin. I can't forget a lot of honest people, half out of their minds.

"Colonel, if anybody ever called you mean or heartless—" here Colonel Bailey sat up straight—"you

301

might want to shoot that person. And yet, at heart, and even though you may not *quite* have known it yourself, that's exactly what you are and were."

Suddenly H.M. swung round to face him.

Colonel Bailey, except that his speckled face again seemed to be like thin paper between the eyes and mouth, merely weighed the Webley revolver in his hand.

"Can you stand hearing," asked H.M., "why you were so smackin' obviously The Widow?"

"You wrote to me," said Colonel Bailey. "Said you knew about my strategy. Didn't say I was The Widow. Well! Like to hear about it!"

"You pride yourself on bein' a strategist," replied H.M., "and nobody can say you're not a good one. But I've spent a good deal of my life at strategy too. I saw through it, and in your nervousness you made one bad slip."

"How?"

"I knew you were guilty on Saturday night, the 13th, the first time we talked together. We were in your study—remember?—and standing beside the big map model beside the windows. You were holdin' a big magnifyin' glass over foot soldiers practically invisible."

"I remember. Well?"

"You gave your first straight-out opinion about the poison-pen writer. You said, *Except for the dam' heartlessness of it—*"

Colonel Bailey stirred.

"I can almost understand the (what-d'ye-call-it) the mindworkings of the fellow who write these letters," quoted H.M. "That's what you said, with one bad slip smack in the middle of your strategy. Every other person I'd met, then or later, distinctly referred to *the woman* or to *she*. They took it for granted The Widow

302

was a woman. You slipped and said 'fellow,' because you knew."

Colonel Bailey said nothing, but looked down at the Webley .38 balanced on his palm. It gleamed in the light of the lantern beside him.

"However!" pursued H.M. "That wasn't all of the sentence you spoke. No, burn me! To turn suspicion away from yourself, you added: *There are a lot of people in this world with black bile inside 'em. Some can get rid of it by pouring it out at the War Office, like me. Others . . . well, you've got the result in your hand.*"

A sardonic twinkle appeared beneath the Colonel's eyelids, but immediately vanished.

"Now," said H.M., "that sounds as smooth as cream. It's supposed to slip past unnoticed, emphasizin' your innocence. But it had the opposite effect on me, and I told you it was the most important thing yet said.

"Because, Colonel, it wasn't true. You can't get rid of bile by writing letters unless the letters have some effect. And in your eternal, endless correspondence with the War Office—set in filing cases along the bookcase—you hadn't even made a scratch on a granite wall.

"You knew you were right. You were frantic in your sense of bein' right. And the thick-headed swine wouldn't even listen. It was agony. The bile was in *you*.

"And so I remembered, which wasn't hard, what you'd said only a little time before that. Remember, Colonel? You were standing in front of the map model, holding that enormous magnifyin' glass over foot soldiers so small they could hardly be seen.

"And 'Power!' you blurted out, entirely unrelated to anything else you'd said. It might have been Hitler himself speaking.

"It wasn't even a slip. You weren't thinking about

me. You were thinking about those foot soldiers, hardly seen, not real human beings and good enough only to be crushed. Much later in the game, Inspector Garlick roughly classified you in his third group of poison-pen writers—though I shut my trap and refused to comment further—when he said, 'Sort of Hitler love for what it can't get.' And in group: 'Mainly men.'

"But that classification wouldn't cover you, not easily anyhow. You were gettin' rid of black bile against most people instead of any one person, because you wanted to hurt people in general as you'd been hurt. But there's one thing you couldn't force yourself to do. On Saturday night I said you were a combination of somebody as innocent as a baby, but as sharp as Boney and Washington together. In a less high-falutin way, that's true.

"For on Sunday morning—cor!

"Well, we got a basket of letters. The vicar had to preach that sermon, though I hoped he'd be milder about it. Do you understand why we never got a letter from any villager, except Rafe Danvers and Dr. Schmidt, who can't be classed as villagers in the way you meant?"

But Colonel Bailey was not listening.

"Hitler?" he muttered in a voice of loathing. His eyes looked old and shrunken in his long face. "But I never meant . . . God knows! What did I mean?"

H.M., in turn, was not the accuser or the avenger. He spoke gravely. Never did he address his companion as "son," or by any informality.

"Do you understand," he persisted, "why none of 'em would submit a scrap of paper to us, Colonel? Because those letters were *too* ugly. You went too far; that was why you killed the Martin gal. You'd be friendly with the villagers, and be sociable, and have a pint with 'em; but that's part of your code. You were

304

the sahib. They weren't. They were commoners.

"On the other hand, you had to send letters to everybody or it would have looked too rummy for anybody's eye. But you couldn't, physically couldn't, honestly hurt anybody you really liked. Remember, I'd persisted in askin' questions about who would believe what, until some people must have thought I was loopy?

"You kept firin' accusations at Joan, about having an affair with the vicar. You pestered West with a charge of intimacy with Stella Lacey. Because you knew ruddy well nobody would believe it!

"Why, Theo Bull and his friends—when they wanted to fight the vicar in the field on Sunday—laughed at any idea of Joan's being mixed up in an affair, which excluded the vicar too. West was accused of carryin' on with Stella Lacey, though I didn't find out about Mrs. Lacey's letters until afterwards. But I assumed it was that. I asked Virtue Conklin (as representin' village opinion) and Marion Tyler (as representin' the gentry) what people thought about it. They both said it was nonsense. And Stella Lacey, whose praises you sang all over the place, wasn't really smirched either. It's why, too, there's a little obscenity in the letters. You knew, or thought, there had to be some. But you're a sahib. *You couldn't do it.*

"But, lord love a duck, we're getting ahead of ourselves. Let's got back to that fetchin' basket of letters gathered on Sunday.

"One interesting part of 'em was the phraseology. Afterwards it bothered the ears off Inspector Garlick, because he knew it was familiar—especially to him— and yet he couldn't grasp it. But it's easy enough, Colonel, if you quote a few examples."

It is H.M.'s prodigious memory which makes him so dangerous in debate or in court. Himself a grotesque figure, with a mackintosh and a face not-yet-clean, he blinked for a moment at a corner of the ceiling.

Then he brought together beginnings of letters we may remember.

"To Dr. Schmidt. Listen: *Pursuant to my last letter, I find*—and so on. To Joan Bailey, omittin' the first, 'Well, well,' we get: *Following inquiries made about you, Joan, I find*—and so on. To the vicar: *Apparently you and Joan Bailey are under the impression*—and the rest."

H.M. looked at the Colonel.

"Can't you hear the echo of, *In reply to your letter of June 1st, Major-General Grass-Ears begs leave to state*—and the rest of it? It's the ding-dong, back and forth, twelve-syllable, high-structure ponderousness of *official letterwriting*. Even you, who speak colloquially, fall into the habit of using it when you write. And you, Colonel, have been corresponding with the War Office for a long time. It comes back to you like a homin' boomerang."

H.M. paused.

"Oh, there's little things!" he grunted. "If you honestly hate gossip, where did you learn all the little or big things to slash the villagers? You included Squire Wyatt among the unimportant people, because you think he's a boor; you stung him so hard he's not recovered yet; but that's by the way.

"Your own niece—remember, I've been moochin' about for a week and gathering bits too—your own niece freely admits she loves gossip and she's at the telephone half the day. Now where's the phone? It's at the end of the passage, very close to your study door, and—as everybody can see and a lot of us notice—there's a space under the door so you can hear clearly.

"One other point about the letters, before we leave 'em for a more fascinatin' business about a disappearance from a sealed room.

"Four went to Dr. Schmidt, calling him a Nazi, and put him into a devil of a stew. The odd thing was that they didn't bother anybody in the village, who simply didn't care because people only laughed at the Horst-Vessel-and-Hanish gang. I bet you, if you asked Marion Tyler or even the vicar now, they'd both say it didn't matter a hang.

"But I saw your eyes, on Sunday night, move over to the files marked 'War Office,' when Dr. Schmidt was mentioned. I saw your face, even if you made a noncommittal remark. Colonel, who else but you would have seen that chunky fool as dangerous? Who but you would have written him letters scarifyin' him as a Nazi?"

Colonel Bailey's eyelids moved, and he clenched one fist.

"He is, isn't he?" the Colonel asked in a harsh voice.

"Sure he is. I can tell you a little secret, because—" H.M. stopped abruptly.

"Well?"

"Anyway, the Special Branch have had him taped for over a year. I don't have to quote instances of his betrayin' himself; he does it every time he opens his mouth.

"But let's go back to that first Saturday night we talked, and connect it with The Widow's appearance and disappearance on Sunday night. As I said, I pitched on you as the guilty 'un from the start. Do you remember how I kept insistin' your niece was in great danger, or thought she was, because of a poison-pen letter—I hadn't seen it yet—she must have recieved that day?"

"Yes, yes, I remember!"

"The following Sunday afternoon, she showed me the letter. It promised a visit, at a few minutes before

307

midnight, from The Widow.

"And (I admit it) the old man was scared. I'd have bet ducats to an old shoe that The Widow was really you. You were goin' to try some hanky-panky that night; and I swore to myself I was going to stop you. But it fitted in with another idea of mine, which I mentioned to you as a warning when we were both sittin' outside Joan's locked door in the dark on Sunday night.

"The idea? I explained how there'd been a rumor in the village, all week, that a big detective was coming from Lonon with a big clue. I showed how it couldn't mean me. I asked why, why, *why* The Widow, who'd lain doggo for a month, fired off two more letters at a time when it might be dangerous.

"Well, there might be a hundred reasons. But one of the letters had been the one which terrified Joan so much—a promised visit from The Widow. A good reason might be this: *The Widow, meaning you, might try to prove that he couldn't under any circumstances have been The Widow, and stop suspicion for good.* There'd be sound logic in that. It might be true, or it mightn't.

"But it did prompt a scary thought. Had you gone off your rocker? Might you possibly kill the gal just to prove you weren't the poison-pen writer?"

Colonel Bailey's eyes opened wide. He tried to push himself up against the rough-stone wall, the Webley swinging wide. He spoke in a husky, barely audible voice.

"Merrivale, for God's sake! You didn't really imagine . . . ?"

H.M. held up a big hand, and Colonel Bailey slid down again.

"I know, I know!" growled Sir Henry Merrivale. "You're honestly and genuinely fond of Joan; you wouldn't hurt a hair of her head. That's true. You thought, in all sincerity, the little game you were goin' to play would hardly scare her at all.

"These Bailey women can stand anything, can't they? They can sit at the siege of Hackaboola and play the mandolin with rifle bullets whoppin' off the strings. But I couldn't afford to think of niceties like that. I had to protect the gal. And, if it's any satisfaction to you, you fooled me completely when I was on the watch for hocus-pocus. Shall I tell you what you did?"

Suddenly, so briefly that it might have been an illusion, there flashed across Colonel Bailey's eyes an unpleasant gleam of vanity as to his own cleverness.

"Doubt if you know what I did," he said briefly.

"No? Then let's take what happened in the study, when you and West and I were talking, before we took up the vigil round Joan's room. West's plan—which you pretended to object to—was your own plan; and as plain as print you'd suggested it to West without his knowing it.

"How do I know that? West says our fourth guard will be Cordy. 'H'm,' you say doubtfully. West whips back at you, 'Hang it, sir, you *said* he was the only one we could trust.' Hear His Master's Voice? When West wants you outside the house, you squash it instantly by saying you and I will be inside, in front of the gal's door. Who suggested the two nembutal pills, which were vital to the scheme? You did.

"Cor—I knew you were up to something, but I sat with you outside that locked door like a dummy!

"We arranged to go in and out, alternately, every ten minutes, to see how Joan was. I couldn't object to that, because I couldn't give my reasons without bein' asked for proof and slung out on my ear. But I kept an eye on the keyhole, seein' Cordy at one window, and you didn't do anything, as I could see for myself afterwards.

"And the last time you went in, which was at ten

309

minutes to twelve—the last time anybody went in until we heard the revolver shots—you didn't seem to do anything but strike a match, blow it out, and hold a long hissin' conversation through the window with West. After that you came out straightaway.

"The clock upstairs struck twelve. All seemed as sweet as a filleted sole. I seemed to be unstuck. As I told you sometime before then, the car was whizzin' at a hundred miles an hour, and I couldn't even tell in which direction."

H.M. paused, considering the long lean kindly appearing figure on the bench. Colonel Bailey's eyes opened.

"Colonel," said H.M. in a heavy voice, "did you ever see an imaginary sketch of The Widow, done by a strolling artist in the early nineteenth century, and often reproduced on postcards?"

"Perhaps," said Colonel Bailey.

Reaching into his trouser pocket, H.M. produced a crumpled postcard. He looked at the leering middle-aged face, eyes and mouth twisted up at the corners, dark brown hair falling snakily to the shoulders: unmistakable, stamped with evil, as he had seen it before.

"Your niece," H.M. said, "has been frightened of this since she was a child. She told us so at Rafe Danvers' shop.

"Half the dirty work you did, Colonel," he went on, "was done in that time you went into the room at a little before ten minutes to twelve, and came out so innocently afterwards. When you talked to West through the window, you were sitting in the position you always occupied: on the edge of the bed, by the head and the little table near the window.

"There was a broad band of shadow across the head of the bed (remember?) but moonlight on the rest of it

310

and moonlight at the sides. A man outside the window hasn't a great deal of vision. West could see the side of your face, past the lamp, as you seemed to be looking alternately at him and at Joan. With lamp and table in the way, he can't see much else.

"Now what was—and is—directly opposite the foot of the bed? I'll tell you. A dressing table, rather high like the bed, with a large mirror above it. I once looked in that mirror, and picked up a comb, to call attention to it.

"Don't you dabble a good deal in water color painting? Yes, you do. You carried in your side pockets three or four, maybe more, little oblongs of paint in their casings. The brush'd go in your inside pocket. If you're bendin' close to a gal's face in shadow, it's not too dark to see the outline of her face with moonlight in the room.

"What was on that bedside table? A bowl of water and a flannel. But you couldn't use that; paint would show. In the cupboard under the table you've got another water bowl and another flannel, planted there in the afternoon.

"You haven't forgotten—*have you, Colonel?*—that Joan's hair was down to her shoulders on the pillow? As we saw it then; as we saw it on her shoulders in costume today. You did a deft job of water color painting on her face. She doesn't wear make up, except powder; it could be done as fast as lightning while you hissed at West, because it required few strokes.

"Any other thing?

"Oh, yes!"

"When you first slipped in there, you'd pushed the dressing table with the big mirror—on castors and a thick carpet—against the foot of the bed. One grab with a handkerchief would have taken the bulb out of the lamp and put it on the table. The painting was a matter of seconds. And you were out at ten minutes to twelve, piously locking the door, while the gal was in a drugged sleep and never noticed anything."

H.M.'s own bedaubed countenance looked as hard as granite. He tore the postcard into pieces and threw them aside.

"What's up next? Twelve o'clock; nothing. Four minutes past twelve; Fred Cordy fires three shatterin' revolver shots just outside the window. What would that blastin' noise do? It'd wake up a dazed gal, even from a drug. She'll sit up in bed, and look straight in front of her—at a big mirror nearly at the foot of the bed. She won't see her own face. She'll see the face of The Mocking Widow, just as in the old terrible picture, in full moonlight.

"Her lips go back as though to scream; so do The Widow's, in menace. She put her hand to push it away. The Widow seems to be reachin' out . . .

"You ought to be a proud man, Colonel Bailey.

"What stumped me for so long was that Joan said the figure was beside the bed, and touched her. It wasn't true; it was hysteria; but she really believed it. Don't you see that's what she feared and exactly what she'd imagined to be true?

"Next, my dear Colonel, let's have a dekko at your own noble conduct. You went chargin' in, right enough. When I thought you were stumbling over furniture with castors, you were really pushing the dressing table a short distance back to the wall. Would anybody hear it bump? No, because the carpet's folded up there. Would toilet articles spill off? No, because long ago—that afternoon, maybe, when you'd planted this paint bowl of water inside the cupboard—you've put hair brush, and hand mirror and the rest of it on the chest of drawers.

"I saw 'em there. Rafe Danvers says he did too. If

312

Joan herself noticed beforehand, which she must have, she was too scared to care.

"Joan, after screamin' several times, slips back into shadow when the drug gets her. West, outside a pane of glass which is always deceptive by moonlight, don't see the changed position of the mirror . . . maybe he don't even notice it . . . between cross lights and shadows. I couldn't see it, because I was behind it and well to one side.

"But the Colonel!

"What's more natural than that he should rush over to the other side of the bed, sit down, and bathe Joan's face? His body hid the face from bein' looked at, even in shadow. (Will you try to wake up, Colonel? I'm speakin' to you.)

"From the cupboard you got the extra flannel, clean, and soaked it heavily in the bowl of clean water beside the bed. You had to get the face of The Mockin' Widow completely washed off Joan's face with one well-soaked cloth. But you had plenty of time, while we bumblers fiddled after the light bulb. Cor, we even heard water splash! The hair didn't matter. Joan's own hair would have looked dark brown and snaky enough in that glimpse.

"I say! D'ye remember how that same scene was played in front of us the day before, only reversed? In the suitcase race, when you were sittin' at the easel, that suitcase of mine jumped on you and smeared your face. Joan, who was laughing, cried out to explain it was only water color and it'd wash off easily.

"Are you laughing now, Colonel Bailey? I *bet* you are!

"You had to shove the paint-stained flannel into the cupboard with the paints, the brush, and the stained bowl of water, and hope to your gods nobody would look in that cupboard before we leave. Well, congratulations. Nobody did."

Colonel Bailey slowly stood up straight, in his old cap and plus fours. His face seemed no less kindly, but the eyes were desperately puzzled.

"I meant no harm to the girl!" he protested. "Never thought of it. I . . . I . . ."

He seemed trying to prove in some fashion that a great wrong had been done to him, which it had, but that he must somehow avenge it on anybody within reach. Slowly he lifted the Webley .38, but he turned it over in his palm, with a shaky smile.

"This is empty," he said.

"Oh, I know that," H.M. replied casually. "Three shots for Cordy to fire, two shots into Cordy, and one fired in here. That's an old-fashioned six-shot; I didn't think you'd reload for me.

"But the very next morning," H.M. went on, trying to hold his eye, "I tumbled to your sealed-room trick. Because why? Because I was in my hotel room, looking at myself in a full-length mirror and seein' myself as an Indian. Then it suddenly hit the old onion with more than one wallop, because you could see more than the trick.

"Y'see, I'd had the idea of murder rollin' round in my head for some time. But, on Monday, you could see the design and you could see the real victim. Before that, I'd been thinking about Joan.

"Then I knew the one who might be in danger was Fred Cordy. Cordy had been the accomplice in the show Sunday night.

"That's plain, surely? Just as the church clock struck twelve, Cordy fired the shots. That smelled of a signal. 'Course, The Widow was supposed to appear a few minutes before midnight. But Cordy couldn't tell about that. He didn't have a watch, as I found out later; and the clock was four minutes slow.

314

"I'm bettin' you a limousine against sixpence," said H.M., pointing at the Colonel, "that when you talked to West at the window you made your request to take the gun away from Cordy a boys-will-be-boys suggestion. You intimated West wasn't to take it very seriously. And West didn't take the gun.

"Later Cordy cut loose with three shots at nothing whatever. West, like anybody who scrabbles about between bushes and moonlight, in a highly edgy state about Joan, is apt to see anything. His 'cursed queer-looking shadow' was sincere. And, if West had been in any way implicated, he wore a wristwatch and could have told Cordy the time. No, Colonel? You and you alone told Cordy to fire those shots, their sole purpose bein' to wake Joan.

"But this looked worse, much worse! If the typewriter was where I thought it was, you'd tied yourself even more tightly to that little acrobat, by having his help to hide the typewriter in The Widow's head. It was his machine. He'd made a brag long ago about throwin' it in the river, when he'd only shoved it away in a cupboard. What's more, Cordy could have told a lot more scandal about village people than you'd ever have heard over the phone. While you tapped away, maybe in the cellar late at night . . ."

"I was the flail of justice," said the Colonel, his eyes opening. "Gad, how I hit and hit and hit! They deserved it. Somebody had to be punished."

"But it was easy to see, by Monday, that Cordy was in an awful dangerous position. He knew too much. If, as Garlick flatly suggested, he tried a spot of blackmail . . ."

"Oh, he'd already done that."

"And you killed him?"

"Naturally I killed him," said the Colonel with a kind of querulousness, as though he considered this of as

315

little importance as H.M. considered it. "First it was five bob, then ten bob or a quid. After firing those shots, he wanted twenty pounds.

"I couldn't pay it, Merrivale. Hadn't got it, that's all. I stole the revolver out of West's cottage. That's my revolver; has been since long before '14; never a registration number. I arranged to meet Cordy as far away from my house as I could. In the park on the south side, up near Wyatt's.

"Dash it, I didn't . . . didn't *mean* any harm. Ever think how that word 'yah,' repeated over and over from some cursed little beast who swears he's going to tell, can make you go mad? I took out the gun and tried to get him by the collar. He broke loose, and ran down the drive.

"I didn't follow. Too dangerous. I cut through the trees of the park, following him toward the northern side. I'm very quick on my feet; ask anybody who's ever seen me play tennis. Like that day when the vicar . . ." The Colonel's shaky smile collapsed.

"Anyway, I got him with two shots over the park wall on the north. Tricky shooting by moonlight. Nearly fainted when he didn't seem to drop. But he dropped, and The Widow too."

Colonel Bailey put his hands over his eyes.

"Y'see, Colonel," said H.M., with much bitterness directed against himself, "my great mistake—and Garlick'll never stop telling me—was not to have had Cordy nabbed as soon as I guessed that typewriter was in The Widow's head, and had you hauled in for questionin' too.

"It's no good saying I was only making a guess; a little midnight climb by one of Garlick's men would have settled the matter. And Cordy couldn't deny it; we had the testimony of the dealer where he'd bought the machine. But we mightn't have got anything out of

316

you, and it would have spilled the beans too soon. Maybe, in my heart (if I've got one), I hoped you'd see warning and shut up.

"On Monday night I went out to Joan's bedroom, and tried to find traces of the water color paintin': the paints, the brush, the stained bowl of water, the stained cloth you'd used on her face. I knew you'd have removed 'em on the night before, when Joan went upstairs to sleep. But—since you did a hurried job in a bad light—I thought there might be paint sloppings from the water bowl inside the cabinet.

"There weren't any. But this mornin' I heard from Masters in town that they can be found and brought out if they get the table in their hands. So, in a way, maybe, I did solve the right problem by solvin' the wrong.

"But, Colonel, you *wouldn't* stop! You'd achieved your purpose, in scarin' the wits out of Joan and proving you couldn't be The Widow. I kept tellin' everybody she was free from harm and she wouldn't see The Widow ever again.

"In that bedroom, on Monday night, I was mad. Good and mad. Rafe Danvers kept driving corkscrew questions into me, like a corkscrew knife. He asked me whether the figure of The Widow had really been in the room. Well, Joan herself *was* the figure of The Widow, though she didn't know it. So I said yes, feelin' pleased, and Rafe shut up.

"But I repeat, Colonel: you *couldn't* stop. Yesterday you fell into an old police trap Garlick and I had set. You bought marked stamps for a last fling at me. The police knew you did. Today the cussed letter must have fallen out of my pocket at West's house, and I haven't any doubt Garlick got it and decided to move in.

"Y'see, I'd asked you to meet me here, when I'd caused a row and not a single soul in Stoke Druid could

317

possibly have noticed you. I wanted to give you . . . well, I still can. But, as far as provin' anonymous letters against you, you're finished. About Cordy . . ."

Colonel Bailey gripped together his long, knuckly fingers. Again he stood up.

"I tell you again," he snarled miserably, "do you think I'm a coward? Do you think I'd mind a decent honest hanging? . . . But these letters! The scandal! I wonder if you've ever noticed that torture wouldn't bother me like scandal."

"Uh-huh. I've noticed it. You've caused a lot of scandal yourself, haven't you?"

"I . . . yes. I deserve it. No argument."

"There's an interestin' thing about our police procedure," H.M. remarked in a musing tone. "If the coppers have got a case built up against a man, and that man happens to die, they never say a word afterwards. Not a word. It makes the press hysterical; but they won't. The English law, that blunderin' old goop we make so much fun of, happens to think this protects the man's innocent relatives."

"But I . . ."

"Colonel, do you remember what you said your friends would do in the Army, thirty or forty years ago, when they knew a man had done something unpardonable?"

"I—I was thinking about the vicar. Wrongly! I—"

"You said they'd leave him alone with a revolver, and give him ten minutes to use it in."

H.M. fished for his hip pocket, which was very deep. He took out the other Webley .38, fully loaded, which he had borrowed.

"As it happens, Colonel," he explained apologetically, "I'm goin' for a little stroll. I'll be back in about ten minutes."

And now you understood why Colonel Bailey had

.eemed in despair every time he touched the empty gun. A sort of radiance crossed the old, weary, half-mad ace; his shoulders straightened, and you would not have seen a finer-looking commander.

"You'll land in trouble for this, you know," he smiled.

"Ho ho," observed H.M. in an expressionless voice.

Colonel Bailey's tone changed.

"Thank you, Merrivale."

"Not at all, Colonel."

H.M. opened the door of the drum tower, which he left slightly ajar. Under a high flooding of moonlight through the western windows, he tramped slowly down the mid-aisle toward the front door. He had not reached the front door before he heard the sound of the revolver shot. H.M. bowed his head for a moment. Then he turned round and went back.